HELL'S BELLES

Jackie Kessler

piatkus

PIATKUS

First published in the US in 2007 by Zebra Books,
Kensington Publishing Corp.
First published in Great Britain as a paperback original in 2011 by Piatkus

A CIP catalogue record for this book
is available from the British Library.

ISBN 978-0-7499-5333-1

Types   ed

Papers   ble
prod   d
in accor   ncil.

Little, Brown Book Group
100 Victoria Embankment
London EC4Y 0DY

An Hachette UK Company
www.hachette.co.uk

www.piatkus.co.uk

Ja...   or...   ...s
humans caught between them, superheroes, supervillains
who pound those heroes into pudding, witches, vampires,
and the occasional Horseman of the Apocalypse. Jackie is
a Deadline Dame, and she lives in Upstate New York,
along with her husband, two children, one cat, and about
9,000 comic books.

For more about Jackie, please visit her website at
www.jackiekessler.com.

Other titles published by Piatkus by
Jackie Kessler and Caitlin Kittredge:

Black and White
Shades of Night

To the memory of Milton Segal,
who told me years ago that
if I wanted to be an author,
I should 'write something juicy.'
I love you, Grandpa.

Acknowledgments

Many thanks to Ethan Ellenberg, super agent, for making this possible; John Scognamiglio, genius editor, for your enthusiasm and exuberance; and Darlene DeLillo, copy editor extraordinaire, for all the fabulous catches.

Hugs and virtual chocolate to Heather Brewer, who loves all happy endings that involve blood; Renee Barr, who has suffered through nearly everything I've ever written; Faith Bicknell-Brown, who stuck with me before, during and after all things *Charles*; Zinnia Hope, who convinced me that yes, I *can* write a nookie scene; Patti Hunt, who taught me that a beat ain't just for music; Caitlin Kittredge, who lovingly coined the term 'flesh puppet'; Joe Konrath, who taught me a very important lesson; everyone at Backspace who helped out along the way, especially Keith Cronin, E.J. Knapp, and Lesley Livingston; and the valiant members of my writing group for their feedback and steadfast support.

Eternal gratitude to Mom and Dad, who have always encouraged me to follow my dreams (even when they lead to Hell); to Ryan and Mason, for sleeping through the nights and not minding that I was a bit tired in the mornings; and, most of all, to Brett, for everything from understanding why I would write until the wee hours of the morning to helping me with my (ahem) research, and everything in between – I couldn't have done it without you.

PART ONE

JEZEBEL

1

Caitlin's House (I)

On the night the Underworld put a contract out on me, a crescent moon dangled overhead like a celestial fishhook and stars bobbed in the sky. Just my luck. I'd been hoping for a raging thunderstorm, maybe some hail. You know, something dramatic. But no. I got picturesque.

Just another sign that Hell had gone to Heaven in a hand basket.

I threw a nervous look over my shoulder, unable to relax even though I sensed only the thrumming energy of Salem, Massachusetts, in the predawn morning. Nothing infernal beeped on my psychic radar. For the moment, I was safe. Desperate and so terrified that I was pissing my metaphorical pants, but safe.

Okay. Deep breath, like the way the humans did it. There. Oh, right. Release it. Mental note: Humans breathe continuously.

Hmm. That was going to be a royal bitch to remember.

I rang the bell and waited, taking in the details of the plain wooden door. The only obvious detriments to the uninvited were a smattering of impressive-looking metal locks. The less obvious barriers included a few nasty hexes and one particularly inventive curse.

Excellent. Just the kind of help I needed.

After a few moments, I felt a presence behind the door – probably scanning me through the peephole. Putting on my game face, I grinned broadly, displaying sinfully perfect teeth.

The door inched open until the attached security chain pulled taut. A face peered through the crack. The one visible eye, very green and very wide, stared at me for a heartbeat. Then it widened even more and took on a glassy sheen. Fear wafted from her like perfume. Yummy.

Stop that, I scolded myself. You need her help. Don't scare her to death. Yet.

'Hi, Caitlin,' I said, pouring on the charm.

I heard her swallow before she replied, 'Hello, Jesse.'

My grin faltered, and I quickly pasted it back on. I'd been banking on her saying my full name. Then she would have fallen sway to my glamour and I'd be inside already, with her dancing a jig to keep me entertained, instead of me still standing on her doorstep, biting back the urge to look over my shoulder again.

Caitlin waited to see what I wanted with her, like she had all the time in the world. Sure, she wasn't the one who had the Scourge of Hell sniffing her trail. That honor was reserved for me.

Okay, time for the mafia tactic. 'You signed a contract with one of my associates. I'm here to collect.'

I heard her breath catch in her throat, and I thought I had her. Then the one eye staring at me narrowed. 'If this were an official visit,' she said, 'you wouldn't have bothered ringing the doorbell. You would've just materialized

4

inside. Besides, since when does one of *your* kind do collections for the Hecate?'

Crap. 'You want an answer, or was that rhetorical?'

'Good-bye, Jesse.' She shut the door.

'Wait!' Hating myself, I said the magic word. 'Please.'

A pause, and then I heard the chain sliding free. Caitlin opened the door far enough to reveal her entire face, round and proud and framed with black curly hair. Let's hear it for insatiable curiosity. I flashed her my best Adorable Female grin.

She said, 'Swear on your name that you mean me no harm, that you'll do me no harm, that you will bring me no harm.'

I checked myself before I rolled my eyes. Friggin' witches and their oaths. 'On my name, I so swear it.' Of course, after tonight, my name didn't mean squat. But I didn't see any need to bring that up.

Caitlin opened her door wide. 'Enter.'

I sauntered through the doorway, my hips sashaying and breasts jiggling. It was part of my Farrah Fawcett look, circa 1978, complete with frosted, flipped blond hair.

'What're you supposed to be?' Caitlin asked as I pranced by, my boobs nearly hitting my chin with every bouncing step.

'A Charlie's Angel.'

I heard a snort, and I glanced over my shoulder to see her hiding a smile behind her hand. Maybe she was terrified of me. Maybe she'd just invited me into her place of power, despite her better judgment. But she still had to admit I had a sense of humor.

Caitlin flipped on a light, and I blinked as my eyes adjusted, taking in the contents of the small living room off the entrance. On the pale walls hung pictures of mountains, pompous in their purples and browns. Candlesticks poked up from holders set on the windowsill to my right; the faint stench of jasmine still clung to the air. Two large sofas, overstuffed with pillows, dominated the space. Each propped against a wall, the couches squatted like bloated spiders. Well, minus the eyes, legs, and webs . . . and overlooking the creamy white coloring.

Okay, so maybe they weren't exactly reminiscent of insects. But hey, I couldn't help but look for the dark in things. You could take the demon out of Hell, but taking the Hell out of the demon required a lot more work. And that's where Caitlin came in.

'Have a seat,' she said.

Choosing the sofa nearer to the door, I plopped down, and my boobs followed. Crossing my long, tanned legs, I leaned back into the pillows and dazzled her with my Farrah smile.

She clearly wasn't impressed. Caitlin glanced outside before she shut and locked the door. A mutter under her breath told me that she'd reactivated her magic wards. Something in my chest loosened as I realized I was under the witch's protection. Not like she'd be much more than a nuisance to my pursuer, but still, it was comforting.

Bless me, I really was getting soft.

Caitlin hid a yawn behind her hand as she approached the other couch. I'd obviously woken her; she was decked out in a green flannel nightshirt, and her curly black hair was so sleep-tousled that it looked like she'd used an entire can of hairspray to get it to stand up that high. Too bad it wasn't the 1980s – she'd have been incredibly stylish.

She sat, folding her legs beneath her and nearly disappearing into the cushions. Because she radiated such power, I tended to forget how small she was physically –

6

maybe she reached five-foot-four. Strong witches really should be taller. She asked, 'What brings you here, Jesse?'

I tried to think of something witty to say, but what popped out of my red-lipsticked mouth was, 'I need your help.'

Mental note: When bargaining with mortals who have something you need, don't tell them how much you need it.

She tapped her chin as she looked at me, her large green eyes thoughtful. Her face had a surprisingly sharp nose and chin, offsetting her full cheeks and cupid-bow lips. Attractive, in a second-glance sort of way. A little makeup, and introducing her hair to a brush, would do wonders. 'What would you ask of me?'

Licking my lips, I said, 'Can you turn me into a mortal?'

She blinked. Then she blinked again. Finally she asked, 'Why?'

'I'm sort of AWOL.'

'You're *what?*'

'And some lower-downs aren't too pleased about that.' Actually, that was putting it mildly. If I got caught, the very best I could hope for was a millennium in the Lake of Fire. I didn't want to think about what the worst would be.

Staring at me, she said, 'What on Earth could make a demon run away from Hell?'

I shook my head. 'Sorry. That's the bonus round.'

'Jesse—'

'Look,' I said, catching her gaze with my own. 'It's like this, okay? I ran away from Hell, just like you said. And now something's after me, ready to drag me back, kicking and screaming. So I need to get off the demon radar and blend with the flesh puppets. That's all you get, Caitlin. Now, can you turn me into a mortal or not?'

Her face darkened as her mouth pulled down into a deep frown. 'If you want my help, you have to answer my questions.'

'And *you* have to understand that there are some things too dangerous for you to know. Unless,' I added lightly, 'you want Hell to come after you too.'

She blanched, and I caught the intoxicating scent of terror. My nostrils flared as I inhaled deeply. Maybe the whole breathing thing had its perks.

'If I help you, what do I get out of it?'

'You mean, besides the pleasure of a job well done?'

She didn't even blink. Bless me, these so-called white witches weren't as altruistic as they claimed. At least, not Caitlin.

I said, 'What about that whole "Do unto others as you'd have others do unto you" thing?'

Her eyes gleamed, and I knew I'd made a mistake. 'So you'd be in my debt? If I help you now, then you need to help me when I need it?'

Crap. 'Sure – assuming it's within my power. I mean, I can't go and make you immortal, or grant you three wishes, or anything like that. And it's a one-time offer. No coming back to me, demanding more and more help. You help me now, and I help you once, when you need it.'

'Deal.' She spat into her palm, then leaned forward, sticking out her hand.

I followed suit. Our palms touched, and my flesh itched where our saliva mingled. Some people think you need blood to make agreements like this. While blood's nice, any bodily fluid would make the contract just as binding.

'Now,' she said, wiping her hand on her nightshirt, 'let's make you a mortal.'

*

I thumbed through a magazine while I waited for Caitlin's potion to brew. The cover story promised to teach me 'ten tantalizing tips' guaranteed to drive my partner wild. I had to see what passed for 'tantalizing' these days. I was willing to bet it didn't include snakes and honey.

'Here we go.'

I glanced up to see Caitlin gliding up to me, mopping back her unruly black curls, looking incredibly proud. In her hand, steam wafted from a large mug. About time. It had taken her a half hour to gather and mix all the ingredients, and nearly two hours for it to do the fire-burn-and-cauldron-bubble thing. I didn't know how long slumming in Salem, hidden in a witch's house, would disguise my presence from my hunter; with every passing moment, my unease had grown. But now it looked like the waiting was about to pay off.

Setting the magazine aside, I frowned at the cup as she thrust it at me. 'What's that smell?'

'Number of things. Moth's cocoon, egg, milk, powdered ivory. Blood, of course. Mercury, but there's no smell to that. Water, a tampon—'

'It's the milk,' I said, wrinkling my nose. 'Ick. How do you people stand that?'

She looked affronted, as if I'd pointed out a pile of fresh dog turds on her area rug. 'Dairy's an important food group. You need milk.'

'Sure, if you're a baby cow. Ugh, revolting stuff.' Making a face, I peered inside the mug. The potion stank to high Heaven, and it looked just as appetizing. Brown with white funguslike flecks, the liquid was just thick enough for me to make out the congealing blood, but still watery overall. 'And this looks like it came out from the baby cow's other end.'

9

'It's Gala Tea.'

I shook my frosted, flipped mane of hair. 'Never heard of it.'

'Actually, the full name is "Potion of Pygmalion." The nickname's just some witching humor. You know, Pygmalion the sculptor? From the myth? Prayed to Aphrodite for a wife just like the statue he carved, and Aphrodite brought the sculpture to life? He named the statue Galatea.' Her full lips twitched into a smile. 'Get it? Galatea, Gala Tea?'

'Sweetie,' I said after a long pause, 'don't quit your day job.'

'You don't have to be mean about it,' she mumbled.

I blew out a sigh, lifting my bangs away from my eyes. 'What, you expect me to be nice? I'm a demon.'

'Not after you drink this, you're not. Now look, here's the thing: this will transform you into whatever your outer image is. So unless you want to be stuck looking like a one-time star of jiggle television, you should probably rethink your appearance.'

I raised my arms high and let a ripple of power wash over me. My hair curled and darkened until it was a thick, tangled mass framing a round face with wide green eyes, a sharp nose, and a mouth with cupid-bow lips. My breasts diminished a cup size, and my frame shrank until I was a petite woman of five-foot-four, small and lean instead of tall and curvy. When I grinned, my teeth clamped down in a slight overbite. *Sayonara*, Farrah. Hello, Caitlin.

The look on her face was priceless. I didn't know if it was because I was wearing her form or because I was naked. She yelled, 'Stop that!'

I blew her a kiss. 'First give me the potion.'

'Fine,' she said, shoving the cup into my hands. 'Here.

Now would you please change into something else? And put on some clothes?'

'In a moment.' The nauseating stench of sweet milk emanating from the mug made me want to gag. 'How's this work? I drink it, and poof, I'm mortal?'

Frowning at me, she seemed lost between answering my question and being annoyed at my temporary appearance. Her pride in her abilities won out. Seven deadly sins – got to love them. 'Well, not exactly.' She ran her fingers through her hair, brushing thick curls away from her face. 'It will lock you into mortal form. No soul, of course. But still human. So you'll have to take care of all your human needs.'

'Like sex?' I perked up. 'I can do that.'

'That's procreation, which you can't do. No soul, remember? No little demonites for you.'

I pouted. Sex was important, even if it wasn't to make babies. It was . . . exercise. Right, exercise. And I had to exercise my new human body. Oooh. This had possibilities.

'Listen,' Caitlin said, dragging me away from lascivious thoughts. 'This is important. If you use any infernal abilities, it will cancel the spell.'

Crap. Why did these things always have a catch? 'Meaning?'

'Meaning that if you use any of your powers, the jig is up, and whatever's chasing you will be able to track you again.'

'So on top of remembering to breathe, I have to restrain myself from seducing men and sucking out their souls? Isn't there a learning curve or something?'

She tapped her chin as she thought. 'Well, if you had an item like a Shield Against Evil, that would do double

11

duty. It would cut you off from your own power, and it'd hide your power from . . . well, your former associates.'

'Perfect! I'll take one of those.'

A smile played across her round face. 'If you want another favor, Jesse, then you need to give me something in addition.'

Ooh, wasn't she the confident little witch? Getting greedy with a creature of the Pit, eh? Sure, I was in her place of power, and I was there to beg a favor. But that didn't mean she should forget who I was . . . and what I could do.

'You're right,' I said, giving her a tiny, helpless smile, setting her at ease. 'I'll give you something.' Then I pushed, just a little – nothing to set off any of her wards, just a tickle of desire. Hetero was way more my thing, but I'd done the Sapphic route in my time. Caitlin was one of those free-spirited mortals who saw the inherent beauty in all living things, blah blah. In other words, she pitched for both teams. A whisper of power, blowing her way, settling over her like dander. She sneezed . . .

. . . and looked into my face, and I watched her eyes darken and heard her heartbeat quicken. I licked my lips slowly, suggestively, and her lips parted in return. A sound escaped from her mouth, the softest of *ohhhs*, as her eyes lost their focus. I caught the spice of her sex as her body responded to my invisible touch, saw her nipples harden beneath her flannel nightshirt, watched her undo first one button, then the next . . .

My voice soft so I wouldn't pull her out of her trance, I purred, 'Say my name.'

Her fingers opened the third button, and her right breast poked out from the opening in her clothing. In a breathy whisper, she said, 'Jezebel.'

Bingo.

'Caitlin, you mentioned a Shield Against Evil.' I kept my voice pitched low; even though calling my name while under my power bound her to me, she was still a ridiculously strong witch. The wrong tone, or pushing her too hard to do something against her nature, could break my control over her. 'Do you have one of those shields here, lying around?'

'Mmmm.' Now her shirt was completely unfastened, and her hand was moving down between her legs. 'Yes . . .'

'Sweetie, I need you to get it. Wrap it up in a towel and bring it to me. Don't touch it directly with your skin.'

Her hand paused, fingers buried in her cotton panties. 'Now?'

'Now.'

With a sigh, she stood and padded out of the room, her open nightshirt flapping around her like a robe.

Okay, she'd give me the shield, I'd drink the nasty brew, and everything would be fine—

A small buzz whined in my ears. I tensed, sitting up straight as I tentatively reached out, stretching my power . . .

. . . and was slapped away.

Shit! I stole a glance out the window. It was still dark out, but the sky already had that lush purple look that meant sunrise was right around the corner. The humans were waking up. A stray car or two motored by, mortals on their way to somewhere; across the street, a light was on in an upstairs room.

And somewhere out there, my pursuer had honed in on me. I didn't know how much time I had before I was found – maybe a few minutes, maybe as much as an hour. In my hands, the mug of witch's brew trembled.

Caitlin walked back into the room, her eyes vacant, her arms wrapped around a blue towel. 'I brought it for you . . .'

Excellent. With both the potion and the talisman in my possession, I could make like a shepherd and get the flock out of there. I wasn't about to put Caitlin at risk, especially not after that blessed oath she'd made me say. Last thing I needed was for the Hecate to come after me; there's nothing like a deity with a hair up its ass to really take the spring out of one's step. 'Much obliged, sweetie.'

I grabbed the bundle from her hands – a bit too roughly, because she blinked once, blinked again and said, 'Jesse . . . ? What—'

The buzzing in my ears turned into a full-blown scream just as something slammed against Caitlin's front door: BOOM, BOOM, *BOOM!*

Casting aside all hints of subtlety, I hurled my power at Caitlin. She gasped, then a dazed look settled over her as she swayed on her feet.

'Hear only my voice, Caitlin,' I commanded her, somehow keeping my voice steady. 'Lie down on the couch and close your eyes.'

Glancing at the door, I saw it still held. For now. Nothing had burst through, which meant Caitlin's ward was way, way stronger than I'd hoped it would be. The beastie outside was only knocking; out of either respect for the witch's power or out of fear for her patron goddess, my hunter was being polite. That meant I had a moment or two to spare. Yay, me.

Turning back to my enchanted witch, I was going to tell her to sleep, but instead I gave her a small gift. I hadn't meant to lead trouble to her door; the least I could do was show her a good time. 'Picture your fantasy lover,

14

the one whom you've always wanted. Your lover is here with you, Caitlin. Your lover is with you now, kissing you up and down.'

She moaned, her body arching, her exposed flesh dimpling from the touch of her imaginary partner. Another crash sounded against the door, like something huge and heavy pounding against it. *BOOM!* The demon outside was getting impatient. Had to be a male; we females were used to waiting.

Over the noise I said, 'Let your lover seduce you, Caitlin. Give yourself over completely, with no restraint.' In a burst of inspiration I added, 'When you climax, you will forget I was ever here. And then you'll sleep for the rest of the day.'

Letting out a cry of pleasure, she moved her body, arms reaching up to encircle nothing.

I'd say that getting Caitlin out of a rampaging demon's way safely counted as me helping her when she needed it. All debts were cancelled.

Again, a *BOOM!!!* against the door, which buckled slightly from the force. I was out of time.

'Right,' I said aloud, the wrapped shield in one hand, the steaming mug in the other. 'Bottom's up.' And I gulped down the potion.

2

Caitlin's House (II)

I've slurped on monkey brains when doing a stint in Taiwan. I've feasted on sweetbreads in France, when one particular client was a chef with exotic appetites. I've even forced down a peanut butter and jelly sandwich, all in the name of doing the job.

But never, in all of my existence, have I had to stomach *milk*.

I quaffed the brew, screwing my eyes shut and pretending there was lemon curdling the mixture, making it palatable. At least the blood and ivory offset the taste somewhat.

With the last gulp, I felt the liquid explode into raw magic, bursting through my body from the inside out. I screamed as heat seared over me, fusing my outer shell to my true demonic form. Pressure bubbled in my limbs as blood and bone and muscle transformed from parody to reality, from infernal to human. Sparks danced across my skin in a wild jitterbug, standing my body hair on end as I felt – really *felt* – every nerve ending tingle. From my

16

scalp to my toes, and everywhere in between, my flesh sang with life, a song resonating with agony and ecstasy. My scream cut off as I gasped, breathed . . .

. . . and crashed to the floor, whimpering, wrapping my arms around my torso. Fuuuuuck. That *hurt*!

I couldn't do anything but tremble as a million sensations hit me at once. Smell, more than anything – a stench of sweat and shit and milk and blood, all mixed into an organic perfume that assaulted my nostrils. Taste – the tangy, salty flavor of my perspiration and sharp sweetness of my blood as I bit through my bottom lip . . . and fuuu-uuuck, the feeling of that bite – bless me, that stung!

A backbeat to my pain was the chill of cool air kissing my skin; the solidness of the wooden floor, and above it the thick bands of the area rug, bumpy and uncomfortable against my bare legs; the undertow of gravity pulling me down, anchoring me to the ground, giving weight to my hands, my breasts, my head . . .

Wetness seeped from my eyes. Raising a hand, I wiped away the fluid, assuming it was blood; with my luck, I'd probably sprung a leak. I stared, dumbstruck, at the water that glistened on my fingers. Tears. Actual *tears*.

Unholy Hell, the witch really did it. Her nasty potion turned me into a mortal.

On the couch, Caitlin let out a series of gasps, ending with a scream of triumphant pleasure. Outside the house, an earthmoving BAM! BAM! *BAM!!!* rattled my teeth and sent candlesticks flying from the windowsill as something massive connected with the warded front door.

Taking a shuddering breath – and marveling over not having to remember to breathe – I looked up. The door still held, but the wood appeared stressed, as if it could splinter with the slightest breeze. On the sofa, the witch

17

sighed in contentment, and her head lolled to the side, her thick curls eclipsing her face. Lights out for Caitlin.

I quickly unfolded the towel. Lying on the blue terrycloth, a thick silver chain winked at me. Clasped to it was a single, large green gem in the shape of an eye. Even in the soft lighting of Caitlin's living room, the verdant color shone clearly, brightly. Not emerald, which would have been a deeper green; maybe peridot.

Biting my lip, then wincing from the fresh bout of pain that brought, I braced myself as I touched the chain.

Nothing. No burst of flame. No instant disintegration.

The door groaned, buckling as the being outside struck it again. Two of the metal locks snapped off, landing near my bare feet. Caitlin's wards wouldn't hold much longer.

Blowing out a nervous breath, I grazed the gemstone with the tip of my finger.

Still no reaction. Either the shield was defective, or I was completely human. From the way overwhelming terror was turning my new blood to ice, I decided to run with the 'completely human' scenario.

Now or never.

I grasped the chain and dropped the necklace over my head. The green stone slipped between my breasts. Gooseflesh dotting my skin, I stood on shaky legs and turned to the door.

Showtime.

I opened the door, remembering at the last minute that I was stark naked. That didn't bother me, but it probably would have upset Caitlin, so I stuck my head out, keeping my nude body behind the tortured door.

Between my breasts, the stone tingled.

On the front porch stood a creature easily the size of a

18

small mountain, immaculately dressed in an Italian-cut black suit. Gold cufflinks by the wrists; gold clasp on the silk tie. Black wingtip leather shoes caught the dawn as they sparkled in the morning light. Wearing a human form, his salt-and-pepper hair was perfectly trimmed, and his face and body were full, the byproduct of luxurious foods. Eyes the color of liquid gold gleamed at me – no pupils, no whites, just gold. Everything about him screamed 'money,' and I easily placed him as a demon of Covet.

I mentally slapped my forehead. Of course. A creature of Greed would be a perfect bounty hunter; everyone knew that nothing stood between a Coveter and its intended object. It made me briefly wonder what sort of price was on my head – as greedy as those demons were, the price had to be right. No one wanted something that wasn't worth the effort.

Cold comfort. Or maybe that was the draft blowing on my nude body.

'Little witch,' the demon rumbled in a rich, cultured voice, 'you have something I want.'

My stomach dropped into my toes, and I swallowed a lump the size of a pigeon. I barely choked down a nervous laugh as I forked the sign of the evil eye, trying to flick my wrist the way I'd seen countless mortals do in the past. Part of me relished the sensation of being horrorstruck; it was fascinating how my limbs wanted to freeze up and my heart nearly stopped beating out of fright. The rest of me told myself to get a fucking grip and deal with the very real threat looming over me right now.

Putting the right amount of respect (completely fabricated) and fear (completely legitimate) into my voice, I shouted, 'Back, demon! You're not welcome here!'

He sneered, looking down at me as if I'd come to dinner

19

dressed in ripped jeans. 'I don't need your welcome, little witch. I need your guest.'

Widening my eyes in mock surprise, I repeated, 'Guest?'

A smile crept across his broad face. 'You know who I mean, little witch. I can smell the slut. I know she's here. Her trail ends at your doorstep. Where is she? Where is Jezebel?'

Even the best lie isn't as strong as the lamest truth. 'She knocked on my door hours ago. She's not here anymore.' So to speak.

He bent down so his head was level with mine. His golden eyes sparkled, and I found myself staring at their reflective surfaces, captivated by the way they shone. All of that gold . . . His eyes seemed to grow into brilliant suns, flashing yellow and white. I felt myself falling into a sea of cold, golden coins, being sucked under . . .

'Are you telling me the truth?'

My voice small, far away, I said, 'Yes . . .'

On my chest, the gemstone flared. Gasping from the sudden heat, my concentration broke and I quickly pulled my gaze to the floor. Bless me, he'd almost *charmed* me! That bastard!

His voice heavy as bars of gold, he said, 'I don't believe you.'

Okay, time to channel Caitlin. How would she react if a demonic presence attempted to compel her?

Based on how she was currently unconscious on her sofa, she'd fold like a pack of cards. So make that, How would Caitlin react if a demonic presence *unsuccessfully* attempted to compel her?

Confident that the shield around my neck would continue protecting me, I pulled myself up to my full height – all sixty-four inches of it – and planted a hand

20

on my hip. Glaring, I said, 'I don't give a damn what you believe. You're a creature of Greed; that's obvious from all your expensive trappings. You have no power over me. I belong to the Hecate. Unless you want to invoke the wrath of the triple goddess, do your golddigging somewhere else.'

Perhaps amused, he stood straight, looming over me as he smiled. 'You're very cute, little witch, posturing in all of your glory. Tell me: Where is the succubus Jezebel?'

If she were in her right mind, the succubus Jezebel would be far, far away from you. Still pretending to be Caitlin, I said, 'I don't know.'

'You smell of sex, little witch. I think you know more than you're saying.'

I lifted my chin high. 'Of *course* I smell of sex. You interrupted me. Last I heard, there was nothing wrong with having intercourse in my own house, on my own time, with a willing partner.'

He stared at me, peered into my eyes as if he could read my secrets. His grin widened, revealing a mouthful of sharp teeth. Eep.

I was out of bravado, so I covered by running out of patience as well. 'Next time, ring the doorbell. Now get out of here before I banish you.'

'You don't have the power to do that, little witch.' His golden eyes flashing hypnotically, he said, 'I could take anything I wanted from you.'

'Anything?' I threw open the door, revealing my nakedness . . . and my necklace. The shieldstone seared my flesh, warding off the demon's inherent Evil. Clenching my teeth, I refused to squirm as I felt my skin burn beneath the peridot.

His gaze traveled the length of my body, lingering by my breasts, but I couldn't tell if that was due to my womanly charms or the amulet that dangled between them. He said, 'Pretty. And a pretty talisman too. I want it. Let me have it, little witch.'

A wave of power crashed over me . . . and washed away. Still, it had rocked me back a step; if I hadn't been holding onto the door handle, I would have fallen. His eyes gleamed gold as they sparkled, inviting me to look deep within.

My throat tight, I said, 'If you can take it, it's yours.'

A grin splitting his face, he reached out and caressed the swell of my left breast. My flesh grew icy where his touch lingered, as if he'd stolen my body's warmth.

I hadn't abased myself to a mortal witch and forced myself to drink milk just to have a Coveter cop a feel. Swallowing my fear, I said, 'Maybe I was wrong about you being a creature of Greed. You're acting more like one of Lust.'

Ooh, that struck a nerve. With a snarl, he grabbed the stone – and screeched, pulling his fingers away. Holding his scorched hand, he glowered at me, his malefic gaze promising to hurt me in ways I'd never dreamed. 'You'll pay for that, witch girl!'

'I'm under the protection of the Hecate,' I said, managing to keep the fact I was utterly terrified out of my voice. 'Harm me, and you'll face her in all her ire.' I made myself believe those words, forced myself to be Caitlin in all of her faith in magic and gods.

And he bought the act completely. Trembling from rage or pain, he spat, 'Where's the slut? Tell me, where is Jezebel?'

Taking a deep breath, I said, 'All I can say is she's no longer here.'

A growl sounded, deep in his throat, and the color of

his golden eyes darkened until they danced with red. Blood money.

I'd gone too far. If I didn't appease him somehow, he would launch himself at me, ward or no. And I was too exhausted to counter a full-blown demonic attack. 'She was dressed up like a television star,' I said quickly. 'Maybe she's on her way to Hollywood. You know, to blend.'

He paused, arching an eyebrow. His unblinking eyes tried to read me, to penetrate hidden meaning behind my words. Finally he said, 'You turned her away?'

'She said something from Hell was hot on her heels. Why would I want to take on her problem?' I even pulled off a passable shrug. All I had to do was keep from passing out, and I'd be home free.

His voice dripping with menace, he asked, 'Did the slut tell you *why* I was after her?'

'I asked twice, but she refused to answer.' Remembering Caitlin's words, I added, 'If she wanted my help so bad, she would've answered my questions.'

After a moment, he nodded. 'I believe you. No matter. I will find her, little witch. If not me, then one of the others.'

'Others?' I asked before I could help myself.

Golden eyes gleaming, he said, 'Oh yes. There's quite the price on her head – either attached or not. So if you see her, little witch, tell her to come back to Hell before it's too late. Or better yet, don't say a word. I'd rather be the one to find her before the others do.' He grinned, then disappeared in a puff of sulfur.

Slamming the door against the stench of rotten eggs, I slid down to the floor, shaking so violently that I thought my teeth would fall out.

Others.

How many were after me?

I rubbed the amulet between my thumb and index finger. It was cool to the touch; nothing Evil was nearby . . . at least, nothing Evil that intended me any harm. For the moment, I was safe. Three cheers for the former demon.

But I couldn't stay. My disguise wouldn't fool everyone; some entities saw the truth of the matter, no matter how deeply or cleverly it was hidden. I needed to lose myself in a sea of humanity, preferably in a place where sinners walked hand in hand with saints. And, if I could swing it, a place where I could get a sweet pair of shoes.

Thanks to my rash action, I was stuck in Caitlin's body. More accurately, I was trapped in a body that was a dead ringer for Caitlin. The lady herself was still leaping in the fields of Slumberland, blissfully unaware of how close she'd been to having a demon of Covet as an enemy.

Since that would've been my fault, I was sort of glad things didn't turn out that way. I might have felt obligated to make things right. Not because I liked Caitlin (I did) or thought of her as a friend (I didn't) but because that would have broken one of the Ten Great Rules. Paraphrasing Rule No. 3, demons could fuck with mortals only if said mortals were slated for Hell, or begged a favor of Hell, or courted the demons of Hell. Caitlin didn't fit any of those categories. Worse, technically she was protected by the Hecate. Smart demons didn't piss off goddesses, period.

I touched my flesh beneath the gem and blew out a relieved sigh when I found the skin unmarred. Mental note: Even if it feels like you're in the Lake of Fire, your body doesn't burn from contact with an active shieldstone.

Mental note, part two: Never ever, ever remove the Shield Against Evil.

Taking a deep breath, I forced myself to stand. The demon had been right – I reeked of sex. Couldn't help it; it was an after-effect of using my power on Caitlin before I drank her vomit-worthy potion.

Right. First things first: Time to bathe.

It took me a few minutes to find which room had the bath (none), and a bit longer to figure out the shower stall. I'd taken my fair share of showers in my time, but they'd all been for (and with) clients. They'd never been about getting clean, just wet. After learning the hard way that twisting the single knob all the way meant scorchingly hot water, I adjusted the temperature, reviewed the various soaping options, and grabbed two dark blue towels from the small closet outside the bathroom. Then I proceeded to take a delicious shower, staying under the water until my skin wrinkled.

Mental note, part three: Showers aren't just for sex.

Toweling dry, I pawed through Caitlin's various toiletries and cosmetics, frowning over the very slim assortment of goodies. It took longer to apply makeup by hand than it did by magic, but I figured I'd get faster with more prac-tice. Turning my thick black hair into a tight French twist, I fastened it with two long bone-colored pins, allowing some tendrils to frame my round face. Then I found Caitlin's bedroom and ransacked her closet and bureau.

Next time I go on the lam from the Underworld, I'm turning to a supermodel for help. Maybe her accessories will lack that certain magical oomph, but I bet she'd have a killer wardrobe.

Finally, I decided on a light blue cotton blouse, dark blue jeans, and brown open-toed sandals. For giggles, I wore a white lace bra and panties. In all of my existence, I didn't think I'd ever worn white intimate garments. Men always seemed to prefer red and black. Maybe white made them think of angels – or worse, marriage.

Finding a suitcase with a set of wheels and a retractable handle (bless me, these mortals were fucking ingenious), I piled in an array of clothing that I deemed bearable, leaving behind the long, flowing skirts, matronly blouses, and dowdy sweaters. Maybe Caitlin was an über witch, but she was also in serious need of a fashionista.

I shoved Caitlin's makeup and personal items into a travel bag and dumped that inside the suitcase as well. In went two pairs of boots, one pair of athletic shoes, and all-purpose black pumps. After scanning her small house, I also added two jackets and a few books from her library. One title in particular had me rolling on the floor: *Lucifer's Hammer*. Heh. King Lucifer never used a hammer.

That thought stopped me cold. In my mind, I heard King Lucifer's voice, decreeing the Announcement to all of Hell. And I remembered the softest brush of lips against mine, the faintest whisper of words: *You really believe that your friend isn't an enemy?*

Shoving the memory aside, I grabbed Caitlin's purse and flipped open her wallet. Then I rolled my eyes. Leave it to me to borrow the identity of the one adult in all America that didn't have a driver's license. What was I supposed to do with a State ID – pick my teeth?

Hmm. But she did have some cash, at least. And ooh, lookie at all the credit cards.

Crap. I should've had Caitlin tell me what her PIN was before I drank that nasty potion. Now I couldn't command her without activating my power – which meant removing my amulet. And it would be, pardon me, a cold day in Hell before I did that. Oh well. I'd make do.

Before I walked out of Caitlin's life, I covered her sleeping body with a blanket. She murmured some nonsensical sleep stuff and rolled over.

Sweet dreams, Caitlin. And don't cancel your credit cards before I max them out.

3

South Station

As I shut Caitlin's door behind me, I realized I had no idea where I was going. I adjusted the shoulder strap to my purse, grabbed the handle of the suitcase, and walked exactly three steps before someone called to me.

'Hey, Cait, good morning!'

I turned to see a little man exiting the house next to the witch's. A scrawny thing, he was dressed in a brown suit that screamed polyester and begged to be returned to the 1970s. With a chicken neck and no chin, the man was a far cry from Adonis. But his smile was genuine, and I found that oddly appealing. His hand was up in a wave.

Flashing him a smile, I said, 'Morning.' Far as I could tell, other than the spectacular shower, there was nothing good about the morning so far.

'Wow, you look terrific!' A mad blush exploded across his face, staining him from ear to ear. 'I mean, you always look terrific. But there's something different about you. Did you change something?'

Heh. A lot of somethings. 'There's no fooling you.'

'Got your hair cut?'

'Styled it differently.'

He grinned, showing overly large front teeth. 'I knew it! It looks really good this way.'

'Thanks,' I said, fiddling with the suitcase's retractable handle. The blessed thing was halfway up, and I couldn't get it to open all the way.

Locking his front door, he said, 'Say, it looks like you're going on a trip. Business or pleasure?'

Survival. 'You could say a little bit of both.'

He chuckled, a sound that was far too attractive for his looks. 'That's the right attitude! You headed to the airport?'

Trapped on a flying coach, with no way out? Er, no. 'I like traveling on the Earth instead of over it.'

'Know what you mean. Besides, security's a real bitch these days. Pardon my French.' Tucking a briefcase under one arm and picking up the newspaper on his doorstep, he said, 'If you're going to South Station, I'd be happy to give you a ride. It's on the way to the office.'

I had no idea what or where South Station was, but if Chicken Neck thought it was where I was supposed to go, I was willing to run with it. Smiling warmly, I said, 'Aren't you the nicest neighbor a girl could have?'

His blush deepened. 'Say, let me help you with that,' he stammered, walking over to me and taking the suitcase. He did something to the handle, a quick push in and out, and the thing worked perfectly for him. Huh. Must be a mortal thing. With a thick newspaper tucked under his armpit, his briefcase in one hand and the suitcase's handle in the other, he looked ridiculously comical . . . and rather sweet.

Ugh, it had to be the milk. I couldn't be this nice in real life.

Next to his large, blue minivan, he released my suitcase to rummage through his jacket pocket. Removing a set of keys, he pointed a device at the car and pressed a button. The minivan beeped twice, and the back door slid open.

Unholy Hell, these mortals were amazing. Such nifty little gadgets! The Almighty really did make humans in His own image, didn't He? Mortals definitely had the creation bug in their genes, whether making babies or making gizmos.

But they also had other genes in them too, didn't they? Darker genes that ate at them like a cancer . . .

Quit it, Jezebel. That's what got you in trouble in the first place. Just leave it alone.

'Say, Cait – you okay?'

I glanced over at Chicken Neck, who threw my suitcase onto the backseat. 'Sorry. Lost in thought.'

He smiled at me, then shut the door. 'You look way too serious for such a nice morning. I know that look. You're thinking about the business part of the trip instead of the pleasure part, aren't you?'

'You could say that.' Feeling the weight of my new body pressing down on me, I tried to smile, but suddenly I felt completely drained.

'Try not to think about business. Think of it as a grand adventure!' He shrugged, looking embarrassed and proud at the same time. 'That's what I like to do. Who wants to go to a convention for dentists? That's boring. But if I think that I'm on my way to someplace new, someplace where I could escape from my life and start over new if I wanted to . . . well, that makes me feel like I'm doing something fun.' He lowered his voice. 'Actually, I pretend I'm doing something dangerous.'

His brown eyes sparkled with joy as he revealed this tidbit, and I couldn't help but smile at his excitement. He was so endearing, like a pet. I resisted the urge to pat him on his balding head. 'Sounds like you make the best of it.'

'Exactly!' He opened the passenger door for me, and I slid onto the seat. 'Say, you never told me where you're headed. What's your destination?'

'Someplace fun,' I said. 'Fun, but dangerous.'

He barked out a laugh. 'Let me guess – New York City, right?'

Why not? I needed somewhere to go. 'You got it.'

'New York, New York,' he sang, 'it's a hell of a town.'

Perfect.

A harrowing ride later – bless me, if all Boston drivers don't have death wishes, then they're certifiably insane – Chicken Neck deposited me in front of a sprawling building laden with Ionic columns, topped by a huge clock tower. South Station, I presumed. The granite structure seemed to take up the entire city block – it curved, as if it were either circular or oval, looking more like an amphitheater than a place that harbored trains. Looking up at the clock mechanism, complete with a massive bird spreading its stone wings as if ready to take flight, I was struck by just how small I was.

How did mortals reach such heights without wings? Or at least a decent levitation spell?

The sculpture atop the clock seemed to look down at me. An eagle, maybe – or an owl. For a dizzying moment, I saw superimposed over the building's façade the towering mountain complex of Pandemonium, home to all creatures of the Pit. The stone bird launched itself off the clock

31

and spiraled down at me, its talons spread wide, murder shining in its black eyes. I bit back a scream as the creature transformed into the half-owl, half-woman shape of Queen Lyssa, goddess of madness and fury, her beak opened as she released a piercing hunter's cry.

Screwing my eyes shut, I told myself that I wasn't in Hell. Even in the deepest part of the Abyss, it didn't smell this bad. Risking a look, I opened my eyes. Once more, the bird was trapped in its stone prison.

Minor panic attack successfully averted. Get going, Jezebel.

Herds of people marched into and out of the massive doorway, all wrapped up in their lives, trying to make their way to their destinations. Gripping my suitcase handle tightly, I joined the flow and allowed myself to be swept inside, caught in the current of human commuters. People swerved around one another as if their feet knew choreographed steps; I, new to the dance, tripped over my own feet and stumbled into fellow travelers. Bags and valises and backpacks and other assorted carrying cases surrounded me, crushed me as we moved forward into a grand concourse.

And there I stopped, too flabbergasted to move. Storefronts and signs and tables and, above all, people milling about, filling almost every available space with color and movement and sound. And the stench! Body odor mingled with perfumes and colognes and deodorants and other camouflages ... and that was just from the humans. From the building itself wafted ammonia, soap, and other cleansers, barely dampening the deeper, richer smell of dirt and decay, buried within the structure's foundation. I inhaled, trying to focus on the earthy scent – something to ground me, help me through the assault on

32

my senses. Someone jostled me from behind, yelling something unintelligible at me as I got shoved to the side.

Glaring, I tried to find the person who'd bumped me, but I would have had an easier time picking a specific grain of sand from an hourglass. Bless me, I knew there were billions of humans on the Earth, but did the better part of that number have to loiter in one building?

I grabbed the handle of my suitcase and walked forward. Now that the initial shock of the place had worn off, I felt amazed instead of overwhelmed. So many stores! Food sellers – many of which seemed closed, but McDonald's and the Boston Coffee Exchange were open and, from the look of the lines of people waiting for service, they must have been giving away free samples. A place called Au Bon Pain also had a lot of business, and as I saw rows of muffins, bagels, and other assorted pastries lying on display, my stomach lurched and rumbled. Saliva pooled in my mouth, and I swallowed it down. It took me a moment to identify the sensation I was experiencing.

I was *hungry!* And not for sex. Wow . . . that was a first.

Ambling inside the pseudo-French *boulangerie*, I paused in front of the baked goodies. My stomach growled again. I grabbed two large muffins, considered the sounds my belly made, and took a third. Following the cues of the humans around me, I stood in a line until it was my turn. The key to blending in, I discovered, was acting as if I knew what I was doing. Apparently, maneuvering through real life was just like sex: When all else fails, fake it.

I showed the cashier my selection. Taking my pastries and putting them into a paper bag, she asked me, 'That all? Any coffee today?'

I'd never tried it before, although I'd heard mortals talk about coffee like it was an exquisite pleasure. I could use a bit of pleasure. Maybe the coffee came with a side order of Cabin Boy to watch me drink it. 'Sure, coffee would be great.'

'Large?'

'Um, okay.'

'Milk and sugar?'

'No milk,' I said quickly.

She pushed a covered, wax-coated paper cup my way, along with the bag of muffins. 'That'll be seven twenty-nine.'

Right, payment. I opened Caitlin's bag and produced her wallet. Inside the billfold were three tens, a twenty, and a few ones. I handed the cashier a ten, took my change along with my purchase, and returned the wallet to the purse.

I just bought my first thing as a human! Woot! I wanted to do a happy dance, but I thought that might call attention to myself.

Suitcase in tow, I hurried out of the shop, managing not to slam into anyone as I searched for a place to sit and eat. Seeing an empty table, I made a beeline for it and threw myself into the seat just as another woman approached. She shot me a filthy look as I placed my bag and purse on the table. I bit back my initial reaction, which was to zap her and giggle as she fell to the floor, writhing as an orgasm savaged her body. Not only was I in disguise, I also had my shieldstone nuzzled between my breasts, which wouldn't allow me to use my power even if I really wanted to. So instead I smiled sweetly at her as I opened my bag of food. Scowling, she turned away, looking for a place of her own. Suck it up, sweetie. I was here first.

Feeling very proud of myself for using such restraint, I took out a muffin. The large pastry had some fruit in it

34

– cranberries and orange pieces, I thought; I'd just grabbed the first ones I'd seen without pausing to read their names. I tore off a chunk and popped it in my mouth.

Chewed.

Swallowed.

Oh . . . unholy Hell, who would have thought a morsel of food could be so succulent? I'd eaten mortal food before, but all as part of the job – it never had any real taste until now. And such taste! Sweet as a man's soul on my lips, solid as a man's shaft ramming inside of me. I ripped off another piece and ate it, savoring the way my saliva began to break down the food even as I chewed, masticating until the bite was nothing more than mush. I swallowed it down and broke off another section, shoving it in my mouth and barely touching it with my teeth before I swallowed, already reaching for more.

Before I knew it, the muffin was gone. As I reached into the bag for another treat, a male voice asked, 'Is this seat taken?'

Hovering next to the empty seat across from me stood a tall man in a white T-shirt and jeans, a steaming paper cup in one hand, a jacket slung over his shoulder. Crowning his head, his light brown hair was cut short, but it was just long enough to curl slightly around his ears. His face was broad, with sculpted cheeks and a strong jaw. Small, expressive sea-green eyes regarded me. Poet's eyes . . . and a fighter's nose, which had clearly been broken at least once in his life.

One side order of Cabin Boy, as requested. *Yuuuuum.*

His thin lips, already curved into a pleasant smile, quirked into an amused grin as my gaze lingered.

'Not taken,' I said, finally remembering to answer his question. 'Help yourself.'

35

He draped his jacket over the back of the chair, then sat, taking a sip from his cup. 'Thanks.'

I smiled at him, admiring how his throat worked as he drank. Then I mentally rolled my eyes. What was I, a former succubus or a wannabe vampire?

To cover my fluster, I removed the plastic cover from my coffee cup and took a careful sip of the hot liquid. Oooooh . . . yum, again!

I must have said something aloud, because the man said, 'Sounds like your coffee's better than mine.'

'I think it's the sugar. Wow, that's good!'

Looking at the advertising on my cup, he said, 'With a reaction like that, from now on I'll get my coffee at Au Bon Pain, too.'

We shared a laugh. His was warm, and hearing it made my stomach flutter and my heart beat a little faster.

He extended his hand. 'I'm Paul.'

When his fingers touched mine, I felt something electric dance over my skin, and the temperature suddenly rose about a million degrees. Instead of telling him Caitlin's name, I gave him the human nickname I'd picked up over the years. 'Jesse.'

His eyes flicked to my suitcase. 'Going or coming?'

My breath caught in my throat as I heard another voice, a deep voice, whisper to me: *Going or coming?* In my mind, I saw a large man, a blue bandana holding his long, red hair away from his lean face. He opened his mouth and asked . . .

'Jesse? You okay?'

Feeling the blood drain from my face, I withdrew my hand from his and placed it between my knees as I shivered. 'Sorry. I'm okay. You just . . . reminded me of someone.'

36

Thoughts flitted across his eyes, but all he said was, 'Oh.'

Shaking off the shreds of memory, I flashed him a smile, but it felt strained around the edges. 'I really should go, get my ticket.'

'Okay.' He raked his hand through his hair, as if he was used to it being longer. A frown marred his brow. 'Sorry I spooked you. It was nice meeting you.'

'You too, Paul.' I grabbed my suitcase and purse and dashed off, not knowing where I was going, just trying to get away from that husky voice inside my head. But even as I finally found the Amtrak board and got in line to purchase a one-way ticket to New York, I still heard that voice inside my mind, repeating the last thing it had said to me:

You're mine.

Collapsing on a red, high-backed seat on the Regional Service Amtrak train, I wrapped my arms around myself. Bless me six ways to Salvation, I was a former *demon*. I didn't get afraid. I *caused* fear. And wet dreams, but that was a side effect.

But I couldn't deny that I was terrified, down to my fragile human bones. How long could I avoid the malefic bounty hunters on my trail? If the Coveter hadn't been lying – always a toss-up when it came to demons – then I was worth a lot to whomever, or whatever, returned me to Hell. With such a high price, how long could I trust the witch's spell and the shieldstone to protect me?

And what would they do to me if I returned?

I inhaled deeply, then let out a shaky breath. I was not going to mind-fuck myself. Caitlin's nasty potion would work because she said it would, and I had to believe her.

All I had to do was not use my powers, and the peridot hanging between my boobs took care of that. I could do this.

I *would* do this.

Feeling a tad better, I struggled to put my suitcase on the luggage rack over the seat. The blessed thing was too heavy. I hefted and grunted and shoved, and let out a few colorful curses. Suddenly the trunk flew out of my hands and into the rack.

Blinking, I wondered if I had accidentally cast a spell somehow – maybe the suitcase had a charm on it? Then I saw Paul grinning at me as he lowered his hands.

'Hope you don't mind,' he said. 'Looked like you could use some help.'

My grin must have eaten my entire face. 'Thanks. Fancy meeting you here.'

'So, if you don't mind, I'd like to start over. Is this seat taken?'

With a laugh, I said, 'Nope.' I scooted to the window, and he sat next to me. Up close, I noticed how broad his shoulders were, how his arms were nicely muscled . . . how he had a musky scent that permeated his entire being. My right arm lay parallel to his left, each on an armrest, and I was fascinated by how tan his skin was, how golden his body hair was, compared with my pale flesh and dark hair. His hand could have swallowed mine and come back for seconds.

'I didn't see any luggage for you,' I said, suddenly burning with curiosity about this mortal – this man with a poet's eyes and a fighter's nose. 'You travel light.'

He smiled, close lipped. 'Boston was a one-day thing. Came last night. Glad to be leaving now.'

'You live in New York?'

38

'Yup. You?'

I bit my lip, which was still sore from when I'd bitten it earlier. 'I will be. Maybe.'

He didn't say anything, just looked at me with those lovely eyes. A silence grew until I filled it with, 'I'm getting a fresh start.'

'Fresh is good.' Something darkened his eyes for a moment. 'Sometimes we have to leave stuff behind, do something new.'

My heart somehow wound up in my head, because all I could hear was it thumping like crazy in my ears. 'Exactly.'

We stayed like that for a small eternity, our gazes locked and tongues tied, silently sharing secrets that we didn't dare speak aloud. The spell broke when the train started moving, and the conductor announced that all tickets should be ready for collection. Smiling sheepishly – and feeling stupid and goofy and excited, all mixed up into a big knot in my belly – I turned away to dig through my bag for the ticket I'd bought with Caitlin's credit card.

Placing the ticket on my lap, I saw that Paul had his ready to go too. He cast a glance at mine, and I could see his mind working. Did he notice the name on the ticket said 'Caitlin Harris' instead of 'Jesse Something'?

The ticket-taker came and went, and I placed the stub inside my purse. For a moment, I leaned back into the seat and watched the scenery outside the window as we rolled past, leaving a blur of color streaming behind. My eyes slipped closed, just for a moment, as I felt the train's vibrations tickle my spine and work its way into my neck.

And just over four hours later, I awoke with my head on Paul's shoulder as the conductor announced over the loudspeaker that we'd arrived at New York City's Penn Station.

4

Penn Station/Hotel New York

I thought I'd seen ordered chaos at Boston's South Station during morning rush hour. That was a sneeze compared with the epidemic of people spread throughout Penn Station. Everyone had somewhere to go, somewhere to be – and they were all late. Even those few people who walked instead of strode, who meandered instead of marched, had an energy to them, a vibrant thrum that I didn't sense in Boston. It filled the air, overriding the stench of humanity and technology.

And the stores! It was like a city block had fallen beneath the surface, an Atlantis submerged in retail and anchored by multiple train lines. Bookstores and pharmacies and shoe stores – ooh, *shoes* – and food . . . bless me, all of the food! Restaurants and small specialty shops and deli-catessens and snack carts and on and on and on. How much value did these mortals place on the appetite? Remembering my recent experience with my breakfast muffin, my mouth watered.

Unbelievable. I was hungry *again*. Maybe creatures of

Gluttony had a better understanding of humans than a former succubus.

Nah. Eating that muffin had been close to orgasmic, but still fell way short of the real thing.

By my side, Paul waited as I looked around like a lovestruck fool gazing at the stars. Leaning against the suitcase's handle, he said, 'You look overwhelmed.'

'Not overwhelmed,' I said as I stared at a doughnut storefront, wondering why Americans purposefully misspelled certain words. It should have been *Crispy*, with a *C* instead of a *K*. And *Kreme* was wrong on two counts. If the owners couldn't even spell properly, what did that say about the quality of their food? 'Whelmed, maybe. But not overwhelmed.'

He laughed, and once again I felt my body react to the sound. Warmth rippled from my belly, reaching up to my breasts and down to touch my groin, then disappeared, leaving my nipples hard.

If that's just from his laugh, imagine what his fingers would do . . .

I bit my lip, hard. The pain was immediate and complete, and it shocked me out of my growing attraction to Paul. I couldn't afford to experiment with my new human emotions and desires. Not yet. Even if what I really wanted was to feel his breath hot against my skin as his mouth kissed my ear, my neck, my –

Crap. Now my panties were damp. Being human meant leaking at very inopportune times.

'Which way are you headed?' Paul asked. 'I could walk you to the subway or a cab, wherever you're going.'

'I . . .' Blinking, I realized I had no idea what I should do. My head began to pound as the reality of the past eight hours came crashing down on me. I'd walked away

– okay, snuck away – from everything I'd ever known. For a gal who admitted to four thousand years, give or take a few centuries, that was saying a lot. What did a long-time succubus do with her newfound life?

And who would have thought that turning my back on Hell would also turn me into an interplaneary fugitive?

One thing at a time, I told myself. As long as I wore the Shield Against Evil and bore the effects of Caitlin's potion, I didn't have to worry about the infernal bounty hunters. At least that was something. 'I have to think things through. Figure out what to do first.'

He looked at me long and hard, those sea-green eyes measuring me. His voice soft, he asked, 'Do you have a place to go to? Friends or family who are expecting you?'

If I saw any of my friends or family, I would run like fuck the other way. 'No, but that's okay. I'll get a hotel room for now while I decide on a more permanent option.'

'So you've got some money.'

I nodded. 'Some.' At least, I did until Caitlin woke up and realized I'd, um, borrowed her wallet.

'Do you have a job?'

The words escaped my lips before I could stop them: 'Not anymore.' With a carefree shrug, I added, 'Guess I have to find a new one.'

He paused, as if he were absorbing my words. 'I'm sure you'll find something.' Smiling, he pushed my suitcase in front of him. 'Come on, I'll walk you to Hotel New York. It's just across the street. I'm not sure what the rate is, but we can find out.'

We. Ooh, I liked that. As we headed through a wall of people, I asked him, 'You always help strangers in need?'

'I serve and protect,' he said. 'It's what I do.'

42

'Romantic. A poet's eyes, and now a poet's words.' Then I groaned. 'Tell me I didn't say that out loud.'

Laughing, he said, 'I won't tell if you won't.' His eyes sparkled when he laughed, like the sun dancing on the ocean. 'You didn't get the reference, huh?'

I shrugged. 'Should I have?' Other than a passing familiarity with recording artists, I was woefully out of touch with pop culture. Mental note: Watch more television.

'Nah, that's okay.' His gaze lingered on mine. 'You know, you look familiar. I'm good with faces, and I'd remember if I'd seen you before, so that's not it. But there's something about you . . .'

A blush crept up my face as he scrutinized me. 'Oh? Maybe it's my dazzling personality?'

'That must be it.' Smiling, he shook his head. 'I swear I've seen you before.'

I looked up at him, at the broad, chiseled lines of his face. I pictured him with his eyes closed, with his hair tousled from sleep and his body gleaming with sweat – there was no air-conditioning or central air in his apartment, and it was a hot night for September in the city . . .

And in that moment, I placed him.

Oh crap, why didn't I recognize him before? And more – what did this mean? If only I could talk to Megaera. Forget about dearly wishing I had my best friend to turn to; she was a Fury, closely linked with the Fates. Meg could read meaning in the clouds. Either that, or she faked it with the best of them.

In my mind, I heard Meg's voice whisper, *We all do what we must.*

And over that, another voice, full of sadness and wounded pride: *If only you were right.*

'Jesse? You've gone pale. You okay?'

43

I turned away from Paul and kept walking, increasing my pace. My heart slammed against my chest like it wanted to burst free, and my throat felt too tight. Did Paul know who I was? No, that was insane. I was in a different body – unholy Hell, I was a different *entity* – from when we last met. And he'd been asleep. There was no way he could know who I really was.

A hand on my shoulder stopped me. Nibbling my lip, I darted a glance at him.

'I know you don't know me,' Paul said, his voice soft as a summer wind. 'And I know you're running away from something, or someone. But you don't have to run from me.'

'I never said I was running away.'

'You didn't have to. It's written all over you.' His eyes locked on mine. 'You in trouble with the law?'

That startled me so much that I let out a full belly laugh, ending with me clutching my stomach and doubling over to try to muffle the sound. Finally I managed to say, 'I haven't done anything illegal.'

'That didn't answer the question.'

Something in his voice froze the last drops of laughter in my throat. 'No, I'm not in trouble with the law.' *Trouble* didn't begin to describe what I was in. *Deep shit* came to mind. And mortal law was the least of my worries.

His gaze softened, and he reached over to brush away stray locks of hair that dangled in front of my eyes. 'Can I help you?'

I wanted to say, Yes. Wrap me in your arms and keep me warm and tell me everything's going to be okay. Kiss away my fears and teach me how to live. Hold my hand as I experience everything for the first time and fill my heart with the sound of your laughter.

44

Barring that, an orgasm would be nice.

I said none of those things. Instead I smiled, perhaps a bit wanly, and said, 'Walk me to the hotel you mentioned.'

He did. And in the lobby, he presented me with my suitcase and squeezed my shoulder once. He took a piece of the hotel's stationery and wrote his name and phone number on it. Folding it in my hand, he said, 'Call me. Whenever you want.'

'You always give your number to strangers?' I asked, trying to be coy.

'The question is, do the strangers call me back?'

'Do they?'

'In your case?' He winked at me. 'I hope so.'

I watched Paul walk out of the hotel lobby, enjoying the way his legs moved, how relaxed he seemed with his jacket slung over one shoulder. Maybe he sensed my gaze on his back (and lower down), because he looked back at me and lifted his hand in a wave. I did the same, and as he walked out of my line of sight my fingers curled into a loose fist that I placed against my heart. Beneath it, the peridot charm was cool, indifferent.

The only thing evil about Paul was the way he made me feel. Ooh, the things I wanted to do to him, to show him . . .

. . . the things I'd already done to him . . .

Blowing out a frustrated sigh, I let that thought go. He'd freaked me out when he said he'd seen me before. I hadn't counted on my very last client to show up in my new life.

Of course, I hadn't counted on taking a place on the Underworld's Most Wanted list. It wasn't like I had done anything wrong. (Well, other than going AWOL.) I didn't know anything that other demons didn't know.

45

Except their loyalty was unquestioned. They were still creatures of the Pit. Because I ran, I was a wild card. And the King of Hell didn't tolerate gambling.

A sharp pain in my hand pulled me out of my dark thoughts, and I realized I'd squeezed my fist so hard that my nails had pierced my flesh. Fascinated, I watched blood seep into the half-moon marks on my palm, transforming them into ruby crescents.

Enough moping, I told myself. Time to take control of your life.

I walked over to the front desk, where a dashing man stood behind the counter, typing on his computer. Glancing at me, he put on a perfunctory smile and said, 'May I help you?'

Pouring on the charm, I said, 'Yes, thanks. I'd like to check in, please.'

His smile warmed, obviously pleased that I wanted to spend money in his establishment. 'Do you have a reservation?'

'No,' I said, standing on tiptoe to lean close to him over the counter. 'But maybe you could scare something up for me?'

He began to type on the keyboard. 'I'm sure I can find something. Single occupancy?'

'For now,' I said, a note of wistfulness in my voice.

With a chuckle, he said, 'Okay, single. How long will you be staying?'

'Oh, I don't know. Let's start with two nights and take it from there.'

Clackety clack clack. His fingers moved so quickly, so dexterously. I wondered what else he could do that skillfully with his fingers. Then I wondered if human females were always in heat, or if that was just me being ... well, me.

'I can give you a standard room for tonight and tomorrow night, at two-fifty-nine a night, for a total of six-oh-five forty-six.'

It took me a moment to realize he was talking about price. Pulling out Caitlin's wallet, I flipped it open and popped out a credit card. 'Here you go.'

'I just need some ID, please.'

Offering Caitlin's Massachusetts State ID, I smiled brightly.

He glanced at it, then at me. My smile broadened as he took the Visa card. The transaction went through, and in a moment he told me I'd been put in room 217. I'd half-expected to get something cheesy like room 666.

'I can't give you the key card yet,' he said, shrugging his shoulders. 'Check-in's not until three. But if you want, you can leave your suitcase here until three o'clock.'

'That's great,' I said, wheeling the trunk over to him behind the counter. 'I have some shopping to do anyway.'

5

Belles/Hotel New York

Whistling the 'I Love New York' theme, I ambled past the club, three overly stuffed shopping bags in tow, before I did a double take, my sex radar blipping. The name was stenciled in silver on the frosted window, as well as on the black awning: Belles. Next to the name was the distinctive hourglass silhouette of a female begging to be on the cover of a bodice ripper.

   Bubbling with curiosity, I opened the door and walked inside. The entrance was dimly lit, making me blink after basking in the afternoon brightness. Up ahead came the distinctive sounds of honky-tonk music. Humming along with the song as I wandered down the hallway, I placed it as a Shania Twain hit. Like most nefarious creatures, I knew who many recording artists were; it was amazing how many young hopefuls were desperate enough to turn to Hell for an edge in getting a foot in the door and launching a career. Unlike many of my former brethren, I knew the names simply because I loved the music. Passion turned to melody, emotion given life in song . . .

ah, ecstasy! Just thinking about it made my G-spot tingle.

With Shania singing loud enough to make my eyes vibrate in their sockets, I took in the large room. A glass-topped mahogany bar sprawled along the left wall; behind it, bottles stood at attention, waiting to be used. Above hung rows of glasses, suspended by their stems. How the crystal withstood the ear-shattering decibel of the music was anybody's guess. Numerous flat-screen televisions decorated the walls around the bar. Off to the side was a foosball table, its players standing half-cocked, just waiting to come to attention and get slap-happy.

Mirrors winked like interactive wallpaper, reflecting the rest of the room *ad nauseam*. To my right, divided from the bar by a mahogany half-wall with a cutout entrance, were rows of round tables, black and cold, each surrounded by three plush gray chairs. The front tables bumped up against a white stage with a runway, the corners adorned with a low, brass rail. A slim pole at the end of the stage caught the targeted beams of multicolored spotlights, casting the silver with hints of red, green, and blue. On stage, a blonde woman danced as she held onto the pole. Either that, or she had a bug in her cleavage she was trying to shake free.

Two people were seated at a table near the stage, a man in an open-necked button-up shirt and a plump woman in a light sweater, both with drinks. The man called over his shoulder, 'For God's sake, Lyle, can't you please lose the country shit?'

'But I *like* country,' a guy's voice boomed from loud-speakers I couldn't see. 'And you never let me play it when we're open.'

The blonde bumped and thrusted as Shania sang that the best thing about being a woman was the prerogative

49

to have a little fun. My kinda gal, that Shania. The dancer wasn't really feeling the music; she moved as if she was trying to find the groove but her feet wouldn't pay attention to the rhythm. Maybe it was the fuck-me shoes. With stilettos that high, if she exhaled too much she'd fall on her ass.

Hips swaying to the beat, the blonde pulled her shirt over her head, revealing a black lace bra barely containing two D-cups. Tossing the garment to the seated man, she flashed a nervous smile when he caught the shirt one-handed. A real pro, that guy.

A grin bloomed on my face. I was in a strip club! Well, no – the decor seemed a bit too upscale for a titty bar, despite the gauche mirror-as-wallpaper motif. More like a gentlemen's club. Flesh as fantasy. I inhaled deeply, imagining smoke and booze and sweat riding the air, hearing whoops of carnal desire over the thumping of the music. No wonder this place called to me. I might not have been a succubus any longer, but my sex radar still worked.

Shimmying to the song, the blonde slid her miniskirt down and stepped out of it. Sheer thigh-highs clung to her curvy legs, held in place by a black garter belt. She performed a slow turn – either in an attempt to move to the beat or to avoid a wipeout in five-inch heels – broadcasting the fact that her black undies were the barest scrap of a thong. Bending over, she wiggled her bare bottom as Shania insisted we forget she's a lady. Her head bobbing between her legs, she fumbled with her bra clasp. Finally unhooking it, she slid her bra off, then sank to the floor. Flipping onto her back, she wriggled like a hooked fish, her large mounds doing their best Jell-O impression as they shook back and forth.

'All right, honey,' the woman at the table said. 'That's fine.'

The blonde sat up, swinging her legs beneath her bottom. She rose to her feet, using the pole for balance. Shielding her breasts with her hands, she licked her lips and waited, shivering either from the arctic temperature in the club or from nerves.

'Lyle,' the man shouted, 'turn that shit off!'

'Sure thing, Roman,' Lyle said offstage, and the music cut off.

'Did I get the job?' The blonde's voice was breathless with hope.

'Of course, love. I'm sure when you get some real music on, your feet'll know what to do.'

The older woman sighed, throwing the man a disgusted look. 'You did fine, honey. You've got a lovely body, and that's what the customers want to see. If you get nervous before your set, knock back a drink for some liquid courage. You'll be terrific.'

The blonde smiled her relief.

'But honey, no throwing your clothes to the customers. You'll never get them back. And I'm guessing you don't want to buy a new outfit for every show. First time dancing, right?'

Her breasts jiggled in time with her nodding head.

'You'll start on the early shift, then. Ease you into things. We open at five, but I'd want you here around four to go over the rules and fees and such like.'

'Fees?' The dancer's face scrunched in puzzlement. Man, she was fabulous at playing a Dumb Blonde. I bit back the urge to applaud.

'Momma here'll explain how Belles works,' the man said, tossing the shirt back to the sweet young thing. 'We'll see you around four.'

She gushed her thanks as she collected her clothing. Dressing quickly, she prattled about how thrilled she was, how this was so exciting, how she's always wanted to dance.

If what she just did on stage was dancing, then I needed a new definition for the word.

She carefully stepped down the stairs on the far left, a touch wobbly in her heels. Sauntering up to me, she gave me a thumbs-up sign. Up close, I saw she was blonde by way of Clairol – platinum all around except by her roots, which threatened to sprout brunette. 'Roman and Momma are really nice,' she said, motioning to the two seated at the table.

I glanced over at the man and the woman, who were bent together, speaking softly. They were nice in the way that diamondbacks were pretty – you still didn't want to get too close. He looked like he was aiming for Mafioso Chic, while she was pushing the boundary on All-American Mom. I didn't take either at face value.

'I was so nervous!' the blonde confided. 'But Momma let me have a shot of whiskey before I tried out. That helped, but I was still afraid they would think I couldn't dance. And I really need this job. I got lucky!'

This girl with her Marilyn Monroe hair wore naivete like jewelry. I was willing to bet one of Caitlin's credit cards that dancing ability was the last thing an exotic dancer really needed. Low body fat and a ready smile were probably more valuable than high kicks. And I wondered whether Roman thought he'd be getting lucky with the new blood later tonight.

I said, 'They wouldn't have hired you if they didn't like what they saw.'

Gah. There I went again with the nice shtick. I didn't want to be nice. Bunnies were nice. I wanted to be less like Thumper and more like Glenn Close in *Fatal Attraction*.

A fluttering smile played on the blonde's face. 'Thanks. My name's Jennifer, but I'm going by Jemma here.'

'I'm Jesse.'

'Nice to meet you. I'd stay to cheer you on, but I've got to get an outfit for later. Good luck, Jesse!' With that, she tottered down the hall and out of sight.

'Hey, love,' the man at the table called out, 'you here to audition?'

It was a moment before I realized he was talking to me. 'Audition?'

'Christ, not another one who doesn't speak English. You know, to try out? Dance?' He made a waving motion with his hand.

Ooh. Me, an exotic dancer? Why not? I needed a job. Caitlin's credit cards wouldn't last forever ... especially not after all of the yummy purchases I'd made at Bloomingdale's. Grinning, I decided to give it a shot. 'Right, audition. That's why I'm here.'

'Well, come here, love. Let's take a look at you first.'

I dropped my bags by the bar and walked over to the table. Momma was older, maybe in her fifties, with a ready smile and warm eyes. Roman, maybe thirty-five, had a lean face and jet black hair. The multitude of rings on his fingers tried to outshine the gold chain around his throat. His open-necked black shirt looked like silk. Style by way of pimp. He radiated money almost as much as the Coveter had. One of the managers, then; maybe the owner.

'You're a bit old for this, aren't you?' His gaze crawled over my body, leaving no curve unexplored. 'What are you, thirty?'

53

Next to him, Momma rolled her eyes. 'Jesus, Roman. Have some class.'

'I'm so fucking classy, I could open a university. I'm just saying the gal's a bit past prime.'

Creep. Never ask a female her age. Personally, I stopped counting after four thousand years, but that wasn't the point.

I planted a hand on my hip and rolled my shoulder back, thrusting my tits forward. Maybe I couldn't tap into my power, but thousands of years of seducing shmucks like this guy meant that I knew how to move my body. Putting the right amount of purr into my voice, I said, 'I might be older than other dancers, but I'm also more experienced.'

Roman swallowed, his eyes locked on mine. A bead of sweat glistened on his brow. Based on how the air-conditioning was set to about thirty degrees, I was sure his reaction wasn't from the temperature in the room. 'What kind of experience you talking about, love?'

My eyes telegraphing all of the things I could do to him if I so chose, I blew him a kiss.

Momma chuckled, a throaty, rich sound. 'Oh, you're good, honey. I love the attitude. And your eyes're lovely, and so's your hair. Can't tell about your figure with your clothes on, but I guess if you're willing to show it off, you're proud of what you've got. Can you dance?'

Turning my smoky gaze her way, I smiled. 'Try me.'

Roman mopped his brow, then shouted, 'Lyle! Put something on. And make sure it has a beat, God damn it.'

'Go ahead, honey.' Momma motioned to the stage. 'Show us what you've got.'

I sashayed to the stage and glided up the five stairs. Standing on the platform, the spotlights in my eyes, I couldn't see a blessed thing other than the stage itself. Probably done on purpose to keep dancers from getting nervous, seeing so many eyes on them. Me, I liked the attention.

From the speakers mounted above either side of the stage, drums tapped out a beat – *bump, ba-bump, bump, ba-bump* – followed by a guitar. Southern rock, maybe country gone the way of blues ... Marc Broussard's 'Home.' A good tune. I let my body pick up the pulse, felt it move through my hips, my shoulders, my neck. Marc began to sing, his voice deep and lush with emotion. Feeling the passion in his voice caress me, I let his words carry me across the stage.

Stopping in front of Roman and Momma, I planted my feet wide and dropped my body down, then rolled up slowly, snaking my hands up my calves, my inner thighs, my belly, my breasts, then raised them over my head, all the while my hips working the beat. I felt Roman's eyes on me, locking onto my hands as they traveled the length of my body, boring through my clothing as if he wanted to eat me alive from the inside out.

That's right, sweetie. Feast on me.

Moving to the music, I pulled the pins from my hair, freeing my curls. My hands swam through my locks, gathering up my hair and letting it crash around my face. I smiled at my audience as Marc sang, feeling as sultry as his voice.

Next to Roman, Momma's head nodded, either to the beat or for my performance. I didn't care which it was – as long as she didn't grab a cane and yank me off the stage, she was encouraging me to go on. And I did, letting my body speak the language of foreplay, promising sweat and tangled sheets.

Marc sang, 'Here we go,' and clapping hands amplified the drumbeat, making my steps bigger, bolder. Crossing my arms in front of my stomach, I grabbed the bottom of my shirt and pulled it over my head, then let it drop to the floor. Hips grinding to the music, I unclasped my bra in a fluid motion and swung it away. Freed, my breasts bounced as I danced, my nipples erect and my skin dotted with goosebumps. My amulet bobbed against my skin.

Maybe it was an icebox in the club, but I was feeling hotter than the Lake of Fire. There was no way I could strip off my jeans while dancing in low-heeled sandals, so I opted to keep them on. Instead I popped the button and unzipped my pants, then mimed peeling them off. Roman's face told me he easily pictured the real deal. He looked like he was thinking with Mister Happy instead of his brain.

Awesome.

Crying out to his audience or his God, Marc begged that someone take him home. I dropped to my knees and arched back, my body undulating to the beat. The sound reverberated along my flesh, teasing me, seducing me, and I opened wide as I let the music fuck me.

And just like sex, it was over too fast.

I held my final pose for a moment after the song ended, thrilled by how my blood pounded, how my breath had quickened. Then I lifted myself up until I was on my knees. Still smiling my Come Here Sailor smile, I planted one foot and rose gracefully, awaiting judgment.

Roman's eyes shone, a wolf contemplating the possibility of lamb chops. 'When can you start, love?'

Feeling proud, I toted my shopping bags as I marched down the hallway of Hotel New York, searching for my room. I was looking forward to my new role as a dancer. Granted, Roman seemed to be a real ass, but I liked Momma. Maybe that's because she'd buttered me up as she'd given me the lowdown about working at Belles.

'You've got terrific sex appeal,' she'd confided after my audition.

'It's my scented body wash,' I said. 'Vanilla. Does wonders for pheromones.'

'Hygiene helps,' she chuckled, clapping a hand on my shoulder. 'But on you, it's more than a smell. You radiate sex. If you're half as confident with a live audience during your shows as you were for the audition, you'll actually score decent stage tips.'

'I'm feeling confident. But I'll buy some new lingerie just in case. You can't help but feel sexy when you're wearing new lingerie. Maybe some new shoes.'

'Shoes are wonderful. Go with a minimum of four inches. Five, if you can swing it – you're a tiny thing and can use the extra height. Break 'em in before you show up tonight. And don't forget to put grips on your heels. Stage floor's polished and can be a slippery bastard. Don't want to see you taking a spill.'

I grinned, bemused by her concern. 'You really are the house mom, aren't you?'

'It's what I'm paid for. Actually,' she added, lowering her voice, 'that's a lie. I work for tips. But my girls are good to me. And I'm good to them. Makeup, hair, costume repair – you name it, I'll do it. I even have spare G-strings, if you ever need one. But those are a dollar a pop. The other stuff is free.'

'Good to know.'

'You'll do well here, honey.' Her eyes twinkled as if she had a marvelous secret. 'I can tell. And you'll find that even though we're small, we believe in quality. And that's not just for the entertainment.' She began ticking off points on her fingers. 'We don't use funny money here, and we've got an ATM on the premises. The music's never so loud that you can't hear your customers talking to you. Our waitresses know better than to hustle drinks, and God forbid the bartenders screw around and water things down.'

I had no idea what the 'funny money' comment meant, but I just smiled like I understood and nodded my head. When in doubt, pretend you have a clue.

'Okay, let's discuss your role. You'll do a minimum of three shows a night, three songs per show. We don't require lap dances, but you'll probably want to work the floor. That and the VIP room's where the money is.'

I nodded again, filing away her advice for later use.

'We're a medium-mileage place for lap dances. The customers know there's no touching your breasts or genitals, ever. You, on the other hand, can touch the customers however you want, just not their crotch. Feel free to grind, if that's your pleasure.'

Hmm. Get them all hot and bothered, with no follow-through. Maybe the place should be called Blue Balls instead of Belles.

'Fees are pretty good, all things considered,' Momma said. 'Only a forty-five dollar stage fee, but it's more if you're late. Roman's a bit of a dick when it comes to that, so do yourself a favor and show up on time.'

'Noted. Thanks.'

'There's no cut for table dances, which usually go for twenty bucks for three minutes. If your men want privacy, there's the VIP lounge upstairs with couches, and the VIP room itself. Ten dollars of every thirty-dollar couch dance goes to the house. VIP room's two-fifty for a half hour, with fifty going to the house for a room rental fee. What you arrange for dances in the VIP room is up to you. No fixed salary, of course. All we have here are house dancers. Features are prima donnas, and they mess up the rotations and put the house girls in bad moods, so we don't book them.'

My head was spinning from all the information. What was the difference between a table dance and a couch dance? And what were the prima donna features? Ah, screw it. I stretched my 'Yes, I understand completely' grin from ear to ear. I'd figure everything out on the job.

'You'll do the last shift, nine to three. Long dresses required before ten. Short dresses from ten till midnight. Then it's lingerie and bikinis from twelve until closing.'

Mental note: Go on shopping spree.

'Like I said before, we're about quality here. We don't want Neanderthal asshole customers, so we expect our staff and dancers to follow certain rules. No hustling drinks; wait for a customer to offer. No hustling private dances. You tell a guy you'll see him in the VIP room, you make sure you show up. Don't have one of the other dancers entertain the customer while you take your time, then show up and force the guy to tip you both. We ask our floor girls to follow tip-rail etiquette – no hitting up the men by the stage for dances when another dancer's performing her set.'

Holy fuck in Heaven, there were as many rules here as there were in the Pit.

'And last thing,' she said as we got to the front door. 'Tipouts. You want to treat the DJ and the bartender right. Don't go any less than ten, unless you want to dance to

Enya on stage and get completely snorkered when your men buy you drinks. Some girls tip the doormen and VIP host. Me, I recommend it. A girl can't have too many friends.'

I knew a hint when I heard one. I opened my wallet and produced a ten, handing it to Momma. 'Thanks for all the info.'

'See that?' she said, beaming proudly. 'I knew you were a natural. You keep us happy here, and we'll keep you happy in return. So what should we call you, honey?'

I grinned. 'Jezebel.'

It had to be the rush of hormones. I would never have been that stupid if I were still a creature of the Abyss. Sure, I walked, talked, and smelled like a human. That didn't mean I should all but advertise what I really was. But I was high on life, so I trusted Caitlin's magic to keep me safe. I was Jezebel.

Pleased with all of my accomplishments so far, I opened up the door to room 217 and threw the shopping bags to the floor. I dropped my purse to the carpeted floor and kicked off my sandals. In my first day as a mortal, I had a body, a job, and a possible love interest. Not too shabby. Now all I needed was to find an apartment and a couple of pairs of killer shoes.

Humming the tune 'Home' under my breath, I turned on the light as the door slowly swung shut behind me.

'Hello, Jezzie.'

My heart stopped as the voice hit me, and the melody died in my throat.

Fuck.

Swallowing, I turned to see one of the seven most powerful entities in all the planes seated in the large art-

60

deco chair near the small table. Her eyes gleamed as they locked on mine.

I stared into the face of my best friend, the Fury Megaera.

PART TWO

MEGAERA

6

A *Client's House*/*Periphery of Hell*

The man rolled off of me, a look of extreme contentment on his face as he stretched his long, muscular body. 'Darlin', you're the best lay I ever had. Some of what you did – man, you took my breath away.'

Way more than his breath, but why spoil his afterglow?

I touched my tongue to my upper lip, then gave him a huge smile. That had been his particular Hook: The smile. For some men, it was the eyes. For others, legs. Tits and ass were right up there too. But my current paramour was all about the smile. I had a particular talent for recognizing Hooks. Hot damn, I loved my job.

'Glad you enjoyed, sweetie.' I put a purr in my throat, just the way he liked it.

'Enjoyed? Darlin', words can't describe how I feel. That thing you did with your toes? No one's ever done that to me.'

That's probably because the act was illegal in his home state. My voice flirty as I wiggled my toes, I said, 'So you could say that I was your first?'

'You bet. Ahhhhh.' That was in response to my fingers lightly tracing patterns just over his pubic hair. The abdomen is particularly sensitive after a climax, and I wanted him to sink into the last bit of pleasure from our short time together.

'That's so sweet,' I said, sucking in his bliss. His emotional reaction was a physical delight for me, and I lapped up his ecstasy like a child slurping an ice-cream cone.

'Man, I'm spent.' He tried to chuckle, but he didn't have the strength to do more than chuff out a weak laugh. 'Feel like I could sleep for a year.'

'Actually,' I crooned, kissing his belly, the outline of his ribs, his nipples, 'you won't be getting any sleep in the foreseeable future.'

He was feeling the effects from our sex play, but even as his body started shutting down, his mind didn't comprehend what was happening. That's usually how it went, assuming my paramours didn't simply fall asleep and wake up dead. He blinked sleepy eyes at me, an exhausted smile lingering on his face. 'I'd love another go, but I just don't have the energy.'

'I know you don't, sweetie.' I kissed my way back down his torso, teasing his penis with my tongue. Even as the rest of his muscles slowly went limp, his shaft stood thick and long. Some succubi liked to leave their customers with a smile. My goal was to have them salute me on the way out. I murmured, 'You taste delicious.'

In the barest whisper, he said, 'Thanks . . .'

Ah, he was slipping away. Time to collect. I sat up, giving him the full view. An athletic man, he preferred his women to be strong, supple, and very toned. He also thought blondes were to die for, so my current form had mounds of flaxen hair that tumbled around my face like a waterfall, and my body was long and lean with dangerous curves. Giving his penis one more squeeze, I mounted him.

He let out a moan of pleasure and closed his eyes.

'Say my name,' I said, my voice husky as I rolled my hips.

'Juh.'

'Come on, lover,' I said, my pace quickening. 'Say it.'

'Jezz . . .'

I felt him throbbing inside of me, his shaft swollen and quivering, moving with a will of its own. My nipples tightened as I sensed the buildup of semen in his testicles. I ran my hands over my breasts as my body pumped on top of his, ramming him into me again and again. 'Say my name!'

'Jezebel . . . Ah!'

He ejaculated, and I shrieked with delicious joy as he came inside of me. Waves of rippling pleasure crashed across my body as I absorbed his seminal fluid and sperm. Succubi don't have reproductive organs; everything inside of us is geared toward fuelling our own bodies, not creating new ones. Actually, demons couldn't create, period. But we could destroy with the best of them.

And, in my case, I could seduce the soul away from a man. Given how nearly all of my lovers were used to charming the pants off of their female conquests, I considered it a perverse form of justice.

Still shivering from my orgasm, I smiled down at the man, whose body was already turning cold. 'Wakey, wakey,' I whispered in his ear.

His eyes snapped open. 'Huh. I must've fallen asleep.'

'Not exactly.' I planted a kiss on his head, then rolled off of him. 'Come on, sweetie. It's time to go.'

'Go? But – whoa!'

At my command, his soul lifted out of his body. From what I understand, the feeling is like slowly pulling an adhesive bandage off of one's skin – sticky and uncomfortable, but not truly painful. His soul glistened like obsidian and cherries in the dim light of his bedroom.

Oh, my. Based on its color, in life this man had been a horrific person. Thievery, physical violence against women – and a lawyer. 'Ooh. You've been a very naughty boy.'

He stared at the ethereal form of his hands. Mouth gaping, he touched his face ... and pushed his hands through his head. 'Ahhh! What did you do to me?'

'I fucked you to death.'

'Ahhh!'

'Oh, really now. Based on your soul, you've fucked over many people in your time.'

'AHHH!'

I crossed my arms. 'Come on, now. So you're dead. No use complaining about it.'

His mouth opened, closed, opened. 'You had no right to do this to me! I didn't deserve this!'

'Uh-huh.' Denial.

'I *didn't*!'

'You liked to raise a hand to the ladies, didn't you?'

Tendrils of scarlet swirled around his form, warring for dominance with the blackness in his soul. Frowning, he said, 'How do you—'

'It's written all over you.' I made a 'come here' gesture, and his soul – temporarily bound to me – had no choice but to obey. 'Enough chitchat, sweetie. It's time to go.'

He licked his lips. 'Go where?'

I dropped my current form, letting it pool around my ankles like discarded clothing. With a wicked grin, I said, 'Where do you think?'

But he was too busy screaming to hear my words. I sighed. Theatrics were utterly wasted on the faint of heart.

In a shimmer of gray light, we materialized outside the Gates of Hell. I could have just zapped my catch directly inside, but there was a protocol to these things. Humans didn't go to Hell by mistake; they had either made an agreement with a demon or had been very, very wicked in real life, so they deserved to get the full treatment. Thus, the first stop was the Gates. Intimidation at its finest.

Out of sight beyond the entrance, the Lake of Fire churned, emanating sulfuric gasses that permeated all of the Pit and its outskirts. I inhaled deeply, relishing the way the brimstone stung my nostrils. Some people liked the smell of frying eggs in the morning. Give me the stench of rotten eggs any time. The staleness of the air made it that much more acrid, and altogether suffocating. Yummy.

A dim light, shifting between indigo and vermilion, flickered above the great Wall that surrounded the Pit. Mortals tended to think that the Underworld was as dark as a black hole. If that were the case, Hell would be called Black Hole. As with the eternal, infernal stink, the glow was thanks to the Lake of Fire, which fulminated blue sulfuric flames amid its pool of lava. It was also the source of the temperature. Situated in the center of the Earth, the Abyss topped the 3,000-degree mark. Anyone who says 'It's not the heat, it's the humidity' has never been to Hell.

From the other side of the Wall, wails of suffering and torment rode the air. The screams of the damned mixed with the raucous laughter of the demons, forming a beautiful cacophony of anguish and gratification.

It was good to be home.

'Ahhh!'

Annoyed at being yanked from my reverie, I clouted my lover's head. Because we had descended to the Underworld plane, his soul had become as solid as his physical shell had been. My hand smacked against his skull with a satisfying *thwock*. 'Quit your whining already.'

'*Ahhh!*'

'You going to shriek all the way to the Lake of Fire?'

'*AHHH!*'

I took that as a yes.

Outside the Gates, a long line of sinners and demons snaked around the Wall, waiting for admittance into the Abyss. Mortals liked to think that we creatures of the Pit are all chaotic, but in truth, we had major rules to follow. Being Evil wasn't an excuse to ignore laws literally set in stone. Our Ten Great Rules were etched into the four walls of Abaddon, their commands legible no matter where one stood (or crawled) in Hell.

Hey, Moses had to get the idea from *somewhere*. But the whole parting of the Red Sea thing, that had been original.

I shoved my charge in front of me as we headed toward the back of the line. Privately, I thought the massive Wall around Hell was pandering too much to the mortals. I mean, talk about overkill. Who in their right minds would break in? Humans had no desire to go to Hell (even though they told one another to do so all the time), and angels would never debase themselves by sinking into the bowels of the Earth. The Archangels left us the fuck alone, which was more than fine by me; they were seriously frightening entities.

That left the damned, the demons, and God. If the damned could escape their punishment, they deserved to leave Hell. Demons had no other place to go, so it wasn't like we were trapped in an Underworld Roach Motel. As for God, well, considering that the Almighty created basically everything in existence, I seriously doubted that the Gates would keep God out.

Even though Hell didn't need the Wall or its Gates, mortals expected them, so we demonfolk obliged. Sweeping up more than ten meters high, the colossal stones of the Wall gleamed, polished to a high shine thanks to the tremendous heat of Hell. At the last Time of Consensus, the Wall stretched more than 7,000 kilometers long. Given that Hell altered its shape to accommodate all the damned, the number was an approximation at best.

'AHHHH!'

My paramour's shrieks increased as he stared at the various denizens of Hell loitering around the Wall, waiting for their turn to be admitted with their charges and pass through the Gates. I easily recognized other succubi and incubi, no matter what physical shape they currently wore. Whether a sixteen-meter gargoyle or a buxom redheaded midget, all Seducers were creatures of the demon king Asmodai, and we all recognized one another for what we were through a psychic seduction sense. I acknowledged my brethren as we passed, giving my ass a bit of a wiggle. They, in turn, answered with assorted lewd gestures. One of the incubi, my pal Daun, did this complicated thing with his thumb and pinky, and I felt my groin tighten in response.

Mental note: Speak with Daun later. I purred just thinking about it.

The rest of the waiting demons were tougher to distinguish. Both the Gluttons and the Lazy had flesh rippling over their various bodies. In their natural forms, the Jealous and the Envious all were shades of green, although Coveters always had hypnotic golden eyes. The Arrogant were easy to spot; they all radiated an unholier-than-thou attitude that got under my skin. I didn't note any Berserkers, but I hadn't expected to; those demons of Wrath always transported their catches directly to the Lake of Fire for judgment. If they didn't, things would get . . . messy.

The various mortal charges, for the most part, all screamed, gibbered, and wailed, no matter which member of the demon horde they belonged to. I shook my head. Mortals. It was so hard to tell them apart. They all looked the same: Terrified.

Cringing before me, my lover raised the volume on his own screeches. His eyes darted about wildly, a fine sheen of panic making them particularly bright. He tore his ethereal hair, which wisped away in smoke after he yanked it from his head. Gazing upon the vast, cratered plain outside of Hell that eventually gave way to Limbo, the man summed up the whole of his situation in one word:

'AHHHH!'

Rolling my eyes, I resigned myself to listening to his cries for the next ninety minutes or so. Screaming was okay – that went along with the territory – but it did get tiring on the ears. Some demons claimed that a mortal's shrieks could sing them to sleep. Me, I'd rather listen to Britney Spears.

'Jezebel! There you are!'

I grinned up at Megaera as she flew down to me. At the moment, she sported long brown hair, pale skin, and blue eyes. A white toga draped around her form; I guessed she was doing the Greek Muse look, which was all the rage with some of the Fallen.

Around me, demons backed away, giving Meg a wide berth. Most of my brethren were nervous around the Furies, but Meg and I went back a long, long way. 'Hey, girl!' I said. 'What's up?'

She would have been breathless if she actually breathed. 'I've been looking all over for you.' She noticed the man next to me, who blanched from the attention. To me, she asked, 'Can you get away?'

I motioned with my chin to my lover. 'I'm sort of busy at the moment. After I turn in my charge, I have to file my receipt.' Waiting to get into Hell was nothing compared with trying to get paid. I had planned on spending the better part of the next three days waiting in line.

Meg blew out a sigh. 'As soon as you're done, call me.' She leapt into the sky and disappeared somewhere inside the Abyss. I had no idea what Meg wanted, but knowing her, it meant she was up to no good.

Most excellent. I loved looking forward to things.

My lover and I walked slowly – the man's abject terror had slowed him to a crawl, so every few meters or so I'd have to give him a push to get his legs working again, to the amusement of the demons around us. More than once, my charge threw himself to the ground, where he'd roll on the black cinders and rocks until I hefted him up by his armpits. It took us nearly fifteen minutes to reach the back of the line.

'Oh God . . . oh God . . . oh God . . .'

A smile played on my lips. 'Wrong direction, sweetie.'

He stared at me, wide-eyed. His soul had taken on a

distinct grayish tone, which dampened the obsidian and scarlet swirls. He was nearly petrified with fear.

So cool.

After a few moments of him trying to hyperventilate, he realized he wasn't breathing anymore. Finally he stammered, 'Can we maybe make a deal?'

'A *deal*?' I blinked, incredulous. 'Really?'

'You get me out of here, I'll give you whatever you want.'

I threw back my head and laughed. Damn, it had been a long, long time since I'd had a charge so completely clueless. After I got my guffaws under control, I said, 'Sweetie, what do you think landed you here in the first place?'

He paled to a sickly ashen color. 'What do you mean?'

'At one point, you made a deal with one of my associates. And here you are, fulfilling your end.'

'But . . . No, I never did that! I never signed anything!'

I sighed. 'Why do mortals always think that you have to sign something to make it binding? You were a lawyer. Haven't you heard of a verbal agreement?'

'But—'

'Look,' I said, 'if you seriously think there's been a mistake, take it up with your Case Worker.'

He swallowed. 'Case Worker?'

'It'll add to the paperwork, but if you're sure there's been an error, we'll have to backtrack.'

Weakly, he repeated, 'Paperwork?'

I put a hand on his shoulder, enjoying the way he flinched from my talons grazing his form. 'Sweetie, this is Hell. We invented paperwork.'

That was a lie, but hey, I was a demon. I was supposed to lie.

My lover's color continued to bleed out, leaving him marbled with shots of pink. Staring down at the blackened ash by his feet, he asked, 'I'm really in Hell?'

I squeezed his shoulder. 'Not yet. Based on this line, we're not getting you inside for about another two hours.'

7

Hell – The Second Sphere/Pandemonium

'Next!'

Ah, finally. I pushed the man forward hard enough that he stumbled to his knees. Part of the fun of waiting for almost two hundred minutes (I counted) was watching the fright settle into my paramour. With nothing to do but wonder what awaited him, he would have scared himself to death if he hadn't already been dead.

To the left of the wrought-iron Gates, a red plaque hung, held in place by severed hands nailed to the bars. The writing on the sign changed whenever the Gateskeeper felt like it. The position was filled on a rotating basis; the current Gateskeeper seemed to be in a literary mindset. For the moment, the plaque read:

ABANDON ALL HOPE, YE WHO ENTER HERE

What a shock – a Dante phase. When I served as Gateskeeper, I liked to have the sign read 'ENJOY YOUR STAY!' I'm a bit of a sadist at heart.

Squatting in front of the Gates, a massive being slobbered, glowing a poisonous green with white pinpoint eyes – a creature of Envy. Shooting me a glare, she sniffed my lover's chest. He squeaked and turned an interesting shade of gray and pink, sort of like a sunburned ghost.

'Thievery!' The Gateskeeper smacked her rubbery lips together. 'Loves thievery!' She snuffled some more. 'Lechery! Pah.' She hawked a green glob of phlegm onto the heat-baked ground. 'Hates lechery. Ooh.' She inhaled, and a look of beatific pleasure spread like a fungus over her face. 'Violence. *Loves* violence.'

Most creatures of Envy simply didn't get the concept of love, which made them suspicious of Seducers at best. Whatever. They didn't know what they were missing. Or maybe they did, and that's why they were envious in the first place. I did a mental shrug; philosophy had never been my strong point.

The demon grunted at the man's chest, directly over where his heart had been in life. 'I guesses it goes to the Cauldron, I does.'

That was my guess, too, but that wasn't her place to say. Or mine. The Case Worker would decide. I pulled my lover away from her snout. 'No touching the merchandise,' I growled. In my arms, the man stiffened, perhaps upon hearing the malefic tone to my voice.

The Gateskeeper snarled at me, and I snarled right back. Finally, she hocked another green-tinged loogy at my feet, then stepped aside. 'Enters.'

Giving the man a shove forward, I blew the Envious a kiss and sauntered through the Gates, making sure to bump my hip against her.

'Bitches,' she hissed at me.

'That's *bitchin*',' I corrected with a wink.

The Gateskeeper bellowed, 'Next!'

Once we passed through the entrance, the stink of brimstone got kicked up from cloying to overpowering. My lover stumbled to the ash-covered ground, dry heaving as if he could save his soul by puking up his guts.

I gathered him up by the scruff of his neck and pitched him forward. He landed roughly on his stomach, grunting from the impact. He lifted his head and let out a piercing scream. Before him, the Lake of Fire seethed. Burning liquid splashed over the lip and slid down the slope lazily, leaving channels in its wake. Strands of molten lava, cooling quickly once freed of the Lake's surface, formed glassy filaments that drifted upward along with the smoke. I watched a strand of dark glass as it floated past my face, dancing on the updraft. With a derisive snort, I batted it away, and it shattered from the impact. It had been nothing more than trapped heat, rage turned brittle. I had no patience for such delicacy.

The man stared at the boiling pool as if hypnotized by the swirls of orange-red. Then, near his face, the Lake's surface erupted into a cone of vibrant blue flame. My lover whimpered and scuttled backward like a crab, his belly sliding over the pitted ground. He bumped up against my hooves. Trembling, he clutched onto my legs, grasping my pelt for support, possibly even for comfort. The thick hair that covered my body from my pelvis down to my ankles served as protection against even the angriest fires of Hell, so the human's fingers didn't even make a dent as they pulled at me.

Still, I was flattered that he turned to me. Yeah, I was a creature of Lust. Even so, I liked to have my ego stoked as much as the demons of Pride. I patted the man's head, as if he were a favorite dog. 'Come on, sweetie. Let's get you to your Case Worker.'

He looked up at me, over my furry groin and flat stomach, over the swells of my breasts all the way up to my face. I didn't look remotely human in my natural form – more like a satyr, minus the goat tail and horns, with a cherry-red hide and green cat's eyes – but he must have seen something caring in my gaze, because he reached up to me, supplicating.

'Please help me,' he whispered.

Demons have hearts, but we don't have feelings in the way that mortals do. That being said, thousands of years of being a temptress had given me an understanding of the human psyche. And while I appreciated absolute fear like any other being of the Pit, I also sympathized with the people new to our plane. Everything they had ever known, gone in a flash of death. And now, on the precipice of judgment, they realized they had a soul ... and that they had sacrificed it for temporary gain.

So I squatted onto my haunches and cupped his face in my hands. 'I'm sorry,' I said. 'I'm not an angel. I don't help humans. But I'll hold your hand while we wait for your Case Worker to see you.'

He looked absurdly grateful, and color slowly bloomed in his form until once again, he was covered in black and red. He didn't thank me, but he squeezed my hand tightly and offered me a smile that slipped into a grimace.

I flashed him my fangs as I pulled him to his feet. 'Come on, sweetie. Let's go.'

Because I was a Seducer, I had to steer my catch to the portion of Hell reserved for mortals damned by their lusts, the Heartlands. Whether my lover would be judged as Lustful remained to be seen.

I could only hope. We had a quota, after all.

We walked slowly, following the Lake of Fire as we made a circuit around the western edge of Hell, passing the area of Sloth. My lover, perhaps dazed by his own upcoming sentencing, hardly seemed to notice the agonized wails of the damned in their snake pits, desperately attempting to climb over the writhing serpents to reach the top and escape their fate. Give us a few hundred years, and we'll scare the laziness right out of you.

Continuing south, we crossed over into the land of Pride. Sure, we could have used a more direct route to get to the southern central area designated as the Heartlands. But mortals got to see only parts of the Third Sphere, the level used for penance and other forms of punishment. That meant no passage through the Second Sphere, Pandemonium: home to demonfolk and other Fallen creatures. The First Sphere, Abaddon, served as the Unholy Court; only the great Kings of Hell gathered there.

Forget the humans, the last place a regular *demon* wanted to be was in Court, surrounded by the rulers of Hell. Gah. I got goosebumps just imagining it. I'd sooner suck face with an angel than willingly visit the First Sphere.

As we walked through the Pridelands, something snapped my lover out of his trance, and he flinched when he saw various instruments of torture in full swing. (In the case of the pendulum, literally.) Demons capered and exchanged gallowshumor jokes as they worked various machines, like the wheel, the rack, and the iron maiden. Trapped within such devices, once-arrogant humans screeched their throats raw as their blood seeped from numerous wounds and their bones cracked.

Just another day in the Pit. I pushed my paramour forward. 'Almost there, sweetie.'

Blanching to a sickly gray, he nodded.

The stench of searing flesh announced our arrival in the Heartlands. Nailed to wooden stakes, humans writhed as they burned. Covered in the kisses of fire, their bodies licked by flames, the damned that had allowed their passions to rule them while alive suffered the affections of the Inferno.

By my side, the man made a sound that caught in his throat.

'Chin up, sweetie,' I said. 'This is just where your judgment takes place. You may not be assigned here.'

'Oh, good,' he said faintly.

One of the demons attending a bonfire noticed us. He stood up, stretched out his back, and picked his way around the various burning humans. Flicking soot from the red armor that marked him as a Case Worker, he nodded to me. 'Jezebel. It's been a human's age. How're tricks?'

'Heya, Zepar. You know – same old, same old.'

Zepar smiled tightly, then turned his full attention onto my lover. Stroking his chin, Zepar said, 'Clearly, he's more of a coveter than a berserker. And unfortunately, the lust is secondary to the greed.'

'I was afraid of that,' I said. 'The Cauldron?'

He nodded. 'Indeed. Oh well. Better luck next time, eh?' Running a thick finger over my paramour's forehead, he etched the symbol of Covet just over the man's eyes. To his credit, my lover barely winced.

As Zepar handed me a body receipt for my catch, I asked, 'We make our quota this quarter?'

Zepar turned, already working his way back to a raging conflagration that engulfed at least twenty humans. 'Barely.

I'm telling you, things that used to guarantee a hot seat now hardly can be called sins.'

'I blame television.'

'No doubt,' he muttered, shaking his head.

'Come on, sweetie,' I said to the man. 'I'll take you as far as the boundary for Covet.'

'So I'm not going to burn?' he asked, the relief obvious in his voice.

'Nope.' He was going to boil in oil. But I'd let him learn that on his own.

As I materialized in front of Meg, I stepped backward, shielding my eyes. This was one of those times her power shone through – most Underworld entities radiated slight power when manipulating forms out of the ether, but Meg, like her sister Furies, were part of the fabric of the universe. Her power was enough to make the brightest of stars go diving for sunglasses.

'Tone it down, girl!' I yelped.

'Sorry. Okay, you can look now.'

I glanced around, seeing that we were just outside of Pandemonium near the Heartlands. Around me, I sensed that my demonic brethren were making themselves scarce. At times, Meg's automatic fear factor had its advantages; it almost guaranteed a private conversation. Blinking, I saw she was still doing the Ancient Greece thing. 'Listening to the Muse today?'

'At least I remembered to get dressed. Come on,' she said, pulling my arm. 'We have to get to the First Sphere.'

'What?' I yanked my arm away. 'You're insane. No way am I going up there.'

Meg rolled her eyes. 'Would I tell you to go to Abaddon if there wasn't a good reason for it?' Leaning in close, she whispered, 'I heard Rosier going at it with Naberius. You know how they get, trying to one-up each other. Well, Rosey said that He's going to make an Announcement!'

I swallowed. Rosier was one of the Principals of Lust, second only to King Asmodai and Queen Lillith. Rosey had nearly as much pride in him as one of the Arrogant, not that anyone would ever suggest that to him; saying that the Proud and the Seducers hated one another was like saying snow was cold. Rosey and Naberius had a rivalry going on more than fifteen hundred years. Neither he nor Berry were stupid, so they boasted only about things that were completely true. So for Rosey to make a claim about Him to Berry meant that it was legit.

King Lucifer was going to make an Announcement. And that meant . . .

My hand flew to my mouth. 'That means all the hordes of Hell will be there!'

'Smart girl.' Meg grabbed my hand. 'Come on. If we hurry, we'll get there before the Call of Gathering.'

8

The First Sphere

Pulling me along, Meg flew us over the Second Sphere. Beneath us, thousands of demons and other creatures of the Pit meandered about, scuttling into or out of the enormous mountain complex that served as Pandemonium. Housing more than seven million nefarious entities, the black crag towered over the Third Sphere, which sprawled around the mountain's edge. If the Third Sphere was the periphery of Hell, the Second was its base – and the First Sphere was its peak. High above us, rocks and dead trees gave way to the polished stones of Abaddon. I swallowed as we approached the summit of Hell. 'You're sure about this?'

Meg looked over her shoulder to grin at me. 'Positive. You afraid?'

'Bless me, yes. You?'

'Anxious, I guess. But if there's going to be an Announcement, I want a good spot.'

'If? What do you mean, if? I thought you said it was definite!'

She chuckled but said nothing, leaving me to stew in my fear of rubbing elbows with our unholy leaders.

Meg circled the pinnacle, giving me the unprecedented opportunity to look at the palace. Abaddon gleamed, its walls of black onyx and fire opals winking. Reflections of the Lake of Fire danced upon its surface, washing the entire castle in flames. The Ten Great Rules gleamed on the walls. Rule No. 1 blazed in an angry red: All Creatures in Their Place.

No shit, Sherlock. That's why I'd never ventured into the dread castle. Everything had its place, and every creature had its station. I was a succubus, and a relatively minor one at that; I didn't dally with the elite or, Pit swallow me, the Kings. Sure, I would (and do) happily screw the pants off of mortal rulers. But the infernal ones? No way. Not on your soul.

Yet there I was, about to descend into the courtyard of Abaddon. Bless me, I must have fucked myself stupid.

Past the outer wall, the great courtyard sprawled, its black stones dull and unassuming. Around it, an inner wall provided three levels of seating boxes, with each section separated by stone columns. From what I'd heard, the upper box seats were reserved for the Principals, leaving the lower rows for the various Dukes, Marquises, and Barons. The wide expanse of the courtyard would be standing room only for the rest of the denizens of Hell. Beyond the inner wall, the palace itself loomed, a dark construction of unspoken menace and captured terror.

Well, I had to admit, the architecture was fucking amazing.

It looked like Meg's information had been correct. Already, creatures appeared in the courtyard – a few Nightmares here, smatterings of ghosts there. A number of demons loitered near the outer wall, as if too nervous to step within the confines of the First Sphere before the actual Call went out.

Meg, being a Fury, had no such reservations. She landed right at the center of the courtyard, directly in front of a granite platform.

I hissed, 'What the fuck are you doing?' I tried to pull away and dash off to the periphery like the others of my brethren, but Meg had an iron grip on my forearm. 'We can't be here before at least some of the Barons arrive!'

Meg grinned at me. 'So worried about poor form, Jezzie?'

'More worried about keeping my flesh attached to my body. Come on, Meg – some of the elite have really, really bad dispositions.' The last time I crossed one of the titled demons had resulted in me bathing in the Lake of Fire for a month. I'd rather be sequestered in a nunnery for the next century than suffer through perpetual burning for any length of time.

'I'd expect nothing less,' Meg said. 'They do have a certain reputation to maintain. But really, Jez – do you think any of the elite would approach you while I'm by your side?' She arched her eyebrow, and flecks of power sparkled in her blue eyes.

Gnawing my lip, I conceded that I was safe for the moment. I'd become close with Meg way before she'd revealed her true nature to me. By then, we had a good millennium of friendship bonding us. Once in a while, I remembered that she was even more frightening than the Archangels. Meg knew my true name, which meant she could easily destroy me in a blink. But that reality peeled away whenever we conspired together and shared our deepest, most secret thoughts. Sure, she was one of the few creatures that all residents of Hell and Heaven feared. But she was also a friend.

Me and Garth Brooks: We've got friends in low places.

With a shove, Meg released me. I rubbed my arm to work some feeling into it. 'You almost severed my forearm. Been working out again?'

Meg made a kissy face.

'What,' I said playfully, 'no tongue?'

She stuck out her tongue.

I licked my lips suggestively, but I was far too uneasy to keep up my usual flirting. 'What do you think He's going to say?'

Meg shrugged. 'Could be anything.' Lowering her voice, she added, 'I heard He's been away for a while. Something about an all-important meeting. But I don't know with who, or about what.'

Darting glances around the Court, I said, 'You sure there's going to be a Call? I don't see any of the elite here yet.'

'I know what I heard.'

Perhaps emboldened by our presence, a few demons took hesitant steps onto the courtyard stones. What a shock – they were Arrogant. Of course they'd be the first to shake off their overwhelming fear; they couldn't stand to be upstaged by a Seducer.

'Oh, look,' I said to Meg. 'Company.'

'You going to start trouble?'

'Me? Never.'

They wore male human forms, each with more muscles than the other. I didn't know how they could strut about without tipping over. I batted my lashes at them, and they sauntered forward, mocking grins plastered onto their smug faces.

'Look at that,' one of them said. 'A whore's sleeping her way to the top.'

'Slumming with a Fury,' said the second. 'My, my. You do have ambition, don't you?'

'Me?' I shrugged. 'Nope, no ambition. I leave that for you boys. You know all about overextending your reach, don't you?'

'Overextending?' The first smiled tightly. 'Not even close, whore.'

I tapped my chin. 'How does it go, something about pride before a fall?'

'Yeah, you would know about falls and tumbles, wouldn't you? It's got to be tough on your back,' said the third.

'And your cunt,' said the first. 'Poor little whore had to be flown here by her friend because her cunt's too sore to let her walk.'

'You do so love that word,' I said. 'Does it get you off to say *cunt*? Is that what does it for you – dirty talk?'

'You know all about dirt,' said the second. 'Tell us, is it true that all Seducers are pox-infested carriers of disease?'

'Not at all,' I said. 'You tell me, is it true that all the Arrogant have their noses so high up in the air, they can't smell their own bullshit?'

'Listen to the tempter girl.' The third leered at me. 'You talk tough for a common slut.'

'Not so common,' I said, putting a throaty growl into my voice. 'Want me to show you just how uncommon I am? What do you say, boys? Any of you demon enough to take me?'

'What are you, fifth level?' The second demon brayed laughter. 'As if I'd let one of your class even touch my flesh.'

'Funny,' I said to Meg. 'They talk about levels, but all the Arrogant look the same to me.'

Meg covered her smile behind a hand.

The second one's eyes lit with rage. 'You shouldn't attach yourself to such trash, Erinyes. It rubs off on you.'

'Temper, temper,' Meg said. 'If I didn't know better, I'd think you were a demon of Wrath.'

He snarled at her, 'Don't you dare associate me with a Berserker, bitch.'

She must have hit a sore spot, because no entity ever, *ever* insulted the Furies. It was rumored that even God kept the Erinyes at arm's length. I pursed my lips, waiting to see how this would play out.

Meg locked gazes with the Arrogant. 'Watch yourself, little demon. Banter is fine, but I won't stand to be called names by the likes of you.'

I saw fear overtake the ferocity in his eyes, but his nature wouldn't allow him to back off – especially not with his brethren standing by his side. 'And what will you do about it, bitch?'

Her blue eyes flashed like lightning in a clear sky. 'Call me that name once more, and you'll find out for yourself.' She ended the threat with a small smile, one that underscored the truth of her words.

Crap. The last thing I needed was a group of the Arrogant holding a grudge against me and my ilk. Pompous asses that they were, they'd probably do something inane like declare a war of Sin. I could see it now: Lust versus Pride, brawling over every mortal soul claimed, tying up the offices of Pandemonium for years in red tape.

Putting a hand on Meg's shoulder, I said, 'Sweetie, think of all the forms you'll have to fill out. Disintegrating a demonic entity without a writ of permit is what, three weeks of paperwork?'

'Six,' she said, the smile still on her face.

The first Arrogant sniffed disdainfully. 'We wouldn't want the poor Erinyes to get writer's cramp. Come, fellows. Leave the whore and her . . . friend.'

The two dragged their buddy away, with him glaring at Meg and me the entire time. They came to a halt by the extreme left of the platform, where the three of them huddled, casting the occasional black look our way.

She glanced at me. 'You do so love goading the Arrogant, don't you?'

'Who, me?'

Meg opened her mouth, but just then a screech rent the air. Shrieking overhead, a flock of Banshees swarmed. *Gathering!* they cried, their voices digging into my mind. *Gathering! To the First Sphere for Gathering! Attend for King Lucifer!* They rocketed away, throwing their Call at all the denizens of Hell.

'I'll be blessed,' I muttered, staring at the receding forms of the Banshees. 'He's really going to make an Announcement.'

'Told you so,' Meg said, smiling innocently.

Creatures of the Pit advanced upon Abaddon, oozing and slouching and swooping, moving in whatever ways they chose to answer the Call of Gathering. The courtyard and box seats filled quickly – one didn't keep the lord of the Underworld waiting. As the sheer bulk of demonic presence pushed me against the edge of the granite platform, my anxiety grew.

What could King Lucifer have to say that merited the attendance of the entire legion of Hell? I could count on one hand the number of times any of the thirteen Kings had demanded an audience. But for *all* of the demon hordes to collect was unprecedented. Partially that was because most of the different types of demons despised one another, and forcing them together was a catastrophe waiting to happen. Picture a cat hurled into a bathtub filled with water. Multiply that by a million. You'd have an easier time getting those million felines squeaky clean than you would corralling all the demonfolk under one roof.

But partially, it was also due to the gravity of the situation. King Lucifer only made an Announcement once before, in all of existence. That had been at the very beginning of Hell, way before my time; I was just a few millennia old – relatively young, as these things were counted.

What did He have to say that was important enough for all demons to leave their charges of damned souls unattended?

Meg's lips on my own snared me out of my roiling thoughts. I opened my mouth to hers, relishing her taste of mint and old parchment. Before my tongue could do more than graze her teeth, she pulled away to whisper in my ear. 'Queen Lyssa's here. Got to go.'

'You dumped me here in front, and now you're leaving me?'

Giggling, she said, 'We all do what we must.'

I squeezed her hand, then watched her fly up to greet her ruler. The Queen was easily recognizable, even with thousands of other beings hovering in the air. A blend of owl and woman, Lyssa soared above the courtyard, her tail streaming behind her. Gray feathers swathed her form, with black stripes rippling across her body. Her wings, like her tail, were pebbled with shots of white on a field of pitch. Orange burst from her body as her feet flexed, her razor-sharp claws putting my own talons to shame. Even from the ground, I felt her gaze upon me. Set in a charcoal face, her eyes blazed, white stars dying in a poisoned sky. Her beak, the same fiery orange as her claws, opened wide as she screeched her disapproval. Everyone knew that the Erinyes weren't supposed to mix with the demons.

Yeah, yeah. And oil's not supposed to mix with water. But then someone invented mayonnaise, and wham – instant mixing. Just call me Jezebel, the condiment of the nefarious.

Around me, masses of creatures bumped and shoved and cursed, jostling my form as they jockeyed for a better position. With Meg gone, I wished I could just sneak to the back and keep the wall company, but there were millions of bodies in my way. I was trapped by the platform.

That blessed Megaera! If I didn't know better, I would have sworn she'd dumped me in front on purpose.

'It's difficult, isn't it?'

I looked over my shoulder to see a large demon smiling at me. He'd chosen a human form, an attractive one with just enough tone to show the beauty of the body without calling too much attention to the muscles themselves. Wrapped in an emerald toga of raw silk, he stood proudly, his chin high. Atop his head, his dark hair practically begged me to run my fingers through its curls. Green eyes shone brightly, hinting at amusement, yet sadness was clearly stamped on his face. At first I thought he was Arrogant. Looking closer, I sensed something about him that touched on Envy, possibly even Lust.

Even with the courtyard uncomfortably crowded, demons had given him a wide berth. Curious, I pushed my way closer to him. Nope, no malefic force radiating from him, no overwhelming sense of threat or fear washed over me. He didn't even smell bad. How'd he manage his own elbow room?

'What's difficult?' I asked him, still trying to get a fix on his affiliated Sin.

His smile broadened, but his mournful eyes belied his mirth. 'Being friends with one of the enemy.'

My nostrils flared. 'She's not the enemy.'

'Of course she is.' He cast a glance at Meg's receding shape, nearly lost among her sister Furies. Queen Lyssa, a goddess in her own right, claimed a top-level box seat with the other Principals, and her cluster of Erinyes flocked by her side. 'Her nature is to avenge, and murder is her birthright. She is one of the few entities that can negate a demon's existence on a whim.'

'I know all that,' I said tightly, feeling uncomfortable for a reason I couldn't name. Maybe it was because he was illuminating my friend in a light that I didn't want to see.

'You think the scorpion won't sting the frog this time, don't you?' He laughed softly. 'But it will. The scorpion will always sting. That's its nature.'

'If you say so,' I said with a shrug, trying to act flippant. When all else fails, go for the Dumb Blonde approach, no matter what form you wear. 'I'm not much of a philosopher.'

'I didn't say so. Aesop did. And I'm no philosopher.'

'No?' I put a purr into my voice, did a little shimmy-bop with my hips that jiggled my breasts. 'Then what are you, sweetie?'

He sighed. 'I'm tired.' Then, lower: 'And I'm bitterly disappointed.'

Ah. Definitely Envy. Normally I had no patience for the Envious, neither the infernal nor the mortal variety. Wah, wah, you've got what I want, wah, wah, I'm so bitter. Cry me a fucking river. You want something so much? Go get it. But something about this demon set him apart from the rest of his brethren, something that I couldn't place right away. But it tickled the back of my mind.

Giggling to cover my disquiet, I said, 'You had me going for a while. I thought you were one from the Pridelands.'

'Did you, now? That's amusing.'

A grin flitted across his face, and for a moment, I saw the cosmos shine in his green eyes. As bitter as he was, he didn't *feel* Envious.

He felt lost.

The tickle in the back of my mind strengthened to a maddening itch. Who was this creature, this being whose Sin was too mercurial to define?

His voice soft, he asked me, 'You really believe that your friend isn't an enemy?'

My throat constricted, and I swallowed thickly before I answered. 'Not that it's your business, but yes I do. Megaera is not my enemy.'

He leaned over and kissed me. Nothing passionate, nothing seductive – just a simple, affectionate kiss. His lips barely touched mine before they were gone. Stepping away, he smiled sadly at me. 'If only you were right.'

My hand flew to my mouth; I felt a tingle where his flesh had pressed against my own. My voice a breathy whisper, I asked, 'Who are you?'

He inclined his head in a brief bow, and then he strode onto the platform.

Around me, the legions of Hell crashed to their knees. Foreheads touched the stones on the ground as demons prostrated themselves, offering complete devotion to the being that stood alone before them. My eyes widened as I understood who He was, that handsome demon whose words had troubled me so and whose kiss still lingered on my mouth.

With a cry, I fell to the floor, hiding myself among the infernal. As one, we creatures of the Abyss called out the name of our dread ruler, the unholy one to whom we all answered:

Lucifer the Light Bringer, the First of the Fallen.

9

Hotel New York

As Megaera stared at me, her blue eyes unblinking, I wondered if I could feign innocence. Of course I could. If I could fake an orgasm on the spot, surely I could muster up some Bambi eyes.

'I think you have me mistaken for someone else,' I said, aiming for Disgruntled New Yorker, but coming across more like Mortal In Fear For Her Life.

Meg arched an eyebrow. 'Really, Jezzie. I know your true name. You think a little thing like a human shell can fool me?'

Fuck.

Squeezing my eyes shut, I waited for the nothingness of oblivion to crash over me. After three heartbeats, I realized that either it took an Erinyes a few moments to summon enough power to annihilate someone, or Meg didn't want to destroy me.

Daring a peek, I saw Meg trying to fend off a grin. 'Honestly, Jez, if I wanted to take you out, I would've gotten you when you first walked in.'

'So you're not after me?' Relief turned my voice into something breathy and high-pitched, like Minnie Mouse after a serious bong hit.

'Not officially. I'm here as your friend.' The grin finally bloomed on her face. 'Girl, what've you gone and done? A *mortal?* What were you thinking?'

With a heavy sigh, I plodded over to the bed and flopped down on my stomach. The mattress was soft yet firm – a good sleeping surface, but not so hot for wild sex. 'I was trying to get off the Evil radar. Between the human thing and the Shield Against Evil, I thought I was safe.'

'You wound up snagging a shieldstone?' Meg whistled in appreciation. 'Nicely done. I can't wait to hear how you managed that.'

Rolling onto my hip, I met her gaze. 'So how'd you find me? Even with our spiffy psychic connection, the shield should be masking my presence.'

Throwing back her head, Meg let out a belly laugh so jolly, Santa Claus would have turned green with envy. Lost in her guffaws, she looked as human as I did, albeit one seriously out of touch with current fashion. Still sporting her white toga, she looked like a poster child for either a Grecian Revival or a fraternity party.

Finally she stifled her giggles enough to say, 'Jez, you're completely hidden from Evil. But I'm an Erinyes. I'm many things, but I'm not Evil.'

I mentally slapped my forehead. Duh. Just because Meg and her sisters resided in Hell, that didn't mean they were truly creatures of the Pit. Heaven had an exclusive membership – only the Good may apply. Hell wasn't nearly so choosy; the Underworld enjoyed diversity. If you weren't purely Good, you either had Purgatory, Earth, or Hell to call your own. Most creatures caught in between opted for Hell; we threw better parties.

I blew out a sigh. Thinking like that was going to get me caught. I wasn't a creature of the Pit any longer.

'Jezzie, what possessed you to run?' Meg leaned forward, cupping her chin in her hand, her elbow on the chair's armrest. 'Now of all times, you had to go and buck authority?'

'I couldn't stay.' Sitting up, I wrapped my arms around myself. 'You should've seen where they placed me.'

A smile flitted across her face. 'I heard. Crossing the boundaries between desire and terror, huh?'

'Inadvertently.' I bit my lip. 'Is she still pissed off at me?'

'What else is new? Lillith gets pissed at everything.' That she could blithely mention the Queen of the Succubi's name without any fear of getting her attention spoke volumes about Meg's power. No nefarious entity in its right mind ever wanted to bother an Erinyes.

Meg's face turned somber. 'Seriously, Jez, this wasn't a good idea. He's looking to make an example out of you.'

I felt the blood drain from my face, and I fought back the urge to vomit all over the pretty coverlet. 'He can fuck Himself until His wings rot.'

She smiled tightly, and it didn't come close to reaching her eyes. 'And here they've been saying you aren't loyal.'

'You know I'm loyal, but not to that—'

'Stop.' She held her hand up, and I sealed my lips shut, forcing my mouth to silence. 'Don't say it, Jez. Don't even think it. They haven't set me on you. Don't give them a reason to.'

Swallowing thickly, I nodded. Having a Fury on my tail would make my new life very stressful . . . and very short.

She rubbed the bridge of her nose for a moment. Then she said, 'Look, for now you're okay. They still have your case posted in Avarice only. But after your little stunt with the Coveter earlier today, it won't be long before you're on top of the list across all the geographies of Hell.' She met my gaze. 'I don't suppose there's any way I can convince you to come back, freely and of your own accord?'

'I can't, Meg.' I shook my head, remembering my final assignment from the Abyss, and how miserably that turned out. 'I can't spend an eternity doing something that I loathe.'

'Did you ask Lillith for a different assignment?'

'She hates me. After four thousand years, I was still only fifth level. If she wasn't going to promote me when I was good at what I did, there was no way this side of Salvation that she would've reassigned me.'

'Technically, it wouldn't be up to her. It's His call.'

'Yeah,' I said. 'And we both know how well that would've gone over.'

She nodded. 'So you're chancing it as a mortal?'

'Yeah.'

'And you won't say anything to the humans?'

I let out a startled laugh. 'Bless me, no. That would be all I needed – both sides after me. No thanks. My life's interesting enough as is.'

For a moment, something flashed in Meg's eyes – a hint of sadness, perhaps. Then a wicked grin unfurled across her face. 'So what's in the bags? Anything naughty?'

An hour later, I was perched over the toilet. It had taken me a moment to understand what the pressure below was desperately signaling; at first, I thought it was just a reaction to the rather frightening hot dog I'd eaten for lunch

– the vendor had called it a 'sewer dog,' and it had tasted like hairspray. By the time I had finally realized that nature was calling, I had to make a mad dash to the bathroom before the special delivery landed in my panties.

In a lot of ways, being a demonic blow-up doll had been easier. Sure, it had been messy at times – sweaty and slick and sometimes covered head to foot in whipped cream. But I'd never had to clean up after myself. A little zap of power, and wham! Instant sanitation. But mortals had to bathe and brush and crap and scrub and dab and scour. And repeat, *ad nauseam*. Gah. Whoever came up with the proverb that cleanliness was next to godliness must've been a demon. At least in Hell, mortals didn't have to worry about cleaning away grime and filth, or washing away old bodily fluids. Of course, they were sort of too busy being tortured to really care about what covered their flesh.

Sitting on the can, I found, was a perfect opportunity for some deep thinking. It's not like there was much else I could do while I waited for my system to finish doing its business. So I thought about what Meg had said to me before she'd left.

She'd heard my dealings with Caitlin (Meg: 'Bonus points for your parting gift'), the Coveter (Meg: 'You were so freaking lucky, it makes my head spin'), Paul (Meg and me: 'Yum!'), and Belles (Meg: Rolling on the floor, help-less with mirth) – overall, she thought for my first day as a human, I was doing fine. When I'd asked her point blank about whether my bumping into Paul had been a coinci-dence, she'd smiled and made a no-no-no gesture with her hand. 'That'd be telling,' she'd said.

Well, duh. That was the point, no? But her lips were sealed on the matter, which led me to believe that Paul had a role to play in my new life. Based on how just looking at him was like foreplay, that was fine with me.

But Meg had left me with some advice on her way out. 'Have fun,' she'd said, 'but don't be a fool. You're human, but you've got no soul.'

'Sweetie, next you'll be telling me I've got no rhythm.'

Her face somber, she'd replied, 'Not funny, Jez. If you get yourself killed, then that's it – no Underworld, no second chance. You're toast.'

'Toast?' I'd said, trying to lighten the mood. 'White, wheat, or rye?'

I'd expected at least a chuckle. Instead she'd given me a look that would've frozen parts of the Lake of Fire. 'I'm serious. One of the joys of being an Erinyes is having an intimate understanding of Fate. Yours is spraypainted in neon. If you die, that's it. Oblivion. So don't be stupid. Keep your shieldstone on, don't tell the humans what they shouldn't know, and keep yourself alive. Who knows,' she added, a tight smile on her face, 'maybe you'll even make it to a ripe old age and watch your body decay and slowly die.'

'That's my Meg,' I said, feeling my stomach somewhere in the vicinity of my ankles. 'Always putting a positive spin on things.'

'You already broke the rules,' she said, her voice as soft as spoiled fruit. 'Don't make it worse. You know I'm rooting for you. But if I'm told to come after you, I'll have to do my job.'

Her blue eyes locked on my green ones, the air between us flashing with a turquoise energy that vibrated with love and fear and despair. Then I grabbed her in a huge embrace and hugged her for all I was worth. I told myself that she'd never betray me. We'd been best friends for more than a thousand years. She wouldn't hurt me. Even if she were set upon my trail, she'd never turn me in.

And I heard King Lucifer's voice whisper in my mind, the memory of a warning: *If only you were right.*

Pasting a smile on my face that felt as fake as Barbie's boobs, I said, 'Then I'd better make sure you don't have a reason to find me on official business.'

She left, and that's when my stomach sent up its first gastronomical SOS. Now, with my butt getting numb on the toilet seat, I thought about how sad Meg's blue eyes had been.

Enough. I didn't have time for malaise. I had to prep myself for my first shift at Belles. Based on how pale my skin was, and how dark my hair was, that would entail a lot of lathering, shaving, trimming, and moisturizing. Then I'd have to figure out which outfits to wear, which shoes to totter on, and what to do with my hair. And finally, I had to decide whether I would do a girl-girl scene, which Roman had begged me to think about.

Being a human female was fucking complicated.

I finished my business, experienced the usage of toilet paper, and flushed. Just like that, defecation disappeared, washed away in swirling water. Mortals had come a long way from simply dumping their refuse into the gutter. A few hundred years back, I'd done the London circuit, and let me tell you, those streets made toxic dumps seem clean. Nothing like going down on a man, surrounded by garbage, feces, and rats, to really turn sex into a dirty act.

Speaking of sex . . .

Before I hopped into the shower, I padded over to my purse. Rummaging through it, I pulled out a folded slip of paper. I picked up the phone, entered the code to leave the internal hotel system, then punched in the numbers scrawled onto the hotel stationery. After two rings, a man's voice said, 'Paul Hamilton.'

A smile in my voice, I said, 'So you said to call you whenever I wanted.'

I could picture him blink before recognition set in. 'Jesse?'

'Heya, sweetie. Is this a good time?'

Paul chuckled. Just hearing his laugh made my toes curl. 'You bet. How's everything going?'

'Good,' I said, rolling onto my back. Teasing my left nipple with my fingers, I purred into the phone, 'So I wanted to tell you about my new job.'

PART THREE

DAUNUAN

10

Belles

Backstage at Belles, five minutes before my shift started: I was elbow-deep in lingerie, and the vanity tables were so littered with cosmetics and brushes and tissues that I could barely find the mirror. Momma's baskets of complimentary makeup and perfumes had been ransacked, leaving only a lonely lipstick and broken wicker. Free facial products apparently brought out the pack rat in dancers.

The yellow paint on the walls looked like urine stains, and the stench of cabbage and peanut oil clung to the air, thanks to the Chinese restaurant next door. Even Momma's cinnamon incense couldn't mask the smell. Ling's brought more than culinary perfume to the dressing room; earlier, I'd seen a cockroach that would've scared the piss out of an alley cat scuttle into a crack in the wall. Dandy. I suspected that the black beans in some of Ling's recipes were more of the *Periplaneta Americana* variety.

But I didn't care about roaches or how cramped the room was for seven women. In a few minutes, I'd be dancing on stage. Men would watch me, their pulses quickening, their sweat gleaming on their foreheads. As I moved, they'd follow my body with their eyes, wishing they had the balls to jump up on stage and touch me. They'd sit there in the dark, worshiping me with their lusty thoughts and hidden hands.

So maybe I couldn't suck out their souls. I could still make them want me. A girl had to exercise her skills, after all.

As I tucked my hair under a black fedora, one of my coworkers let out a curse that would've had marines take note.

In a thick Jersey accent, another dancer asked, 'What's the matter?' *Whassamatta?*

Lorelei, a top-heavy, brain-dead beauty pouted so deeply that her lower lip touched her boobs. 'My fucking hairspray just died!' Sure enough, half of her copper tresses were teased higher than a man's erection, and the other half was as limp as that same dick, two minutes after ejaculation. 'Where's Momma when you need her?'

'Jesus, Lori, what'd you use, a whole fucking can?' Candy rolled her eyes. I didn't know how she managed it; her lashes were so gunked up with mascara, it must've felt like her lids were toting bricks. 'Know what that shit does to the ozone layer?'

Lorelei's pout sank to her knees. 'Candy, you don't even know where the o-fucking-zone layer is.'

'This from the girl who thinks 'ozone' is the place where you get an orgasm,' Circe said. Circe, whose legs reached her chin, was the brains of the Belles dancers; she'd told me no less than three times that she was in law school, and dancing paid a hell of a lot better than waitressing. 'At least here if the guys grope me,' she'd said, sucking on a cigarette as if there were better drugs than nicotine buried within, 'they usually stuff a fiver between my breasts. And then I get their asses thrown out for touching me.'

Trying to scare her hair to new heights with a comb, Lorelei muttered, 'Christ, all I want is some fucking hairspray. You guys don't have to be so fucking mean about it. Where the fuck is Momma?'

'Here, use mine.' I tossed Lorelei my can of Rave. No, I wasn't being nice. I would've done anything to shut them up for a moment. I couldn't tell if the banter was friendly or not; some of these gals scored so deeply with their barbed words that the floor should have been tacky with their blood.

Umm, pools of congealing blood. I sighed with longing. Bless me, I missed home.

Candy grinned at me, her white teeth a startling contrast to her ebony skin. While Aurora, the Jersey babe, had a rich café au lait coloring to her skin, Candy was pure dark chocolate – thus her stage name. She said, 'Careful, Jez. You get footprints all over your back, the men won't tip so much.'

'Much obliged, sweetie.' I blew her a kiss, then returned my attention to the film-encrusted mirror.

'Footprints they dig,' Aurora said, shaking her head. 'Scars they love. But don't you dare bruise. That makes you a damned leper. Can't figure that shit out.' It was like a foreign language: *Canned figgur dad shitout.* Good thing demons (even the former kind) automatically spoke, read, and cursed in all known (and many forgotten) languages.

'You trying to understand men?' Candy snorted. 'Please. You're in it for the money. Who gives a rat's ass why the men like what they do? As long as they pay, who cares?'

'I'm going to barf,' Jemma said. 'I'm going to vomit all over my shoes.'

'Girl, you don't want to do that,' Faith said as she fluffed her white-blonde locks. She liked doing the angel-as-temptress thing; the feather wings attached to her white bustier were sort of a giveaway. 'Those shoes look like they cost more than my rent.'

Exotic dancers – flexible and practical. Who'd have guessed?

'I'm just so nervous,' Jemma said, her face a picture of lament. Sitting on the threadbare sofa, she wrapped her arms around her legs and propped her chin on her knees. 'I barely made it through my two sets so far. How do you guys do it?'

Three of the strippers chuckled. 'Some nights I strut out of here with almost a thousand in cash,' Faith said. 'And that's after tipouts and giving Dick his house fee.'

Dick, short for Dickhead, was Roman. Apparently, he thought with Mr Happy even more than I'd credited him with.

'Good hours, good money,' Candy said, buckling the strap on her heels. 'Makes anything bearable.'

'And there's nothing like knowing you got a roomful of guys just begging to get into your G-string,' Circe added with a sly wink.

'Damn straight,' I said, grinning as I adjusted the rim of my hat. I was doing the spy versus spy thing for my first show – fedora, trench coat, and killer lingerie. I'd lose the hat and coat by the end of the first song, the teddy and peek-a-boo bra for the second, leaving me clad in my G-string, garters, nylons and heels for the last song. And my amulet, of course. Nothing would ever get me to remove that baby. The peridot nuzzled between my breasts, cold and hard.

110

'So, you been in the business' *(da bizniz)* 'awhile?' Aurora asked me, pulling up her thigh-high boots.

'You could say that.' I stood up and cleared away from the crowded space by the mirror, practiced a few steps in the new heels. 'I'm more used to one-on-one attention.'

'Jez, you know Dick don't go for soliciting here, right?' Beneath layers of eye makeup, Candy met my gaze. 'He'll show you the door, let it hit your ass on the way out.'

Lorelei snorted, but said nothing.

'Guy asks you how much for a blowjob,' Faith said, applying fuck-me-red lipstick to her mouth, 'you tell him that all we do is dance.'

I laughed, shaking my head in disbelief. 'Sweetie, I've never asked a man for money in my life.' My collections had been a purely spiritual thing.

'So we don't . . . um, you know?' Jemma looked like she was going to cry.

'Hell no,' Candy said, shaking her head. 'You want to get busted for prostitution? Shit, the place is crawling with undercovers.'

Jemma looked like the Governor had just called to save her from the chair. 'Okay, good. But you know, Roman sort of, um, made a pass at me. So I thought that he sort of, you know, was encouraging me to, um. You know.'

'Girl, Dickhead wants nothing more than to bang his dancers, have one draped over each arm,' Faith said, shaking her platinum tresses.

'Man thinks with his cock all the time,' Lorelei said, chucking my can of hairspray into a trash bin. 'But you got to tell him no. Man's like a fucking tic. You let him into your pants once, you need a fucking crowbar to get him out.'

'So you guys haven't slept with him?' Jemma asked.

The ladies shared knowing glances. 'All I'll say 'bout that,' said Candy, 'is you don't ever want to accept a drink from Dick.'

'He likes 'em spaced out,' Aurora said, as if that made any sense, even with the thick Jersey accent.

'Dickhead,' Circe muttered, and the ladies all agreed.

The curtain between the dressing room and the dark hall that led to the stage parted, and Joey lumbered in, doing the Arnold Shwarzenegger thing from the original *Terminator*. One of the three Belles bouncers, he was all muscle and, according to Candy, all heart. A walking teddy bear, swore Aurora. If you asked me, he was a poster child for raunchy dreams. Yummy!

'Momma's on the way with some JD,' he boomed. 'Then it's the Cabaret Bow.'

I asked Candy, 'What's that?'

'Stupid shit,' she said. 'We all get out there, do a bow as Lyle introduces us. Stage is too damn small for eight of us.'

'Ten,' Faith said, dusting her cheekbones. 'What with Jemma and Jezebel here.'

'Momma says it's advertising.' Circe shrugged. 'Whatever.'

'Joey,' Lorelei said, her motor purring and her eyes screaming JUMP ME NOW, 'can you get the clasp on my necklace?' She motioned to her throat, where she held a row of faux pearls in place with her other hand.

Aurora, Circe, and Faith rolled their eyes. Candy said, 'For fuck's sake, Lori, the man's gayer than Liberace.'

Joey shrugged, and his shoulders moved like boulders rolling downhill. 'No problem, Lori.'

As Joey's thick fingers fumbled with the clasp around her long neck, Lorelei's face had that smug 'drop dead'

112

look, the kind worn by tigers about to munch on small children.

Momma bustled into the room, holding a tray with a bunch of shot glasses and a bottle of Jack Daniels. 'Here we are, my bellerinas.'

Bellerinas? Groan.

'A toast to today's latest additions to the lineup. Speaking of which, here's the order. We've already got Selina, Josie, Harmony, Aurora, Circe, and Jemma doing their shows.' She paused, giving Jemma a critical eye. 'Honey, you're looking a bit green. You've been doing fine on stage, but you really should talk to the nice men, get some lap dances.'

'I've never done that,' Jemma admitted, looking miserable. 'I'm scared I'll do it wrong.'

'Heaven knows the other girls'll thank you for limiting yourself to the stage, but still you have to think of yourself.' Momma sighed as she poured out the whiskey. 'Better take a few swigs, hon. Courage in a bottle. Does wonders.'

'That'd be great,' Jemma whispered, her voice thick. Poor girl really was going to lose her lunch, wasn't she?

'So. Selina, Josie, and Jemma clock out at eleven. Circe, Harmony, and Aurora are here until one. Everyone else is here until closing. So the lineup is Candy, Selina, Aurora, Josie, Jezebel, Jemma, Circe, Harmony, Faith, and Lorelei.'

Man, she was good with the names. Me, I would've had to write them on my palm or etch them on someone's forehead to remember the order. I noticed that Momma didn't offer a glass to Joey, and he didn't ask. Maybe bouncers stay away from booze while on the clock.

'First shift dancers have only one more mandatory show, by the way. Jezebel and Jemma, remember to tell Lyle when you're heading up to the VIP area so he can skip your name until you're back. You don't want to miss your rotation. Roman'll charge you extra for the missed show.'

I nodded, turning the shot glass around in my hand. Rules, rules, rules. There were always rules. Jemma looked like she'd rather be anywhere else.

Momma beamed at the seven of us. 'Here's to lusty men.'

As the mortals say, Amen.

'Between your shows,' Momma said to me as Joey collected our used shot glasses, 'work the crowd. Talk to the nice, lonely men. You remember the pricing?'

I nodded, but she kept on talking.

'Lap dance by the tables is up to you, but if you ask for more than twenty for a song, they're going to get their expectations up. Thirty gets them a private dance upstairs in the VIP lounge. Two-fifty for thirty in the VIP room. Roman gets his cut before you go home. Got it?'

'You bet,' I said.

'Now go on out there, ladies. Say hi, give them a hint of what's coming. Make some money, and make Momma proud.'

Sheesh. She laid it on thicker than lubricating oil, didn't she?

Candy grabbed one of my hands, and Lorelei took my other. 'Quick little hustle on stage holding hands, a bow, that kind of thing,' Candy said as the other dancers all grabbed hands. 'Then we all scoot off, and my act starts.'

'You got a theme song?' I asked her, my heels clomping on the wooden floor as we seven trotted down the dimly lit hall.

Grinning, she whispered, 'Candy Girl.'

Of course.

114

Suddenly we were on stage, the spotlights dazzling my eyes like paparazzi flashbulbs. I barely made out the three other dancers joining us from the floor – it looked like the Cabaret Bow wasn't optional. Amid a backbeat of drums blaring from speakers above the stage, I heard the appreciative claps and whistles of our audience. Inhaling, I breathed in cigarette smoke and booze-heavy air, peppered with the spice of sex. *Ummmm.*

'Say hello to the lovely ladies of Belles!' Lyle's disembodied voice boomed out, and the men in the crowd let out a cheer. 'Belles is proud to present Aurora! Candy! Circe! Faith! Harmony! Josie! Lorelei! Selina! And two new additions – please welcome Jemma and Jezebel!'

The shouts filled my ears, echoed through my body as the audience applauded and whistled. Drunk on the sound, I pulled my hand away from Lorelei's and waved at the men I couldn't see, grinning madly as I did a little shimmy-bop and tipped my hat.

Lorelei snatched my hand back. Just before we all pranced backstage, my eyes adjusted to the lighting, and I was able to make out some of the faces in the packed room. I locked gazes with Paul, who was about two rows back. Smiling, he dropped me a wink and saluted me with his glass.

Paul! Oooh. My Cabin Boy returneth. Woot!

Back in the hallway, Lorelei hissed at me, 'That was okay, 'cause you're new. But don't you fucking upstage me again. Hear me?'

Bitch. I was tempted to pull out my hat pin and puncture one of her silicon-inflated tits.

'Jesus, Lori,' Candy groaned, 'give it up, will you?'

'Go fuck yourself.'

The opening of 'Candy Girl' rang out, threatening to

liquefy my eardrums. Candy fixed a smile on her face and glared at Lorelei with cold, shark's eyes. Lyle announced her, and she headed toward the stage, bumping her hip against the buxom redhead's as she bopped past her. Lorelei snarled and looked like she could have happily plucked out each of Candy's mascara-crusted lashes with her teeth, but Faith put a hand on her shoulder and whispered something in her ear.

Lorelei's nostrils flared, but she kept her mouth screwed shut. Looking pissier than a pit bull with a cavity, she flounced onto the showroom floor, ready to dole out the charm and back rubs.

As Warren Zevon would've said, disorder in the house. But who gave an angel's feather about potential catfights between strippers? *Paul* was in the audience.

A wave of heat crashed through my body, leaving my nipples hard and my panties wet in its wake.

Life was damned good.

After my first show of the night finished to the final chords of 'Start Me Up' and wolf calls from my appreciative audience, I collected my garments and hustled backstage to throw on my bra and spandex evening gown, and to tuck my tips into my shoulder bag. Then I ambled onto the showroom floor, ready to make casual conversation and see if anyone wanted me to gyrate on their laps.

A group of businessmen at tables six and eight hailed me, and after some flattering conversation on my part (all bullshit) and theirs (all true), I used my knee to spread one guy's legs and then wiggled along to Bon Jovi, running my body up and down the customer's. On stage, Lorelei was in the middle of her Big Hair set, doing the Hard

Rock Whore thing. Frankly, I shook it up like bad medicine way, way better than she did. Then again, I wasn't toting around tits the size of watermelons, either.

One of the guys got a tad too close for Joey's taste. As I plucked his fingers away from my boob, Joey grabbed the guy by his pinstriped shoulders and hauled him away from the table. Joey's buddy Ben – an iron man so full of muscles, I was amazed he could cross his arms in front of his chest – hovered by tables six and eight. His body language dared the businessmen to make another inappropriate move. None of them took him up on it. Wimps.

Well, rich wimps. They each tipped me ten bucks for three minutes of dancing and not even shrugging out of my dress. Cha-ching! One of them even asked if we could go to the VIP room later that night. But of course, sweetie!

After we arranged a time for our VIP rendezvous, I sidled up to Joey and Ben, giving them a peck on their cheeks. 'My heroes.'

Ben blushed to the top of his bald pate, looking like a sun-burned thumb. But Joey just smiled and shrugged. 'You're one of the family now, Jez. We won't let any guy touch you like you shouldn't be touched.'

Ooh, wasn't he the sweetest thing? I could see why Lorelei wanted to ride him like a bronco. And here I'd thought that sensitive men had gone out of fashion in the late 1990s. Silly me. Mental note: Show the love when it's time to tip out.

Ambling around the main room, I stopped by table one. 'Excuse me,' I said to the hottie in the pocket-tee, 'is this seat taken?'

'Not at all.' Paul grinned at me. 'Have a seat.'

'I've got to say, I'm not used to dancing in four-inch

heels.' I laughed, but it came out more like a giggle. Eek. What was I, a schoolgirl with a crush?

'Hazards of the job, huh?' A smile bloomed on his face. 'They really lengthen your legs.'

'With all this flesh in your face, you were watching my legs?'

'Among other things.'

Crap, now I was blushing. What the fuck? I'd been a succubus for longer than all the men in the room had been alive combined. I used to eat guys like these for breakfast. Literally. Snap out of it, Jezebel!

'I never would've pictured you as a stripper,' Paul said, keeping his eyes on my face. 'At the train station, you seemed so . . . I don't know, naive. Innocent.'

I barked out a laugh so hard that my eyes teared up. 'Sweetie, I'm pretty sure that's the first time anyone's ever told me that I was innocent.'

Those magnificent eyes warmed as his grin softened into something incredibly kissable. 'But you are. There's something about you, something . . . I can't put my finger on it. You're like a real sex kitten. Playful and . . . I don't know. Young. God, that sounds stupid.'

No, it didn't. Maybe I was an experienced succubus, but I was still a newborn as a human. 'A sex kitten, huh? Maybe I should buy me a catsuit.'

'Mmmm.' His mouth made the right sound, but his eyes whispered something different. I couldn't tell if he was trying to read me or if he was casting judgment on me.

A hand clamped down on my bare shoulder. Points for me that I didn't jump. 'Love, if you have a moment, I'd like a word.'

I glanced over my shoulder and up at Roman. He was

sporting black like it was going out of style, with enough gold jewelry winking on him to give rappers an inferiority complex. With a smile as sweet and fake as saccharine I said, 'Sure thing, Roman.'

Paul's hand reached out and touched mine, covering it completely. 'Actually, I was just about to ask Jezebel for a private dance.'

Still watching my boss, I saw something dark flash in his eyes. Then he grinned like a hungry barracuda, showing all of his perfect teeth. 'Hey, the customer always comes first. Especially if my girls do their jobs right.' He squeezed my shoulder, then oozed away to annoy the other dancers.

Paul's gaze tracked him, and the look on his face made it clear that he thought Roman was right up there with plague-infested rats.

I cleared my throat. 'So, you said something about a dance?'

He looked back at me, and his eyes softened from a stormy green back to sea foam. 'Show me the way.'

Ooh, the things I could show him . . .

A smile on my face told Paul I'd be right back. I dashed over to the DJ booth as fast as I could in stilettos. Getting Lyle's attention, I mimed that I'd be going upstairs for a bit, and I pointed to Paul seated at the table. Lyle gave me a thumbs-up. A man of few words was Lyle. Maybe that was due to the speaker mounted directly over the DJ booth.

Then I led Paul to the stairs that headed up to the VIP lounge, my arm wound around his. On the way to the stairs, I caught Roman staring at me, his eyes hard as diamond chips. Maybe it was just me – the air-conditioning was set to nipple-hardening temperatures, so my internal thermostat was way off – but for a second, I thought the peridot stone felt hot against my skin.

No, it was cold, as cold as the smile that flashed on Roman's face as he winked at me.

11

Belles (II)

At the front of the lounge, the VIP host loomed in his chair. Don't ask me how any mortal could loom while sitting; this giant in bouncer's clothing pulled it off beautifully. 'Evening, sir,' Dalton rumbled.

Paul removed a bill from his wallet and flicked it toward Dalton. 'Evening.'

The bouncer's eyes lit up. 'Much obliged, sir,' he said, palming the tip.

My Cabin Boy doth have charms I hadn't expected. Sweet. I wondered what else there was to Paul that was just waiting to be discovered. Ooh, the possibilities . . .

Dalton rose to his feet – a feat unto itself, rather like watching a mountain form before my eyes. 'Follow me.' Pocketing his cash, he led us past two other booths, where Candy and Faith were grooving to the beat, their customers drooling with desire. In the far back corner, just outside the VIP room, Dalton motioned to the plush sofa, small circular table with two matching chairs, and a slim, metal pole that connected the floor to the ceiling.

'Enjoy your dance, sir.'

'He will, sweetie,' I told him with a wink. Dalton, obviously unimpressed with my wry wit, lumbered back to his bear cave at the front of the lounge.

The music piped in from the overhead speakers changed to the Eurythmics' 'Sweet Dreams.' Nice. I wrapped my arm around Paul's waist. 'So tell me, you want me between your legs or on the tabletop?'

He smiled, and my nipples nearly burst out of my bra. 'They both sound tempting.'

Yay, tempting! 'Sweetie, you tell me what you want. I'm happy to do it for you.' I wished I was taller; how was I supposed to blow in his ear to emphasize my point when his ear was a good five inches above me?

'Really . . .' The way he said that single word gave it layers of meaning.

'Really.' I bumped my hips to the heavy synth beat. Annie Lennox's voice rang out, smoky and lush and sexy enough to make me take note. Sweet dreams are made of this, she declared. Who was I to disagree?

'Anything?' Paul's eyes sparkled like moonlight on the water. Ooh, my Cabin Boy was entertaining naughty thoughts. Yum! 'But we've got an audience.'

I glanced at the others in the lounge. Candy's customer was nearly blind with passion. Faith, sitting on her man's lap, giggled as she sipped from his glass. Off by the host station, Dalton tried to look fierce as he hid a yawn.

'Sweetie, I'm betting we're all but invisible to them. So name your poison. Lap dance? Maybe something on the table?'

Paul smiled up at me as he slid onto the couch. 'You really don't have to dance.'

'No? Maybe a massage? I give good massage.'

'I'd really like to just talk.'

Boring! He paid to be with me . . . and he wanted to talk? Oh, but bless me, he looked so earnest. I leaned forward, giving him an eyeful of my cleavage. Beneath my gown, my bra was a black satin demicup that shoved my boobs way up, defying gravity and a few laws of magic. 'Talk? Sure. Do you speak body language?'

His smile was the stuff of sonnets. 'Willing to learn.' He leaned back in his seat, measuring me with his eyes. 'Interesting job you've got.'

Grinning, I sat on the table, rolling onto my hip and propping my head in my hand. Tabletop centerfold in training. 'Believe me, it's nothing like my last job.'

'Oh? What'd you used to do?'

I trailed a tapered nail along the tabletop. 'Collections. I like this better.'

'Yeah?' His lovely poet's eyes deepened to a true emerald. I wondered what he was thinking. 'Why'd you change jobs?'

'Oh,' I shrugged, 'I didn't see eye to eye with management.' Not liking where this was going, I changed the subject. 'What about you? What's your ball and chain?'

'I'm a consultant.'

'What do you consult?'

'This and that. How's it go, jack of all trades, master of none?'

'Handsome and modest,' I said, wanting to do more than just talk with him. 'My, my.'

'Modesty's my best quality.'

Not even close. That strong jaw, the bump on his nose . . . oh, those eyes and his large hands . . .

His voice pulled me out of my fantasy. 'So, do you do more than dance?'

Ooh, a man who cut to the chase. Me like. 'Sweetie, I do almost anything once,' I said, blowing him a kiss. 'Why? Have something in mind when my shift ends?' Sex! Sex! Let's have sex!

His eyes met mine. Expectation, anticipation . . . something dark and wet and hungry made those sea green eyes flash like heat lightning.

A pregnant pause, then he said, 'Maybe. When do you get off?'

Now, just from watching you. 'Closing time. Three.' Visions of him and me in my king-sized hotel bed nearly made me swoon.

He drummed his fingers on the tabletop, two inches away from my right breast. 'Too late for me tonight. Maybe tomorrow?'

Crap. How could my Cabin Boy have no stamina? 'I'm working middle shift tomorrow. Seven to one.' I perked up. 'Maybe we could grab some dinner?'

'Can't. Got a long afternoon meeting that's going to stretch into the evening. Maybe lunch? Like around one-thirty?'

'I'd like that.' I rolled onto my belly, cupping my chin in my hands as I gazed at his face. 'I'd like to know more about you, Paul the Consultant.'

'And I'd love to learn all about you, Jesse the Dancer.'

Love? *LOVE?* WOOT!

The rest of the half hour, we made small talk and moon-eyes. Nothing more. No touching, no kissing, no breathy promises that neither of us intended to keep. Just staring that was so physical I could feel his gaze caressing my body, my face, my hair. Paul had a tiny scar beneath his left eye, one that you couldn't see unless you stared really closely at his face. I wanted to know

124

how he got it. I wanted to know whatever he was willing to tell me.

After, I walked Paul to the host's station. I tugged on Paul's shoulder until he lowered his head enough for me to kiss his cheek. 'Talking was lovely, but next time I'd love to dance for you too.'

'That would be great,' he said, his voice low and soft, making me think lusty things. How could a few spoken words turn my insides to jelly? Was this the effect I'd had on my former clients before I sucked out their souls?

If so . . . then damn, I'd been *real* good.

Paul pulled out his wallet from his back pocket. Ooh, the way he wore those jeans! Slurp, slurp! Grabbing a bunch of bills, he folded them into a square and tucked them into my cleavage. His fingers barely touched my skin, but it was enough to send shocks of heat blasting through my body.

He smiled as if he knew the effect his touch had on me. 'Tomorrow, for sure.'

My voice about three octaves higher than it should have been, I said, 'I'm marking my calendar.'

He winked, then he shook Dalton's hand before he ambled out of the lounge. I should have escorted him downstairs, but I was too busy melting into the floor in a pool of presex juice.

'Oh, Jezebel.' Dalton laughed from his host station. 'Getting a crush on the customers is a bad idea.'

'Yeah,' I said, thinking about how Paul would look wearing my ankles as earrings. 'But I'm a bad girl.'

Bent backward, with my tits over my head and my hair whipping against the floor like an automatic dust mop, I mused that being an exotic dancer meant that I was reduced to being nothing more than a creature of sex – an object, a toy. Just something that men thought of as a potential receptacle for their seed. They didn't see my smile, they saw my blood-red lipstick and imagined what it would be like if I sucked their root until they exploded in my mouth.

Uber cool.

I finally didn't have to tailor my costume to each individual client. I could dress however I wanted, as long as a G-string covered my bush. For that matter, I didn't have to actually sleep with anyone (not that I ever really got any sleep with my former clients).

Maybe I should have become a call girl instead of a dancer.

But then I wouldn't be dancing, unless it was between the sheets. And then I was back to doing one-on-one jobs (unless I got very lucky). I sort of dug the whole bespell-the-entire-room thing. Maybe I was just a sexual object . . . but I was a fucking powerful one.

Being a dancer definitely had its pros and cons. But I was willing to bet that the pros – most of which were stuffed in my garter – outweighed the cons. Nothing like swinging from a stripper's pole to really get some perspective.

Someone called my name. I swung to the left, gripping the pole tightly, and I stretched my smile wider than a football field as my upside-down gaze fastened on Roman by the tip-rail. I'd forgotten that he'd wanted to talk to me before – being with Paul had turned me into a creature of the moment. Oopsie.

'When you're done with your show, love, stop by my office.'

'Okay.'

Crap. It wasn't even one in the morning. I hoped I wasn't going to be fired; another hour at this rate was going to line my panties with the better part of five hundred dollars. Not that I counted or anything.

I swung away from Roman and pulled myself upright, then danced away from the pole, shimmying to Melissa Etheridge. She wailed about some other gal, wondering if she does it like the way I do. Better believe it, sweetie.

After the song ended, I gathered my clothes and my tips, bid *adieu* to my adoring fans, and sashayed offstage to clear the way for redheaded Lorelei, whose tits appeared about three feet before the rest of her body. In the dressing room, I put on a blue satin robe and cinched it tight. Then I made my way upstairs to Roman's office.

I rapped my knuckles on the door. His muffled voice said, 'Come.'

As if I could on command.

I opened the door and hovered in the threshold. The man himself was sitting at his desk, his legs crossed by the ankles and planted on top of a stack of papers on the desktop. A cigarette clung to his lips like a desperate lover; the entire room stank of tobacco, with a deeper odor of . . . something. Not sweat, exactly, and not sex. I couldn't place it.

'Ah, Jezebel. Come in, love.'

Momma, behind Roman, straightened up and patted her graying hair. 'What can we do for you, honey?'

'Roman asked that I stop by after my set.'

'Did he now?' Momma shot Roman an appraising look, which ended in the tiniest of nods – if I hadn't been watching for it, it would've looked like her hair just shifted back into place. 'Well then, I'll leave you two alone.'

'Close the door behind you, would you, Momma?'

'Of course, Roman.'

Momma smiled at me, then sauntered out and shut the door. Wondering if he assumed he was getting in my pants, I stood with my hands clasped in front of my body. The room was tastefully done – tasteful, that is, if you're into wood paneling and tan Naugahyde couches. I was surprised the carpeting wasn't shag.

'So, how's your first night going, love?'

I smiled politely. Don't piss off the boss on Day One. 'Fine, Roman. I like dancing, and the men aren't too grabby.'

'Yeah, I've been watching you.'

I knew I'd felt little rodent eyes on me all night. Now I had the source.

He was watching me now, searching my face as if looking for something he'd lost. His eyes narrowed as he crushed out his cigarette. 'You're a fine dancer. Most girls don't know shit. They get on stage and sort of bounce their tits and shake their ass, and they call that dancing. But you actually move to the music. That's nice. I like that.'

Not sure where he was going, I said, 'Thanks.'

'You give any thought to my suggestion, about doing an act with Faith? She's got the angel thing going, maybe dress you up like a devil?'

Somehow my heart wound up in my throat. I swallowed it and said, 'I don't know, Roman.' I stretched my smile wider, trying to ignore the icy fingers creeping up my back. Bless me, I was afraid. It had to be coincidence. Nothing more.

Except there was that smell, just under the surface of the Pimp Motif, a smell that was so familiar, yet completely elusive. I'd heard the expression 'Right on the tip of my tongue' before; until now, I'd assumed it had to do with fellatio.

'Think about it, love,' Roman said, standing. 'You're both around the same height, and you've got similar figures. Originally I'd wanted Jemma for this. She and Faith could be twins, if you look at them after a couple rounds of Jim Beam. But she's too green for that. You, though. You know how to move that body of yours. Same as Faith. You two are actually for-real dancers.' He spread his hands wide. 'It doesn't have to be too raunchy. Hell, I don't want to lose my license because of a girl-girl scene. I was thinking something . . . classier. Like a mirror image show.'

He was moving now, coming around his desk and walking behind me. His hands on my shoulders, he whispered in my ear, 'Just think about it. That's all I'm asking.'

His hands moved down to my breasts. He got one squeeze before I pushed his hands down and away.

'Roman, don't.'

'No? Are you sure . . . Jezebel?'

Something about the way he said my name made me want to turn and run, but my legs felt rooted to the floor. His tongue darted against my earlobe, and he hit a zinger of a spot because my knees buckled. Pressed against him, I felt his erection against the small of my back.

Finding my voice, I said, 'This isn't a good idea, sweetie.'

'There we go.' He kissed my neck, sending electric shocks across my skin. 'I knew it was you, babes.'

My throat constricted, and pretty white stars blinked in front of my eyes. Swallowing thickly, my heart boomed as 'babes' echoed in my ears. My voice a harsh whisper, I said, 'Daun?'

'In the flesh. Heh. Flesh pit.'

Suddenly I was falling backward, but he caught me, held me in a dip. Staring into Roman's brown eyes, I watched as they gleamed red . . . and for a second, I saw the incubus buried within the man.

My boss was possessed.

'Babes,' Daun said, his breath hot on my neck, 'I've missed you.'

12

Pandemonium

I dropped off my lover at the edge of Covet. He gave my hand a final squeeze before one of the Greedy eagerly led him to the Cauldron. He'd been sweet, in a sickeningly cloying sort of way. Sort of like rotting honey.

Content over another job well done, I headed toward the Second Sphere. As I was groaning over the thought of waiting on line for days just to file my body receipt, a presence slid through my mind: *Hey, babes. You busy?*

I grinned from the slick feeling of the thought, which left an impression like scented oil. My buddy Daun always knew how to get my sweet spots. Reaching across the psychic link between Seducers, I replied: *Heya, sweetie. I have to file some paperwork. Payday's right around the corner.*

Oh well. I thought I could tempt you with wild, rampant sex.

So who needed to get paid? *You know what? I need me a good bout of loving.*

That's my hot-blooded little succubus. I'm in the District. Come on over, babes.

I fixated on his presence until I clearly pictured his

131

location within Pandemonium. And then I blinked myself to his side.

Daunuan the incubus stood before me, arms folded in front of his broad chest. Like me, he was in his natural form. One of Pan's brood, Daun was a satyr, complete with horns, hooves, and tail. His turquoise skin offset the brilliant gold of his hair and eyes. A pelt of thick, sandy curls covered his lower half, with finer hair covering his torso and arms. A smile played across his face, full of silent temptation and unspoken promises. In stark contrast, his dick spoke volumes as it stood proudly. My nipples hardened in response. Body language at its finest.

He'd found an empty chamber within the Red Light District of Pandemonium, reserved to those affiliated with Lust. Although the elite had personal quarters that they decorated however they wished, lesser-ranked demons made do with spartan rooms containing only a sleeping pallet. None of these bedrooms were assigned; it was strictly first come, first served. The chamber itself, like all such pods, smelled of the deep earth from which it was carved. And sex, of course; all rooms in the District smelled of sex.

I sidled up to Daun and reached out, stroking his member, his flat stomach, his chest, tracing the outline of his jaw. 'Heya, sweetie.'

'Babes.' His voice rumbled in his throat, the lazy growl of a somnolent grizzly bear. Without touching me, he rubbed his thumb and index finger together, and I cooed as I felt ghostly fingers brush against my clitoris.

'Oooh. I like.'

'You're supposed to.'

He rubbed his finger up his thumb and wiggled the digit, and I purred with delight as I felt a ghostly finger probe inside of me. Nearly melting against him, I wrapped my arms around his waist and planted my mouth on his, sucking greedily. Before I could mount him, he gently pushed me away.

'Slow, babes,' he said, chuckling. 'I've been working on a new fantasy. You game?'

Many of the infernal liked to try out their various temptations on other creatures of the Pit before they plied their wares on targeted humans. But agreeing to act as the unsuspecting mortal in a demon's fantasy was risky for the player. The one controlling the scene had complete control over the situation . . . and over the demon going along with it. On top of that, there was a chance the player could get lost in the fantasy and forget everything about having been a demon.

Hazards of the job. Besides, Daun was worth the risk. Along with being a pal, he was the best lay this side of the Pridelands. I squeezed his shaft once, then let go. 'For you? Always.'

'Excellent.' His eyes glimmered as he said, 'Get dressed.'

'Who am I?'

'Good girl, engaged, true to her man, but curious about what another lover would be like.'

I raised my arms over my head and tilted my face toward the ceiling, closing my eyes. Power rippled through me, starting at the top of my head and working down to my feet, weaving my costume. Short, dark hair. Round, wholesome face. Long frame, but slightly chunky. Pert breasts. Round belly and hips. Curvy legs. Dainty feet. For an outfit, I selected a white T-shirt beneath a V-necked blue sweater and dark blue jeans. Matching bra-and-panties set. A gold bracelet winked on my left ankle. A thin band of gold, with a tiny but bright diamond set in its middle, hugged the ring finger of my left hand. Small gold hoops hung from my earlobes. A whisper of makeup, just enough to accent my brown eyes and long lashes; nothing too fancy. I wiggled the toes of my bare feet, enjoying the ticklish sensation.

I loved playing dress-up.

'Sweet,' Daun said, giving me the once-over. 'Okay, babes. Ready?'

Anticipation fluttering in my stomach, I nodded.

His long nail grazed my forehead, and I *shifted*.

A sensation like falling, which ends with me shuddering. In the back of my mind, I know I am still the demon Jezebel. But now I am also Molly Ridgewood, twenty-three, and newly engaged to Jeff Loren. I still can hear his tremulous voice whisper in my ear when I remember him asking, *Will you marry me?*

A doorbell rings.

I open my eyes, surprised to be standing in the hallway of my cramped apartment. Of course I'm here, I tell myself. Jeff and I just moved in yesterday. He's at work, and I'm unpacking. Where else would I be?

Boxes clutter the foyer and the kitchen; even more crates barricade the bedroom. The smell of new paint mingles with the stale city air blowing in from the open windows in the living room. It's far too hot for my sweater, and I peel it off as I approach the door. Moving is sweaty work; I should have remembered that.

Blotting my forehead with the sleeve of my sweater, I open the door. Hulking in the doorway, a man smiles down at me. A blue bandana holds his long, red hair away from his lean face. Beneath a sleeveless leather vest, a dusty

134

white T-shirt pokes out. Ripped jeans cover his lean legs. Over-sized black boots shod his feet. A voice in my head giggles. Shitkickers, they're called shitkickers. I swallow the nervous laughter that accompanies the thought. I *never* curse. Good girls don't curse.

'Yes?' I ask, fear peppering my curiosity. Jeff and I were living in the big city now; who knows what this stranger wanted? He could be anyone, could do anything, and I would be helpless. The phone won't be in service until tomorrow, same as the electricity. My cell phone has no charge. If there's a problem, all I can do is scream . . . and everyone knows that in the big city, no one will risk themselves to help you. In the city, you're on your own.

The thought makes me giddy. I've never been on my own before.

His eyes sparkle in the dim light of the hallway. 'Found your purse outside.' His voice is rough, a rumble that reminds me of a motorcycle revving down a nighttime street. 'Thought I'd do a good deed and return it.' He raises his hand, and sure enough, my beaten up shoulder bag dangles from his fingers.

With a startled gasp, I reach for it. 'Thank you! Gosh, I didn't even know I'd dropped it. Where'd you find it?'

'Just outside your door. I was leaving another apartment and I saw it lying on the ground. Took a chance that it belonged to whoever lived here.'

'Thanks,' I say again, smiling up at him. He's so tall. Jeff's my height. I like having to crane my head to meet a man's eyes. 'You're a Good Samaritan.'

'I like to think of myself as a knight in leather armor.' He grins, motioning to his leather vest. Smoker's teeth, I think as I laugh, too, crooked smoker's teeth. I never smoked, always thought of it as a dirty habit. A dangerous habit.

He holds my gaze for a moment, then glances at the numerous boxes around me. 'Going or coming?'

'Coming,' I say, staring his face. I can't decide if his eyes are green or hazel. 'We just moved in yesterday.'

'We?' He glances at my hand, spots my ring. With a wry smile, he says, 'Congratulations.'

'Thank you.'

'Lucky guy here helping you?'

'He's at work.' A tattoo peaks out from beneath the man's sleeve. Something stirs in me, low down, near my crotch. Tattoos are so sexy. Jeff doesn't have a tattoo, wouldn't dream of ever getting one. Sweat beads on my forehead, and I mop my brow again with my sweater.

'Bringing home the bacon,' the stranger says, arching his brow, 'so you can fry it up in a pan.'

He's so different from Jeff. Where Jeff is clean-cut, this man sports a two-day growth of stubble. Jeff is easygoing, unassuming. This man radiates dominance ... and hints of danger. My heartbeat thumps in my ears as I think about what it would be like to be dangerous. A thin scar trails down one of his cheeks. I imagine stroking the white line, brushing my fingers over its pattern of old pain. My breath quickens as I wonder if his kisses would be like Jeff's – soft and loving, if sloppy – or if they would be forceful, insistent.

'You've got such beautiful eyes,' the stranger murmurs.

His words hit me like ice water, and I clear my throat. I am marrying Jeff Loren. I love Jeff Loren. What does it matter that I find this man, this tall stranger, fascinating – even desirable? Maybe I'd dream about him tonight. Something secret, something wicked. But nothing more than that. I'm a good girl.

136

'Listen,' I say, my voice cracking, 'I'd like to give you something, to show my appreciation for returning my bag.' I rummage through my purse and take out my wallet.

When I look up, he's laughing silently. 'What's so funny?'

'I don't want your money,' he says, a bemused grin on his face. 'That's really not necessary.'

'Oh. Um . . .' I'm at a loss of what else to offer. I know I don't want him to leave yet, but there's no way I can have him stay. He's a stranger, and I'm engaged.

His eyes darken to a rich, chocolate brown. How could I have thought they were hazel? His voice low and seductive, he says, 'What I'd really like is a thank-you kiss.'

Thoughts of Jeff dance in my mind, whisper of betrayal, even as my breath catches in my throat.

'Isn't that what fair maidens give their knights on white horses?' A smile quirks his lips, his full, cupid-bow lips, lips that promise to be soft yet strong. 'A kiss?'

It would just be one kiss. That's all. Even good girls can give kisses. 'Sure,' I say, and I stand on my tiptoes. Tilting my head up, my lips brush against his.

Magic rushes through me as the world catches fire. His tongue thrusts forward, parting my lips. My tongue touches his, and they probe each other, turning in maddeningly slow circles. The kiss strengthens as our tongues roll faster, shooting waves of heat into my breasts, my stomach, my groin. I've never felt so alive!

He starts to break away, but I grab his long hair and pull him back to me. His lips leave mine as he kisses his way to my ear. He whispers, 'What about your man?'

'Fuck him,' I pant, wanting him, needing him to kiss me again.

'I'd rather fuck you.' His breath tickles my neck, and I gasp in startled delight as he licks the hollow of my

137

throat. 'Is that what you want? You want to feel my cock inside of you? Want me to fuck you?'

'God, yes . . .' His tongue flicks out, licking my earlobe, stealing my voice.

'"God"? My, you *are* far gone, aren't you, babes?' He chuckles softly, and just as I'm about to question his words, he leans down and sucks my nipple, right through my shirt and bra. Moaning, I lean back, thrusting my chest into his face.

He nuzzles between my breasts, then he moves to my other nipple, teasing it with his mouth and teeth. My hands clutch his shoulders as my hips jerk forward, moving in rhythm as he sucks. His mouth leaves my breast and he whispers, 'Lose the shirt and pants.'

My face is flushed with heat. Breathing heavily, I pull my T-shirt over my head and throw the garment to the floor. Then I unclasp my jeans and yank the zipper down so hard that I break it. I wiggle out from the denim and kick it away. Standing in the hallway of my tiny apartment with the door wide open, I'm clad only in my pale blue bra and panties. And I don't care that my new neighbors could see me, don't care about my fiancé possibly walking in at any second. All I can think about is this man, this powerful stranger with long red hair and soft lips, and how I want to feel him inside of me.

'Nice,' he says. Then he grabs my arms and crushes me against his body. Kissing me deeply, he lifts me up. I wrap my legs around his waist as he kicks the front door closed. Sucking in his breath like it was a drug, I kiss him even harder, faster, bruising my lips. I can't get enough of him; I want to drink him down until he fills me.

He throws me onto my ancient sofa. I stare up at him, my lips parted, my body tingling all over. With a practiced motion, he unbuttons his fly. His penis pokes up, and I gaze at it, marveling over its thickness, over the way it seems to pulse with a life of its own.

Climbing on top of me, he kisses one of my nipples as his hand reaches behind my back and unfastens my bra. He flings it off of me and sucks at one breast, fondling the other. Writhing beneath him, I moan as my body responds in ways that I've never known before. He licks down my chest to my belly to the edge of my underwear. His tongue runs over the swell of my stomach before he catches my panties in his teeth and yanks down, exposing the triangular patch of dark hair between my legs. Working my underwear off my legs, he drops my panties to the floor.

Oh God, I'm doing this, I think as he kisses up my calf, then my inner thigh, sending shocks of pleasure through me. I'm actually here with a stranger, and he's about to make love to me, and I don't even know his name.

Then his mouth finds my sex, and I can't think at all as his tongue darts out and licks between my inner lips. My hips buck beneath him as I cry out, and my hands ball into fists as I feel something huge and wild building inside of me, begging for release.

He grabs my hands and pins my wrists above my head. Maneuvering on top of me, he gives me a knowing smile as he plunges his staff inside of me.

I squeal as he pounds me, as he fucks me, as I move beneath him and with him. 'Ahh!' I shout with every thrust, 'Ahh! AHH! *AHHHH!*' A dam bursts inside of me, and I arch my back and scream as my sex explodes in liquid fire. I shudder as my groin pulses, the tsunami of pleasure too intense to describe slowly winding down to lapping waves.

139

Oh . . . bliss. A smile spreads across my face as my body relaxes. Breathing deeply, my eyes slip closed.

His breath is hot on my neck. 'Call my name.'

Sleepily, I murmur, 'Don't know your name.'

'Yes you do, babes.' His penis shifts inside of me, sending aftershocks between my legs. 'Say it.'

And, as if by magic, I do know his name. My mouth opens, and I whisper, 'Don Juan.'

'That's my good girl.' His lips touch mine, but I'm too sleepy to do more than let him kiss me. 'You're mine.'

'I'm yours,' I agree as I feel sleep dragging me down. Before I lose myself completely, I feel his finger touch my brow.

Shift.

A falling sensation, ending with a violent shudder wracking my body.

My eyes opened to find Daun's face above mine, his golden eyes gleaming with satisfaction. 'Welcome back, babes.'

I felt him, huge and throbbing, inside of me. Blinking, I shed the vestiges of my dress-up character, shaking away the last characteristics of Molly Ridgewood like a dog ridding its fur of water. Daun's cock bumped against my cervix, sending ripples of pleasure interlaced with pain through my body. Wrapping my legs around his waist, I sank my talons into his shoulders. He grunted, then flashed me his fangs in a huge grin. He liked it rough.

'Sweetie,' I said, my voice a throaty purr, 'you were amazing.'

'Flatterer.'

'You actually got me to say your name,' I said, feeling awed and incredulous . . . and, truth be told, a touch uneasy.

140

Female Seducers were firm believers in the one-night stand – meaning we had one chance to snag our intended target. Our male counterparts liked to suck their victims dry over the course of many visits. Even so, that initial seduction was key. Once a human female willingly kissed an incubus, that was the end of her willpower; he'd be able to fuck her six ways to Salvation, and she'd beg for more. Once she called his name, she was bound to him until her soul belonged to Hell.

In all the times I'd played along in Daun's fantasies, he'd never gotten me to say his name at the end. And while I didn't have a soul to lose, the idea that someone had complete control over my desires, even just in play, was disquieting.

I was Jezebel. No one owned me.

Well, except for King Asmodai and Queen Lillith. But why split hairs?

'You're getting better,' I said, pumping beneath him, trying to yank myself out of my dark thoughts with every thrust of my hips.

'Always.' He kissed me deeply, ending with him sucking my lower lip. Then he pulled back to meet my gaze. 'You were gone way before the end, though. You actually mentioned the G-word.'

'I remember,' I muttered. Gah. If anyone found out I'd cried 'God' in the middle of a fantasy, I'd never hear the end of it.

Knock, knock, Jezzie.

I froze as Megaera's voice kissed my mind. Even though she wasn't a creature of Lust – as a Fury, technically she wasn't even a demon – we had our own bond, formed out of friendship. A thousand-plus years would do that to anyone. *Heya, sweetie. I'm sort of in the middle of something.*

141

More like you're in the middle of someone. Thought you were going to call me when you were done.

I sort of got sidetracked.

You mean you sort of forgot. This is important. Can I summon you?

Meg didn't need my permission to yank me to her side – she was way, way more powerful than me and could basically do whatever the fuck she wanted. But because we were friends, she always asked my permission. At times, I thought she was too nice to be a creature of the Pit. *Give me a sec to say good-bye.*

Apologies to Daun. Kisses from his Auntie Meg. Her presence caressed my mind in a farewell hug, soft as velvet. Then it was gone.

Tensing my internal muscles, I squeezed Daun once, then pulled away from him. I sighed as his erection slid out of me. 'Meg's in a tizzy, sweetie. Got to go.'

His smile lingered, even though his eyes narrowed. 'Sometimes I think your priorities are screwed up, babes. What's more important than fabulous sex?'

'That's what I'm about to find out.' I crushed him to me in a final kiss, then Meg summoned me and Daun was gone.

13

Belles (III)

Roman's breath, Roman's voice, but Daun's words: 'Babes, I've missed you.'

I squirmed out of his grasp and spun around to face him. Yes, it was right there in his eyes: The red-rimmed glow that had nothing to do with drink, drugs, or exhaustion. How could I have missed it?

Easy. I hadn't been looking. I was so confident that Caitlin's magic would protect me, I'd forgotten to watch out for signs of the Underworld. Stupid. Now I placed the subtle odor in the room: Brimstone.

'Daun,' I said, hating how high-pitched my voice was, like I'd sucked on helium. 'How'd you find me?'

In Roman's body, Daun grinned: A slow unfurling of his lips, radiating sex. A tiger's grin. 'Your friend Meg is very worried about you. She asked if I could pop by, see how you were doing. Me, I never argue with a Fury.' He looked me up and down, his gaze heavy on my skin. 'Seems to me like you're doing fine. Looking fine, too. I like the innocent façade. Very nice. Very . . .' His hand reached out and cupped my cheek. '. . . tempting.'

I released a breath I didn't know I'd been holding. Leaning against Roman's desk, I closed my eyes. A shudder worked its way through me, more intimate than Daun's lingering touch. Lucky, lucky girl. This could have been very bad.

No. Ring around the collar was bad. This could have been the end of everything. Reality check for the former succubus.

'Got to say, babes, you're a ballsy one. Going by your name? And in a place like this? You do so love to take chances, don't you?'

Chances, nothing. It appeared that I had a subconscious death wish. My voice tight, I said, 'I live for it.'

'Yeah, speaking of that. Nice move on your part, shuffling onto the mortal coil. Very well played. Doubtful the lowerdowns would consider that.'

'That was the idea.' Opening my eyes, I resolved to be more careful. Chances were, the next creature of the Pit that I came across wouldn't be a friend. Mental note: If I see anything remotely Evil, get the fuck out of Dodge.

Roman/Daun was giving me the once-over in slow motion. As much as I wanted to fall into my old flirtatious role and flash him my boobs, something inside me whispered that would be a bad idea – right up there with waving a red cape at a charging bull. So I did Bambi eyes instead of bedroom eyes, going for the whole I'm So Helpless look.

'We go back forever, babes. I'm surprised you didn't sense me.' Something flickered in his red-rimmed eyes. 'Or that I didn't sense you, even with Meg's description to help me out.'

'I know,' I said, aiming for charming innocence, 'you thought I'd be taller.'

'Cute.' He rubbed his chin, his gaze boring a hole through me. 'I should've honed in on you. But even now, with you right here in front of me, I'm getting nothing.'

'You sure know how to make a girl feel special.'

Eyes locking on mine, he said, 'It's more than just you doing the mortal impersonation. What's your secret, babes?'

I should've played dumb and shrugged. I could've said something witty along the lines of, 'That'd be telling.' But what did I do? I pulled my amulet from under the robe's lapel. 'One Shield Against Evil, courtesy of a friendly neighborhood witch.'

It had to be the rush of hormones. Or maybe the full moon.

I *couldn't* have been that idiotic in real life. At the rate I was flirting with danger, I would be a contender for a Darwin Award before I could say, 'Gee, is this thing loaded?'

'Ooh, Jezzie's playing with power.' Daun chuckled softly, his presence turning Roman's voice into something sexy and dangerous. 'Nicely done again. A shieldstone. You're effectively cut off. Only those who know where you are could find you.' His eyes flashed red, hinted of Lust. 'Guess you better be nice to me.'

'Guess I better,' I said, telling myself to relax. This was Daun. My bed buddy, my fuck friend. The Keymaster to my Gatekeeper. Demons didn't have siblings per se, but the incubi and succubi were as close as they came to mimicking brothers and sisters. Well, more in the incestual sense than the ancestral. Still, if there were ever a family reunion in Hell, the Seducers would all be lumped together in one huge infernal orgy. Kissing cousins, sexual siblings, what have you. If I wasn't safe around Daun, then I'd never be able to let my guard down.

'What're you doing in Roman?' I batted my eyelashes. 'Slumming?'

'Sort of. Like I said, when a Fury gives me an order, I hop on it. Meg mentioned this club, so I checked it out for myself. Once I thought I found you, Roman here was the best body for me to test drive.' He patted his chest. 'Bad boy, this one. Definitely going to be a toss up whether he gets the Rack or the Bonfire when his time comes.'

'Really? He's that proud?' I tsked, shaking my head. 'Would've pegged him for the Cauldron.'

'Nah, he's not that greedy. Prouder than a peacock, and definitely a mortal swayed by the evils of Lust.' He grinned. 'My kind of guy.'

I stood up and stretched, thinking that I should head back out, work the tables some more. 'Not unless you're after a piece of ass.'

'Actually, now that you mention it . . .'

Before I could blink, he was on top of me, kissing my neck, my collarbone, my breasts through my robe. His hands pressed down on my shoulders, forcing me down until my bottom touched the desktop. Nuzzling the fold of my robe with his nose, he pushed the material aside, exposing my breasts.

'Dau– *ooh*.' His mouth on my nipple stole my words. Arching my back, I couldn't figure out if I wanted to get away or jockey for a better position. He made the decision for me as he kissed down my belly, around the knot of my sash. Parting the satin robe, his tongue trailed down to the top of my G-string. Lifting one hand off my shoulder, he grabbed the material and yanked it off. That wasn't

146

very hard to do, considering the undies were roughly the size of an adhesive bandage.

'Whoa, cowboy,' I said, 'I'm not sure this –' I meant to finish with ' – is a good idea,' but then his tongue found my sex and all I could do was gasp. For a small eternity he teased my most sensitive spot, making my insides turn to mush and my flesh tingle from the roots of my hair to my toes.

Ah! Sweet mystery of life, at last I've found thee . . . Tangling my hands in his black hair, I moaned as my hips moved beneath his head, his sloppy licks turning into precise kisses. Delicious heat pulsed through me, hinting at building into something bigger, hotter. Then he sucked between my inner lips, taking my clit into his mouth, and I threw back my head and bit my lip to keep from shrieking in pleasure as my blood caught fire.

Oh, unholy Hell . . . this was beyond words. I've had sex for thousands of years. I've inspired men to leave their wives. I've sucked souls out from lips still wet with my saliva. But never, in all of my existence, had I ever felt every part of me sizzle from desire.

Being on the other side of the whole seduction thing? Pretty fucking awesome.

Kissing his way up my hip, my waist, the swell of my breast, his lips worked on my body.

Ooh, me like. Me like a *lot*.

His breath tickling my neck, he said, 'Why don't you take that thing off?'

My fingers worked at the knot of my sash. Crap, it was on tight. I was a dancer, not a Girl Scout; how was I supposed to untangle this?

'Not that, babes. The stone around your neck.'

As if someone flipped a switch, my sex drive turned

off and my survival sense kicked in. Spluttering and wheezing, maybe, but there all the same. Feeling goose-bumps dot my arms and breasts, I said, 'Why should I do that?'

'It itches, babes.'

The wildfire in my blood flickered and died, and my heartbeat kicked out a crazy rhythm. 'So go scratch.'

Calm down, I told myself. If he'd been out to hurt me, the shieldstone would've done quite a bit more than make him itch. After the magically charged peridot vaporized him, I'd have been wearing *eau d'incubus*.

But if the amulet was affecting him at all, then he wasn't exactly looking out for my best interests.

Men. Whether human or demonic, they really did think with the wrong damned head, didn't they?

'Take it off, I can do you right.' He pulled away from me enough to look at me. I saw his eyes glowing a soft red, felt his hands between my legs and how wet I was down there. 'Take it off,' he whispered, his finger inching inside of me, 'and I'll make your body sing.'

'I don't think so.' I wiggled backward, knocking stacks of paper to the floor. Clutching my robe closed, I vaulted over the side and landed on my feet behind the desk. I nearly twisted my ankle in the process; fucking heels weren't made for action shots.

He stared at me, demonic eyes set in a human face. The smile playing from cheek to cheek held no hint of mirth. 'Jezebel,' he purred, 'don't you trust me?'

Fuck, no. 'Sweetie, you got to learn that when a girl says no, a girl means no.'

He dropped me a sly wink. 'No worries, babes. You've had a long day. I'll come back another time. Maybe you'll be more . . . receptive then. Oh, and Jezzie?'

'What?'

'You keep your mouth shut. You don't want to come back to Hell, fine. But don't go telling the mortals about the Announcement. If you do, it'll go poorly for you.'

Clenching my jaw, I said, 'You threatening me, Daun?'

The wide smile opened into a huge grin. With a hearty chuckle, he said, 'Oh, babes. I'm here as your friend. Friends don't threaten each other.'

'Then what was that, a fucking soliloquy?'

'If that were the case, I'd still be talking about how bad it'd be for you.'

He had a point.

'I *am* your friend, Jez.' He spread his arms wide, as if he were taking in the small office. 'But I'm also an incubus. You have to admit, seducing a one-time Seducer is an amazing opportunity.'

'If you say so.'

'I made you call my name once, when you played mortal.' With a grin so evil that he must have practiced it for ages, he asked, 'Want to see if I can make you do it again, now that you're not playing anymore?'

Feeling like I was going to faint, I said, 'Not particularly.'

'Wonder what would happen if a human with no soul calls my name when under my power.' His eyes sparkled like broken rubies. 'Wonder if you'd be bound to me until you died.'

'Wonder if I could squeeze your balls to oatmeal before you had the chance to try it.'

'You're so cute when you're nervous.' He winked at me again. 'Later, babes.'

His eyes flashed, and then Roman crashed to the floor.

*

149

'Fuck me,' my boss said, 'did you get the name of that Mack truck?'

I helped him to his feet. 'You okay, Roman?'

He looked at me like I'd sprouted bat's wings. Which, of course, was impossible, thanks to my amulet. 'I don't know, love. What happened?'

'I . . .' What did I say? Mentioning that my former brethren went all Exorcist on him probably wasn't a great way to ensure job security. 'I'm not exactly sure. One minute, you were asking me about doing an act with Faith, the next—'

'Ah.' He glanced at his desk, then picked up my discarded G-string. Swinging it on his finger, a thoughtful expression crossed his face. 'Love, you must be the best lay I've ever had. No one's ever made me pass out before. Not counting the time I did the thing with the belt.'

I blinked, wondering how to play this. 'Roman—'

'Shhh.' He stopped playing with my panties and looked at me sharply, his gaze assessing my body like a banker did a pile of gold. 'You'd mentioned that you were experienced. You like showing men a good time?'

'Sweetie,' I said before I thought better of it, 'I ruin men for all other women.'

'Excellent. I have to finish up here, but let's talk more tomorrow, before we open. Come by around three. I want to hear about your previous work. Go on. And close the door behind you.' He handed me my underwear, and as I took the garment, he rubbed his finger suggestively against my palm.

Hoo-boy.

Smiling so much that my cheeks threatened to rebel, I said, 'See you, sweetie,' and scooted out of the office.

The rest of the shift passed in a blur of music, men,

and money. I got back to the Hotel New York by three-thirty and collapsed on the sinfully soft king-sized bed.

Mental note: Dancing in four-inch heels for six hours is murder on the feet.

Staring at the insides of my eyelids, I reflected over the events of the day. Human form? Check. Additional protection again nefarious entities? Check. Job? Check. Cash?

Hmm. Check – made about five hundred tonight. But I really should visit the bank in the morning, make sure I have a monetary buffer. To Do List, Item One: Go to bank.

To Do List, Item One-A: Search through Caitlin's wallet to see which bank she uses.

Let's see.

Place to live? Er. Not so much.

To Do List, Item Two: Find an apartment.

Meet sexy Cabin Boy and get his phone number?

Check, with underline and three exclamation points.

Overall, for a first day as a mortal, I could have done a lot worse. Granted, Meg was keeping tabs on me, and Daun was sort of being creepy and seductive. But as long as I stayed in line and didn't blab about stuff I wasn't supposed to blab about, I'd be fine.

Assuming that Meg was exaggerating about the King of Hell wanting to make an example of me, that is.

Oh, so this is what it felt like to fret.

Stop that, Jezebel. Don't waste time stressing over things you can't control.

So instead I thought about Paul. With a grin on my face and one hand in my panties, I fell asleep.

PART FOUR

LILLITH

14

Hotel New York

My eyes opened before I realized I was awake. For a moment, I just lay there, blinking like a drunken owl, wondering what had happened to the lovely vision of me and Paul in a tub filled with whipped cream. The real stuff, not the junk in a can.

On the nightstand by the bed, the phone rang. I screwed my eyes shut and buried my head beneath a pillow. I didn't want real life. I wanted the yummy dream. And a few more hours of sleep.

The phone rang again.

Gah. Apparently, I was not a morning person.

Somehow, my questing hand found the telephone and managed to grab the receiver. Trying to sound like I hadn't been yanked out of a solid sleep (and confectionary dream), I pulled the mouthpiece beneath the pillow and mumbled something akin to 'Hll.'

'Jesse? Did I wake you?'

Paul's voice turned the vestiges of my dream into

confetti. 'Heya, sweetie. That's okay. Just thought we'd be talking closer to lunchtime.'

He chuckled, and the low chuffing sound made my toes curl. Yum. 'Don't know how to break it to you, but it *is* closer to lunchtime.'

'Than what, teatime?'

'Actually, that's a toss up.'

I glanced at the clock radio on the other side of the bed, and then I did a double take. 'That can't be right. It's really one-thirty?'

'No.'

I let out a relieved sigh. 'For a moment, I thought I was running late.'

'It's one-thirty-three.'

I bolted upright, sending the pillow halfway across the room. 'AHHH! Where did the time go?'

'Um, the Land of Nod?'

'AHHH! Don't be witty! I'm late! I don't have time for wit!'

'Deep breath, Jesse.'

I inhaled.

'Now, what do you want for lunch?'

'No idea. Coffee. Ooh, another of those muffins from the fake French bakery.'

'That's breakfast, not lunch. Tell you what: I'll swing by with some lunchables. You start doing the morning routine that women have perfected over the centuries, and I'll be by in a half hour. Sound good?'

'I can't hear you, I'm already halfway to the shower.'

'See you soon.'

'Bye.'

I untangled myself from the bedding and dashed into the bathroom. Skidding to a halt in front of the shower, I

156

fiddled with the nozzles and got a blast of icy cold water in my face. With a screech that rightfully should have put the Banshees out of business, I adjusted the temperature and stepped away, already stripping off my silk nightshirt and undies. A quick toilet visit and brush of teeth later, I was in the shower, lathering, rinsing, and shaving.

Crap. Crap! *Fuck!!!*

And bleeding from multiple tiny nicks.

Mental note: Don't do my legs and bikini area when I'm in a hurry.

Finally I shampooed, conditioned, and rinsed. Yay, all of last night's sweat and booze and smoke and sex odors were finally off of me. Just in time for me to see Paul and get my panties soaked, but hey, that's why some enterprising mortal had invented panty liners.

Mental note, part two: Buy some panty liners.

Out of the shower, I wrestled the dripping, tangled mass that served as my hair into a thick white towel, twisting and tucking the material so that I had my own terry cloth turban. Just as I started patting myself dry with the oversized body towel, someone knocked at my door.

I wrapped the towel around my torso, style by way of MuMu. It wasn't for my modesty (I had none); my skin was still damp. And while it was one thing for Paul to get me moist, meeting him halfway took all the fun out of it. So, blotting dry in a fuzzy peach towel, I opened the room's door.

Paul stood in the hallway, his leather jacket unzipped, holding a large, flat cardboard box in one arm and a paper bag in the other. I didn't know which made me salivate more – the hidden contents of the box, or Paul dressed in a green button-up shirt, black slacks, and black boots. The shirt turned his eyes into liquid emerald; the dark

157

pants and boots made the stubble on his cheeks and chin seem almost dangerous. His just-a-shade-too-long sandy hair kissing his ears and neck was the icing on the cake.

Or, based on my interrupted dream, the whipped cream in my bathtub. *Slurp!!!*

He grinned at me, his eyes checking out my legs briefly before locking politely onto my face. 'Someone here order a pizza?'

Stop staring at him like he was the hottest thing since Adonis.

Uh-uh, I told myself, wondering if all mortal women had silent conversations with their psyches. He'd give Adonis an inferiority complex that would eclipse Mount Olympus.

Oh, please. Get past the hot factor. You're a former demon. Hot for you would make suns feel chilly.

But those eyes . . . !

At least pick your jaw up off the floor and say something clever.

I opened my mouth and said, 'Hi.'

That's it, the little voice in my head snorted in disgust. *I give up. You're hopeless.*

Paul's grin stretched wider. 'So, can I come in, or do you want to eat in the hallway?'

Stepping aside, I held the door for him to enter, the yumalicious odor trailing after. My stomach growled loud enough for Paul to laugh.

Stupid body. Unless you start projecting 'Have sex with me now' signals, shut up and leave the conversation to me.

Right, my little voice whispered. *Because you're so quick with the snappy one-liners.*

Putting the box down on the huge desk, Paul said, 'I'll

set up lunch while you get dressed. I think I forgot to get napkins.'

'I've got towels. If you don't mind damp, that is.'

'Used towels,' he said with a grin. 'You sure know how to sweep a guy off of his feet.'

Nah. If that were the case, I'd throw the towels to the floor and drip dry. 'For you, only the best.' I debated shucking off the peach wrappings right there, but I decided against it. My most prominent appetite of the moment was hunger . . . for food.

Bless me, being a mortal really was fucking up my priorities.

'I don't get how milk can be so nasty, but pizza could taste so good,' I said, working on my second slice. We were sprawled on the carpet, our banquet of pizza and soda set out in front of the bed. Between the steam from the shower, the heat from the food, and the way my body temperature hit the stratosphere whenever Paul smiled, all of the bones in my body had melted into gush.

'You wouldn't say milk was nasty once you've had it with Oreos.'

'What're Oreos?'

'Bad enough you've never had pizza before,' Paul said around a mouthful of melted cheese. 'But you mean to tell me you've never even heard of Oreos?'

'I was sort of deprived growing up.' Well, more like depraved. But what's one vowel?

'Let me guess. Minister's daughter, raised in the heartland of America. A romance went sour, and now you've run away to the big, bad city to experience a life of sin.'

His words startled me so much that I started choking on mozzarella. Tears welling in my eyes, I swallowed the bite of pizza and reached for the bottle of Coke. Bless me, he'd even pegged the Heartlands. Was he some sort of psychic, able to pick up on the truth of my identity through my aura? Or was it really just a coincidence?

Gulping the sweet beverage, I decided I didn't care. Let Meg be the one to babble about Fate; I refused to waste my mortal life by searching for hidden meaning.

Either in agreement or indifference, my body let out a massive hiccough.

BLECH!!!

Mental note: Cola-flavored backwash is gross.

'Was the face for my guess about your background?'

With my left hand, I clasped the peridot hanging between my breasts. Nope; still cool. So the evil grin on Paul's face was from a wicked sense of humor, and nothing more. It was nice to know that the man I wanted to have sweaty animal sex with wasn't out to eat me alive (and not the fun, cunnilingus way).

'Don't give up the day job, mister. You're close, but still way off base.'

'Yeah?' He grinned, and I noticed that it was deliciously lopsided, as if he had this fabulous secret that he could barely keep contained. Oh, how I wanted to kiss those lips until his mouth opened and his secrets came spilling out, thrilling me and filling me . . .

For Hell's sake, get a grip. He's just a mortal man.

Yeah, but he could be my Cabin Boy . . .

The infernal voice in my mind made retching sounds.

'So tell me,' Paul said, 'what part did I get wrong?'

'Well, the whole minister thing was way off.' In more ways than he'd ever know. 'And the romance was just a kiss. But you got the Heartlands right. And the life of sin, that I'm working on.'

160

'So you left home because you kissed the wrong guy?'

For a heartbeat that stretched into an impossibly long time, I said nothing as I remembered the feeling of King Lucifer's lips on mine, how my mouth had tingled even after He'd pulled away from me. And then He'd made the Announcement . . .

No. Stop that now.

I felt the weight of Paul's gaze on me, but I couldn't look at him as I spoke. My voice soft, I said, 'I left home because I learned something that upset me. I guess you could say I didn't handle it well.'

I paused, wanting to tell him more, feeling this burning need to spew the truth and bask in a momentary catharsis before my life would be forfeit. Then I pushed that need down deep inside and locked it away. It squirmed, but down it stayed.

'At first I tried. The rest of my –' I took a deep breath, wondering how to explain my brethren '– my family took it in stride. Some of my sisters embraced it, like it was this excuse to forget everything they'd ever known. But I couldn't do that. I couldn't just pretend that the past never happened, that everything I'd ever done was meaningless, useless.'

'Who told you that?'

Paul's voice was whisper-quiet, and that's when I realized I was crying. Ah, shit. I scrubbed at my tears, hating the salty drops that trickled down my cheeks.

'It doesn't matter,' I said. My breath hitched, and a full-blown sob escaped my lips. I swallowed it down, choked back my rage and my sorrow. I couldn't be this upset. I was a creature of the Pit, I was Evil, I was stronger than this!

No, that blessed voice said in my mind. *You're only human.*

I closed my eyes and fought the bitter sadness that threatened to crush my heart. Strong arms circled me, and I leaned against a broad shoulder and cried – loud, terrible wails that shook my body and stole my breath. The suffocating feeling in my chest loosened with every gut-wrenching sob, and my overwhelming grief eventually diminished, settling into a bone-deep ache. My gasping breaths soon turned to quiet sniffles. Paul hugged me tighter, one hand stroking my back as he murmured into my hair, 'It's okay, it's okay.'

Settled in his embrace, tears still streaming from my eyes, I realized just how weak I'd become. Not just soft – fragile. Delicate. Like the strands of molten lava that floated in the updraft from the Lake of Fire, I'd transformed into a brittle shell, nothing more than trapped heat, frozen flame.

If this heartache was part of the package, then I hated being human.

'Don't hate it,' Paul said, his breath warm on my hair.

Oh, bless me, I'd actually spoken aloud.

Still stroking my back, Paul said, 'It's better to be a real, feeling person than some cold, unfeeling thing. Even when that means feeling sad, or disappointed.'

Stiffening, I pulled away from him. 'There's nothing better about . . . about this!' I motioned to my tear-stained face. 'This is just *weakness*, just useless emotion that does nothing but show how soft I've become.'

'You're not soft.'

'I am! He said so! I didn't believe Him, but He was right!' Remembering that horrible judgment, the way His voice had sunk into my form and echoed in my mind, I balled my hands into fists. Snarling, I said, 'I used to be so strong, and now I'm as fragile as a porcelain doll!'

Paul's hand touched my fist, and my fingers relaxed in his grip. 'Jesse, you're not a doll. And you're stronger than you give yourself credit for.'

Staring at him with my swollen eyes, I said, 'How do you figure that?'

He smiled, and the tenderness I saw in his eyes nearly started my tears anew. 'Look at you. You've come a long way to start over.'

'I ran away, Paul. How's that being strong?'

'If you ran away from people telling you that everything about you was soft and useless, then running away was the best thing you could've done.'

'No,' I said, 'you don't understand—'

'Don't make excuses for it.' His face hardened, turning his sea-green eyes into raging storms. 'You're not useless, Jesse. Don't let anyone ever tell you otherwise.'

I tilted my head back and took a deep, shuddering breath. 'It's not that simple.'

His hands pressed down on my shoulders until I looked into his face. 'Yes it is.'

'I'm supposed to be a creature of Lust,' I whispered. 'Not some frail, emotional girl.'

'Jesse,' he said, his voice thick, 'you are the most damned gorgeous, desirable woman I've seen in a long, long time.'

'You're saying that because you saw me naked at the club.'

'I'm saying that because it's true. It's not just your body. Don't get me wrong, your body is nice. Really nice.'

Great. Now I ranked up there with bunnies and rainbows.

Paul said, 'But it's more than that. It's the way your eyes sparkle like diamonds, like you're always laughing

163

inside. It's the way you moved on stage, so damned confident in yourself. It's your smile. It's *you*, Jesse.'

My heart thumped so loud in my chest, I barely heard my own words. 'You don't even know me.'

'I'd like to.'

That's when I pulled his face to mine and kissed him with all of the soul I wished I had.

Paul started to melt into the kiss – I felt his body respond to me, heard his surprised grunt turn into a melodious *Uhm*. But just as I parted my lips to strengthen the soft kiss into a deep, passionate tonsil-hockey suck, he gently pulled me away.

'Jesse, don't.'

My brows knitted as I searched his face for meaning. Finding none, I asked, 'Why?'

'This isn't how it should be. You're upset right now.'

'Damn straight I'm upset,' I said, my voice rising. 'And I'm getting more upset. Why don't you want me to kiss you?'

'I do.' He put his hands out in a supplicating gesture. 'But not like this. After you've had a chance to calm down, then you bet. But I won't take advantage of you.'

'Do it, please, I'm begging you. Take advantage.' I yanked my shirt over my head and threw it to the floor.

'Jesse—'

'Show me that I'm not useless.' My hands fumbled behind my back at my bra clasp. The blessed thing wouldn't unfasten. Fucking underwire monstrosity.

'Jesse.' Paul reached around me to put his hands over mine. 'Please stop.'

Pressed close, I smelled his aftershave and his sweat and a deeper, more primal scent that was purely male. I inhaled, drowning my senses with his intoxicating scent,

164

and then I planted a kiss on his mouth. He released my hands, and I pushed him to the floor and straddled his body, my pelvis over his.

His eyes locked onto mine, and I saw his desire at war with his conscience. Deciding to help his desire along, I moved my body, rubbing my sex against his, feeling his penis take note of my intention. Even though we both wore jeans, there was no mistaking the effect of my affection; beneath me, his shaft hardened.

'Touch me,' I said, my voice husky.

'Jesse . . .'

'Touch me!' I grabbed his hands and put them onto my breasts. Arching my back, I leaned into the touch, letting him caress my swells, feel how hard my nipples were beneath his fingers. Yes, this was what I wanted, what I needed. What did it matter that I'd given up everything I'd ever been, that I was on the run from all I'd ever known? All Paul had to do was love me, fuck me, and everything would be all right. Fuck me, I thought, fuck me long and fuck me hard.

Prove that I'm not useless.

He pulled out of my grip and seized my shoulders. Rolling, he knocked me off of him and onto my back. Leaning over me, he started at my face, looking like he wanted to either kiss me or slap me.

'I'm begging you,' I said, my voice that of a little girl. 'Please touch me.'

'Oh, Jesse.' His words were as gentle as rose petals. 'I'm sorry.'

The pity in his voice nearly killed me. 'Get out.'

'Jesse . . .'

'Get out! Leave me alone!'

Fuck, I was crying again. Being human really, really sucked.

165

With a sigh, he let me go. I stayed on my back, on the floor, but I turned my face away from him.

'Jesse, I didn't mean to hurt you.'

Hurt, nothing. He made the demons of Pride look like amateurs.

'I'm sorry.'

'Go away, Paul,' I said, closing my eyes. 'Just go away.' I felt like someone had plucked my heart out of my chest, chewed it up, spat it out, and planted it back inside me. I hated this feeling, this utter sense of helplessness and despair. How did mortals deal with this?

'I'll see you later.'

'Don't do me any favors.'

I heard him gather his jacket and walk out, but I didn't open my eyes until the door slammed shut.

And the thing that really stank to high Heaven was that when I opened my eyes, I hoped he'd still be there, waiting. But of course, there was only me, my misery, and a half-eaten pizza pie. Staring at the cooling food and thinking of the pity in Paul's eyes, my stomach lurched. I barely made it to the toilet before I vomited.

It only went to prove that anything with milk in it led to disaster.

15

New York City/Belles

By the time I cleaned up after my stomach cleaned itself out, I had twenty-five minutes to get to Belles. I grabbed my outfits for the night and my broken-in four-inch heels, and I stuffed it all into a Victoria's Secret shopping bag. And if I used a little more force than necessary to jam silk and leather into the bag, sue me.

Fucking Paul I-Know-Everything Hamilton. Him and his sorries. Who did he think he was? How dare he hold me and soothe me and have me bare a soul I didn't own, and then shove it right back in my face?

I should kill him. I should chase him down, rip off my Shield Against Evil and fuck him to death.

No, I should make him want to fuck me and then refuse to sleep with him, and make him so depressed that he would throw himself in front of a bus during rush hour. And the bus should back up over him five times.

No, I should go down on him and bite his cock off at the root, then shove it down his throat and lap up his blood

167

before I took his soul and spat it into the Lake of Fire the way he spat away my advances.

Why didn't he want me?

I bit back a sob, crumpling a satin teddy in a shaking fist. No fucking way was I crying again. I didn't have that much hydration in my entire body. And I'd be blessed if I had to wash off my makeup and put it all back on again.

No wonder mortals invented waterproof mascara.

He'd like to know me, he said. Well, there's one way to know a succubus, and that's intimately.

I paused in my unholy anger. I wasn't a succubus any longer. My fingers danced on the peridot stone, feeling its cold, slick surface. All it would take was one pull, and the chain would give. And then I could use my power, and Paul would rue the day his father sired him.

My little voice whispered, *Settle down, Jezebel. You're spouting words like* rue.

Screw that. I'm four thousand years old. I'm allowed to throw in the occasional archaic word into my narrative.

But that voice was right. I had to calm down. I wasn't going to jeopardize my human life because of Paul Fucking Hamilton. And I wasn't going to be late meeting Roman because I was so busy plotting Paul's demise that I lost track of time.

Jamming my feet into loafers, I grabbed my purse and the shopping bag, remembering at the last second to make sure I had my wallet and key card. Then I was out the door and on my way – still fuming, still wishing all sorts of painful deaths on Paul, but at least I was also mobile.

As I marched down the city streets, the wind gusted around me, kicking up litter and pollen as well as tangling my dark curls. I didn't care; the haggard look fit my mood. I'd doll myself up once I got to Belles.

168

A fragile, porcelain doll.

My blood simmered in my veins and slowly cooked my heart. Oh, how I hated Paul Hamilton.

'Spare some change?'

I glanced over at the pile of rags that was a human slumming in the dark, narrow alley between buildings. Stronger than the lingering odor of garbage, his – her? – unwashed body radiated disease. Open sores covered his face, with a particularly impressive pus bubble by the corner of his mouth. His hand shook as he held it out.

Look at that, Jezebel. Some folks have it worse than you.

And in my mind, His voice whispered, *And what kind of God allows His children to suffer so?*

I squeezed my hand into a tight fist. Stop. Do not go there. Period.

'Miss? Got some change?'

The creature was nothing more than bones loosely held together by festering skin. My chest felt odd, almost as if my heart had melted into a warm puddle. Sighing, I decided that if I was going to wallow in my own humanity, I might as well do the Grinch thing and let my heart grow three sizes. 'Sure, sweetie. Hang on.'

'Sweetie? That nice. No one call me nice names.'

What, did I have NICE HUMAN tattooed on my forehead? 'I'm not nice,' I said, digging through my purse. 'You call me nice, I won't give you anything.'

'You want I should call you a bitch?'

'If you don't mind.'

'Give me a five, I call you anything you want.'

I cleared my throat to cover my giggle. Maybe he was a walking cesspool of infection and destined to die a lonely, painful death. Maybe his body odor was rank enough to

169

overpower garbage dumps. But he belonged to Lust. I dropped a twenty into his filthy palm.

The beggar grinned, displaying blackened teeth and gums the color of a boiled eggplant. 'Rich girl. You got a nice necklace.' His licked his chapped lips, leaving a thin line of spittle dangling from the corner of his mouth. 'Maybe you so rich, you don't need one more necklace.'

For a dizzying moment, I was tempted to give him my amulet. It would be so easy. Just yank it off, drop it in his hand and be on my way. Shed this mortal flesh and wreak vengeance on the man who'd wronged me. Maybe tear up the town a bit. Show the customers at Belles what they wished they could have, with no G-strings to mask what they so dearly wanted to touch, to suck, to fuck. And for the right price, give it all to them. Give it to them until they screamed . . . .

Then my survival instinct overrode my death wish. 'I don't think so.'

'Thanks for the money, rich girl.' The wretched creature leered in a way that would've given the Marquis de Sade nightmares. 'Maybe I give you a kiss, show you my 'preciation.'

I grinned, and even though it was tight on my face, it felt good. 'Sweetie, you want to show me your appreciation, go get yourself something to eat. But stay away from milk.'

'Yeah, stuff spoils too quick.'

Wasn't that the ever-loving truth.

My jaunt into the Land of the Good Samaritan reminded me that I needed money. Sure, working the tables at Belles would keep me flush with beer-soaked tens, but that wouldn't be enough for me to land an apartment. So I had to make a pit stop into Caitlin's bank and make a teensy withdrawal.

As a demon, I'd picked up a lot about humans and their fabulous inventions. Being draped over some slob's arm had its advantages; I studied ATM interactions, I watched personal checks get filled out, I absorbed credit card transactions. So I knew that without Caitlin's PIN, the bank card in her wallet was useless. But I didn't quite know how to dip into her account without that PIN. So I needed to play the Helpless Female role and score some cash.

Not too much, of course; I was a former Seducer, not a one-time Coveter. I needed just enough to set me up without wiping Caitlin out. She didn't deserve that. What's more, the Hecate would probably overlook a dash of theft, but not full-scale larceny.

As I entered the bank, a wave of emotion crashed over me. It took me a moment to identify the feeling as guilt. Bless me, I felt *bad* about taking the witch's money. Yesterday I ran one of her credit cards into the space station, but today I was uncomfortable about borrowing – okay, stealing – her hard-earned cash.

What the fuck was wrong with me?

You're becoming human, that tiny voice whispered. *Not just in form – in feeling.*

Crap. I didn't want to develop a case of morals. That could be very hazardous to my health. Not to mention to my sense of humor.

I approached an available teller, a sheepish grin on my face. 'Excuse me, but I must be having a bad day. For the life of me, I can't remember my PIN.'

The well-dressed representative sniffed. Based on the tight smile he wore, either he had hemorrhoids or his underwear was too tight. 'If you fill out a withdrawal slip, you can access your account. Checking or savings?'

'Um, checking.' He said it first, so it must be more common.

'Here's a blank slip. All you need to do is fill in your account information.'

Staring at the instructions on the small piece of paper, I felt like I was thrown into the Tower of Babel. 'Er, I'm not sure what my account number is.'

The teller wrinkled his nose. 'May I have your driver's license, please?'

I opened Caitlin's wallet and rooted out the plastic State ID. 'Sorry, I don't drive.'

'I see,' the man said, the tone of voice clearly indicating he equated nondrivers with nose boogers. He pierced me with his gaze, scrutinizing my features and comparing them to those of the woman smiling on the identification card. 'One moment, please.'

Based on the clacking sounds, he must have typed something on a keyboard. 'Miss Harris, could you please tell me your address?'

I rattled off Caitlin's home address, which I'd memorized from her State ID.

'Thank you. All I need now is your mother's maiden name, please.'

Blinking, I said, 'Excuse me?'

'Your mother's maiden name, please.'

My mind drew a complete blank. 'Um, Harris.'

The teller sniffed. 'Thank you. Your mother never changed her name when she married, I see.'

I didn't know if I was more relieved over my sheer luck or annoyed at the little prick of a man for being so condescending. 'Actually, my mother was brutally raped by a traveling gang of Satanic bikers. She died giving birth to

172

me. The hospital, in its infinite wisdom, assigned me my mother's name.'

The teller paled. 'I,' he said. 'I. I. I had no idea.'

'And now you do. So, if you have all the information you need, could you please take out two thousand dollars for me?'

'Certainly,' he said, his voice a nervous wheeze. 'One moment while I access your account.'

Maybe I should become an actress.

After a few more clackety-clacks, the teller frowned. 'Miss Harris, it seems that you closed your account.'

I froze for a heartbeat, then said, 'Excuse me?'

'It seems that sometime this morning, you closed both your checking and your savings accounts.' He darted a glance at me. 'You have no recollection of this?'

'I've had a very bad morning,' I whispered, feeling all of the blood drain out of my face and pool in my toes.

Caitlin must have woken up and discovered that her purse was missing. Bless me, I thought I had at least another full day before she realized that she didn't have her wallet.

Crap.

No money . . . and if Caitlin closed her bank account, she probably also cancelled her credit cards.

Double crap.

I took back my State ID and fled the bank, hoping that Roman wouldn't fire me for being late. Yesterday, the job had been a lark. Today it transformed into a necessity.

Triple crap on toast. This day couldn't possibly get any worse.

Dashing into the club, I heard Hank Williams Junior singing that all his rowdy friends were coming over tonight.

Some singers had all the luck. I wondered if Lyle was really a Good Ol' Boy, or if he'd always wanted to grow up to be a cowboy.

Peeking into the showroom, I waved gamely to the dark DJ booth. 'Heya! Anyone home?'

Over Hank telling me he had a little whirlpool just made for ten, Lyle's voice boomed, 'Hi, Jezebel! You're early!'

'Looking for Roman,' I called out.

'Office. You think I'd be allowed to play this stuff if he was sitting in this room?'

Invisible Man had a point.

A minute later, I was seated in Roman's office, staring at Dickhead himself. No telltale smell of brimstone, no redness to his eyes; I was willing to bet that the man was demon-free. Excellent. Last thing I needed was for Daun to make an appearance. After what happened with Paul and then with the bank, I doubted I had the strength to fend off a serious attempt at seduction, even with the Shield Against Evil. My head throbbed just thinking about it.

Now I knew where 'Not now, hon; I have a headache' came from.

Still doing the Johnny Cash thing, my boss was swathed from head to foot in black, looking like he was a walking advertisement for trendy mourners. He finished typing on his keyboard, shut his laptop, and looked at me as if I were his favorite dessert.

'Thanks for coming in early, love.' He tapped his lips with a finger, staring at my face, then dropping his gaze lower down. 'I see you're happy to see me.'

'Sweetie, the temperature's set for North Pole standards. My nipples would be poking out even if you were the Queen of England.'

'See, that's what I like about you, love. You've got attitude. And when you're on stage, you demand to be watched.' He dropped his hand to his desk, where he began to tap, tap, tap. 'You're not the prettiest girl here.'

My eyes narrowed.

'And you're definitely the oldest girl here.'

Only by a couple thousand years or so. But it was fucking insensitive of him to say so. 'Boy, Roman, you're a real sweet talker.'

'What I'm saying is that you've got all that against you. But still, you were on fire last night. What'd you walk away with, about four hundred?'

Five hundred twenty-seven. 'About.'

'That's fucking amazing. Most girls, until they find their rhythm, they're lucky to earn carfare home for the first two weeks. But you, you know how to move, how to smile, how to talk to the customers.'

I shrugged. 'I speak body language. It's sort of universal.'

'You know it's more than flashing your tits and shaking your ass. It's knowing how to make the guy feel like he's the only one in the room, that you've singled him out because there's something about him that's appealing. Touchy-feely bullshit like that.'

'I like touchy-feely bullshit.'

'I bet you do, love.' He leaned forward. 'You mentioned yesterday that you were experienced. You been a dancer before?'

'Not exactly.'

'Then what?'

Hmm, how to explain that I used to target my prospective clients, seduce the pants off of them, and lead their souls to Hell? 'Let's just say that I made house calls.'

175

'Really.' His eyebrow arched. 'We are talking about the same thing, right? The adult entertainment industry?'

Entertaining for me, an industry for the Pit. 'Right.'

'You worked where, in a massage parlor?'

'More like an independent contractor.'

'And you had no, you know, business manager?'

King Asmodai and Queen Lillith. 'We sort of had a parting of the ways.'

His eyes flashed dollar signs. 'Maybe we can help each other out. You want to make more money?'

After the fiasco at the bank, want had nothing to do with it. After tonight, I had to leave the hotel. And unless I planned on slumming on Roman's Naugahyde sofa, then I needed a place to live. That meant I needed a lot of cash, quick. 'Yes.'

'See, I knew you were a businesswoman. You use that special gift of yours, love. You keep dancing and making the men feel like they own the fucking world. You get more of them into the VIP room, you do what they want you to do. *Whatever* they want you to do. But it will cost them more than just what they pony up for the privacy and your company. You understand what I'm saying?'

This was definitely getting interesting. Unless I was grossly mistaken, Roman was giving me the go-ahead to screw the customers' brains out. 'You want me to solicit them?'

'No! Oh, love, never that. That's illegal. But if they want maybe to have you show them some affection, just make sure they tip you appropriately. Say, fifty for a touch of such affection, a hundred for a special kiss. And, hypothetically speaking, if a customer wanted to get the full Jezebel experience, that's at least two hundred for thirty minutes. On top of the VIP room rate.'

176

'Uh-huh.'

He wagged a finger at me. 'And make sure they tip you first. No trading favors for cash. That's prostitution. And we don't believe in that here at Belles.'

'Then what do we believe?'

'In having customers get their money's worth. And me, too, of course. Whenever you have these special arrangements, my house fee goes up. Forty percent on all such transactions.'

'That's a lot for just providing some privacy, no?'

'Privacy, clientele, security.' He spread his hands. 'You've been around, love. You know how the world works. You want to play nice, that's fine. But if you want to score big, you have to put out.'

Let's see. The former succubus was being asked if she'd like to make money by sleeping with her customers. Hmm. Let's think.

Before I could say, 'Hell yes,' the small voice – which I was starting to suspect was either my conscience or the first sign of schizophrenia – whispered in my mind. *Yesterday, the dancers had been pretty clear that Roman didn't tolerate, let alone encourage, prostitution at the club. So what was the change of heart?*

Maybe he recognized someone who was an expert in the art of seduction. Maybe, as a mortal creature of Lust, he had his own sex sense when it came to other Seducers.

And maybe not, the voice whispered. *Daun told you you're taking too many risks, and he was right. You've got Hell sniffing after you, even with your human shell and your shieldstone. How long do you think it'll take for word to get out that a dancer named Jezebel is fucking her customers? How long before your brethren start popping in, just to see who this mortal Jezebel is?*

177

This fucking conscious thing sure knew how to rain on a parade. 'I'll think about it.'

'You do that, love. Go on, scoot. I'll see you during your shift.' He tapped his lip again. 'Understand that if I'm ever asked, this conversation never happened.'

'Of course.'

'Last thing. If you're looking for some, ah, business advice, you talk to Momma.'

That caught me off guard. 'She knows?'

'Love, it was her idea.'

As I rose from the vinyl chair, I realized that the old saying was correct: You really can't judge a book by its cover. Maybe Roman was a what-you-see kind of guy, minus the occasional demonic possession. But Momma, the middle-aged, sweater-wearing madam actually being a madame blew my mind.

And that was free of charge.

16

Belles

'Jez? You okay?'

'Huh?' Blinking, I realized I'd been staring at nothing as I started applying my lipstick, my hand frozen midstroke. 'Oh. Sorry. Lost in thought.'

Candy grinned, her white teeth brilliant in the frame of her dark lips. 'Fuck lost, girl. You so far gone, you're in another dimension.'

'Yeah, I guess.' Sighing, I dropped the tube of lipstick on the cluttered vanity, then tried to do something to make my hair less Medusalike. Momma's baskets of hair accessories had already been pilfered so completely, a Coveter couldn't have done it better; to tame my mane, I was on my own. 'Today's been a shitty day. Thought I had money, now I don't. Thought I had another job opportunity, now I'm not sure it's a good idea. But the thing I keep coming back to is this fight I got into with this guy.'

'He pop you?'

'What?' At first, I thought she meant in the cherry sense, but then I realized she was talking about physical violence.

'Oh, no. Well, he rolled me onto the floor. But that was to get me off of him.'

Her chocolate-brown eyes measured me. 'You pop him?'

'No. Tried to jump his bones.'

'And?'

'White guys can't jump.'

Letting out a belly laugh, Candy shook her head. 'Girl, you're a dancer. Who gives a shit if one guy doesn't want you? You got a roomful of men who give you money because you tickle their fancy.'

'Yeah, but I wanted to tickle *his* fancy.' I stuffed my boobs into my bra, a red satin demicup that made my breasts defy gravity. After I tucked and arranged, I turned away from the mirror and faced Candy. 'Am I ugly?'

'Shit.' Candy rolled her eyes. 'Jezebel, you listen to me, all right? You aren't ugly. If you were, Dickhead wouldn't have hired you to flash your tits on stage. Hear me?'

'Then why—'

'Jesus, girl, who cares why? He didn't want to. He had his reasons. Best thing you can do, go out there, dance your ass off, get a lot of tips. Break a lot of hearts.'

'You think so?'

Chuffing laughter, she winked at me. 'Jez, trust me. I know it 'cause I've been there. Move on. Lots of fishes in the sea.'

I glanced at my reflection in the mirror. Heavy shadow and blue eyeliner hid the redness in my eyes; mascara pumped my lashes out almost as far as my nose. My hair was a lost cause, but whipping it around on stage would give it that windblown, stylish look. And my lips, while perhaps not as bee-stung as Angelina Jolie's, still had that blowjob glossy look to them.

Okay, so all was not lost.

Momma stuck her head in the dressing room. 'Jezebel. Come on, hon. Your show's about to start.'

Frowning (carefully, so as not to smudge the lipstick), I said, 'Jemma's on now. She just started not even two minutes ago. Isn't she doing a full three-song set?'

'She's fading fast. Says she's got a cold or a flu bug, and it shows. She's barely moving her legs. Come on – Lyle said he's got the perfect opening tune for you.'

'Get out there, Jez,' Candy said with a wink. 'Give some guys a couple wet dreams.'

Blowing a kiss to Candy, I jiggled after the house mom.

Offstage, I peeked at Jemma's performance. Momma had been kind in her assessment – Jemma looked like the walking dead. And that's coming from someone who's seen her fair share of zombies. Jemma's blond hair was the most lively thing about her – her face was ashen, making her bright red lipstick all the more dramatic; her body swayed, sort of in time to Berlin's 'Sex,' looking like a slight breeze would topple her onto her ass. How she balanced in those five-inch heels, I had no idea. She wasn't trying to score any tips, even with a few hopefuls waiting by the tip-rail. Definitely ill, or maybe on drugs.

Momma looked over her shoulder at me. 'I'll tell Lyle you're ready to go. If Jemma doesn't get the hint, I'll have Joey escort her offstage.'

'Thanks, Momma.'

She took off at a clip, and I marveled how a plump woman could move so lightly. Before I ducked back, I swept my gaze over the showroom. Not bad for a Thursday evening, I decided; not filled to capacity, but well over half-full. Maybe sixty men, all wanting some entertainment. A few groups of businessmen clustered around various tables, their ties loosened and their money flowing, judging from the number of beer steins on the tables. A group of stray cats hovered by the tip-rail, gazing at the swaying blonde, lust in their eyes and singles in their fingers. Yes, tonight would be a money night . . .

Hold the phone. At table three, toward the back, that wasn't . . . Paul?

No. No, no, no. He wasn't allowed to be here.

Lyle's disembodied voice sliced through the showroom. 'Give it up for Jemma! Thank you, Jemma, we love you. Right. And everyone tip your hats to Joey, one of our doormen, who's a perfect gentleman.' This last as Joey, who'd bobbed on stage, tucked Jemma's arm over his and quickly escorted her back-stage.

I was so wrapped up in my own dark thoughts over Paul that I dismissed the tingle from the shieldstone as Jemma and Joey brushed by me. It was nothing – just my body already humming with the electricity that came with being on stage, being the center of attention.

The center of Paul Fucking Hamilton's attention.

'And now,' Lyle's voice boomed, 'please welcome back to the stage, the one, the only, Jezebel!'

Electric guitar screamed out from the speakers, with drums pounding out a beat. The audience whistled in approval as the singer let out a 'Woooooo!' I let the sound ride my body for a few drumbeats, and after the band called out 'So good!' I shimmied on stage. Gene Loves Jezebel's 'Desire' boomed out loud and hard, pulsing, passionate. Perfect song for me, indeed.

The spotlights dazzled my eyes, turning all the faces in the audience into specters, shadows. So Paul was there, eh? Well then, I'd put on a show that would make him regret not taking advantage of me in my moment of weakness. He wanted to be noble around a former being of the Abyss? Fine. Time for him to stew in his choice.

For the next ten minutes, I moved my body in ways that made women burn with envy and men wet their shorts. Hips grinding, tits bouncing, ass wiggling ... I did it all, and I did it all damn well. I gripped the stripper pole and tilted back far enough to let my hair brush the stage as I swung round and round, a sexual whirling dervish. My floor work turned the act of miming sex into an art form. I high kicked and low dipped, I ran my hands over my body as if my fingers were discovering new planes and curves.

'Desire' melted into 'Mysterious Ways,' and I slowed my movements until my body was one with the new tempo. Rolling my hips, I ran my fingers through my curly hair, feeling Bono's voice tease my skin. I stripped off my red teddy and dropped it to the floor. As I danced in my bra and G-string, the humans called for me, whistling and waving their money by the tip-rail, begging to caress my flesh, even if it was only to stuff their dreams into my garter belt.

'Bad Touch' thundered from the speakers, and I unclasped my bra and swung it over my head, basking in the gaze of the audience. Even though I couldn't see their features, I sensed their open mouths, their hungry looks. I smiled at every man there, at every male who wanted nothing more than to have me fuck him until he exploded inside of me, and I grinned with shining lips as I imagined the taste of their souls.

The spotlights flickered, and for a moment I saw every face in the audience as clearly as stars dotting a midnight sky. At table three, I locked gazes with Paul. If that wasn't raging desire I saw flashing in his eyes, I was a cherub.

My show ended, and I gave the men a parting butt-shot as I bent from the waist to retrieve my discarded clothing. I sauntered offstage, riding the wave of monstrous applause. Howls and hoots rang in my ears, made my nipples vibrate. Ah, my adoring fans.

Fuck you, Mister Paul Hamilton. And the horse you rode in on.

One by one, I worked the tables. Around me, the other dancers strutted their stuff, performed their shows, and sucked money away from the customers. Some, like Candy, were model strippers, so to speak. She talked to her customers, laughed with them, and more often than not led them upstairs either to the lounge or the VIP room. Others, like Aurora, never let the men forget they were ATMs with dicks – her big line, delivered in a thick Jersey accent was, 'Gimme some love, baby. Put a ten right here.' And then there was Lorelei. Her idea of a sales pitch was, 'Wanna dance?' It blew me away that she got as many offers as she did. One line I heard her purr was something like, 'You got my number, and I answer my pages.' No idea what that meant, but obviously the guys did. It always seemed to lead to the VIP room.

I strutted by table eight, smiling at this kid barely old enough to shave let alone know what to do with his rod. His hand shook when he asked me if I'd perform a lap dance at the table; between his fingers, a crisp twenty trembled like a virgin. I took his hand and gently pushed it between my breasts. After a moment, I said to the Lovestruck Young Thing, 'The idea, sweetie, is to let go.'

'Oh . . . sorry.'

The bill whispered its song of money on my flesh. Smiling deeply, I began to dance for the LYT. I took his hands and moved them up my legs, over the material of the slinky short dress, coming to rest on my torso. His fingers twitched beneath the swells of my breasts as I rocked against him, his penis pushing against his jeans and pressing into my belly. Beneath his mop of black hair, his eyes sparked like polished glass. Even though I couldn't smell his fear, it was obvious the poor boy was utterly terrified. Two days ago, I would have gotten off on that. But now it made me feel a bit sorry for him.

Holy fuck in Heaven. I was a sad, sad little ex-demon.

'Just breathe, sweetie,' I said, blowing in his ear. 'I won't bite.'

'Really?'

I winked. 'Not unless you pay me.'

When the song ended, I stroked his hair. 'Thanks for enjoying the dance.' Against my stomach, his erection cheered.

He let out a squeak. 'I think I love you.'

'No, sweetie. You don't. But I'm guessing the next girl who's lucky enough to grab you will have herself a fine, fine time.' Ugh, I was so fucking nice, bunnies seemed vicious in comparison.

'Here,' he stammered, handing me another folded bill. 'Thanks. I mean . . . thanks.' This time, he knew how to tuck the tip into my cleavage properly. Fast learner.

Leaving the smitten LYT in my wake, I moved to the next table, where an overweight, middle-aged man pounded back his third drink. A wedding ring gleamed on his left hand, and thoughts of fornication twinkled in his eyes. Cha-ching!

'Pardon me,' I purred, 'do you mind if I sit for a moment? These heels are murder on my feet.' Not a lie; how strippers didn't spend a portion of their earnings on orthodics, I'd never know.

He cleared his throat. 'You go right ahead, Ms Jezebel.'

Ms Jezebel. Wasn't he the cutest little flesh puppet? I smiled my thanks as I sank into the chair opposite him. 'Looks like you're thirsty tonight.'

'It's Thirstday, don't you know.' He chortled at his own cleverness.

One of the two cocktail waitresses working the room sashayed up to him as I settled back in my seat. 'Sir, would you like to buy the lady a drink?'

'Ah! Ms Jezebel, forgive my poor manners. Would you care to quench your thirst?'

Hmm. Would I like him to spend the money on booze for the house, or on me for my Former Demon Relief Fund? Let's think. 'I'm good, sweetie. Thanks anyway.'

'We're all set for now,' he said to the waitress. She smiled tightly at him and shot me a glare that should have evaporated me on the spot. Then she slunk away, on the prowl for other victims.

Chuckling softly, I flipped my hair over my right shoulder and started working out the kinks of my left by moving it in slow circles. 'You enjoying the show?'

'Very much,' he said to my boobs. 'You're really good, Ms Jezebel.' Maybe he realized his gaze was doing things to my nipples, because he noisily cleared his throat and looked me in the face. 'You dance like you love it.'

'I do. There's something about being on stage that makes it feel like the music pulses through my body.'

'You make it look . . . what's the word. Sensual.'

'Why, sweetie, I'm an exotic dancer. I'm supposed to make it look that way.'

We both laughed – just two people sharing a joke,

nothing seductive or manipulative. At least, that was the goal. Make every customer feel like he's the one you really connect with – that's the secret. But I'd never tell.

Jowls quivering with mirth, he said, 'Well, you're a damned fine dancer.'

'Thank you.' I leaned back in my seat and slowly crossed my legs. The hem of my micro skirt slid up to my crotch. Massaging my neck, I rolled my head to the left – and saw Paul at table three, smiling at red-haired Lorelei, who looked like she was having an epileptic fit as she flailed on top of his table. If she wasn't careful, her silicon-heavy tits were going to smother her. What a pity.

As if he sensed my presence, Paul's eyes darted my way. Paul Fucking Hamilton. When I'd offered myself to him, he'd been all holier than thou. But there he was, with a half-assed stripper dry-humping his tabletop. My eyes narrowed, and maybe I was crazy, but I thought he shrugged and sort of rolled his eyes at Lorelei, who was now making a big show of sucking her fingers. Either that, or she was trying to yak all over him. Not that I could blame her.

I turned back to face the heavyset man next to me, and I stretched my smile as wide as it would go without cracking my cheekbones. 'This is going to sound like a line, so forgive me. Come here often?'

His startled grin revealed smoker's teeth. 'Every once in awhile. When the mood strikes me.'

Absolutely not thinking about Paul and Lorelei, I repeated, 'The mood?'

'To see some pretty girls dance.' His eyes sparkling from drink, he added, 'To dream about doing more than watching them dance.'

I lightly touched his arm. 'Sweetie, you don't have to dream about it.'

Beads of perspiration erupted on his forehead. 'No?'

'If you like, we can go to the lounge, or if you prefer, the VIP room. I'd be happy to dance for you. Or with you.'

He licked his lips. I guessed that in all the time he'd come to Belles, he'd never had the balls to pay for a private dance. His voice cracking, he asked, 'How much would this dance cost?'

'Depends. If you want a dance in the lounge, that's thirty for the one dance.'

'My. So, um, for three dances, that's what, ninety dollars for ten minutes?'

'Sweetie, don't tell the managers, but I'm more of a by-the-song girl than a clock watcher. Tell you what,' I said, one conspirator to another, 'for you, I'll give you four dances for a hundred.'

Fingering his wedding band, he said, 'And we'll just . . . dance?'

I patted the man's hand. 'Never underestimate how sexy a good dance can be.'

Leaving the VIP lounge a hundred fifty dollars richer – the fellow insisted on showing his appreciation for the extra dance – I bumped into Candy by the foot of the stairs.

'Wanted to tell you, the guy at table three's been asking for you.'

Paul.

My face must have looked like I'd quaffed a milkshake with extra cream, because Candy said, 'What's wrong? You know him?'

'Remember I told you I'd gotten into a fight with this guy?'

'Yeah – shit, you mean that's the white boy who can't jump?'

'Yep.'

We both glanced surreptitiously at table three. Meeting my eyes, Paul lifted his beer in a salute. I turned my back on him. Bastard. He wasn't supposed to catch me sneaking a peek at him.

'Looks like he wants to make up,' Candy said.

'It's going to take a lot more than a toast to get me to walk over there.'

'Girl, you serious?'

'Excuse me, Candy. Nature's calling. I guess seeing him's bringing out the best in me.'

I clomped my way to the dressing room, pretending every time my stiletto heel hammered the floor it was really skewering Paul's eyeball. Or maybe his scrotum. Whichever would make a better popping sound.

On the threadbare sofa in the back of the dressing room, Jemma sat with her hands around her knees, shivering violently. Even with the temperature at see-your-breath levels and her little scrap of clothing she was almost wearing, she shouldn't have been shaking so much. 'Heya, Jemma. You okay?'

'Cold,' she said, teeth chattering.

No shit, Sherlock. 'Sweetie, you should go home. You're sick.'

'Not sick. Need the money.'

Before I could think better of it, I offered her the cash I'd just scored from the lounge. 'Here.'

She stammered, 'What's that?'

'A wad of boogers. What do you think?'

Shaking her head, she said, 'No.'

'Will you take the flippin' money before I talk myself out of this?'

She sniffled so deeply that she should have choked on her own mucus. 'Can't. Yours.'

'Oh, for fuck's sake.' I grabbed her hand and shoved the money into it. Her perfume immediately attacked my sinuses, and my eyes watered. Sickeningly sweet, like milk, but with a hint of something more foul beneath it, maybe like fetid breath or an unwashed body. Looking up at me, her redrimmed eyes puffy and distraught, Jemma looked sick and lost – a little girl abandoned in a hospital by her mother.

'No need to pay me back. Now go on, go home. Shoo. Put on something disgustingly cute like flannel jammies and bunny slippers, bury yourself in bed, and get some sleep.'

She pulled her arm away and clutched herself. 'Not sick. Just cold.'

'Then buy a blessed sweater,' I muttered, walking past her to the tiny bathroom. After I flipped on the light and shut the door, I banged my head against the wall. It felt sort of good, so I did it again. I needed money, almost as badly as a creature of Greed. So what in all the levels of unholy Hell had possessed me to give any of it away?

I was getting so soft that my spine was going to melt.

After I did my business, I opened the door to find Momma hovering right outside. 'All yours,' I said, motioning to the toilet.

'No thanks, honey. When I have to take a crap, I use the VIP room. Better toilet paper.' She took me by the arm. 'Come on, Jezebel. I've got to show you something.'

She gently but firmly led me out of the dressing room

at a clip that would've have made soldiers beg for mercy. We zoomed onto the showroom floor, weaving our way around customers and my coworkers. And at table three, she stopped me dead and put out her palm.

Paul, grinning like an angel with a new halo, dug out a bill from his wallet and put it in Momma's hand.

'Thanks a bunch,' I said, spitting out the last word.

Smiling at the face on the greenback, Momma said, 'You should be flattered that the gentleman wants to see you so badly, he gave me a twenty for the privilege.'

As she meandered away, I called over my shoulder, 'You should at least give him a lap dance for the twenty!'

She shouted over the din, 'Honey, my dancing days are far behind me.' Then the crowd and the music swallowed her alive.

'Hi, Jesse.'

Refusing to look at him, I crossed my arms over my breasts and stared at the foosball table tucked into the back corner of the room. Did anyone really come here to play foosball? I sniffed, 'Hello, Paul.'

'Will you at least look at me?'

'Depends. You going to make me feel like throwing myself in front of a truck?'

'Not if I can help it.'

'Okay then.' I glanced at him. His hair was a little shaggy, his cheeks and chin a little stubbly. His poet's eyes beck- oned with odes and epics; the bump on his nose that spoke of fights in his past cried out for my fingers to touch it. And that mouth ... Bless me, the man was so fucking sexy I wanted to throw him down and suck him dry.

Oh, wait. I'd already tried going that route.

'Your sets are fabulous tonight,' he said. 'I thought you were good yesterday, but damn, tonight you're on fire.'

'I bet you say that to all the strippers.'

'Just the ones I like.'

'Uh-huh.' I made a big deal of tapping my foot – which, in four-inch heels, is a royal pain. 'I have to get back to work. You know, dancing for the guys who actually fantasize about me kissing them.'

He ran his hand through his curling brown hair. 'Listen, about before. I'm sorry. I didn't mean to upset you, or embarrass you.'

'Embarrass me? Why? Just because I threw myself at your feet and you said no?'

He blew out a sigh. 'It's not like that. God, if you only knew how much restraint it took for me to walk away . . .'

'Yeah, my heart bleeds for you. See you, Paul.'

'Wait, please.'

Hating myself, I waited.

'Let me make it up to you?'

Ooh. Possibilities abounded. 'How?'

His lips quirked in a suggestive smile. 'For starters, can we see if the VIP room's available for a private dance?'

Nonplussed, I said, 'Sure. Want me to get Lorelei for you? I saw you drooling over her seizure on the table before. I didn't peg you for a boob man.'

'Boobs are nice,' he admitted. 'Especially on sexy brunettes with green eyes.'

My heartbeat quickened, and when I licked my lips I tasted perspiration beaded over my mouth. Bless me, did Roman actually turn up the heat in the joint? Or was Paul getting me hot?

My body said to me, What do you think?

Stop that, body. I'm pissed off at him. He's not allowed to turn me on. Got it?

My body, treacherous thing it was, ignored me. My

192

nipples nearly exploded through my bra. Between my legs, a hint of wetness lapped at my G-string.

'What do you say, Jesse? Me and you, in the VIP room for a half hour.'

I barked out a laugh. 'That's two-hundred-fifty dollars. You sure you want to start making up to me by me robbing you blind?'

'It's worth it.' He stretched out his hand, and I took it, helping him to his feet.

After a pit stop to inform Lyle of my whereabouts, Paul and I headed to the VIP room.

As we approached the back room, he leaned close and whispered, 'I know I've seen you before.'

Goosebumps broke across my flesh. 'Really?' I said lightly. 'Where?'

'I don't know. But I feel it in my gut. I know you.'

'Sweetie, that's probably just hunger pangs.'

He laughed – oh, that laugh! – and said no more about it. But as I led him into the VIP room, I thought about how he'd looked, twisted between his bedsheets, his hair sleep-tousled, his breathing ragged.

And I remembered how his agonized shrieks had echoed in my ears.

17

Paul's Bedroom

Materializing into an unknown space entails a bit of risk. It's not as dangerous as, say, calling an Archangel 'fuckhead,' but it's more nerve-wracking than planning a few laps in the Lake of Fire. Thing is, when you don't know where you're about to appear, you could solidify inside an object or a being that's already occupying the space. Granted, I wasn't alive in the technical (read: breathing) sense of the word, but even so, suddenly sharing space with an oak tree or a moving city bus hurt like a bastard. I don't recommend it.

So when I materialized inside of a pitch black closet and found a sneaker, a basketball, and rumpled clothing poking out of my hooves and legs, I bit back a yelp and yanked the dirty laundry out of me. Fucking mortals and their fucking possessions. And not in the cool demonic sense that was always a scream at parties.

It's your own fault Lillith's voice sniffed in my mind, her thoughts as hard and shining as diamonds. *You shouldn't be solid. You're a Nightmare, remember?*

Moping, I tossed the shoe to the floor. *I'm a succubus acting like a Nightmare.*

And what difference does that make? I imagined her full-lipped smile as she projected her thoughts to me – Lillith, Queen of the Succubi, thought she was the epitome of wit. Yeah, right. And Jim Carrey was the Pope. *Call it what you will, your role now is to terrify sleeping humans. Think you can do that, Jezebel? Or should I speak to Him about placing you as a ghost?*

Balling my hands into fists, I replied, *That won't be necessary.*

The silence stretched longer than a mortal's small intestine. Lillith hissed, *That won't be necessary . . . what?*

Whoops. Maybe she was the ruler of all female Seducers, but she had pride that would put any demon of Arrogance to shame. *That won't be necessary, my Queen.*

Better. You don't have to like me, Jezebel. But you do have to respect my position.

Which, based on her reputation, meant straddled over King Asmodai and sucking his dick while she wiggled her ass in his face. *As you say, my Queen.*

Now do your job and terrify the flesh puppet.

Her presence winked out of my mind, but I knew the connection lay there, waiting to be activated. She was watching me. Bitch.

Hating one's supreme ruler wasn't the best way to enjoy an immortal existence. I didn't know what I'd done to earn her wrath; smart demons didn't question such things, they merely accepted it and did their best to avoid said ruler whenever possible. For whatever reason, Lillith attacked my confidence like a cancer did a human's body. She ate away at my ego and ravaged my assurance in my abilities. If I nabbed three clients, it should have been five; yet if I brought in ten, then I was sacrificing quality for quantity. If I maneuvered my lover into calling my name when I was riding him, then I was relying on demonic power instead of my own skill. And if I didn't tempt a mortal into saying my name as he ejaculated inside of me, then I obviously didn't take my role seriously. And so on.

And here mortals thought that Joseph Heller had invented the Catch-22.

Maybe it had to do with Lillith not being a proper demon. One of the few humans who transformed into a nefarious entity, Lillith had been the first woman. As in Adam's first wife. Never one to choose subservience, she had insisted on taking the dominant position when they consummated their union. Adam, instead of lying back and enjoying the ride, had bitched to God. What a wuss. Frankly, most of the men I'd entertained had been all too happy to let me slide up and down their poles. So Adam asked God to kick Lillith out of Eden and get with the begatting of a new wife. Along came Eve. And everyone knows how well *that* turned out.

Adam, like most mortals, didn't know just how good he had it until after he fucked it up completely.

Lillith, story had it, made her way across the world, offering her body to any creature that wanted her sex . . . for a price. The Queen of the Succubi was the first real working girl, proving that prostitution, and not mother-hood, was the oldest profession since Creation. Lillith was so good at her trade that King Asmodai himself wooed her, and lo and behold, Hell had a mortal woman in its midst. A couple of centuries was all it took to transform her into a demon, but human blood still coursed through her veins.

A demon queen with PMS. Talk about a living Hell.

I let the basketball drop to the ground, where it bounced halfheartedly, its movement hindered by the piles of junk in the closet. Especially with Lillith watching me, I had to nail this assignment. Which meant getting my ass out of the closet.

Letting my eyes glow a malefic red, I set my mouth in a fang-flashing grin and opened the door slowly, allowing maximum squeakage. And then I stepped out of the closet.

A scan of the room – alcove, really – told me the immediate things I needed to know: The man was deeply asleep in his bed; the man was alone in his bed; the man was a mouthbreather. The last was über important when sucking out a soul; mouth-breathers made the job easy.

Stop that, I told myself as I slowly walked away from the closet. You're not a succubus anymore. No more soul-sucking kisses. No more seduction. No more . . .

Ooh, look at the sleeping man. Sculpted cheeks. Strong jaw. Broken nose. Tangled hair that begged for a trim. Muscular neck and shoulders . . . lots of chest hair peeking up beneath the sheet. The one arm tossed over his head was wonderfully formed – sinewy without being too bulked up. Yummy. I wondered what he looked like without the sheet covering him.

No. Bad ex-succubus. You're not here to sleep with him. You're here to scare the bejesus out of him.

Oh, but look at how his chest rose and fell, rose and fell – so rhythmic, almost as if he was dreaming about sex.

Taking slow, languid steps, I circled the bed, my hooves muffled by the worn, wall-to-wall carpeting. Queen-sized mattress, but a black rail frame; probably a futon. A white sheet clung to the man's body, outlining his form with its tangled embrace. On the floor in a heap, a thick comforter lay discarded. Maybe the lovely human had a flare for violence and he kicked off his blanket in a fit of unconscious rage.

There, look at how his muscles rippled, how even in repose his body thrummed with animation – a vivid dream captured him. Hmm. Maybe being a Nightmare had its perks.

In the window, an air conditioner stood sentry, but even though it was a warm night for late September, the box was off; instead, a second window stretched open, frozen in a yawn. Conserving energy, then – careful with his money. On his beech dresser, a Bose stereo perched, silent, waiting to fill the room with soft tones or throbbing backbeats. Not cheap; a man who preferred to spend his money on things he considered worth it. Nice.

Looking at his slumbering form, I thought I could be very worth his while. I wanted to lick every inch of his body and watch his face to see his reaction when he woke up with his balls in my mouth. *Ummm.*

Next to his bed, I brushed my fingers against the surface of his nightstand. Coming across a framed picture, I picked it up. A woman, young, with short brunette hair. Good smile; thin face. I glanced at the sleeping man, then back to the woman. If there was a family resemblance, I missed it. Sure, it was dark in the room, and not even moonlight streamed in, thanks to the overcast weather. But demons didn't need carrots for good eyesight. We saw equally well through the entire spectrum of light. Made my job easier, especially when more often than not they ended in the middle of the night, with all the lights out. It would be majorly embarrassing to lean over for a final kiss and miss the mouth completely.

And now that I was a blessed Nightmare, seeing in the

dark was a fucking job requirement. Right along with inspiring terror and causing panic attacks, not to mention the occasional heart failure. In other words, Malefic Standard. No creativity, no thoughtful planning, no passion. Just fear. Just my fucking lot in the Afterlife. And it was all because of the Announcement.

I let out a frustrated sigh. No point in dwelling on what I couldn't change; for the foreseeable future – which meant the better part of forever – I was a bottom-level Nightmare.

A breeze whispered its way through the screen. The man, perhaps reacting to the windy kiss, stretched his arms and rolled onto his left side. I stared at his back, delighting it its broadness, wondering how it would look decorated in scratches from my talons . . .

My eyes gleaming with lascivious thoughts, I cast the picture of the smiling brunette to the floor and glided toward the bed. Approaching him, I saw his face. Beneath his closed lids, his eyes rolled and flicked. His brow wrinkled, and a soft moan sounded in his throat. A bad dream. About to get much worse.

Wondering whether I should kiss him awake or just shout 'Boo!' I trailed my fingers over his jaw. Oh, such a powerful jaw, such sensual lips. How would they taste? Would remnants of his toothpaste cling to his teeth? Did a smoker's shadow cloud his breath? What was his unique flavor, one that mirrored the taste of his soul?

Beneath the smells of daytime exhaustion and nighttime worries, I took in his musky, human scent. And I grinned.

Maybe I was a Nightmare, but it wasn't written anywhere that the entire experience had to be terrifying. In fact, the fear factor would be all the more intense if it started out pleasurable. The whole no-light-without-darkness thing.

So I did what I did best – I climbed on top of him and planted a kiss on his lips.

His eyes popped open, and so did his mouth. I took advantage of the new space by thrusting my tongue between his lips and running it over his teeth. No toothpaste; just a little sleep fuzz. I held myself over his body with my left hand propped on his shoulder; with my right, I traced slow circles down his chest, tickling his nipple and working down to the patch of hair over his sleepy shaft. Wakey, wakey, sweetie.

He tensed beneath me as he tried to suck in air through his mouth, except my tongue and teeth and lips were in the way. Crap – he was going to shout, and not in the spine-tingling way.

Remembering the image from the photograph, I let power wash over me, transforming my red, leathery flesh into pale human skin. Short black hair crowned my head and fell thickly over my dark eyes. My face thinned and my fangs receded. Talons softened into tapered nails. My hooves rippled into small, tender feet. The curly hide on my legs, ass, and pelvis faded to reveal shapely, bare legs, with the smallest triangle of dark hair over my sex.

I deepened the kiss as my costume settled into place. Once I felt the image lock, I gently pulled away and looked down at his stunned face.

'Tracy?' His voice, thick from sleep, rumbled softly in the tiny alcove.

Smiling, I said nothing as I stroked the stubble along his cheek and jaw.

'Tracy. Tracy!' His voice cracked, as if strangled with sobs. 'Oh, God. You're here. You're really here.' He wrapped his arms around me, crushed me to him in a hug that should have broken my spine. I felt a shudder run through his body as he pressed me close. I patted his back softly, soothingly, a trusted lover providing comfort.

He whispered into my neck, 'I've missed you so much.'

'Me too.' When you don't know the speech patterns of the human you're dressing as, your best bet is to keep the conversation short. Even better is using body language for the small talk. Which I did – I cupped his face between my hands and kissed him, letting my mouth and tongue do all the speaking.

Strong hands covered mine, pulled them away. His eyes searched my face. Brow wrinkling, he asked, 'How?'

'Who cares about how?' I said, keeping my voice pitched low. 'I'm here. That's all that matters. Now kiss me.'

Pressing my lips to his, I kissed him as deeply as his closed mouth would let me. Sometimes men thought too much, even in the middle of a passionate act. I figured it came from having two heads; there were bound to be times when the wrong one did the serious thinking. To encourage his gray matter to take a backseat to the red zone, I rocked my hips, bumping against his shaft. Yup, Mister Happy was starting to do his morning stretches.

He pulled back, a frown pulling at his face. 'This can't be happening. You're dead.'

The framed picture on the nightstand; the lack of a ring on his finger, of a woman by his side. The click was so loud in my head that my eardrums should have burst. 'So maybe this way you and I can both finally rest in peace.'

It must have been the wrong thing to say. His eyes narrowed, and his shoulders tensed. Then he turned his head away, anger radiating from him like summer heat off of blacktop. 'Why now, after two years?'

'Sweetie,' I crooned, touching my finger to his chin

and gently nudging him to look me in the eye, 'don't think about it. Just let your body do what it wants to do, what it needs to do.' I rubbed against him, feeling his penis swell with blood and heat. After kissing his lips again, I darted my tongue across his cheek until my mouth found his earlobe. There I nibbled playfully while I reached down to rub the tip of his erection with my fingers.

His hands grabbed my shoulders, and before I knew what was happening he rolled me onto my back, with him on top of me, pinning my hands by my head. Ooh, my man liked it rough, eh? I flexed, blowing a ripple of power over him. His eyes widened, and for a moment I thought he saw my true form. Then he kissed me hard enough to make my lips bleed.

I opened my mouth, and his tongue thrust against mine, dueling more than tumbling, as if he were at war with the passion that enveloped him. Still pinning my wrists, he kissed down my neck, the hollow of my throat, down to the curve of my left breast. Licking the underswell, his saliva tingled coolly on my flesh. I cooed with delight as he gave into the desire raging through his body, as his mouth latched onto my nipple and sucked.

My back arched from his attention, and I threw back my head and bucked my hips. He moved to my other breast, his teeth grazing the nipple in a dangerous tease just before he gave suck. A wet heat bloomed in my groin, and I let out a moan.

It wasn't supposed to be like this. I was supposed to be doing the seducing. 'Let my hands go,' I whispered, 'and I'll ride you until you explode.'

He released my breast and paused, his gaze locked on mine. His eyes were dark with passion, but through the haze of lust, something glittered brightly, something I couldn't place. 'You're not Tracy.'

Lie, or tell the truth? Meet him halfway. 'No, sweetie. I'm a dream.'

Pushing his cock hard against my belly, he said, 'This is no dream. You're here, you're real.' He pushed again, and I felt his erection straining to burst from his shorts. His voice gruff, he said, 'Who are you?'

'For now, I'm your lover.' Wrapping my legs around his torso, I pulled his body down to mine. With a flick of my wrists, I freed my hands and grabbed his hair. Then I yanked his head to mine and I kissed him deeply, imagining the taste of his soul against my lips. He rocked his hips, all hesitation gone as his movement increased in speed, in force.

Yes, sweetie. That's right. Fuck me hard.

Just as I was about to pull off his pajama shorts with my toes, Lillith's voice screeched in my mind: *YOU'RE SUPPOSED TO SCARE HIM, NOT SEDUCE HIM! TERRIFY HIM NOW, OR I'LL SEND YOU TO THE LAKE OF FIRE FOR A CENTURY!*

Her words sliced through my mind, lacerating my thoughts. My physical shell reacted to the psychic attack, and I shook violently, my teeth chattering loudly.

'What's wrong?'

I looked up at the man straddling me, biting my lip to keep my teeth from clattering out of my mouth. That made me shiver even harder.

A calloused hand stroked my cheek. His eyes brimming with concern, he said, 'You're trembling.'

Even awash in my power, the man had pulled himself out of his burning hunger – a hunger that should have been consuming his will – to ask me if I was all right. His compassion stunned me beyond my ability to speak. Something loosened in my chest, and I struggled to understand the emotion filling me to the breaking point.

No, this was *wrong*. I was a demon. I didn't feel things for people . . . for flesh puppets. I used them and discarded them, I collected their souls like trading cards.

I didn't care about them.

I *didn't*.

In my mind, His words echoed, disdainful and full of scorn: *You are too soft*.

Oh, bless me six ways to Salvation, He'd been right.

'Please,' the man said, his hand stroking my face. 'You're crying. Did I hurt you?'

Momentarily flummoxed, I gazed into his eyes, his beautiful sea-green eyes, and said, 'I'm so sorry.'

Then I shrieked, releasing my confusion, my fear, my shame – and my mouth and chest erupted in blood as if my heart had exploded. Maybe it had. Nothing made sense anymore.

Above me, the man's screams joined my own, his terror and agony riding the cool September breeze. My blood splattered his face and chest, baptizing him in horror.

His anguished cries echoed in my ears, even after I materialized in Pandemonium.

Better, Lillith whispered. *Go file the case as complete.*

Shivering, I reached up and touched dampness on my face, but in the red-tinged heat of Hell, I didn't know if it was blood or tears that stained my fingertips.

I took a step toward the administrative wing of Pandemonium, then another, and then my feet stopped. My human feet; I hadn't shed my costume.

An eternity of this.

Forever and ever, wondering what side I was really on.

King Lucifer's sad eyes, telling me something that I couldn't understand. King Lucifer's kiss, lingering on my lips.

The King of Hell, telling us . . .

Cutting off the thought, I turned away from the administrative wing and marched out of Pandemonium, heading toward the Gates. I didn't know where I was going, but one thing was certain: I couldn't stay in Hell any longer.

18

Belles (II)

'Okay,' I said, shutting the door to the VIP room, 'it's your dime. What's your flavor – striptease or private dance?'

'How about we just talk?'

I flounced over to one of the plush fake-leather sofas and sank down, crossing my legs and my arms. Me defensive? Never. 'Okay, sweetie. Talk.'

With a deep sigh, Paul ambled over and sat next to me – within slapping distance, but a bit of a stretch for swapping spit. 'I want to talk about what happened earlier today.'

'You mean when you had my heart for breakfast then puked it all over my new shoes?'

'Christ, Jesse, will you stop being pissed off so that I can just talk?'

That quenched the fire in my gut. Softening, I said, 'Okay.'

He ran his fingers through his hair, away from his face. I wondered what he'd look like with long hair crashing over his shoulders, wearing a leather duster instead of a suit jacket. Not meeting my eyes, he said, 'You caught me off-guard before. I really just meant to comfort you, to let you know that I heard you. And then you were all over me like a kid on candy.'

Taking a deep breath, he continued, 'And it was just as sweet. God, you have no idea how desirable you are.' Blinking, his lips quirked into a smile. 'What'm I saying? Look at where you're working. Of course you have an idea.'

I wanted to raise my eyebrows in amusement, to let him know that I got he was trying to cut the tension. But I was still too angry with him; the fire sparked once again into a steady simmer, one that could either suddenly boil over or die out completely, depending on how it was fed. So instead of encouraging him, I stared, hard, waiting for his next words.

'But the timing was damned lousy. You'd just bared your soul to me – how could I take advantage of that?'

I couldn't help it; I let out an angry laugh. Baring my soul was pretty damn easy, considering I didn't have one. 'I told you it was okay. I begged you to take advantage.'

'I know. I was there. But I couldn't do that to you.'

'Why?'

'Because there are some things you just don't do. It's in the rulebook. You don't make a play on a woman you really like when she's drunk or depressed.'

I swung my leg as I considered his words. 'You have a rule-book?'

'Of course we do. Comes with the union card. I think it's chapter eight: Times When You Never, Ever Make a Pass.'

Despite my best efforts, the right side of my mouth lifted up into a half-smile. 'Isn't that chapter six?'

Clucking his tongue, he said, 'Man, someone let you see the book? One of the rules is never to show the rule-book to a woman.'

Now my entire mouth was in on the smile. 'I can be very persuasive.'

'I know.'

Crap. Full circle again. My smile deflated until it flapped off of my face.

'It'd be different if I just wanted something physical with you.' His mouth twisted into a tight grin. 'If it was just about sex, that'd be a no-brainer. I'd never have walked out of that hotel room.'

'But you did,' I said.

'But I did. Because I don't want it just to be about a quick fling and making plans that never happen.'

'You're not into casual,' I said. 'I get it.'

'No, you don't. It's been a long time, Jesse.' His voice was so low, so soft, that I had a hard time hearing it over the Pink tune blaring from the overhead speaker. 'I've had plenty of casual nights. But only one real relationship. And that ended two years ago.'

Remembering the photograph on his nightstand, I asked, 'Who was she?'

'College sweetheart.' His eyes shone, and I saw love sparkling there. I didn't know his old love, but at that moment, I hated her. 'Tracy and I were in the same poly-sci class at Boston U. freshman year. We just clicked, as if we were meant to be together. After graduation, we kept dating. And it kept getting more serious. Next thing you know, I'm spending two months' salary on a ring and we're talking about setting a date.'

Already knowing the answer, I asked, 'What happened?'

His face pulled into a grimace, and he closed his eyes.

'I left for work early, like always. She was still sleeping, so I didn't give her a kiss, because I didn't want to wake her. Next time I kissed her was in her coffin.' His eyes opened, but he was focused two years in the past. 'Hit and run, when she was out for her morning jog. Happened on a side street, so it wasn't called in right away. No one saw it happen. She was dead before they got her to the hospital.'

'I'm so sorry.'

He took a deep breath, then blew it out slowly. 'The first few months were tough. Her family took it hard, and her mother still blames me for not being there.'

'How could you have been?'

A smile flitted over his face. 'Not the point. Grief does strange things to people. Makes them say horrible things. Makes them do unpredictable things they might later regret.' He looked me dead in the eye.

Ouch.

Okay, so maybe I'd been off the deep end when he rebuffed my advances in the hotel room. It wasn't my fault; I'd never been rejected before. Considering that I hadn't ripped off my amulet and fried him into a crisp, I thought I'd handled it pretty well.

'After a few more months, I started accepting that Tracy wasn't coming back. A year after she died, I moved to New York. Part of it was to get away from her family – her mom especially had a way of just showing up at places like the supermarket when I'd be shopping, and she wouldn't say anything at all, just stare at me with those haunted eyes, like she was judging me and finding me guilty, over and over. I had to escape.'

Boy, could I relate. 'It's not just escaping judgment. It would have killed you.'

'Maybe,' he shrugged. 'But it was more than leaving the bad stuff behind. I needed a fresh start. And that meant walking away from my past. I got established in New York pretty quickly. And I like it here. I met a couple people who've become good friends. I went out on a few dates, nothing too serious. And I was good for a while. When the second anniversary of Tracy's death came around, I took the train to Boston to visit her gravesite. To let her know how I was doing.'

As a demon, I'd never understood the need for humans to convene with the dead. Unless they spoke through mediums, the dead were way beyond the mortal coil. And the handful of true mediums I'd met over the millennia all agreed that spirits were flighty at best and downright vindictive at worst. The whole séance thing was pointless; spirits of the deceased couldn't provide any comfort or real answers. When an entity is transparent physically, it was a good bet that mentally and emotionally, it would be just as empty.

Even so, humans continued to reach out to their dead. Small wonder there weren't more charlatans out there, bilking people away from their money for the promise of a few moments with their ethereal loved ones.

But now . . .

Maybe it was because I was human. Or maybe it was because it was Paul telling me this, and as much as I wanted him to be just my Cabin Boy, he was growing into something more meaningful. Like a Gardener, or even a Butler.

'To be honest, I hadn't even been planning to go up to see her,' Paul said. 'But I had this dream a few nights ago that had me thinking about her all the next day.'

All the blood in my face pooled down in my toes. Trying

to ignore the pretty black dots swimming in front of my eyes, I asked, 'Are you still in love with her?'

A smile bloomed on his face. 'I'll always love her. But I've also said good-bye.' He spread his hands wide, a helpless gesture that looked so odd on a strong man. 'I've made my peace with it. But I hadn't counted on you.'

I squeaked, 'Me?'

'I don't know what it is, but there's something about you. I knew it from the moment I saw you sipping coffee at South Station. When I saw you again on the train, something inside me just, I don't know, connected.'

He leaned close to me. 'God knows, I've wanted to kiss you as soon as I met you. But there's more to you than just sex appeal.'

More than just sex appeal? My hands shook. Never in all of my existence had anyone suggested something so . . . blasphemous. All I knew was sex and desire; there was nothing more to me.

'I *know* you, Jesse. Somehow, deep inside, something about you just feels right to me.'

My throat constricted. This was way more than I'd bargained for. Yes, I wanted him in that wonderful Biblical sense – but more than that, I wanted him to be right. I wanted there to be more to me than just a roll in the sack.

I wanted to be loved.

My heart slammed against my chest like it couldn't stand being in my body. Shit! Humans and their icky emotions! This *sucked*! I was born and bred in the Pit – warm and fuzzy feelings were supposed to be an anathema!

'I want to discover what that thing about you is,' Paul said, 'what makes you resonate with me. I want to discover who you are.'

I whispered, 'Maybe I don't want to be discovered.'

He reached out and clasped my hand, swallowing it completely in his own. 'I think you do. I think you're waiting for the right person to find you.'

'You don't know anything about me,' I said, finding it hard to breathe.

'But I want to.' His hand tightened on mine. 'I want to know whatever you're willing to share. Whenever you're ready. I want to know *you*.'

Feeling like I was going to cry my fool head off, I said, '*I* don't even know me.'

'So let's learn together.'

I looked into his eyes and saw waves of green swell and recede into an ocean of dark blue. My voice barely louder than a mouse's squeak, I said, 'How?'

'I can start by making up to you about before, in the hotel. What should I do?'

Let me ride you like a bronco. 'I don't know. No one's ever tried to apologize to me.'

'Well . . . what do you like?'

I nibbled my lip, thinking. Finally, I shrugged. 'I really don't know.'

'Okay, I'll guess. Chocolate?'

'Very yummy.' At least, I assumed it was.

He inched closer to me. 'Flowers?'

'Very pretty.' And they died so quickly, which was rather thoughtful of them.

Now his hand was draped over my shoulder. 'Wine?'

'Maybe . . .' Especially if he poured it over my navel and lapped it up.

Eyes darkening, he said, 'Dine?'

'Hmmm.' Too many delightful possibilities to consider.

His breath on my neck, he asked, 'Dinner and a movie?'

'That sounds nice . . .'

'Jesse? I'd really like to kiss you now.'

'Have at it.'

And he did.

Time was ridiculously relative. In this particular instance, the thirty minutes flew by.

We'd kissed and cuddled, but we didn't let it get any further than that. Part of it was because I was a dancer, not a hooker (even though Roman had invited me to be one), and I was on the clock. More important, I was terrified of pushing Paul away by moving too fast.

Ugh. I was a pathetic former malefic entity. Even angels would have attacked Paul by now.

When time was up, we approached the door together, hand in hand, and shared a lingering kiss. 'When's your shift over?'

'One.'

He sighed. 'Can't stay the whole time. Maybe until midnight.' An unspoken thought danced in his eyes. 'I need to get me some sleep tonight. Have a big day tomorrow.'

'Okay. You going to stick around here a while longer?'

'For a bit. Maybe watch one more of your sets before I call it a night.'

I led him downstairs, back to the showroom. Near the DJ booth, he asked me, 'So, when're we going to get together for dinner and a movie?'

My mouth stretched into a very happy grin. 'I'm off Sunday and Wednesday.'

'Sunday it is. It's a date.'

Date. Oooh, shivers!

He squeezed my hand, and I gave him sappy, moonstruck eyes. This was turning out to be a decent night.

Which is why I was stunned when my peridot stone suddenly flared against my breast.

My hand flew to the shieldstone. Hot, screamingly hot . . . then dead cold.

Feeling nausea roll in my stomach, I pasted a smile on my face while I glanced around the crowded showroom, trying to pinpoint the source of Evil. On stage, Circe's eyes bored into me as she made love to the stripper's pole. Offstage, stretching her hands over her head, Lorelei glared at me like she'd happily tap dance on my grave. Too many men to count – most lusting, some leering – letting their gazes roam freely over my shape. By the foosball table, Roman's eyes narrowed dangerously as he glared at me, then at Paul, who seemed blissfully unaware of all the heated, hateful looks.

Bless me, it could be *anyone*.

I hoped it was only Daun doing the jealous incubus thing inside Roman's body. Daun I could handle.

'Jesse?' Paul nuzzled his nose against my neck. 'Either the lighting's bad, or you just turned green.'

Green. As in a creature of Envy . . . or Greed. I looked around the crowded room, Depeche Mode thumping in my ears, suggesting we play master and servant. But with the shieldstone on, my power lay beyond my reach . . . and my sense of the Underworld was cut off, stripped.

'I'm okay,' I lied, feeling like a vice was slowly pressing against my heart. 'I'm okay.'

19

Belles (III)

Feeling completely rattled, I gave Paul's hand another squeeze. 'See you later, sweetie. Got to visit the little girl's room.'

'I'll definitely say good-bye before I head out for the night.'

I grinned up at him, thrilling over how his smile showed in his eyes. 'See you later.'

With a parting squeeze, I sashayed off the showroom floor, Depeche Mode's Dave Gahan insisting that domination was the name of the game. My shieldstone remained cold, indifferent. Maybe it had been a momentary blip on the Evil radar, like a psychic solar flare.

Uh-huh. Right. And maybe Tammy Fay Bakker would be seen in public without her layers of makeup.

Heels clacking against the bare floor, I trotted down the dark hall toward the dressing room. Each click-click of my shoes grated at my nerves, shredding them until I thought I would scream. Mental note: Consider wearing sneakers at work.

When I felt a hand press down on my shoulder, I almost hit the roof. Whirling, I drew back my fist, ready to slam it into a mouthful of fangs.

'Christ on a pogo stick! Don't hit me!'

No demonic entity in its wrongful mind would ever say the C-word. Scowling, I lowered my fist. In front of me was a scrappy girl who looked like she'd stuck her finger in a socket. With dyed black hair, heavy eye makeup, and more piercings than exposed skin, she was a prep school's worst nightmare. Even without my shieldstone doing nothing more than nuzzle between my breasts, I knew she was only human. No demon would try to blend with the flesh puppets by wearing enough jewelry to set off a metal detector.

'Sorry,' I said.

She blew a relieved sigh in my face, bathing me in spearmint and tobacco. 'I was just going to ask where's the ladies' room. Christ, you're a jumpy one, aren't you?'

Shrugging, I said, 'Thought you were someone else.'

'Christ, I sure hope so! So where's the ladies' at?'

I hooked my thumb over my shoulder. 'Got to use the one in our dressing room. There's only a gent's room off the main floor.'

'Isn't that, you know, sexist?'

As if I cared. I shrugged again. 'Maybe. Most of our customers need urinals instead of tampons, so maybe it's just good business sense.'

'Seems pretty fucking sexist to me. What if I'm a lesbian who's into dancers?'

'Are you?'

'Nah. Here for a fucking bachelor's party.'

My eyebrows rose all the way to the roots of my hair.

'Yeah,' she said, 'I know. What can I say? I'm a fucking groomsmaid. How fucking gay is that?'

'It'd be gayer if you were a lesbian.'

'I know. I'm just one of the guys, I'm surrounded by tits and bush, and I'm so unturned on that my fucking sex drive's dead.' She sighed again. 'Christ. Life's just not fair. At least I didn't have to pay the cover charge.'

'Come on,' I said to Goth Girl. 'I'm headed to the bathroom.'

Together we clomped, me in my stilettos, she in her steel-toed workboots, down the hallway that led to the dressing room. Inside, Aurora and Candy were muscling each other out of the way for a better helping of mirror as they touched up their makeup and hair.

'Who's that?' Candy asked, motioning with her mascara wand toward Goth Girl.

'Just passing through,' I said. 'She needs the facilities.'

'Yeah, well she's got to wait her turn to facilitate. Jemma's in there.'

'Jemma's *still* in there,' Aurora said, rolling her eyes. Then over her shoulder, she called out, 'Yo, you fall asleep in there or what?'

'Sick,' came the muffled reply.

'Shit. Don't go stinking the place up with vomit. Bad enough it always smells of fried cat in here. Last thing we need's puke on top of that. Even Momma's incense won't cover that up.'

'Christ, you're all fucking heart,' Goth Girl said.

'Ain't that the truth,' Candy said. 'Since that Julia Roberts flick way back when, guys expect dancers to have a heart of gold.'

'Thought that was hookers.'

'Same shit. Except I'm paid to be on my feet, she's paid to be on her back.'

She and Aurora cracked up over the display of wit. Me,

217

I really had to pee. I strode over to the bathroom door and knocked. 'Come on, sweetie. Don't die in there. Shitty way to go.'

Candy and Aurora fell over themselves with laughter. Just call me Jezebel the comedienne.

As I considered the possibility of exchanging my heels for a microphone, the door banged open, crashing into the wall and chipping the plaster. I had a moment to see Jemma glare at me with hate-filled eyes before she grabbed me by the throat and slammed me against the wall.

Clawing at the vicelike hand pressing against my windpipe, I tried to scream. What came out was a strangled 'Eep.'

In front of me, Jemma's eyes glowed a bright, wet red, like fresh blood on a white satin pillow. Her lips pulled into a leer, and from her mouth came a sultry voice that oozed sex and screamed death. 'Hello, Jezebel. I've been looking all over for you.'

Oh, fuck.

The voice hit me like a spike in my spinal cord. In Jemma's body, Queen Lillith grinned at me.

Jemma's hand squeezed tighter, her fingers digging into my neck, cutting off my air. I pried at her fingers, to no avail; my nails sliced her flesh, but all she did was bleed and smile. Switching tactics, I tried to punch her, but she held me aloft and away from her body. My feet – dangling off the ground – swung out in crazy arcs as I thrashed.

'Hey! Let her go, you crazy bitch!'

I tried to warn Candy to stay away, but I was too busy trying not to let Jemma crush my throat.

Not deigning to look behind her, Jemma threw back her free hand. Candy sailed backward and landed hard against the vanity table. Lillith stretched Jemma's grin wider.

Shit.

Someone, either Aurora or Goth Girl, screamed for all she was worth. Whoever it was had a set of lungs on her. Terrific. Except we were in a strip club where the rule of thumb was to keep the music just above teeth-rattling level. It was extremely doubtful that the cavalry would be arriving anytime soon.

Lillith turned Jemma's head, glancing at the dancer and the patron. Sizing them up. Maybe thinking about taking them out, just for giggles; a creature of the Abyss always had time for a little wanton destruction. The scream abruptly stopped, cut off by the monstrous sight of Lillith's red gaze dancing in Jemma's eyes. Humans had this thing about possession: It terrified the fuck out of them.

Someone muttered, 'Christ.' Goth Girl. Either a curse or a prayer. I would have happily accepted either, but all the word did was make Jemma's hand tighten on my throat.

Okay, Jezebel. Distract the psychotic demon queen.

In a choked whisper, I asked, 'How?' Considering that I couldn't breathe, getting the one word out there was a real feat. Gold star for me.

Turning back to me, Jemma's grin reached her ears. I must have amused her. Goodie. 'How what, Jezebel? How did I find you?'

Maybe she took my silence as something other than me desperately trying to stay alive, because she answered her own question. 'Your friend, the satyr. I knew he'd come find you. So I watched him. And I learned of this place. So I waited, biding my time until I could identify you. Nice trick, becoming a human.'

219

'Thanks,' I whispered. I felt my face turning purple.

'I don't know if it's just the sex, but the satyr seems genuinely to care for you.' Her eyes narrowed, telegraphing what she thought about such nasty feelings.

Keep the bitch talking. The more she talked, the less she was killing me. 'What. About. Shield.'

The Queen of the Succubi laughed, a low, throaty chuckle that would have given serial killers a hard-on. If I hadn't been slowly strangling, I would have been equally as impressed as I was terrified. 'Your little necklace does nothing against *me*.'

I coughed out, 'Why?'

Her grip around my throat tightened, wringing out the last vestiges of air from my windpipe. Eyes glowing, she said, 'I'm not a creature of Evil.'

My heart thumped madly in my ears. Blood pounded in my head like someone had mistaken my face for a bass drum. As my body realized there was no oxygen coming in, my limbs flailed all the harder, as if with a life of their own. Which was a good thing, because my own life was being choked out of me.

No. No *way*. I didn't just start breathing a day ago only to have a possessed stripper force me to stop.

Focusing my waning strength, I managed to place a snap-kick to her stomach. The stiletto sliced the soft flesh of her belly, but she either didn't notice the blood seeping out or didn't care.

Fuuuuuck. This was really, really bad.

Purple blossomed in the corner of my vision, lilacs creeping up to the irises in my eyes. Gasping, I batted at Jemma's hand. A boneless kitten would have had more strength than me.

In Jemma's body, Lillith smiled. 'You've been a very

bad girl, Jezebel. He's been asking for you. The price on your head is enough to turn any demon into a Coveter.'

Her fingers pressed into my throat. Now black flowers joined the lilacs.

No choice.

Feebly, I reached for the peridot stone – the cold peridot stone – ready to use the last of my strength to yank it off my neck. Between being a hunted demon and a dead human, the former had a slightly better life expectancy.

As I touched the shieldstone, Goth Girl smashed something against Jemma's blonde head, making a thick, mushy sound.

Jemma's hand snapped open, and I fell against the wall and slid to the floor, wheezing and gasping for breath. Blood roared in my ears, drowning all other sound in a frantic *thump! thump! thump!* My throat was raw, and each gulp of air seared like a kiss from the Lake of Fire. Tears stung my eyes and trebled my vision. Hands shaking, my fingers tap-danced against my neck, trembling delicately over my bruised flesh.

Oh, air – bless me, I could breathe again.

Jemma lay sprawled on the floor, the back of her head a tangled mass of red. I frowned. Slicing her had done nothing. Then how . . . ?

Standing over her, Goth Girl cradled one of her boots, wielding it like a bat. Blinking, I stared at the bloody workboot. The steel-tipped bloody workboot.

Iron.

Some of the nefarious are very sensitive to certain metals. Apparently, Lillith's personal allergy was of ferric origin.

Looking up at Goth Girl, I whispered, 'Thanks.'

'No problem.' She glanced down. 'Except I fucking wet myself.'

Aurora came charging through the door, Momma and Joey on her heels. Apparently, she'd run out for reinforcements when Lillith was gloating and Goth Girl was gearing up for batting practice.

Joey sank to my side. 'Shit! Jez, you okay?' His strong hands fluttered by my neck, afraid to touch.

'Been. Better.' I dropped my hands from my throat, wincing as I swallowed. Fuuuuuuck. That hurt!

Gingerly, Joey probed my throat. 'Looks like you'll have some pretty colors on your neck. You able to breathe okay?'

'Think. So.'

'Oh my God, oh my God, oh my God,' Aurora intoned, wobbling in her heels. 'Oh my God, oh my God.'

'Fucking crazy bitch,' Candy muttered, picking herself up from the floor. 'Why she hate you so much?'

Because she was a deranged malefic entity with an inferiority complex the size of Texas. 'Thought. I was. Someone else.'

On the ground, Jemma's body began to flop like a landed fish. Momma turned the blonde head to the side. 'Aurora, get me your eyebrow pencil.'

'My . . . ?'

'Eyebrow pencil. If you please.'

Aurora did as she was told. Pencil in hand, Momma pried open Jemma's mouth and stuck the pencil between her teeth. Jemma's body jitterbugged faster, her arms and feet drumming against the bare floor like a machine gun's *tatatatat*.

'Seizure?' Joey asked, glancing at the fallen dancer.

'Based on the track marks on her arm,' Momma said, 'probably more like a bad drug reaction.'

They were both wrong. Jemma's body was reacting to the sudden flight of her host. Lillith was gone. For now. I rubbed my throat, staring at Jemma's flailing arm. The drugs explained how Lillith could have possessed Jemma; narcotics weakened a human's will, made them susceptible. Jemma'd been an easy mark. And now she was paying the price.

Aurora asked, 'What's the pencil for?'

'In case she *is* having a fit, this way she won't bite off her tongue.'

'Crazy fucking bitch deserves it,' Candy spat. 'Must be doped up on something. She barely touched me, sent me flying.'

'Her eyes,' Aurora said. 'They were red.'

'Bloodshot,' Momma said. 'Drugs.'

Jemma's thrashes turned to erratic jerks. The red stain looked horribly dark in her tangled blonde hair.

Momma sighed. 'Doesn't this just blow monkey chunks. Candy, you okay?'

'Hip hurts like a bitch.'

'But you'll live?'

'Hell yeah.'

'Okay.' Glancing at Goth Girl, Momma said, 'What about you, honey? You all right?'

'My fucking pants are goddamn soaked. And my boot's dinged up.'

'Joey here's going to get you a couple drinks on the house. Warm you right up.' Momma's eyes met mine. 'You okay, Jezebel?'

Tears streaming down my face, I nodded. Even that made my throat burn.

'You want a doctor?'

I whispered, 'No.' Just because I was human didn't

223

mean that I wanted someone to take a close look at what made me tick. For all I knew, a doctor might be able to see hints of the demon I really was. I couldn't risk it.

Grimacing, Momma's face made it clear what she thought of my decision. But what she said was, 'You should go home. Get some rest. Me, I'll take the drug queen here to the emergency room. If it's okay with you ladies, I'd like to keep the police out of this. Okay?'

Wincing, Candy rubbed her hip. 'Last thing I need's some cop poking his nose where it don't belong.'

Aurora and Goth Girl agreed that the police were the enemy. Me, I just nodded – and I barely had the energy to do that. Bless me, I was absolutely exhausted. I felt like I could sleep for a year.

'Joey, can you help me get Jemma to my car? Then take care of our guest here. Get her whatever she wants, for the rest of the night.'

'I want a dry fucking pair of pants.'

'Get her almost whatever she wants.'

Joey helped me to my feet, then he and Momma carted Jemma away.

'Just look at this shit, my makeup's all over the place,' Candy muttered, hobbling as she gathered up her things from the floor. 'This jar cost me ten bucks, and now it's cracked and moisturizing the floor. That fucking psycho bitch from hell.'

She had no idea how right she was.

As I changed into a regular bra, my hands shaking so bad that Aurora had to work the clasp, I realized I was screwed six ways to Salvation. Lillith had made me. It wouldn't be long before she returned.

And she'd said it herself – she wasn't a creature of Evil.

Residing in Hell had altered her, but at her core, she was still a human.

The shieldstone wouldn't protect me from her.

I quickly got dressed, exchanged my stilettos for sneakers, and gathered my belongings. Candy let me borrow a bright green scarf to hide the damage to my neck. When Joey came back, drinks in hand for me, Aurora, Candy, and Goth Girl, I pounded mine back without bothering to ask what it was. I barely felt the liquid slide down my throat. It must have done something, though, because my nostrils pinched and my eyes watered.

I thanked him and the girls, then I headed out, meaning to duck quietly past the showroom and hoof it to the hotel, where I'd pack my few possessions and bust a move like there was a hellhound on my trail. Because there was – the biggest bitch of the Underworld was on the case. Which meant that I was no longer a target only for creatures of Avarice. Now I was Number One on Hell's Most Wanted list. And that meant only one thing.

I had to run.

PART FIVE

PAUL

20

Hotel New York

'I still want to know why you were slinking away.'

Sighing, I opened the door to my hotel room, Paul in tow. He'd caught me as I did the tiptoe thing across the showroom floor. Burly Cabin Boy-Slash-Gardener that he was, he insisted on escorting me back to Hotel New York, claiming there were evil people out there who could hurt me if I walked alone at night.

Evil people I could handle. Evil entities that ate said people for lunch? Not so much. My confidence in the shieldstone was greatly lacking at the moment.

And Paul made chivalry so damn appealing. It helped that I wanted to fuck his brains out. So I reluctantly agreed to let him play bodyguard. I hadn't counted on him yammering at me the entire time to find out why I'd been sneaking away.

I flipped on the lights as Paul shut and latched the door. In my absence, the bed had been turned down. Why did mortals bother with such trivial things? I'd just mess up the covers when I slept in the bed, so why make it look neat at all? A small item rested on the overly large pillow.

'Jesse? Are you going to answer me?'

'For the millionth time, I wasn't slinking away. I was sneaking. That's why I was in sneakers. To, you know, sneak. Otherwise they'd be called slinkers.'

I strode over to the bed and picked up the tiny foil-wrapped square. What was this supposed to be, something to make the pillow smell nice? I put the item to my nose and took a whiff.

My salivary glands imploded in ecstasy. Mouth tingling with anticipated pleasure, I tore off the silver foil and popped the brown square into my mouth.

Oh, the feeling of it on my tongue – bliss! I pressed the treat against the roof of my mouth, delighting at the taste as it slowly melted. Swallowing, I shivered as thick, liquid sweetness coated my throat. Unable to restrain myself, I set my teeth into it and chewed, chewed, chewed until it was nothing but a pulverized mass of disintegrating confection. Its aftertaste thick on my tongue, I searched my pillow to see if there were any more foil-wrapped squares. Finding none, I pouted. Only one? Greedy bastards.

I blew out a frustrated sigh, lifting stray curls from my forehead. I had a new understanding for creatures of Gluttony.

'Let me guess,' Paul said. 'You've never had chocolate before now.'

'Is that what that was?' My toes curled in pleasure. 'Now Valentine's Day makes a lot more sense.'

'How could you never have tried chocolate before?'

'There's a lot I've never tried before.' I flopped down spread-eagled on the bed, feeling like I'd screwed an entire pro-football team. At one shot. Okay, I'd rest for a moment, get Paul out of the room, and then grab my things and go.

Somewhere.

Paul sat next to me, his fingers slowly tracing the curve from my hip to my shoulder, and back down to my hip. 'You're a mystery.'

'Wrapped in an enigma.' By my waist, Paul's fingers did this flutter-thing – oooh! 'That tickles.'

'Sorry,' he murmured, his eyes telling me he wasn't sorry in the least. His hand slid over my stomach, inching upward. He gently traced the mound of my left breast, then moved his hand to the side, sliding over the bumps of my ribcage. 'Better?'

His fingers progressed upward, brushing my shoulder. Wrong direction, I wanted to say, go back down and touch me properly. Caress the full swell of my breast. Rub my nipple with your palm. Make my back arch with pleasure. Instead, his hand pressed gently against my shoulder, kneading the muscle.

'Mmmm.' I closed my eyes, smiling as his fingers drummed against my skin. Ohhh, that felt good. Feeling tension melt with his touch, I turned my head away from Paul, giving him more room to work.

His hand pressed, pressed . . . and trailed a path to my borrowed scarf. Too late, I realized he was pushing aside the material. Opening my eyes, I swatted his hand away and rolled away from him.

'Who did that?' His voice was flat, empty. 'Who did that to you?'

Crap. 'Sweetie, come on, it's nothing.'

'It's *not* nothing! You tell me who did that to you!'

Flinching from his anger, words fell from my lips before I could catch them. 'At the club. Jemma. But it wasn't her fault, she wasn't herself.' Literally.

'Jemma.' He said the name like it was a disease. 'That's

231

the blonde who one of the managers and the bouncer helped out at the club. Said she'd passed out, too much booze before the show. What the hell happened, Jesse?'

I sat up on the other side of the bed, my fingers tracing the flesh beneath the scarf, where Lillith had nearly strangled me. Even the soft touch of my fingertips was enough to make me hiss under my breath. Fuck me, that was tender. Swallowing, tasting the remnant of chocolate coating my tongue, I thought about what answer I could give him.

'Jesse.' In that one word, I sensed Paul's building fury, a whirlpool thickening into a maelstrom. 'Tell me.'

On top of everything else, my little voice whispered, don't anger the one human you have yearnings for. Angry Cabin Boys tend to piss in the pool.

I licked my lips before I spoke, carefully choosing my words. 'Jemma was doing drugs.'

'Drugs? Snorting lines before the show?'

Shaking my head, I said, 'I don't know; Momma said she had track marks. I never saw her do anything. But today she'd been acting sick. I tried to get her to go home, even gave her some cash so she wouldn't go home empty-handed. After I saw you, I went back to the dressing room. She was holed up in the bathroom, and I made a joke. I must've said the wrong thing, because she burst out of the bathroom and grabbed me. Started choking me.'

Gooseflesh dotted my skin, and I rubbed my arms, trying to work some warmth into them. I could still feel her hand pressing against my windpipe, her fingers digging into my neck.

'One of the girls got her off of me, and then she went crazy, like she was pitching a fit. That's when Momma and Joey came in, and they took her to Momma's car, to

232

bring her to the emergency room. Momma thought she was having a bad drug reaction.'

I felt Paul's gaze pierce my back. Stiffening, I clutched my arms tighter.

'That's what happened?'

'Yes.'

'Jemma just freaked out?'

'Yes.'

'So why were you slinking out of the club?'

Sighing, I looked up at the ceiling – for what, I didn't know. I'd seen countless mortals perform that gesture, rolling their eyes Heavenward as if God could see them.

As if God cared about them.

Tearing my eyes away, I turned my head toward the wall, away from Paul. 'I told you before, I wasn't—'

'Fine. Sneaking. Whatever.' His hand on my shoulder made me jump. 'Jesse, what are you hiding from?'

I closed my eyes and said nothing.

'Earlier today, you said you learned something back home, something that upset you. You mentioned someone, some guy who said terrible things about you.'

His words, cold as winter's breath: *You are too soft.*

'Is that guy trying to find you?'

My lower lip started to tremble. Even though my eyes were screwed shut, tears managed to squeeze through the closed lids. Unholy Hell, how much moisture could this one body hold?

'What did he do to you?'

'Nothing!' I realized I'd said it too fast, that he wouldn't believe me. 'Nothing. It's not like that. He just . . . wants me to go home. But I can't. I won't.'

Paul's hand pressed against my shoulder, its weight comforting, reassuring. 'Did he do something bad?'

The absurdity of the question brought nervous laughter to my lips. Smothering my giggles, I shook my head, but that made me cry harder. When I could finally speak, I said, 'It's not like that. He didn't do anything wrong. He just turned my life inside out.'

Taking a shuddering breath, I faced Paul. Lightning flashed in his eyes, a storm at sea. Waiting, he said nothing.

I asked, 'Have you ever learned something that was so devastating that you didn't know how you could go on?'

His face hardened, and he dropped his hand from my shoulder. 'I buried my fiancée. So yeah. I understand.'

Heat flushed my cheeks, but I kept talking, even over my embarrassment of forgetting Tracy's death. 'He didn't kill anyone, but He may as well have killed me. Everything I'd ever known, ever believed in, gone with His words.'

Thoughts flitted behind Paul's stormy eyes. 'What did he tell you?'

'That's not important,' I said, shaking my head.

'Yes it is.'

Ignoring him, I spoke quicker. 'I tried. I really tried to accept the way things were going to be from now on. But I just couldn't.'

Remembering the sound of Paul's shrieks, I darted my gaze to the floor. 'I couldn't do it. I couldn't pretend to be something I'm not.' Clenching my teeth, my breathing came in ragged gasps. My heart felt too tight in my chest.

'Jesse—'

I let the words spill out of me, as if that action would give my heart the room it needed to keep beating. 'I was good at what I did! And I loved it! I loved making them feel so good, loved reeling them in and making my catch. But I loved *them*, too, and I didn't know it. It was supposed to be just business, but I started caring about them, started having *feelings*, bless me, feelings for them. Like I was supposed to be an angel.'

Please help me, I heard my lover's voice plead as he reached up to me, supplicating. Grimacing, I shoved the memory away. 'And then He came and ruined everything! And now I'm supposed to hurt them, make them scream. And I can't, I won't, I won't do it!'

Just like that, my words died. I had no more to say. Instead of feeling tight, now my heart seemed hollow, like I'd lost something in the rush of words that escaped my lips like water gushing from a broken dam.

'Jesse,' Paul said, his voice soft, 'were you a prostitute?'

A wan smile flitted across my face. 'Not exactly.'

'Not exactly.' What, is that like being a little bit pregnant?'

I sighed, feeling my entire body deflate like a balloon. 'I've slept with a lot of men, Paul. I've done things that would make you squirm. But until I worked at Belles as a dancer, I never took money from my customers.' Their souls, yes. But never money.

'What about at Belles? You doing more than dance there?'

'Not that it hasn't been suggested to me, but no.'

Paul stared at me hard, absorbing my words. 'This guy. From back home. He make you sleep around?'

'I keep telling you, it's not like that,' I said, anger bubbling in my gut. Paul's nobility rubbed me raw – he was like those holier-than-thou angels with their halos of gold and purity in their eyes. Who was he to judge me?

'Answer me. He make you do that? Did he pimp you out?'

'No. In fact, He made me stop.'

'What?' Surprise was so clearly stamped on his features,

the word may as well have been etched onto his forehead. 'But—'

'What the fuck am I doing? I don't have time for this. I've got to go.' I scrambled to my feet, but Paul grabbed my arm, pinning me to the bed. 'Let go.'

'No. I want to understand what's going on.'

'Sorry, but that's not on the agenda. I've got to pack.'

'Why? You don't have to run again, not with me here.'

'Damn it all to Hell, I don't have time for you to go all white knight on me!' I tried to pull my arm away, but he held on like a pit bull. 'Don't you get it? They know where I am. I've got to leave!'

Paul masterfully displayed selective hearing as he ignored what I said. We might as well have been married. 'He doesn't want you sleeping around, you said. He wants you to hurt them, you said, make them scream.' Paul's eyes roamed my face, searching for meaning. 'What does he want you to do to your johns, Jesse?'

'Paul—'

'Tell me. Who is he?'

Meg's warning hummed in my mind, with Daun's flagging it. 'I can't!'

Voice soft, he said, 'You can trust me.'

A sob burst from my lips. With my free hand I covered my mouth, turning my head away from him. 'It's not about trust. It's about protection.'

'I'll protect you. I swear, as God is my witness, I'll protect you.'

'God doesn't watch humans,' I whispered. 'And you can't protect me. As long as I don't say anything, at least I can protect you.'

An eternity of silence, then I felt Paul's hand cup my cheek, brush away my tears. I inhaled his musky scent, taking him deep inside me. Bless me, I didn't want to leave him.

No, stop thinking about how you feel. Survival first. Leave.

But I want to stay with him. I . . . oh help me, I care about him.

The best thing you could do for Paul, the little voice whispered, *is get the fuck out. Now. Or do you want to bring Hell to his doorstep the way you did to poor Caitlin?*

'Jesse. Please look at me.'

I did, tears streaming down my face.

'You came here for a fresh start, not for a temporary resting stop. You don't have to run again.'

'But they know where I am. They'll find me again.'

'So it wasn't Jemma who did that to you.'

Biting my lip, I dropped my gaze from his face. 'It was. Ask Aurora or Candy. They'll tell you. They were there.'

His hand touched my chin, tilted it up until I met his eyes. 'I promise they won't hurt you again, whoever they are.'

'You can't make that promise. You don't know them, what He can do.'

'I don't care. I won't let them hurt you again.'

I came so close to telling him the truth – about me, about the Announcement, about why Hell was willing to move Heaven and Earth to return me to the fold. But then my life would be forfeit . . . and Paul's would too. As my heart thudded in my chest and my mouth dried up, I realized that I cared about Paul far, far more than was healthy. I had to leave.

Maybe Paul felt my arm tense, understood that I was ready to bolt from the room. Eyes pleading, he whispered, 'Please trust me, Jesse.'

A demon trust a human? Unspeakably funny. The only

creatures that lied even more than demons were humans – and that was because demons didn't lie to themselves.

But I wasn't a demon anymore.

If I trusted him . . . what would happen? I bit my lip as I briefly imagined what it would be like to let myself be human all the way and fall in love. To allow myself to be that vulnerable.

To be with Paul.

My voice breaking, I said, 'I want to trust you. You have no idea how much I want to believe that you can keep me safe.'

'I can. I swear it.'

'Please don't swear. I . . . I don't like thinking about you swearing something and then breaking your word.'

'Then believe in me. Believe that I'll keep my word when I say that I'll protect you.'

'I do believe you. You're the only thing I want to believe in.' Sniffling, I said, 'Great. Now I sound like a greeting card.'

He smiled, lighting his eyes until they sparkled. 'You sound like *you*. Please don't run again. Let me protect you.'

'If you really want to do something for me, hold me.'

He embraced me, pressing me against his chest. I felt his heart pumping, inhaled his scent until it made me giddy.

I pressed my lips against the rough stubble of his cheek, tasting the salty tang of his skin. 'Make me believe that it's all going to be okay.'

His hands cupped my face, turning my head to his. Meeting my gaze, he said, 'I swear to you, Jesse, it's going to be okay.' Then he kissed me.

Hands touching my face, my hair, my shoulders; my hands touching the sculpted planes of his cheeks, his strong jaw, his thick neck. His tongue rolling with mine; his lips sealed against mine. We were hands and tongues and lips, our bodies moving in sync as we explored each other. Kissing me, Paul stole my breath. I chased his tongue with mine, trying to steal it back.

I didn't need to breathe; I sucked the air from his mouth, sucked him into my body. His life sustained mine with an electricity that made every nerve ending sizzle. His kisses set my skin aflame.

We tumbled onto the bed, limbs locked around each other. Paul pinned my hands above my head as he straddled me. He pulled back, drinking my passion with his eyes as his gaze roamed my face.

On my chest, tucked beneath my shirt, the peridot stone slept.

'Are you sure?' he asked.

'I've never been surer of anything in my life.'

He kissed me again, his lips on my mouth, now on my chin, my jaw, moving up. His tongue flicked against the tender skin behind my ear, and I let out an *ummmm* as my lower body clenched in response. The sound changed abruptly into a delighted gasp as he sucked my earlobe. I wanted to grab his hair and kiss him hard, suck him into me, but his hands held mine, trapped them like birds.

'Let me touch you.'

'Shhhh,' he whispered in my ear. 'Let me make you feel good.'

No way – I was the Seducer. I opened my mouth to tell him, command him, to let me go, but his tongue jammed between my teeth, his kiss silencing my words.

Okay, so maybe I should just lie back and enjoy . . .

His kisses slid down my neck, deftly avoiding my scarf. Over the collar of my shirt, he lapped at my flesh, tracing the scoop-cut of the fabric. Between my legs, my sex released a splash of wetness, followed by tiny waves of heat. My breathing quickened. Beneath his body, my hips began to move, dancing to music I couldn't hear.

Moving my hands together, he pinned both my wrists with his left hand. With his right, he brushed his fingers over my cheek, then my shoulder. He slid down, licking my right nipple as his free hand caressed my left breast.

I moaned like a sexed-up poltergeist. Oh bless me, my blood was on fire!

He released my hands, but all I could do was arch beneath his attention. My brain told my body to start showing him some love, but my body told my brain to shut the fuck up.

Pulling away from my breasts, Paul tugged at the bottom of my shirt, yanking it up. I sat up, helping him remove the garment from my body, easing it over my bruised neck. He stripped off his T-shirt and tossed it to the floor. I gazed at his broad chest, marveling over the curly hair that covered him.

'Bless me, you're so gorgeous.' I reached over, ran my fingers through those curls, loving how they tickled my palms.

'You should talk.'

He wrapped his muscular arms around me, crushing me to his chest. I inhaled, breathing in his musky scent. As his hands fumbled behind my back, I kissed his skin sloppily, leaving my saliva on his body. Nuzzling down, I sucked his nipple, relishing the soft moan that escaped his mouth. I grazed that tender spot with my teeth, and he gasped. I loved the sound.

Fueled by my teasing, he tore away my bra and peeled it off my body. For a moment, he stared at my breasts as if memorizing them, then he set to them with his hands and lips and tongue.

And I made very loud, appreciative noises.

My fingers curled in his hair as he suckled. The gentle waves of heat between my legs spread up my torso and down my legs, a steady simmer gradually increasing to something hotter, wilder. I wanted to run my nails down his back, but I didn't know how he'd react. So I bit my lip and held onto his hair, trying to control the tension building in me.

He moved down, his tongue tickling the outline of my ribcage, then traveling over the concave form of my belly. By the top of my jeans, he paused.

'Want to take these off?'

'Only if you do the same.'

Sharing a smile, we quickly unsnapped, unzipped, and undressed. I stared at the shape of his erection, stretching the front of his boxer briefs. I wanted to touch it, kiss it, run my tongue around its thickness and lick his balls.

He rolled with me on the bed, our bodies on fire. I wound up on top, and as I straddled him I stroked his shaft, wanting desperately to remove his cotton underwear and really feel him in my hands. His breath ragged, he reached up and touched me between my legs, his fingers finding my clitoris on the first stroke. He pressed, and my jaw dropped as the simmer in my blood immediately kicked up to a roiling boil. He pressed again, and I threw my head back and cried out, bucking my hips as his fingers worked magic.

'I've got to taste you.'

He rolled with me again, this time with me landing on

my back, staring up into his face. He moved away, out of my line of sight; then again, I was seeing stars, thanks to his amazing touches. I felt my panties being removed, and then . . .

Oh . . .

The world stopped as my sex erupted with his kiss. The orgasm took me completely, my flesh singing, my body trembling in its wake. Paul moved away for a moment, but I didn't see anything but the insides of my eyelids. Feeling aftershocks of pleasure ripple through me, I finally understood why an orgasm was called a small death; at that moment, Lillith herself could have slaughtered me, and I would have died a happy exdemon.

Paul returned, tearing open a small package of foil. At first, I thought he brought me more chocolate, which would have been the perfect ending. Then I realized it was a condom.

Grinning, I snatched the contraceptive from his hand. 'Please. Let me.'

He did. Before I slid the condom on, I took his penis in my mouth. If I was going to put on the rain gear, at least I could make sure it was wet outside. I sucked him, Paul's groans encouraging me to take him deeper.

'Stop, I'm going to come.'

I licked him from tip to root. 'Please do.'

'No. I want to be inside you.'

Removing the condom from the package, I unrolled it over his swollen rod. Once it was in place, I mounted him. He throbbed inside me, filling me, sending new waves of pleasure through my body. As I rode him he fondled my breasts, cupping them as they bobbed in his hands. His breathing quickened and I moved faster, urging him with every thrust to come on, sweetie, come on.

He opened his mouth, said, 'Jes—'

I stopped the word with a kiss.

As if that were a signal, his back arched, lifting me up as he climaxed. He bucked, shuddering beneath me until he collapsed on the bed.

Gently moving off of him, I snuggled against his body. He wrapped his arms around me, a grin spreading over his face. Our sweat mingled, making small talk for us.

Eventually he said, 'I've got to get rid of this thing. Be right back.' He kissed my forehead, then got up, heading to the bathroom. My body immediately missed his warmth. I dove under the comforter, aching to be in Paul's arms again. My fingers touched the peridot hanging from its silver chain. Still cool.

If I wasn't safe with Paul, I'd never be safe.

He came back to me, free of the used condom. Burying himself in the heavy blanket, he held me close and stroked my hair.

'Paul?'

'Hmmm?'

'I believe you.'

'Good.' He kissed me softly, sleepily. 'I swear it's going to be okay.'

That I thought was a lie. But I wanted to believe in that lie, so I said nothing and held him until I fell asleep.

21

New York City

Lips pressed against my mouth, then a soft, deep voice called out, 'Jesse.'

'Mmmm.' I opened one eye and saw Paul smiling at me. Ah, yum. That sight alone was worth being nudged from my delicious dream of bathing in chocolate, with Paul washing my back. 'Heya, sweetie.' Actually, what came out was more like 'Hhhaswuh.'

His lips brushed mine once again in the lightest of kisses. 'Got to get to work. Couldn't leave without saying good-bye.'

See, right there, that proved he was a keeper. I wanted to tell him that, but all that came out was, ''Kay.' I really wasn't a morning person. Or at least my mouth wasn't.

'Go back to sleep, hon. I'll call you later.'

I closed my eye. ''Kay.'

'Jes?'

'Mmmm.'

'Don't go to work today.'

My eyes popped open, and I stared at his face, taking

in the thin, serious line of his mouth. 'Why?'

That line softened into a warm smile – but his eyes were hard as diamonds. 'You should go to a doctor, get that bruise checked. Just to make sure there's no real damage. And you should rest.' His fingers grazed my neck, trailing over my scarf, and I barely controlled a wince.

'I'm fine,' I said. 'It's just sore.'

'Humor me?'

'Really, I'm okay. Just sleepy. What time is it, anyway?'

'Eight-thirty.'

'Gah. How do you get up this early and still function?'

'Usually I don't go to sleep after two in the morning. So you'll take tonight off?'

'I really can't. I need the money.'

He frowned, his sea-green eyes clouding over. 'Fine. What's your schedule?'

'Late shift. Nine till closing at three.'

'Okay. Maybe I'll stop by tonight, see how you're doing.' He kissed me again, with a hint of tongue. 'And we've got to set a time for Sunday. Dinner and a movie.'

'And chocolate,' I murmured, closing my eyes.

'For you? Anything.'

I was half asleep when he called out, 'Hey, Jesse, there was a note under your door. It's your receipt. Looks like you're checking out today.'

My eyes popped open again. 'Oh. Oh, crap!'

By the door, Paul said, 'What's wrong?'

'I forgot to find an apartment! Crap, crap, crap!'

Paul's chuckle brought a flood of warmth in my belly. Ooh, waiter, I'd like some of that, please. 'Well, I know what you'll be doing this morning. See that – you really should take tonight off, go apartment hunting.'

'Crap!'

Paul walked back to the bed, sat by my side. 'You know what? It's a sign. No dancing for you today. Read the classifieds in the paper, get settled first.'

Feeling his fingers twining in my hair, my body both relaxed and coiled, wanting his hands to roam the planes of my naked body. I reached my arms up and stretched, arching my back. The comforter rolled down, exposing my breasts.

Paul's hand traced a path down my cheek, dancing over my neck, until the backs of his fingers brushed my left tit. A small shiver rippled through me. He rubbed his thumb and forefinger against my nipple.

Swallowing thickly, I said, 'Stay.'

'Can't.' He leaned down, darted his tongue against my nipple, and I moaned as heat pulsed between my legs. 'Got to go to work.'

One last suckle, then he left my breast and kissed my mouth. I grabbed his hair, feeling it curl in my fingers as my tongue rolled with his. Then he gently pulled away, untangling my hands from his hair.

'Why don't you extend your stay in the hotel for another day, take the pressure off?'

'Maybe. I'll figure something out.'

'I have no doubt.' His eyes, dark with passion and something else I couldn't place, locked onto mine. 'I really, really enjoyed last night.'

'This morning,' I corrected with a smile. 'Me too.'

'You've still got my number?'

'Yes.'

'Call me. Let me know what's happening with an apartment. And maybe we'll get some dinner tonight.'

'I have to work, remember?'

He winked. 'Only if you get an apartment first, remember? Call me.'

'I will.'

We kissed once more, then he was gone.

Going back to sleep was out of the question; I was way too anxious. How long did it take to find an apartment? Screw that; how did I go about *finding* one?

Fuck. Human beings really should come with instruction manuals.

I jumped out of bed and padded into the bathroom to take care of the necessities: toilet, teeth, and total body relaxation in the shower until my skin fell off. Wrinkly clean, I did the hair and cosmetics thing: Wisps of hair curled around my face with the rest pulled back into a sloppy bun; lots of eye makeup that made my orbs appear huge and appealing; pale gloss on my lips.

Examining the results in the mirror, I approved of the Helpless Waif look. Heck, if I were an apartment superintendent, I'd rent me an apartment based on my high-cuteness factor alone.

Next: Clothing. I slid on a matching satin bra-and-panties set. Fuck-me red. Helpless Waif Goes Trolling. After rummaging through my various garments, I selected a light blue denim shirt and faded jeans, shoving the rest into Caitlin's large, black suitcase. Then I dressed, leaving the top two buttons of the denim shirt open and the tails untucked. The tight jeans showed off my legs without advertising what lay between them. Socks, covered with tan suede boots.

Look out, New York: Jezebel's stepping out. Checking out. Whatever.

Last: Packing. A two-minute scan revealed that I already had all of my belongings in the suitcase, my Victoria's Secret shopping bag, and my purse. I considered snatching

247

the Bible in the desk drawer to peruse it as bathroom reading, but I decided against it. If I really wanted to read something funny, I'd scan the headlines in today's news.

Okay, done. I shrugged into my leather jacket – inhaling the intoxicating scent of new leather as I did so – and doffed my black fedora. Time to go find a new place to hang my hat. I tossed two twenties onto the desk by way of 'thank you' to the thoughtful maid who'd left me that sinfully delectable square of chocolate. Then I bid *adieu* to the king-sized bed and the magnificent shower. And the room said a brief *fare thee well* to a few towels, tubes of shampoo and conditioner, and four single-serve coffee packets. Mementoes.

Down in the lobby, I steered my way around a cluster of people and waited my turn to speak with one of the clerks by the front desk. And waited. Although this was a spit in the bucket compared with waiting a few short lifetimes in the administrative offices of Pandemonium, I still found myself tapping my foot and blowing out an impatient sigh. I had an apartment to find, a job to get to, and a lover to corral. I didn't have time to waste while some ancient thing with blue hair argued over her pay-per-view fee.

Look at that. Mortal in the Big City for only two days, and already I was an expert in the New York Minute. Must have been osmosis.

Finally it was my turn. Wheeling my suitcase behind me, I shuffled up to the desk and plopped down the overstuffed shopping bag. Mental note: Buy another bag for my work-clothes. The same dashing young thing from two days ago smiled the same perfunctory smile at me.

I put the check-out form on the desk and slid it forward.

'Heya, sweetie. I don't suppose you could extend my stay for another day?'

He took the paper and read it quickly. 'I'll check, Ms Harris, but we're pretty full. Friday nights are usually packed.' Clackety-clacking on his hidden keyboard, he squinted at an equally hidden computer screen. 'You mind a smoking room?'

After four millennia of Hell, smoking was second nature to me. 'Whatever you've got is fine with me. A little carcinogen never killed anyone overnight.'

A quick flutter of a grin, then back to the tight-lipped impassive look. More tapping, both from his fingers and my foot.

'Okay, Ms Harris, I think I can squeeze you in for tonight. Three hundred seventy-nine for tonight.'

'Maybe I'm crazy, but I think your rates multiplied faster than horny rabbits.'

That earned me a chuckle. 'Weekend rates are more expensive.'

'I'm just glad you've got a room,' I said with a relieved grin. 'I packed up just in case, but I was still hoping.'

'Looks like today's your lucky day. Credit card, please.'

Feeling the blood drain from my face, I pasted my grin tighter. 'Can't you just add it onto what you already have?'

'It doesn't work like that, I'm afraid. I have to run everything through again.'

'Seems awfully inefficient, doesn't it?'

He shrugged, an apologetic smile on his lips. 'I don't make the rules, Ms Harris. Would you like me to book you the room, or not?'

With a sigh, I dug through my purse and removed the wallet. Hoping my luck would continue, I offered the clerk one of Caitlin's three credit cards. He took it and did more computer magic. After a few heartbeats, he frowned. Some clacking sounds, then a deeper frown.

'Ms Harris, may I see some photo identification?'

Uh-oh. I pulled out Caitlin's State ID and slid it over the desk.

He picked it up, scrutinized it, then stared at my face. Then back to the photo on the identification card. Pursing his lips, he handed the ID back to me. 'Well, this is a bit tricky, I'm afraid. Your credit card has been reported as stolen.'

Crap on toast.

Okay, Jezebel. What would a wronged New Yorker do?

Spluttering from the indignity, I said, 'That's ridiculous! Who reported that?'

'According to the creditor, *you* did.'

'I never did anything of the sort!'

'I'm sorry, Ms Harris. You should contact your creditor and get this straightened out. But I'm afraid I can't help you.'

'Fine,' I said with an exaggerated sigh. 'Can I have my card back, please?'

'Er, I'm afraid I have to confiscate it.'

Sniffing my disapproval, I wheeled my suitcase away from the counter and paused near the lobby door to replace the State ID in my wallet. Granted, I had enough cash to pay for the room tonight, but after what just happened, I couldn't stay here. Maybe I was a former creature of Lust, but I still had my pride.

Okay, this confirmed that Caitlin had cancelled her cards as well as closed her bank account.

Shit. I hated getting caught.

Look at the bright side, my little voice suggested. *At least you got caught by the mortals. Imagine what would happen if it had been creatures of the Pit who'd found you out?*

Yeah, that made me feel loads better. I was just completely broke, except for the eight hundred dollars I'd scored from two nights at Belles. I peeked in my wallet and did a quick count. There was more in there than I'd thought: Just shy of a thousand dollars.

Hmm. Okay, that should be enough to get some sort of an apartment, shouldn't it?

Now, how did I go about doing that? I tapped my chin. Paul had said something about reading the classifieds in the paper. So maybe there would be a section that advertised apartments for rent.

The clock on the wall said it was a quarter to ten. Surely I'd be able to find an apartment before noon. Right?

I stumbled out of a greasy spoon diner, barely able to keep my breakfast down. The eggs had been fabulous, the sausage a little frightening (and coming from a former demon, that's saying something), the toast sodden with butter. The coffee had been a sad, sad thing, but it wound up perking me up, more so than the tiny squeeze of orange juice in a glass about as tall as my pinky. The food had been marvelous, both in scent and in taste.

The thing that was making my stomach lurch was my scan of the real estate section from today's *New York Times*. Apparently, a thousand dollars wouldn't get me a closet to put my shoes.

Bless me six ways to Salvation, how the fuck did mortals afford to live in New York City?

Mental note: Acquire a sugar daddy.

I walked, I thought. If I worked my ass (and bra) off at Belles, I could score a lot of money. Especially if I started hooking. There was a couch in the dressing room. Screw that – there was a fucking suite in the VIP room, complete with shower and a whirlpool bath. I could slum at the club for a few days, save my money, squirrel everything away.

All I had to do was stay alive and off of the Evil radar for a few more days. Would Lillith return to Belles? Goth Girl had thwoked Jemma pretty good with that spiffy boot of hers; getting forced out of a human body usually laid up a demon for the better part of a month. And Lillith was proud enough to keep her information to herself; she wouldn't want to share her prize with any of the Underworld.

You're being stupid, my small voice scolded. *Lillith made you. Daun made you. You have to run.*

A lump the size of a kitten lodged in my throat. Even with my survival sense driving itself into a frenzy, I knew I wasn't going to run. I didn't want to leave Paul.

He's just one man, the voice whispered. *You were with him for just one night. Leave him. Flee before Hell returns.*

In my daze, I didn't know where I was heading. People and streets faded into a background color of sludge, city noise nothing more than a background hum, city smells blended into a sour haze of sweat and desperation.

You're so reluctant to leave Paul, my small voice said, *so call him. Ask him for help. Have him find you a place to hole up. Ask to stay with him.*

No. Definitely not. I didn't want him to think of me as weak.

As I crossed the street, my voice snorted. *Since when do you care about what mortals think of you, Jezebel?*

Since I first saw him at South Station. Since he gave me his number and offered his help. Since he opened his heart to me about his fiancée. Since he listened to me as I cried and held me when I shook. Since I felt him deep inside of me. Since I thought I was falling in love with him.

Oh, bullshit. You're in love with the idea of being in love. You're too new at being a human to try to understand the emotions raging inside of you.

Maybe. But I'm not calling him to cry about not having a place to live.

Fine, the voice said in a huff. *Don't use the one resource you have. Be that stupid.*

I'm not stupid.

No? You going to run?

My fingers flew to the shieldstone. No.

See that? You are *stupid,* my voice told me. *You want to get caught.*

No. I want to be with Paul.

Oh please, the voice said, rolling its mental eyes. *Why? Because he's the first mortal to fuck you raw while you're playing at being human?*

As I considered the voice's words, I paused beside a foul-smelling alley sandwiched between two storefronts.

You think you gave away your heart when you spread your legs?

It's not like that. He's different. I want to be with him.

The small voice broke into peals of laughter. *I don't believe it. You, a Seducer, allowing yourself to be seduced by a mortal. You really* do *have a death wish.*

'Hey,' someone called, 'rich girl.'

Hearing the physical voice yanked me out of my silent conversation with myself. I turned to face the alley, where a pile of rags addressed me. 'Yeah, thought it was you. Still want me calling you a bitch?'

I smiled at the diseased human. Even though looking at him festering beneath his clothing was enough to make

253

me want to shower for a month, he'd successfully shut up my small voice. Blessed conscience, or whatever it was. If all mortals had such voices in their heads, it was no wonder that humans as a race were so completely fucked up.

'Heya, sweetie. How's it going?'

The beggar shrugged, sending piles of rotting clothes upward. 'No worries. You so generous yesterday, my thirst is all quenched.' He motioned to a mostly empty holder of beer bottles. At the bottom of his mound of rags, empty bottles glittered in the late morning sun.

'As long as it's not milk.'

'Hate that shit.'

'I hear that.'

'You gots any more generosity in you, rich girl?'

I held out my hands. 'Wish I did. Just got kicked out today. Got to find me a place to live.'

'Sucks to be on the street, rich girl. Share a drink with me?'

I took a few steps into the alley. My nostrils pinched as the stench of putrefying garbage washed over me. Grimacing, I stepped closer. The man offered me an unopened brown glass bottle. Eyes watering from the clashing odors of filth and pestilence, I said, 'You sure?'

'Yeah man. Go ahead, share a drink with me.'

'Thanks.' I twisted off the cap, we clinked bottles, and I took a sip. Warm beer frothed in my mouth, and I swallowed it down before my gorge could suggest otherwise. Almost as nauseating as milk.

'Hell of a life, isn't it?'

I chuckled. 'Yeah.'

'See you still gots that pretty necklace, rich girl.'

'Yeah.' My throat dried up, so I took another sip of the nasty beer.

'You should sell that, get some money.'

'Can't. It's precious.'

'Yeah, I sees that. Hey, that guy there knows you?'

I turned, wondering if Paul had been following me. Blinding pain flared at the back of my head; something wet soaked my hair as I crumpled to the ground, falling over my shopping bag. My head throbbed in time to colors shooting before my eyes. Too stunned to move, I lay prone, surrounded by rotting boxes and cans of refuse.

Grime-covered hands grabbed at my neck. My chain pulled taut, snapped. My shoulder burned as my purse was brutally ripped away. The ground shifted as my shopping bag was pulled out from beneath me.

I tried to stand, but white stars blinded me, robbed me of my strength.

'This for you, rich girl.'

A twenty-dollar bill fluttered to the ground by my face, followed by an empty beer bottle.

The beggar chortled as he walked out of the alley. I heard the squeak of the suitcase's wheels over the garbage-riddled concrete. When I could finally move without the world shifting with me, the man was long, long gone.

Along with my money, my suitcase, and my Shield Against Evil.

22

Belles

'My God. Jezebel, what happened?'

I looked up from the doorway of Belles to see Roman hovering over me. At least, I thought it was Roman; he was kind of blurry. 'Been a bad, bad morning.' My voice cracked as I spoke.

He hunkered down. 'You smell pretty bad, love. You drunk?'

'No, but the guy who hit me with his beer bottle was.'

'Shit.' He glanced at my head, which I cradled with one hand. 'You should go to a doctor, get that checked.'

'Can't. Guy stole my money. Can't pay for a doctor.' I blew out a sigh, and that made my head pound worse. 'Guy stole everything. Didn't know where else to go.'

'Why didn't you call the police?'

Because the last thing I wanted was for human authorities to sniff into my identity and find the real Caitlin Harris in Salem, Massachusetts. 'All I really want is a shower. Could I use the one in the VIP room?'

'Love, why don't you go home, get cleaned up?'

My lip trembled before I spoke. 'I sort of don't have anywhere to go. I'm sort of screwed at the moment.'

'Hmmm. Well, we can't have you loitering in front of the building. Bad for business and all that.'

'You're not open yet.'

'Figure of speech. Come on in, love. Let's get you cleaned up.'

He helped me to my feet. I barely swooned. Points for me.

Frowning at me, Roman said, 'Glad I decided to come here this morning, get some paperwork done. You'd have been hanging outside for a good couple hours otherwise.'

I whispered through clenched teeth, 'Guess this is my lucky day.'

He unlocked the front glass doors, then escorted me inside. I leaned on him more than I would have liked. Me strong former demonic entity. Me no need puny flesh puppet for support. Yeah, right. My arm looped around his shoulder, he guided me upstairs to the VIP room. I must have looked like shit and smelled worse, because Roman didn't even cop a feel. For Dickhead to be a gentleman, I knew I was in trouble.

No, *trouble* didn't begin to describe what I was in. Shit Creek without a paddle, maybe.

He sat me down on a fake leather chair. 'Be right back, love. I'm just going to get the water going in the shower.'

I dropped my head between my knees and told myself not to be sick. I had a feeling I wasn't going to have a good meal in the immediate future, so I didn't want to vomit up my lovely breakfast. Well, lovely except for the sausage. That had looked like (and smelled like) humans after a go in the Pridelands, chopped into itsy-bitsy pieces and hung out to dry. Ropes of intestines, linked like sausages, roasting over the Lake of Fire . . .

My stomach lurched. Down, boy.

'Here we go. Some Tylenol, super strength.' Roman dropped three capsules into one of my hands, then shoved a glass into the other. 'Come on, love. Down the hatch.'

I popped the medicine into my mouth and washed it down with tepid water.

'Slowly, love. No ralphing on the furniture, please.'

'You're all heart,' I whispered.

'Now, now. No insulting your guardian angel. Come on, Jezebel. Let's get you clean.'

Roman helped me up, then walked me into a bathroom fit for the sultan of a small country. Marble floors and counters, mirrors everywhere there wasn't marble. He steered me past an enormous whirlpool bathtub, coming to a halt by a large stall shower. The water poured out, steaming up the glass door.

'There's towels and a bathrobe for you here,' he said, motioning to a small pile on the toilet cover. 'The robe'll be falling off you, but I don't have your size here. Shampoo and all that stuff's in the shower. You need any help getting undressed or cleaned up?'

Swaying on my feet, I shook my head. That made me dizzy, so I reached out, clutching for anything to keep me steady. Roman's shoulder did the trick nicely.

'You sure you don't need help?'

I thought I detected a hint of lust in his voice. I was probably misreading his signals; getting knocked upside the head could do that to a person. Still, I just wanted some quiet time in a long, hot shower. 'I'm good. Thanks.'

'Right,' he said. 'So I'll be just outside, listening for the heavy thump of your body hitting the floor.' He left me alone. Imagine that: Dickhead really was being a gentleman. The world was going to Hell, no doubt about it.

I stripped and stepped into the steaming spray. I gingerly washed my hair, going slowly over the tender knot where the beggar had clocked me. My head hurt like a bastard, and for all I knew, the shampoo was making the pain worse. But I'd rather have extended agony and clean hair than a throbbing head reeking of stale beer and garbage.

Then I lathered up and scrubbed every inch of skin. No matter how hard I rubbed, I still thought I stank of rotting food. I scoured my flesh, feeling the beggar tear away my shieldstone, hearing his taunting call. *This for you, rich girl.*

Disease infested scum-sucker. If I'd been thinking clearly, I'd have fried him where he stood. I'd have ripped his tongue from his mouth and fed it to him. I'd have torn off his dick and plugged up his ass. I'd . . .

Blinking in the hot stream of water, I realized the scope of the theft. The shieldstone was gone. I could use my power any time I wanted.

And then cancel the witch's spell. Which meant Hell would be able to hone in on my presence.

Crap.

I slammed my fist against the tiled wall. And that made my hand hurt worse than my head.

Double crap.

One thing about showers: They wash away your tears.

By the time I emerged from the shower, the capsules that Roman had given me started kicking in. My head no longer throbbed like it was going to explode. Instead, my brain felt swathed in cotton. Or maybe cotton candy. A definite

259

improvement. They should bottle that stuff and sell it. Oh wait. They already did. Heh.

I frowned, pressing a hand against my forehead. My thoughts felt loose in my head, drifty. Just the medicine working, I told myself. Let it work. Drifting wasn't so bad.

After I toweled dry, I wrapped myself up in the huge robe. Stealing a glance at myself in the foggy mirrors, I thought I looked abysmally cute. All I needed was over-sized bunny slippers to make it complete. Yuck. I stuck out my tongue. My reflection did the same. How unoriginal. I ran my tongue slowly over my lips, feeling the wet pressure against the sensitive flesh, watching my image mimic the movement.

I lifted my hand up and touched my saliva-slick lips, remembering His kiss. Nothing passionate. Nothing seductive. Just a kiss, a sad farewell. *If only you were right.*

Right about what? It was so hard to think.

My hand slid away from my face, down to my chest, where the peridot stone had hung. First I drummed my fingers over my breastbone, enjoying the gentle *tap tap tap* sound they made. Then I brushed my fingertips along my collarbone, tracing the outline, entranced by how my flesh softened my frame. Mortals had such beautiful forms. Bones were so hard, yet the body had so much padding, so many curves and crevices. Like secret passageways of the skin. I wondered if my birthmarks, Caitlin's birthmarks, were really a code that showed travelers where those hidden doorways were.

Someone knocked at the door. 'Love, how're you doing in there?'

'Fine,' I called, my voice sounding strange, tinny. Maybe my ears were clogged from the shower. 'Clean. Less headachy.'

The door swung open, revealing Roman in his mafia-wannabe outfit of black shirt and black slacks and flashy pinky rings. 'Look at you, pretty as a picture.'

'You really should knock,' I said, fascinated by how his rings caught the bathroom's light.

'Please, love. Look at where you work. You show more flesh to our customers. Even your doctor doesn't see you so naked. Speaking of which, you sure you don't want to go to the hospital?'

'I'm good. Thanks.'

'That's what I thought. Love, come into the main suite here. Let's discuss your options.'

Options. I wondered what that meant. Then I realized I didn't care. I was floating, drifting. That was all that mattered.

As I padded into the large living room, I gnawed my lip, worrying it between my teeth. My mouth felt swollen, my tongue too large and too fuzzy, as if it were wearing a sweater. A wool sweater. Did that make me a woolhead?

'Looks like the medicine's doing the trick.' Roman pressed a glass into my hand, ushered me to one of the sofas. 'Good, good. No throbbing head for my Jezebel. Well, not that kind, anyway.'

I sank onto the cushioned seat and sniffed my drink. My eyes immediately watered. 'What is this?'

'Scotch. Thought you could use one. The good stuff, too. Eighteen year.'

Usually, I preferred a little Scotch wearing a kilt and no knickers. But I'd take the liquid variety today. I knocked it back, relishing the way it scorched my throat and immediately set fire to my belly. Sniffing deeply, I handed the empty glass to Roman. Bless me, the stuff was strong. My head was spinning. Whoo. Whoever invented alcohol

261

should be one of Hell's elite; this stuff was potent. Such clever beings, mortals were. No wonder I wanted to be one. Was one.

What was I?

'So.' Roman sat heavily next to me, his own drink between his thick-knuckled fingers. 'You said the asshole what did this to you, he stole everything. Meaning what, exactly?'

I ran my hand through the tangles of my black curls as I tried to focus on his words. 'Meaning my purse, my suitcase, my jewelry. Everything.' My hair was smooth, silky in my fingers. Bless me, how could there be so much texture in strands of hair?

'Suitcase?'

Something about the tone in his voice pulled my attention away from my hair. Roman's eyes gleamed, and for a moment I thought they looked red. He asked, 'You going somewhere?'

'I was looking for an apartment,' I said, trying to shrug, except my shoulders didn't want to move.

'With a suitcase in tow?'

I hid a yawn behind my left hand, my right one still playing with my hair. 'I travel light.' My tongue blended the double L sound, turning it into one word: *travelight*. 'Was looking for something in move-in condition.'

Roman pursed his lips, thinking. 'Ah. And your previous place of residence?'

My fingers untangled themselves from my locks and trailed over the back of the leather sofa. *Ummm*, the material was deliciously soft. Everything was soft. I snuggled in my seat, drawing my robe close around my body. It was like being swathed in a cloud. Yummy. Maybe the angels had the right idea, hanging out in Heaven with all the fluffy clouds.

Roman's voice, right by my ear: 'Jezebel?'

I started, blinking. Had I fallen asleep? 'Sorry, what?'

My right sleeve was bunched up by my elbow. Roman's hand was stroking my forearm, his fingers pressing into my flesh. Ooh, that felt good. He asked me, 'What happened to the place you were staying?'

Being comfortable must have loosened my tongue, because I said, 'The hotel had this thing. You know, about credit cards that don't work. They didn't like it.'

'Stolen?' This with an amused grin.

'More like borrowed.'

He leaned back in the seat, looking at me, his hand still stroking my bare arm. His dark eyes darted back and forth, as if he could read something on my face. 'And the robber? You know him?'

'No,' I said, yawning again. Between the shower, the medicine, and the Scotch, my body was all warm and fuzzy. Sleepy. Nice. 'Saw him yesterday, gave him some cash.'

'Guess that'll teach you. No good deed goes unpunished.'

It didn't seem like he asked me a question, so I didn't bother answering. I was too busy stroking the soft, soft couch again. It made the pads of my fingers tingle.

'So you need money and a place to live.'

'Hmmm? Oh. Right.' His words sounded thick, like syrup. If I closed my eyes, maybe I could hear him better.

'Jezebel, love? You been giving any thought to what we discussed yesterday?'

'Mmmm. Yeah.'

'And? Do you think it's a good idea?'

Agreeing with him felt like the right thing to do. My mouth didn't want to form the words, so all I said was, 'Uh-huh.'

'That's my girl. I'll make sure that customers with special needs come see you. VIP room only.'

''Kay.'

Hands pressed down on my shoulders, kneading. I leaned my head back, enjoying the way my muscles responded. Those hands slid down inside my robe and fondled my breasts. It felt nice.

'Now that you're relaxed,' Roman breathed on my neck, 'let's have us a little fun.'

'Mmmm.'

'You're mine.'

His fingers rubbed my nipples, pinching them. It sort of hurt, but I didn't really mind. The pain was far away. My body was far away, and I was floating . . .

'Now this isn't right,' a deep voice said. Hands cradled my face, lifted my chin. 'Babes, can you hear me?'

Funny. That sounded like Daun.

'Doping you up is cheating. And after you got your head bashed, too. This guy's such a fucking loser, I can't wait until he burns. Come on, babes. Time to wake up.'

I tried to open my mouth, but it didn't work.

Daun's voice let out a sigh. 'Well, I owe you one anyway for accidentally setting the queen bitch on your trail. Glad she's waylaid for a bit. Man, is she pissed off at you. Okay, let's see, what've we got here?'

My body tingled, and I let out a contented sigh.

'Hmmm. Valium mixed with some booze, all muffling a nasty concussion. Could have been much worse.'

I wanted to ask Daun what he was talking about, but that would have required way too much effort. So I just floated.

'Heads up, babes. This is going to hurt.'

A finger brushed my forehead . . . and I gasped as heat

seared my body, scorching every muscle. I bucked beneath that touch, my gasp stretching into hitched, sharp inhalations. Every nerve ending flared, and I shrieked with all the strength in me. Thrashing, my limbs flailed in all directions, but my head remained still, melded to that fingertip touching my forehead. Sweat and seared meat stung my nostrils, and I screeched all the harder knowing that the foul stench emanated from my jittering body. The flames shooting through me burst into wildfire, cooking my heart. My tongue blackened; my eyeballs popped. Just as the agony was too much to bear, it abruptly ended.

I was alive. I – oh, shit! OW! *OW, OW,* OW*!!!*

I sat up and leaned over, cradling my head in my hands as steam wafted from my flesh. Oh, fuck me raw, that hurt! Between my hands, my head throbbed so hard that I debated the possibility of decapitation.

A deep voice chuckled. 'Clean and sober, I see.'

My cooling body shivered, bathed in a sheen of perspiration. Teeth chattering, I glanced over at Roman, who looked smug and as content as a mosquito at a nude beach. A red gleam danced in his dark eyes. Faintly, beneath my own sweat and the lingering odor of frying burgers, I smelled rotten eggs. Brimstone.

'Heya, Daun,' I said, my voice sounding pitifully weak. But even that bare whisper was enough to send fresh waves of pain through my head. Biting my lip, I groaned as I buried my head between my knees.

'Sorry I couldn't do anything about the concussion,' Daun said. 'I burned away the drugs, but I can't make your body heal.'

'Drugs?' Blinking, I tried to make sense out of what he said. 'What're you talking about?' Every word I spoke made colors creep along the edge of my vision.

'Your boss is a real peach, babes. He likes his ladies dopey. He was going to rape you thoroughly, and you wouldn't have remembered a blessed thing.'

'Dickhead,' I muttered, closing my eyes. Better. The colors went away if I stared at the insides of my eyelids. 'If he would've just made a pass, I probably would've let him fuck me.'

'Nah, that's not his style. He does all the overtures, acts like he's the real gigolo. Bangs whoever he can, when they're willing. But the ones he really wants to possess, he drugs. He gets off on it.' Daun paused. 'Want me to kill him for you? Get his soul down to Hell ASAP?'

Aw. For a demon, Duan was downright considerate. 'Thanks, sweetie. But no.'

'You sure, babes?'

'I may be mortal,' I said slowly, for the benefit of my aching head, 'but I still know about how much paperwork's involved when a demon kills a human without preapproval.'

'Things are changing, babes.' Something about Daun's voice made me look up, momentarily ignoring my pounding skull. Behind Roman's eyes, Daun looked . . . nervous. 'He's not a big believer in the old rules. He blasted them right off of Abaddon.'

You are too soft.

I swallowed thickly, a bitter taste coating my throat. 'So now it's okay to just go and slaughter humans?'

Roman's eyes narrowed. 'You left the fold, babes. You want to come back, I'm happy to escort you to Abaddon, get your marching orders from Him directly. But until that time, you're mortal. And demons don't talk shop with flesh puppets.' A grin bloomed on his face, and he leaned over until we were eye to eye. 'A demon influences flesh puppets. And an incubus ... well. You know what an incubus does.'

His hand brushed up my inner thigh, and I gasped from the sudden touch. His fingers curled, lightly drumming just beneath my groin.

Commanding my heartbeat to slow down, I said, 'Look at that. I'm naked. What happened to my robe?'

One finger slid over my sex, sending ripples of heat through my body. Daun said, 'Burned away when I cleaned your system of the drugs. Poof, all gone. Occupational hazard.'

My breathing quickened as Roman's finger probed between my legs. 'Sweetie, this isn't a good idea.'

'No? Why not?'

'I think I'm in love with a human.'

Inside me, the finger paused. 'Well, well,' Daun said, staring at my face. 'The fellow with the big shoulders, right?'

'Right.'

Roman shimmered, and when I blinked, Paul leaned over me, his sea-green eyes wicked, his kissable mouth set in a smirk. 'Better?'

Visually? No comparison. But . . . 'Daun, don't.'

'Why not, babes?' The finger crooked inside of me, nearly blinding me with pleasure. 'A little bit of sex'll do you good. Help you take your mind away from your poor little head and your various worries.'

He stopped talking to suck my nipple. Moaning, I tangled my hands in his hair, my hips moving beneath his as his tongue and lips worked magic. Yes, my mind going on a brief vacation sounded like just what the doctor ordered. Forcing myself to think clearly, I stammered, 'What do you get out of it?'

He broke suction with a parting kiss and looked into my eyes. 'I get to see if I can make you call my name.'

My hands still wrapped in his hair, I yanked his head down to mine and kissed him hard.

Three orgasms later, the only name I'd called was Paul's. Daunuan said he didn't mind. He liked a challenge.

23

Belles (II)

'Here,' Faith said, handing me a bundle of clothing. 'Try these on.'

Blinking over the variety and the amount of garments, I said, 'You sure?'

'See, now I know you got hit on the head. I know you're not questioning whether I'm this generous in real life. Right?'

'You bet. Thanks.' I started pawing through the material, separating the street clothes from the intimate stage costumes. Silks and satins mixed with flannel and denim. Something for every occasion.

'You're actually doing me a favor,' Faith said, returning to applying her makeup. 'I had most of that shit cluttering my closet for years, not getting touched. My closet appreciates the breathing room.'

I pressed a bright green long-sleeved shirt against my torso: V-necked and form-fitting. Yummy. 'This is really, really terrific. I'll give it all back after I get settled and back on my feet.'

Faith rolled her eyes. 'You really got yourself some brain damage there. No backsies, chickie. Got it?'

'You're the best,' I said, blowing her a kiss.

'Girl, you're still dumb for not going to the hospital, getting yourself checked out.' Candy eyed me suspiciously, then continued pumping up her lashes with mascara. 'I don't like the docs any more than you do, but someone starts fucking with my head in the nonpsychological sense, I'd get myself checked.'

'No,' I said, rummaging through the pile of clothing and selecting a white sequined bra. 'I'm not spending the money on some intern sticking a light in my eye and telling me I bumped my head. And by the way, thanks for the loan.'

'Don't mention it. You know, between Jemma getting all psycho on your ass yesterday and now you getting mugged in broad daylight today, I think you got yourself some shit-ass luck.'

I found the matching G-string and set it and the stage bra aside. Faith and I were going to try out the mirror-image thing. We both thought that there was major tippage potential; guys liked the idea of a girl-girl scene, and we liked the idea of guys being dazzled by our moves. 'Yeah, I read something like that in my horoscope this morning.'

Candy grinned. 'At least you still got yourself a sense of humor.'

I rubbed the back of my head, feeling the swell of the knot where the mugger had slammed me. 'I think some of it leaked out.'

'Tell us true,' Circe said as she jiggled into her scarlet stage bra. 'Did Dickhead really treat you like a gentleman?'

'Yep.' After Daun possessed the fuck out of him. Literally.

Circe shook her head. 'I can't believe it. Our Dickhead, not taking advantage of you.'

'Our Dickhead calling us, asking if we could help you out with clothing,' added Faith. She shrugged. 'Maybe he got himself some religion. It *is* the Christian thing to do.'

'Oh yeah,' Candy chortled. 'That's our man. Father Dickhead, strip club owner and poster boy for charitable causes.'

The ladies shared a chuckle. Me, I smiled tightly as I held up another outfit, thinking about how Father Dickhead would burn, baby, burn. The major reason why I'd stopped Daun from killing Roman after our fabulous afternoon of sex and sweat was because I knew what lay in store for the man after he died. Just thinking about his shrieks riding the wind over the Lake of Fire brought a smile to my lips.

Yes, some things were definitely worth the wait.

The short-term good news was that I didn't have to worry about Roman getting any more ideas over what he could do to me. Daun, still feeling responsible for leading Lillith to me in the first place, said he'd make it up to me by stowing away in Roman for the time being. Close to the surface, he promised – just enough to keep the man off his game and distracted, but not enough to make his eyes flash red. My fingers drummed against my collar-bone, still missing the shieldstone. Without my protection against all things Evil, having Daun at my back (and watching my backside) was a relief.

Not enough for me to relax completely, though. I didn't think I'd completely relax until I was long gone from New York City. The new plan was for me to work all shifts tonight, score as much cash as I could, then head directly to Penn Station after my shift and catch the first possible train to Anytown, USA. Daun thought I was being stupid.

'You should pack up and go now, babes,' he said after two hours of rampant animal sex that would've made bunnies look like prudes. 'Don't wait until tonight. If this is about money, I'll have Roman here give you whatever you need. Say the word, I'll have him sign over his house to you. Screw that, I'll have him buy you a new one.'

'Thanks, sweetie. I really do appreciate the thought. But no.'

'Why?'

I shrugged, trying to understand and explain the nagging feeling that had eaten at me when I'd wanted to take money from Caitlin's bank account. 'Because it's not right. If Roman wants to give it to me, that's one thing. But to force him to do it against his will, that's just . . .'

'Evil?'

'Spot on.'

'Babes,' he purred, nuzzling my ear, 'I *am* Evil. It's what I do.'

Sighing, I snuggled deeper into his arms. 'I know. But it's not what *I* do anymore. I've . . . changed.'

'You know, I figured that out once you hightailed it onto the mortal coil.'

I frowned, even with Daun's fingers dusting my nipples. 'It's more than my form. It's . . . bless me, Daun, I think I have a conscience.'

'Fuck. Is it contagious?'

I shrugged away from his touch, all sorts of pissed off that he wasn't taking me seriously. 'Don't you see? I don't know what I am anymore. Not a demon, but not really human. Mortal, but without a soul. What does that make me?'

'Incredibly conflicted.'

'Thanks.'

'If I may suggest, babes, that you play the soul-searching game after you've relocated? You don't have the luxury of self-discovery at the moment.' He traced patterns on my stomach, and I closed my eyes, enjoying his touch. 'Maybe because you're a human, you're coming to grips with morals and ethics and bullshit like that. But I'm still a creature of Lust. And I smell the truth on you, babes. You've got it bad for your mortal man. You don't want to leave without seeing him again.'

'Busted.' I was banking on Paul keeping his word and stopping by tonight before Belles closed. The slip of paper with Paul's number was inside my wallet, which did me a fat lot of good now that the beggar had it (along with all my other possessions). If Paul didn't show up tonight, I'd never see him again.

My stomach fluttered from the thought. Of course he'd show. He said he would. My Cabin Boy/Gardener/White Knight had to keep his word. It's what mortals like him did.

'Look at that,' Daun said, laughing softly. 'Jezebel's in love. Poor babes.'

'If this is love,' I said, burying my face in my hands, 'it sucks. I don't want to think about him, about seeing him, about fucking him. But I can't help it. It's like he's burrowed into my brain and is setting up shop.'

'Sounds painful.'

I turned to face Daun, who still wore Paul's form. 'He's stolen part of my heart. I don't know how he did it, or when. And what stinks to high Heaven is that I don't want it back. I want him to keep my heart, to wear it next to his.'

'Jezebel the romantic.' His eyes flashed crimson – sunset over the ocean. 'You want to risk yourself even more than you are, all because you think you're in love, fine. You still belong to Lust, no matter what body you're wearing. I can't blame you for being led by your feelings.' He placed his hand on the center of my chest, pressing against me as if he could touch my heart.

'Thanks.' Maybe it was the warmth of his hand; maybe it was his words. But for whatever the reason, something inside me loosened, relaxed.

'Tell you what,' Daun said. 'You won't accept anything from Roman here, how about I at least have him call your dancer friends? Play the Good Samaritan. Maybe they'll help out in a pinch. Money, clothes, that sort of thing.'

So he had. Faith had come to work with two duffel bags stuffed to bursting. Circe donated an old purse, two pairs of shoes (one for work, one for play), and a trench coat. Candy brought cold, hard cash – nothing too extravagant, but enough to start my emergency nest egg. Daun as Roman left a message for Momma, but she hadn't shown up for work yet. Leave it to me to get assaulted and robbed the one day that the house mom was unavailable.

'Earth to Jezebel.' Faith snapped her fingers in front of my face. 'You having a whatchacallit, an episode?'

'Huh? Oh, sorry. No. Just lost in thought.'

'Well, get un-lost. If we're going to do the mirror image thing, I want to rehearse a bit.'

I put on the heels Circe had given me and wrapped the ties around my ankles. Suddenly I was five inches taller. 'Holy crap, I'd forgotten what it's like to be above armpit level.' Taking a few practice steps, I found I could balance better when I exaggerated the sway of my hips.

274

Spinning to face Faith, I did a shimmy-bop and planted my hands on my waist. 'Okay, sweetie. Let's dance.'

Heavy synth pulsing, drums thumping a beat through my body, I gripped the stripper pole and arched backward. Opposite me, hands crossed over mine, Faith shadowed my movements. Together we spun, our hair fanning out in a drastic pattern of platinum and obsidian, a follicle yin and yang. Sliding down to the floor, Faith and I rolled onto our bellies and crawled to the edge of the stage like matching jungle cats, radiating heat.

Purr, baby.

The customers dug the whole mirror image thing, based on the beads of saliva leaking from their mouths as Faith and I danced. Most excellent. On my side, I kicked my leg straight up and held the pose, running my hand up my curves, teasing its way over the white satin of my G-string, up my bare stomach, over my breast, up to my hair. Lowering my leg, I pushed my body up until I sat up on my knees, riding the music as my hands lifted my curls away from my face. Feeling eyes lock onto my crotch and my tits, I smiled broadly, showing the men how much I appreciated their attention.

I pivoted to face Faith. We held our hands up and out, pressing against each other as we lowered our arms. I swayed right; she swayed left. Back the other way. Wrapping our arms around each other, we arched backward, our boobs high and pert, our hair brushing the floor.

Ooh, the men, they like the girl-touch-girl scene. Green crashed over the tip-rail as customers waved their money.

Faith and I straightened until we were tit to tit. Swaying in the spotlights, we untangled our limbs and raised our arms high, our gazes fastened. Her eyes danced wilder than her body, and her mouth locked in a grin wide enough to swallow Thunder the Wonder Horse. I didn't know if it was from our performance or from the sound of money rustling in the air. Me? I was loving the whole thing.

We finished the set to deafening applause, Lyle's voice over the speakers demanding that the customers give it up for us. And they did – the money flowed like blood from an artery. Intoxicated from the cash and the sexual tension in the showroom, I gathered my clothes and the tips while mentally clapping my hands for joy.

Offstage, Faith and I giggled on our way back to the dressing room, where we'd squeeze into thin gowns and get ready to work the floor. 'Oh my God,' she said around her giddy laughter, 'I think we're rich!'

We bustled into the small room. By the vanity table, Lorelei wrinkled her nose at us. 'Holy shit, is that all your stage tips?'

'You bet,' Faith laughed. 'The guys loved us! I can't wait to get my ass back out there, get going in the VIP room.'

'Uh-uh,' Lorelei said. 'I already got me a date in the VIP room in five. I'll be there for at least an hour. Use the lounge.'

I sauntered over to the worn sofa and dumped my pile onto the cushion as Faith and Lorelei dickered over who got dibs on the VIP suite. Ooh, look at all the lovely dead presidents. Opening my purse, I stuffed wads of singles, fives, and tens inside. I'd count later. For now, I just wanted the money put away, and some clothing temporarily put on. After that smoking set, the crowd would be eager for my affection. And as long as the money beckoned, I'd be happy to oblige.

Because let's face it: This would have to be my last

foray into the land of the exotic dance. It was one thing to take a chance when I was protected by the shieldstone and still flighty from my transformation into a mortal. Now, with a couple of days of experience and lacking the peridot, I knew better. Hell would be sniffing out all such human temples of Lust. I was lucky in that only three entities knew my location, two of which were (sort of) on my side, and the third was licking its wounds.

So tonight would be the money shot. Tonight would be my blaze of glory as a Seducer before I walked away from that life completely.

Can you do it? my little voice asked. *Can you really turn your back on all of this?*

Sweetie, I told my pathetic conscience, it's not like I'm becoming a nun. I'll still have sex. But seduction-as-occupation would have to go.

It's who you are, the voice insisted.

Maybe, I admitted. But if I'm going to survive, I have to do what I must.

We all do what we must, the voice whispered. *Jezzie's finally growing up.*

My heart lodged in my throat, and my purse slipped from my numb fingers. *Meg?*

Hey, girl.

Oh fuck me. *All along, it's been you in my head?*

In my mind, I felt Meg shrug. *Sometimes. I had to keep tabs on you.*

I didn't know if I was relieved not to have a conscience after all, or if I was pissed off at Meg's invasion of my privacy. Bubbles of disappointment rolled in my stomach. Bless me . . . I couldn't possibly be upset that I didn't have a stupid voice helping me think things through, could I?

Someone parted the black curtain that walled off the

dressing room, but no one entered. 'Knock, knock. You girls decent in there?'

Faith and Lorelei exchanged a look before the redhead called out, 'Roman, since when you ever worry about whether we're decent? Your day's not complete unless you cop a feel.'

A warm chuckle from the other side of the curtain, then: 'I'm a whole new person. What do you say, love? Can I come in?'

Faith frowned. 'Shit, maybe Dickhead really did find religion. That's just not like him.'

'Maybe he got himself a good screwing,' Lorelei said, eyeing me.

I ignored her. *Meg? You still there?*

Nothing. Crap, crap, crap. A headache knocking between my eyes, I sighed as I tucked myself into the white sequined bra. 'Hang on a sec, Roman.'

'Take your time, love.'

Faith shook her head as she shrugged into her white gown. 'I'm telling you, he's found God.'

That made me chuckle.

'All right,' Faith said as she zipped up. 'We're covered. Come on in.'

The curtain parted, and Roman strode inside, beaming from ear to ear. 'I just had to tell you both that your act was hot. Good stuff, loves. Shame we lost Jemma, she's more your coloring, Faith. Now that would've been a fabulous mirror image.' He smiled and shook his head.

I wondered about the casual mention of Jemma. Was Daun trying to tell me something? Or was Roman really in charge, with the incubus staying below the radar?

'Yeah, and I hear some guys're really into snuff,' Faith

said with a frown. 'Me, dance with that psycho? I don't think so.'

Lorelei had the same reaction. 'You fired her ass, right?'

Roman spread his hands wide, helpless as a baby rattler. 'She's sick, girls. Once she's clean, I'm sure she'll be a real asset to the club.'

'Really fucking charitable,' Lorelei muttered.

'Told you,' Roman purred. 'I'm a new man. Anyway, good show. Lorelei, aren't you due in the VIP room?'

'I'm going,' she said, grabbing her purse and giving her dress one final tug. How her boobs stayed covered was anyone's guess. If I hadn't known better, I would've sworn there was a levitation spell on her cleavage.

Roman's gaze wandered over my body. 'You look good in white,' he said. 'Pure. I like that.'

Faith glanced at me. 'You coming out to do the tables?'

'Be right there,' I said, picking up a red gown. 'Just got to slip this on.'

'You go ahead,' Roman said to Faith, his eyes not leaving mine. 'I need a word with Jezebel anyway.'

Frowning deeply, Faith strolled out.

As soon as she left, Roman's eyes gleamed red. 'You've got to hurry up, babes. Your case is all over the Underworld. I heard Rosey and Berry going at it, gloating over who would be the one to bring you in. Rumor has it that He's getting ready to send the Hounds out on you.'

My eyes widened at the word. Hell Hounds. That was code for the Furies. My body went ice cold, and I sat down hard on the sofa.

'It's not too late,' Daun said, his voice as soft as a caress.

'Come back with me now. Maybe claim the Rapture took you, or some celestial bullshit like that. He'd buy it.'

Biting my lip, I shook my head. 'No. I won't go back to that. I can't.'

'Maybe He'll reassign you.'

'He won't. You know it. And it's not just that anymore.' Rubbing my arms didn't bring me any warmth. 'Knowing the truth behind everything ... I can't go back there, Daun. Not with Him in charge.'

'Why? Does knowing the truth really change things that much?'

'Yes!' I stood up and paced, my heels making angry clicks on the bare floor. 'It changes everything. Before, every creature had its place, its role. Its purpose. Now everything's all fucked up, and nothing makes sense. I don't know what to believe anymore.'

'*Believe?* What does belief have to do with anything? You're not some flesh puppet born on the mortal coil, in for a short trip before moving on to the next stop. You're a demon, no matter what form you're wearing. You know better.'

My voice a whisper, I said, 'Not anymore I don't.'

I felt him watching me. Turning to face him, I saw confusion in his red-rimmed eyes. 'What's the issue, babes? So some of the roles changed. New jobs, same company.'

'No, bless me, it's *not* the same company at all!' Hearing my words echoing, I realized that I'd been shouting. Clenching my teeth, I lowered my voice. 'It's not the same.'

'Maybe you weren't really paying attention during the Announcement,' Daun said. 'It *is* the same. And maybe *that's* what's got you all in a bunch.'

Glaring at him, I said, 'What're you—'

The look of surprise on his face killed my voice. Surprise turned to fear, and he shouted, 'Run, Jez! She's coming! She's coming for—'

His words stretched into a screech. Roman's body flew backward as if a truck had plowed into it. He crashed into the bathroom door and landed in a heap, his body jittering. The stink of rotten eggs made my eyes water as I cried his name.

Dashing to his side, I helped him up. He shook his head, wiped away spittle from his lips. 'Holy shit, what happened to me?'

Roman's voice, not Daun's.

Something had torn Daunuan out of Roman's body.

24

Belles (III)

'Jezebel? Love, you've gone pale. I'm the one that passed out. What's wrong with you?'

Dazed, I helped Roman to his feet. Very few entities were strong enough to pull a demon out of its host. Usually it required something that repelled the nefarious; holy water was a biggie, as was silver and iron. But that was all on the host's end of the equation – an exorcist used the repellent to banish the malefic presence.

For something to rip a demon from its host without such a tool, that required power. And lots of it.

My heart pounding, I started shoving my borrowed clothes into the two bags that Faith had given me. I had to leave. Now.

'Jezebel?'

I brushed Roman aside to grab the black trench coat and pull it on. No time to change. My throat constricted, and for a moment I couldn't breathe. Don't panic, I told myself. If you panic, you die. Just pick up your bags, like that, sling the purse over your shoulder, like that, and leave.

Two steps to the curtain, Roman's hand on my shoulder stopped me. 'Love, where're you going? And in such a hurry?'

Shrugging out of his grasp, I said, 'No time. Got to go.'

Suddenly Paul was in the doorway, blocking my path. For a moment I thought it was Daun wearing his form again, and I nearly hugged him in relief. But there was nothing red about his stormy green eyes. All in black, a bulky vest covered his torso. Brandishing an open wallet with a picture of a shield in one hand, and a gun in the other, he stared hard at Roman.

'Police! Roman Tuvell, you're under arrest for operating a house of ill-repute. Put your hands where I can see them.'

I nearly tripped over my jaw as it hit the floor. Before I could ask what the fuck was going on, Roman shoved me right into Paul, then pushed past me and took off like a Banshee, screaming his damn head off.

Paul wrestled me off of him, cursing under his breath. Barely sparing me a glance, he said, 'You okay?'

'Yeah, but—'

'Good. Stay here.' Then he took off in a sprint.

For a moment, I just blinked, trying to process what just happened. Then I decided that it didn't matter; getting out of Belles, pronto, was the only item on the agenda. Grabbing my bags, I trotted down the hallway to the show-room floor, where I froze.

INXS blared from the speakers, but onstage Circe wasn't moving to 'Pretty Vegas.' She and the fifty some-odd patrons in the audience were all watching the six men dressed in black, with oversized blue vests and shiny black guns. Faith, paler than her white gown, stood next to a group of businessmen by table six. Joey, Ben, and the two cocktail waitresses hovered by the bar, where two bartenders stood looking like they'd been poleaxed. Marching down the stairs, two men firmly escorted a nude, squirming Lorelei and a worried-looking man (also naked as a jaybird, but his feet weren't in stilettos) toward the exit. Dalton followed, followed by still another man in black.

Rooted to the spot, I spotted two more men in black as they led Momma across the showroom floor, coming from the direction of Roman's office. Look at that, she'd been here all along. Momma looked mad enough to spit fire, but she held her head high . . . until she saw me.

'You,' she hissed, her eyes glowing red. In the split second it took me to understand that Lillith had possessed Momma, she lunged at one of the two men and snatched his gun.

Fuck.

Next to her, the other man screamed, 'Drop it!'

I dove to the ground as two guns fired.

Hitting the floor, I scrambled behind one of the tables. My heart jackhammered and blood roared in my ears, yet I heard everything around me clearly – the men with guns yelling, the frightened shouts of the other people assembled in the room, JD Fortune's sultry voice telling us all that the party was over and the road was long. Footsteps thudded on the floor as a group of customers went for the exit; footsteps screeched to a halt when the men with guns ordered them to stop. The terrified yammering of the humans pitched high, like a mosquito's whine. Biting my lip, I took a slow, deep breath to try and calm myself down enough to think, and . . .

Unholy Hell.

The sharp, sweet smell of blood filled my nostrils. Even

as I recoiled from the odor, a deeper part stretched up and grinned, relishing the scent as I *ummm*ed.

No matter how I tried, wanted, to be human, how I fooled myself into thinking that a witch's brew could completely transform me into a mortal, my reaction to the bloodshed proved that at my core, I was still a creature of the Pit. Tears of despair streamed down my face, the salty water mingling with my nervous sweat.

Enough of the game, my core whispered. Shed your mortal costume.

No! I covered my ears with my hands, opened my mouth and screamed.

This is a temple of Lust. Blood and sex ride the air; music thrums along your flesh. Touch your power and revel in the destruction to come. Be a demon once more.

NO!

Ripping my heels from my feet, I grabbed my purse and tore ass out of the showroom. Behind me, the men with guns yelled something, but I didn't listen. I had to escape, to flee before my willpower faded and I surrendered to the desire bubbling within me.

The scorpion will always sting, King Lucifer whispered in my mind. *That's its nature.*

Blindly, I ran down the hallway and threw open the glass doors to Belles. Outside, a group of police cars waited, lights pulsing red in the night like a demon's baleful gaze. Breathing hard, I took a moment to see where there was a gap between the patrolling officers and the curious bystanders, and I took off like a shot. Behind me, someone called my name, but I kept running.

I had to get away.

My bare feet slapped the pavement, cutting the tender flesh. Clutching my purse with one hand and my coat closed with the other, I sprinted. Where? It didn't matter. Away. Get away from the lights, the sounds, the smells. Around me, people jumped aside, cursing and complaining. Those who didn't move fast enough I shoved out of my way. Get away, I thought at them. Get away.

Surrender to yourself, Jezebel.

Go away.

Release your power. Reveal your true form.

GO AWAY.

Show the flesh puppets your true nature.

Someone barreled into me, and with a grunt I sprawled to the ground. Landing heavily on my forearms, I hissed from the burning feeling of my skin scraped raw. Wriggling away from the person who'd crashed into me, I clambered to my knees, then to my feet. As I was about to run, strong hands turned me around.

Paul stared at me, long and hard. 'I told you to stay put.'

I tried to shrug out of his grasp, but the man's hands held me like a vice. 'Let go!'

'Damn it, Jesse, you could've gotten hurt!'

'I have to go, Paul. Please!'

'No. Not until you tell me what's going on.' His gaze locked onto mine, tried to read the secrets in my eyes. 'Tell me. I can't protect you if I don't understand.'

The world seemed to freeze, giving me all the time I needed to consider telling Paul the truth ... about me, the Announcement, everything. Bless me, I wanted to. I wanted to let the words pour out, wanted to feel the burn of my catharsis.

Show him, my core suggested. Bask in your power once more.

Paul's sea-green eyes compelled me to trust him.

Trust the man who'd lied about who and what he was.

Humans lie. Lie to others, lie to themselves.

They deserved the truth.

Power, just within my reach. All I had to do was touch it . . .

Paul said, 'Jesse.' The tenderness and concern in his voice brought tears to my eyes. I shut them, trying to make sense of everything I was feeling.

Show him! Something in my heart stirred, and within me, my power beckoned.

I said a prayer. I didn't know to whom I prayed, or why. *Please.* Please what? I didn't know. Just that one word: *Please.*

A large hand touched my cheek.

Opening my eyes, I reached up and clasped Paul's face, bringing it down to my own. And then I kissed him. Nothing passionate, nothing seductive – just a simple, affectionate kiss. Pulling away, I whispered, 'I'm so sorry. But I can't tell you.'

I turned to flee.

And stumbled to my knees.

I looked up to meet Megaera's icy gaze.

She floated above the sidewalk, her sandaled feet inches off the ground. Over her white toga, she wore a silver breastplate tooled with a heart and an arrow balancing on the scales of judgment. A silver helm covered her head, shadowing her face; even so, her blue eyes shone brightly, radiating power. In her hand blazed a silver sword.

All the trappings of her office.

'Paul,' I whispered, 'run.'

Behind me, Paul said, 'You, drop the weapon!'

287

Megaera glanced over me. 'Mortal man.' Her voice echoed like thunder in a valley. 'This does not concern you. Leave us.'

'Go to hell!'

A flicker of amusement shone in her blue eyes. 'Momentarily.' She flexed, and I felt a wave of power crash past me, hitting Paul.

Crying out, I turned to see Paul frozen, his gun leveled at Meg. I reached out, touched his face. Ice cold. No reaction in his eyes, his body.

'Jezebel,' Meg said with a sigh. 'I wish you'd come back.'

I was going to die.

My heart full of sorrow, I gently kissed Paul's mouth. Maybe he'd remember me in his dreams.

I felt her sword touch my back. Meg said, 'Answer me one question.'

I slowly turned to face my best friend, my executioner. The sword point pierced my skin, directly over my heart.

She asked, 'Why didn't you tell him?'

My throat horribly dry, my voice came out as a croak. 'Because it wasn't his place to know.'

She stared at me, through me, reading the truth behind my words. Her sword pressed against my chest as she measured me. Finally she said, 'He wants to make an example out of you.'

I swallowed thickly before I answered. 'I know.'

'Will you return with me now?'

Biting my lip, I wondered why she was giving me a chance at all. Friendship? Or maybe she, too, found His words distasteful? Lacking the strength to speak, I shook my head.

She lowered her sword and approached me. I stood my

ground, although my legs felt like rubber. Wondering if oblivion hurt, I closed my eyes and waited.

The softest brush of lips on my own. Then nothing.

After five heartbeats, I opened my eyes. Meg was gone.

Taking a shuddering breath, I touched my face, my chest, my lips. I was still alive!

Why?

Behind me, Paul stammered, 'Where'd she go?'

Tears running down my face, I let out a whoop of joy. Then I spun to face Paul, who looked in every direction, trying to find Meg. I crushed him to me and hugged him fiercely. 'I'm not running anymore,' I said, laughing and crying, turning my words into a hiccoughing jumble.

He must have understood me, because he lifted my chin up with his hand and kissed me. I kissed him back, my heart soaring. It was all going to be okay now! Meg had released me.

I was free.

'Your fault.'

The voice came from behind me, and I quickly placed it. Roman's.

In my arms, Paul stiffened. 'Put the gun down.'

Gun? No. This is my happy ending. There aren't supposed to be guns in happy endings.

'It's all your fault,' Roman spat. I looked over my shoulder and saw him pointing a gun at me.

That Dickhead.

'Jezebel, walk away from him.' Roman didn't look at me. Instead his eyes burned a hole in Paul's forehead.

No, I realized, he wasn't pointing the gun at me. Not at me – at Paul.

'Roman,' I said, feeling cold tendrils creep up my spine, 'please. Put it down.'

'Move away from him now, Jezebel.'

'Do it,' Paul said to me, his jaw clenched.

My stomach churned, and rage bubbled in me, dissipating my fear. How dare this man threaten Paul?

'You ruined everything,' Roman snarled. 'Just a few more years, I would've retired a rich man.'

'You were running a prostitution ring,' Paul said, his voice tight.

'Like that's so bad.'

'It's illegal,' Paul said.

'It's business! That's all – business!'

'It's over.'

'Oh yeah, Mister Undercover Vice Cop.' Roman's eyes gleamed, and I hoped to see the telltale sign of Daun. If Daun were in Roman, then I could talk him down, tell him to back off. But no, there was no red glow, no hint of sulfur. What Roman did now was of his own accord. 'It's over, all right.'

He wasn't going to hurt Paul. I wouldn't let him.

I hurled myself at Roman. I saw the surprise in his eyes as he fired.

Something seared through me, blindingly hot. My body flew backward slowly, gracefully. I heard my blood splatter on Paul's face and chest, heard his shrieks, and for a moment I wondered if I was still a Nightmare, still visiting Paul in his bedroom.

Then the roar of another gun, and my body hit the ground.

This should hurt, I thought.

Paul's bloody face over mine, telling me something, his voice urgent, desperate. I wondered what he was saying. Tears sparkled in his poet's eyes, their sadness transforming them into precious jewels.

290

Don't cry, sweetie.

Don't cry, love.

His face blurred into streams of color, and I let that stream pull me down.

PART SIX

LUCIFER

25

Abaddon/Pandemonium

'My brethren.'

At once a whisper and a cosmic shrill that filled the whole of Abaddon, King Lucifer's words echoed in my head, my ears, my body. My groin clenched as heat filled my belly; my nipples throbbed, swollen from the touch of His voice.

'Many of you have been with Me since we descended from Heaven. Many more of you joined us only in the last few millennia.'

Bless me, I'd been flippant to King Lucifer! I'd jiggled my boobs in front of His face! Why hadn't I sensed who He was?

'Some of you may not know the true purpose of Hell.'

With every word, His malefic presence crashed over me, drowning me. Waves of desire rippled up my limbs, and I moaned as I felt my body respond to the power of His voice. I swallowed, trying to focus on the content of His words instead of the physical effect of His voice.

'And it has been brought to My attention that some of you have forgotten what you once knew.'

Concentrate, Jezebel. Your supreme being is soliloquizing. Pay attention.

'I used to be Satan, serving as Adversary to the Almighty. Some of the Fallen may remember Me in that role, standing at the left hand of God.

Do you remember why that changed? What is the purpose of Hell?'

Purpose? Why, to torture human souls until they no longer contained sin. Everyone knew that.

'Do any of you truly remember the Devil?'

I bit my lip, wondering about His words. Some mortals confused King Lucifer with the Devil. They were wrong. But why was He mentioning the Nameless One?

'God creates,' King Lucifer said. 'But the Devil destroys. It has always been so. From the moment when the Almighty first shaped life, the Devil plotted its destruction. Life, death. Balance in the universe. The only things that the Devil could not corrupt were God and the angelic body – just as the only thing that God could not influence was the Devil. And so it went. God created, and the Devil destroyed.'

He paused. I still felt His kiss on my lips. Why, by all that's unholy, did He kiss me? No, stop that. Listen to His words.

'God created life, culminating with humanity. Unlike His other creations, humans were different. He bestowed upon mortals pieces of Himself, giving them souls. He thought that these souls would prevent the Devil from destroying them.' He sighed. 'Even the Almighty can be wrong.'

My eyes widened. God ... wrong? Not that I served God in any way, but the very thought of the Almighty making a mistake was enough to rock me to my core. Some things simply *were*. Lucifer was King of all Evil. The Almighty was the Creator, the Benefactor of all Good. Such embodiments of Good and Evil weren't able to make mistakes.

'Creation, from what I understand, is a very draining thing. So it should have been no surprise that eventually the Almighty grew tired. Tired of creating new vessels for the souls of the once living, tired of constantly rebuilding forms that the Devil would only destroy again. In His exhaustion, He considered simply calling all souls not just back to Heaven, but back into Himself. Washing His hands of His work and being done with it. A moment of Rapture, and then humanity would come home. Forever.'

My eyeballs nearly popped from their sockets. No more mortals? But what would happen to the demons without mortals to torture?

'But I, God's closest friend, His Satan, offered an alternative. Instead of invoking the Rapture and ending all life, I suggested that instead what was needed was a distraction for the Nameless One. That way, God could rest.'

I risked a glance at the platform. King Lucifer stood calmly, hands clasped behind His body like a schoolboy as He spoke. The emerald green of His toga paled in comparison to the brightness of His green eyes.

'Souls exist forever, whether in mortal shells or in Heaven, side by side with the lower angels. What if there were a place where souls would go for purification *before* they were admitted into Heaven? What if, before they were purified for God, they atoned for their sins through punishment, in a land of despair and fire? Would the Devil be amused by such things? Would Its attention be diverted from the living to be entertained by the dead?'

He spread His hands wide. 'Thus God created Hell. And I was appointed its King. I chose seventy-two of My closest comrades from the angelic body, and we descended into the Abyss and began the work of repentance.'

He turned my way, and I quickly dropped my gaze. Like a lover, His voice caressed my flesh, dotting my skin with goosebumps. 'God created all of you to help us on this mission.'

I had never thought of myself as a creature of God. I belonged to Lust; I tempted mortals with sex and I seduced their souls. Damn me, I was *good?* I mean, really on the side of Good? I shivered, rubbing my arms for warmth. I'd never thought that I could be cold in Hell.

'For thousands of years, we have tortured the damned. Their shrieks filled the plane, and the Devil was content. I wondered, as we did our worst to the damned, how the Almighty could bear it. What kind of God allows His children to suffer so? But I never asked. And God never spoke of it.'

Rubbing my arms faster did nothing to alleviate the chill running through my body.

King Lucifer snorted in disgust. 'But all of our work, all of the pain – it wasn't enough. Look at the mortal coil. Humans slaughter one another on an epic scale. Their passions rule their actions. They steal, they lie, they destroy.'

Bowed to the ground, I shifted uneasily as I considered His words. Other than barracudas, humans were the only living creatures that killed one another for reasons other than survival. They were such fickle creatures, so easily led by their emotions. I should know; I helped them feel those emotions.

'In the past century, they have created weapons of

destruction so powerful that they could obliterate their world completely. Do you understand what that means? The humans could destroy their world.'

Oh. Oh boy. Rubbing my flesh raw, I wondered if mortals were really that stupid. Could they truly allow their momentary passions to obliterate the world?

'It's all too clear that in the past ten decades, the Devil has become bored with Hell. Its attention lies firmly on the mortal coil, and Its influence is felt more with every passing day. Something drastic needs to be done to keep It from leading the humans to end their own existence on a global scale.'

I heard King Lucifer sigh, a sound filled with disappointment and pain.

'The Almighty has decided that it's time for a new regime. I have been called back to His side for reassignment.'

I gasped, and I heard my noise echoed a millionfold as all of the Abyss reacted in shock.

'And so I introduce to you now your new King of Hell: The Archangel Michael.'

No. Oh bless me, no. Not that.

A new voice filled the Pit, smooth and intoxicating as honeyed mead: 'You are too soft.'

His judgment washed over me, filled me with dread. Soft? Demons weren't *soft*.

'You are too close to humanity. You have been among them too long for you to be effective in your roles.' The Archangel sniffed, and I felt His disdain pour down on me like a summer thunderstorm. 'The twelve Kings of Sin and Land will see Me now. All others are dismissed until further notice.'

I looked up, and for a second I met the sorrowful gaze

of my former lord and supreme ruler. Lucifer smiled at me, and if I were mortal, my heart would have broken.

Then the Archangel clapped His hands once. With that resonating sound, I was banished from Abaddon.

I found myself falling. Before I could get my bearings, I splashed into boiling lava.

Fuck!

With violent strokes, I swam up and broke the surface just as my flesh caught fire. Shrieking, I cut a path through the burning water and headed toward shore. Shoots of blue flame burst around me, suffocating me in sulfur and cutting off my screams. A multitude of demons blocked my path as they, too, first materialized in and then evacuated from the churning waves. Pushing and snarling, I forced my way forward. When I finally reached the water's edge, I jumped onto the shore like a leaping bonfire. Once both my hooves touched dry ground, the flames that bathed my body extinguished themselves.

Trembling from pain and rage, I let out a murderous screech. That holier-than-thou bastard had dumped me in the Lake of Fire!

Others emerged from the boiling pool, gasping and cursing, shoving me aside. Still shivering, I plodded down the slope. Seeing stakes laid out and humans burning on them, I realized that I'd been sent back to the Heartlands. Glancing behind and overhead at the wretched forms streaming from the Lake, I noted that all the nefarious with me belonged to Lust. That stopped me in my tracks.

The Archangel had been powerful enough not only to banish the demonic but also to categorize us by our affiliated Sin. Maybe – *maybe* – King Asmodai could separate all the Seducers from the rest of the nefarious, thanks to

300

the psychic awareness all creatures of Lust have with one another. And possibly King Lucifer could have accomplished such a feat; after all, He was . . . no, had been . . . the unchallenged ruler of the Abyss. But no other entity was nearly that strong, that skillful.

And now the Archangel was our King. Heaven controlled Hell.

That alone was enough to make me consider walking back into the Lake of Fire and staying until my form disintegrated, however many millennia that took.

Worse, the Devil's influence touched humanity daily, and it was a toss up whether or not mortals would destroy themselves before the Almighty summoned their souls in the Rapture. And God, that epitome of all that was Good and Right, seemed to want His children to suffer even more, just so that He didn't have to bother with the Devil.

That wasn't the way it was supposed to be. Good can't control Evil. They're polar opposites, by their very definition.

Evil cannot serve Good.

But it does. It always had.

Good cannot be indifferent about Evil.

But . . .

I pressed my talons against my forehead. There was a reason why I wasn't a philosopher.

Feeling the first tendrils of panic creep up my spine, I rubbed my arms. What did this mean for all of us? Screw that – what did this mean for *me*?

I found out an hour later.

'Reassigned,' I panted as Daun fucked me silly. 'I can't believe I'm – OOOH! – going to be a Nightmare!'

'Try not to take it personally, babes,' he grunted. 'It's

not just you. It's all the succubi, and a good chuck of the incubi.'

'Why'd you get to keep your job?'

He thrusted deep and hard, and for a moment I saw stars. Smiling, he said, 'Because I'm one of the best, and King Asmodai knows it.'

I moved with him, fretting too much to take (prolonged) pleasure from our sweat. Around us, the walls of the District vibrated with passion and the air was thick with the sounds and smells of sex. With all female Seducers reassigned, Pandemonium had temporarily become one huge orgy. Going out with a bang, and all that.

'I can't believe that the Queen herself got bumped,' I said.

Daun's self-congratulatory smile stretched into a shit-eating grin. 'Well, if you believe the stories, the Almighty never did favor her. You don't kick your favorites out of Eden on a whim. I can't expect the Archangel to feel any differently.'

Just thinking about Michael, I bared my fangs. 'That rat bastard replaced us with fucking angels! What does an angel know about seduction?'

'Don't know. What does an Archangel know about Hell?'

I stopped bumping and grinding. 'What do you think's going to happen now?'

Daun nibbled my ear. 'Starting in about three hours, you'll be a Nightmare, and I'll continue plying my trade and enticing mortal women into saying my name. But until then, let's you and me get more sweaty.'

'You may have to twist my arm.'

Winking, he said, 'Turn of phrase? Or do you want me to go de Sade on you?'

'Surprise me.'

26

The Lake of Fire/The Gates

I sat in front of the Lake of Fire, holding a stick over the churning waters. Attached to the stick, a male forearm slowly crisped. Sighing as I turned the homemade spit, I watched the skin bubble and blacken, smelled the fat as it pooled and burned. I didn't have any appetite, not even for sex, but I needed to think. Making a light snack gave me the excuse to just sit and try to make sense of my roiling thoughts.

I was trapped.

Unless I really wanted to be a ghost, my only option in Hell was pulling this stint as a Nightmare – *stint* loosely defined as until Judgment Day. And while being a foul-tempered dream forever was bad, stuck as a transparent nonentity hovering around graveyards, old houses, and insane mortals was infinitely worse. Because then I'd be alone for the better chunk of eternity, barring the occasional ethereal conclave and Halloween. And the thought of being alone, fading slowly over the ages, was too much for me to bear.

But terrifying mortals, with no other purpose but to make them scream, was so blessed pointless.

I dunked the meat into the Lake. What was the big deal? I scared humans as a matter of course. I was a demon, after all. And mortals fear demons. So why was being a Nightmare so bad, really?

Because I wasn't created to scare them. I was created to Seduce them. That was what I thrived on, what made my toes curl in pleasure (when I had toes). But it didn't matter that I had thousands of years of experience under my garter belt. The Archangel called us soft, had replaced us without a second thought.

Closing my eyes, I heard the man's shrieks echo as my chest erupted in blood.

I hated my Afterlife.

'Hey, girl.'

'Heya, sweetie.' My voice came out like a sigh.

Megaera's hand touched my shoulder. 'I like the outfit.'

'Huh?' I opened my eyes in surprise, then I realized she meant my human form. I hadn't changed after I'd terrified the man with the lovely eyes. 'Oh. It's from my last assignment.'

She sat next to me, tucking her pale legs beneath her bottom. 'What's wrong, Jezzie?'

Lowering my head, I didn't answer her. It wasn't that my feelings and thoughts were so jumbled together that I couldn't make heads or tails out of them. Meg was a Fury. And one didn't tell a Fury that she was seriously considering running away.

I felt her blue eyes boring a hole through me. We shared a connection, thanks to being friends for a millennium. Did that mean she could read my mind, my heart, without even trying?

304

'Give it time, Jezebel,' she said. 'He needs to stretch His wings and get used to the Pit.'

'And the Pit needs to get used to Him,' I said, not able to keep the bitterness from my voice.

'Yes.'

'Where's King Lucifer now? Do you know?'

'I do,' she said. 'But it's not my place to tell you.'

'He's . . . okay?'

She chuckled. 'The former lord and master of Hell is in a new role. Like you. And like you, He's learning to adjust. He'll be fine.'

'Oh. Good.'

I removed the spit from the Lake and stared at the charred meat. The aroma of cooked mortal did nothing for my mood. 'Hungry?'

'No, thanks.'

Heaving my arm back, I pitched the food across the Lake. It soared gracefully over the bubbling water, then landed with a hissing splash. I watched it sink beneath the fiery surface.

'A waste, no?'

'Lost my appetite.'

'Hmmm.'

We sat in silence, listening to the screams of humans, warming our bodies by the turbulent Lake. When Megaera finally spoke, she didn't look at me.

'Things are in flux. He's calling for all sorts of changes. It could be that after time, you'll embrace your new role.'

'When humans fly,' I muttered.

'Humans do fly,' she said. 'They use marvelous machines to do so. Airplanes and helicopters and gliders and parachutes and the like. But they do fly. They just had to learn how.'

'They are creative, aren't they? Such fascinating creatures.'

'They say God made them in His own image.'

'But they also destroy.'

'True. They're easily influenced. But in the short time they have, more often than not they do something powerful with their lives, even if it's just to create new lives.'

I thought about that. And about how there were billions of mortals walking the Earth, with more joining the mortal coil with every passing day.

I wondered how easy it would be to pick out a demon from the flesh puppets.

'If you do it,' Meg whispered, 'He'll come after you.'

Clenching my jaw, I said, 'I don't know what you're talking about.'

'Maybe He comes from Above,' she said as if I hadn't spoken, 'but He's just as insecure as a mortal in a new role. He won't tolerate any dissension, not now. He'll put out a contract on you, force you back.'

Biting my lip, I flashed through my options. If there was a way I could really blend with the humans, hide myself from Evil . . . 'I'm just one demon. What sort of damage could one demon do?'

'You could inspire a revolt in the Pit. You could incite the mortals on Earth.'

Picturing myself with a pitchfork in hand, leading a stampede of angry mortals down to the Gates of Hell, I burst out laughing. 'I'm not the type to inspire anything other than lascivious thoughts.'

'You'd be surprised,' she said. 'And you know too much to be allowed to roam free.'

'I know just as much as all the nefarious.'

'The others aren't considering what you are. The others

are complaining, moping, taking out their frustration and rage on the damned. But none of them are contemplating the possibility of other options.'

I glanced at her. She gazed at me somberly, her hair flying in the updraft from the Lake. She looked like a windswept nymph, waiting to aid strangers through the forest or the water. I said, 'Millions of demons, including the elite and the various Kings, and none of them have any thoughts of . . . questioning the new status quo?'

'None.'

Hell, apparently, was composed of demonic sheep. Shaking my head in disgust, I turned back to the Lake.

'We all do what we must, Jezebel.' Her lips touched my ear. 'Be careful,' she whispered.

I turned to face her, but she was already gone.

Sauntering up to the Gates, my heels crunched over scattered bones. I hid my distaste by pasting a huge Farrah smile on my face. Obviously, Hell was now all about the shock and awe – in the one day that the Holy Roller had been King, the entire Third Sphere stank of refuse, and you couldn't move without knocking over precariously balanced heaps of skeletons.

Granted, the incoming damned were beside themselves with terror. But still, to me it smacked of overkill. I preferred the subtle approach to horror rather than the in-your-face variety. But hey, no one had asked for my opinion.

I jiggled up to the Gateskeeper – the same Envious from the other day, oh joy – who was busy snuffling a female human. The mortal cringed against her demon captor, a creature of Avarice based on the eyes. A quick glance at her soul told me she'd been a con artist in life;

based on how yellow her form was, she'd been damned good at her job.

Seeing me, the Gateskeeper straightened. 'Where does you thinks you're going?'

'Hollywood, sweetie.' I flashed my Farrah grin, jiggled my Charlie's Angel boobs. 'Supposed to terrify some television bigwig. Something about reality television replacing all programming until Salvation.' Shrugging, I channeled Dumb Blonde. 'Got to do my research. Can't scare the poor things until I understand what scares them, right?'

'You stink of sex,' the Coveter said, his eyes gleaming. 'What of it, slut? You going to sleep your way up the path of knowledge?'

I blew the demon a kiss. 'Carnal knowledge is something you'll never obtain, Greedy.'

He growled at me, and things might have gotten a bit hot. But at that moment, his mortal charge collapsed to the ground, quaking in fear. With a final snarl at me, the Coveter bent down to gather up his human. I took the opportunity to prance away, hips rolling as my long legs took me out of Hell.

I headed for the blasted plains, which divided Hell from Limbo. Most demons preferred to leave from Pandemonium when they had to work on the mortal coil; me, I wanted as much privacy as possible.

Jezebel, where are you?

I ignored Queen Lillith's question and kept walking.

You're supposed to be in Pandemonium, filing your paperwork!

Increasing my pace, I remained silent.

I see you, Jezebel, walking along the edge of the blasted lands. Where are you going?

Out for a morning stroll, I told her. Then I pushed her mental probe aside and severed the connection.

Crap. I'd hoped for a bit more time. But cutting the psychic connection between Seducers – well, former Seducers, anyway – all but announced my intention to run.

Okay then. Time to initiate the plan of action.

Step one: Formulate plan.

Pursing my lips as I marched, I decided that I couldn't just blend with the humans. What I needed was really to become a human. The lower-downs wouldn't expect that. Yes, that was key: I had to become a mortal.

Which meant I needed a witch. And I knew just the person to help me.

Grinning, I lifted my arms and let my power wash over me, spiriting me away to Salem, Massachusetts. With the new regime, I figured there'd be some protocol involved before Hell got its act together and sent the appointed Scourge after me.

At least, I hoped that would be the case.

As it turned out, it gave me a three-hour head start. By the time my hunter found me, I was safely in human form, with a spiffy Shield Against Evil hanging between my breasts.

27

Limbo

'Hello, Jezebel.'

The soft, deep voice pulled me up from my river of swirling colors, and I clung onto it like a lifeline. As I rose, I felt myself becoming solid, more real. When the colors dropped away, I found myself lying on my back. I tried to move, but I couldn't feel my body.

I didn't think that was a good sign. Then again, I was surprised I wasn't dead, so maybe it wasn't all that bad.

'Go on. Open your eyes.'

The voice was maddeningly familiar, yet I couldn't place it. My eyelids felt heavy, crusted, and it took me a few tries before I could open them. When I finally did, all I saw was rolling gray mist, as if I were floating in a cloud. Maybe I had died after all – Roman had shot me, and I'd felt the bullet tear through my chest.

'Am I dead?' My voice sounded strange, thin.

'Not yet.'

My body felt heavy, as if weights lined my skin. I tried

to turn my head, but I might as well have been trying to shift a mountain. 'Where am I?'

'Limbo. I wanted to talk with you. If you don't mind.'

I didn't seem to be in the position of minding anything. 'Why can't I move?'

'You're dying, Jezebel. Paul's hands are covering the hole in your chest, but your blood seeps between his fingers. Medical authorities are on the way, and will arrive momentarily. But when they do, it will be too late.'

'Oh.' I hadn't even had a chance to tell Paul good-bye.

'You're crying, Jezebel. Do you fear death that much?'

'No.' I realized I wasn't speaking with my mouth – but neither was it the psychic connection I'd had with the Seducers. Whatever this communication was, it was more intimate. 'I'll accept my fate, whether it's punishment or oblivion.'

'Then why are tears falling from your eyes?'

Imagining the feeling of Paul's large hands enveloping mine, I said, 'I wish I could see Paul once more.'

'Ah.'

'Will he be okay?'

'You're dying, Jezebel. Do you really care about what one mortal will suffer?'

'Yes.'

'He will be devastated.'

'Oh . . .' My voice faded into a sob. I didn't want Paul to hurt. Had there really been a time when I wished I could kill him?

'He doesn't understand why he was so drawn to you from the first, how you could have affected him so powerfully in just a matter of days.'

'I don't understand it, either.'

The voice seemed to smile. 'Love is stronger than magic, whether mortal or infernal.'

'So Paul and I . . . just fell in love?'

'Yes.'

'Why?'

This time, the voice clearly laughed – a rich, sonorous laugh that made me think of a soft kiss brushing my lips. 'Perhaps it was to show him that he can still love, even after the death of his fiancée. Perhaps it was to show you that mortals are, indeed, worth caring for, even if you are a demon. When lust becomes love, passion burns all the brighter.'

Worth caring for. Yes. I knew it, had known it all along. Yay, me.

'Perhaps there was no reason at all, and you both simply found each other.'

While I liked that possibility the best, I hoped for the first one. If Paul learned from our time together, then maybe he'd go on with his life, find someone new. Maybe now he'd finally put Tracy to rest, find another woman to grow old with. I hoped he did.

I wished it could have been me.

'Tell me, Jezebel. Are you disappointed over your friend's action?'

'My friend?'

'The Erinyes.'

Megaera. I remembered her kiss, her warning, the feeling of her sword's tip digging into my heart. 'She let me go.'

'No, Jezebel. She fulfilled her role. She led you to kill yourself. That's what the Furies do, ever of old. They drive mortals to their deaths.'

I wanted to be angry, to defend my friend. But all I felt

was sadness, and a bone-weary exhaustion. 'She didn't make me do anything I didn't want to do.'

'She led you to your death. Are you saying you wanted to die?'

'No. I wasn't thinking about me. I just couldn't let Roman hurt Paul.'

'Why?'

'Because I love him.'

A pause, then: 'You sacrificed yourself for love?'

I hadn't thought about it like that, but given the circumstances, that's exactly what happened. 'Yes.'

'Sit up, Jezebel.'

And like that, I could move. Using my arms, I propped myself up. Seated beside me was a large man with jet black hair and dazzling green eyes, wearing a white shirt and slacks. His smile made those emerald eyes sparkle, but it was a sad smile all the same.

I felt my eyes widen as I placed his face, and my mouth dropped open. 'King Lucifer?'

'King no more, Jezebel,' He said with a laugh. 'That mantle is no longer Mine to wear.'

Not knowing whether I should prostrate myself, I stammered, 'Then what role is Yours now, Unholy One?'

His smile stretched into an amused grin. 'There's nothing unholy about Me. I am the Morning Star, as always. Bringer of Light.'

Dropping my gaze, I whispered, 'Lord Morning Star.' King Lucifer was here, next to me! If I hadn't been almost dead already, I would have died on the spot.

His hand touched my chin and tilted my head up until my eyes met his. 'Please. I am Lucifer. And you are Jezebel.'

I squeaked, 'Yes, Sire.'

With a sigh, He dropped His hand. 'Stubborn one, aren't you?'

I'd been called worse. 'You will always be my King, Sire.'

'No, Jezebel. But you may call Me sire, if you wish.' He smiled, shaking His head sadly. 'You and I, we are similar in many ways.'

'Sire?'

'We both befriended ones far stronger than us. And we both felt the loss when those friends were true to their natures instead of to us.'

'Please, Sire,' I said. 'I don't understand.'

'God removed Me from My role to do what He felt was best for humanity. That is His nature.'

His green eyes flashed, and I clearly saw that He still felt betrayed, raw. I wanted to touch His hand, tell Him that He didn't have to be bitter. But He was Lucifer, and I was just a one-time demon, a mortal without a soul. Who was I to tell Him anything of the sort?

'And Megaera led you to your death, as she was directed to do by the King of Hell. That is her nature. Duty over friendship. Nature over nurture.' He sighed. 'The scorpion will always sting the frog.'

'But Meg gave me the chance to return. I was the one who said no.'

He nodded, His eyes thoughtful. 'True.'

'Did . . .' I licked my lips, wondering if I dared ask. Before I could think too much about it, I said, 'Did the Almighty give You a choice, Sire?'

Gazing at me, a smile quirked His lips. 'Perhaps He did.'

A wave of pain washed over me, and I doubled over until the feeling passed.

King Lucifer touched my hand. 'The moment is coming, Jezebel. You are about to die.'

I closed my eyes, waiting for the inevitable. I thought of Meg and her attempts to help me, of Daun and his touch. And Paul, his lovely eyes and gentle smile, the broken nose that hinted at the violence in his life. 'I thank you for this conversation, Sire. It's . . . nice not being alone at the end.'

'You were never truly alone, Jezebel. Tell me: You offered to die for love once. Would you care to live for it now?'

My eyes popped open. Not daring to look up, I asked, 'Sire?'

His hand squeezed mine. 'Your sacrifice entitles you to a soul, if you wish it. A chance to be truly human in every way.'

'Oh . . . Sire, what I wouldn't give to be alive again . . .'

'Done.' He chuckled softly. 'One thing about change, Jezebel. It means the old rules do not necessarily come into play.'

'Sire, what of Hell, and the contract on me?'

'Why, that contract is for the demon Jezebel. And you will no longer be she. That particular contract is null and void.'

'Really?'

Smiling rather wickedly, He said, 'I know something about laws and agreements. Michael will have to move on to other things, like running His new Kingdom.'

'Sire, what of . . .' My voice broke, and it was a moment before I could continue. 'What of the Devil?'

His smile faded. 'Either Michael will succeed in His directive, or He will not. Either the Devil will be distracted by the damned, or the Devil will lead humanity to its destruction.'

I wondered if mortals had a chance to beat the Devil. They really were so clever – maybe they had a chance in Hell.

Releasing my hand, Lucifer said, 'Be human, Jezebel. Live and love.' His fingers brushed my brow, and my form shimmered. 'And I will see you again when it is your time to die.'

'Thank you, Sire,' I said, my voice faint.

As I faded, I thought I heard Him call me *daughter*.

But really, if a piece of God is inside us all, aren't His angels part of us as well?

28

After Life

I didn't remember Paul's hands keeping my heart from dying, or being lifted into the ambulance. I did recall his voice promising me that I would be okay.

I remembered flashes, like snapshots, showing me people's faces. Mostly they were of people I didn't know, but sometimes I thought I saw glimpses of red in the eyes that made me think of Daun. And Paul's face, above all others, his poet's eyes full of hope.

And after some indeterminate time passed, the snapshots became moving pictures. And soon after that, they became real life.

Three days after I'd been admitted to the hospital, I woke up.

And Paul was waiting.

'More flowers for you,' Paul said, putting another arrangement on the table. He placed the roses in front of the others there, so that I could see them.

'Pretty,' I said, my voice weak. Paul told me I sounded

sexy when I was all breathy. Me, I'd rather be breathing hard while having sex. All things in good time. 'Thanks.'

'You're very welcome.' He sat down in the chair by the bed and took my hand in his. 'How're you feeling today?'

'Better,' I said, lying only a little. Seeing him made me feel better. For all other times, there were truly spectacular painkillers.

'Good.' He smiled, his eyes sparkling like sunrise over the sea. 'We'll get you out of here in no time.'

'Not too fast,' I said, feeling tired already. 'Still need a place to live.'

'Maybe I can help you with that.' He lifted my hand to his lips and kissed it. 'If you're nice to me.'

'Me? I'm always nice.'

'That's what I like best about you.'

'Thought you liked the wild animal sex.'

'Close second.' He offered me my cup of water, and I took a small sip. 'When you're all better, we have to reschedule that date. Dinner and a movie.'

'And wild animal sex?'

'Maybe for our second date.'

I smiled just thinking about it. Yum.

He kept holding my hand, gazing at me and me at him. At one point, I'd have to figure out what to tell him about my past, explain how I had the looks and name of a woman living in Salem. And I'd have to figure out what to do with my life.

Even without the pressure of Hell on my heels, it felt daunting.

Relax, I told myself. I had time. I had time, and a soul, and a life. A life, hopefully, with Paul. I'd figure out the rest.

Paul smiled, squeezed my hand. 'You look wrecked, Jes. Go ahead, close your eyes.'

318

'Don't want to. I'll sleep when you're gone.'

'You can do that too. You're still recuperating; you need your sleep. Go ahead,' he said, kissing my brow. 'I don't mind.'

So I closed my eyes for a minute. When I opened them three hours later, Paul was long gone. He'd left a note on my lunch tray, saying he'd be back to visit after five. I started counting the minutes.

My stomach suggested that lunch would do me a lot more good in my body instead of in front of my face. I lifted up the tray over my lunch, and I wrinkled my nose at the milk container. Blech. No way.

'Oh, I see you're awake.'

I smiled at the nurse checking the various machines I was strapped to. 'Temporary condition.'

She smiled at my humor ... and bloomed into vibrant colors. Swirls of pink, shot through with green and blue. And like that, I knew she was going to be pregnant within the month and have a son.

Oh ... crap.

'Jesse? You okay? You've gone pale.'

'Fine,' I said. 'Just imagining things.'

So I was seeing her aura. Not a big deal. It was probably the spiffy drugs they were feeding me for the pain. That stuff was strong enough to bring the Northern Lights to the South Pole.

That's when I knew I was completely human. Demons didn't lie to themselves.

'That's a wicked smile on your face if I've ever seen one.'

'Wicked? Nah. Just ... glad.'

'I don't know,' she said with a giggle. 'You've got yourself a grin like the devil himself.'

319

I thought of King Lucifer, of his gentle kiss, of how He said we were similar. Touching my smiling lips, I said, 'Maybe I do, at that.'

Please turn the page for an exciting sneak peek at
Jackie Kessler's
THE ROAD TO HELL
coming soon from Piatkus

Prologue

On the Precipice

Whoever said you see your life flash before you when you die was full of crap. You don't see your entire life. Just the most important parts.

Or, in my case, just the most recent parts.

As I die now, feeling strong arms holding me tight, hearing a voice whisper that it's okay, my mind plays back the events that set me on the road to Hell, good intentions and all.

Faces flash behind my closed eyes, almost too fast to follow – the incubus's fang-filled grin, the Erinyes hissing with reptilian fury, the angel crying fat, salty tears.

My love, my White Knight, a name on his lips that isn't mine.

Darkness pulls me down, my heart slows, stops . . . and once again, I'm in Spice.

1

Spice

'I'm from Death Valley.'

'Really?' I smiled as I poured champagne into two long-stemmed flutes. *Death Valley* Heh. People had such a sense of humor when it came to naming things. Take Slaughterville, Oklahoma, or my personal favorite: Hell, Michigan. There's also Paradise, Pennsylvania, but I don't hold that against them; they also have the spiffy town of Intercourse.

Handing a glass to the dark-haired man seated across from me, I said, 'I've never heard of anyone actually being from Death Valley before. Scorpions and vultures, sure. People, not so much.'

He grinned, and a blush crept up his cheeks until it stained his big ears. Bless me, he was so endearing – he embarrassed easily and he was free with his money. What more could a girl ask for?

'Actually,' he said, 'I just work there. I'm a park ranger.'

Ooh, a do-gooder. The last ranger I'd met had been of the bow-and-arrow variety, many years ago. Different beastie altogether. That ranger, a Royal Forester by trade, had been all too happy to bloody those he'd been sworn to protect in between bouts of raping women. Charming fellow. Sexy, in a pond scum sort of way. Remembering forest and frost and picking twigs out of his beard before our last romp in the crisp snow, I sank back onto the black leather sofa, feeling a smile stretch across my face.

Those had been good times.

'A ranger,' I said to my latest client, rolling the word on my tongue. I tucked my legs beneath my body as I inclined on my left elbow, making sure my boobs almost, but not quite, spilled out from my low-cut red gown. Why give something away when Ranger here would be all too happy to pay me? I flashed him my best Utterly Smitten smile. 'I'd love to hear more about what you do.'

His blush deepened. 'I guess that depends on what day it is. Sometimes I'm a tour guide. Sometimes I'm a naturalist. And then there's times I have to be a cop.'

Ah. No wonder I'd taken a shine to him. Thinking of my own cop – who would actually be home tonight the same time I was, huzzah! – I asked, 'Is there really that much trouble in the desert?'

'Well, not so much as in the cities. But we get our share.' The redness faded from his ears and cheeks as he spoke, and something hard and proud flickered in his brown eyes. Watching Ranger transform from a blushing boy into a seasoned man sent a delicious tingle up my spine. Yum.

Stop that, Jesse. Don't get all hot and bothered by the nice customer. A friendly chat, a little drink in the mega-expensive Champagne Room, a private dance or two, clothing optional. No more. 'What kind of trouble?'

'We get our ravers, our smugglers, our scrappers. We even get our full-fledged homicidal maniacs.'

Ooh, really? How cool was *that?* 'What sort of maniacs? Serial killers?'

Okay, nipples, that's enough. Down, girls.

'Well, the Manson Family hid out in the Panamint Valley.'

'That part of Death Valley?'

'It's part of the larger park, yeah.'

'Sounds like it can be dangerous,' I said, putting an extra purr in my voice.

He shrugged, but the flush returned to his cheeks. My Ranger was modest. 'I patrol in a Hummer, and I wear a bulletproof vest. That's with the temperature soaring well past a hundred degrees. And my M-16 of course. I wouldn't go anywhere without it.'

Broiling hot sun, combined with assault weapons. Sweet!

'Tell me more,' I said, taking a tiny sip of champagne. I hated the stuff – it was so light and airy that even angels would have bitched about it – but my current Tall, Dark, and Handsome had ordered it as soon as we'd entered the Champagne Room. Maybe he thought it was obligatory. 'Why'd you become a ranger?'

'I'm third generation. My parents both were rangers, and my grandpa before them. I love being part of the park service. And I love our mission.'

'Mission?'

He took a deep breath, then said in a practiced singsong: 'To conserve the scenery, and the natural and historic objects, and the wildlife therein, and to provide for the enjoyment of the same, in such manner and by such means as will leave them unimpaired for the enjoyment of future generations.' He grinned at me before taking a deep swig of champagne. 'Congressional Organic Act, 1916.'

'Impressive.' Me, I preferred the Orgasmic Act of the

here and now. 'It's good that you're doing something you really believe in.'

'What about you, Jezebel? Why'd you become a stripper?'

'Oh, I needed a career change,' I said, toying with my drink. 'I love dancing on stage, feeling the music moving through me. And I like taking off my clothes,' I added with a wink. 'So I decided to become an exotic dancer.'

He said nothing for a moment as he stared at my face, a goofy smile on his lips. Based on how he was making with the soulful looks, Ranger seemed more turned on by my large green eyes than by my breasts doing their own rendition of 'June Is Busting Out All Over.' Crap, I'd guessed wrong – I'd been sure he was a boob man. There'd been a time when I automatically knew what hook worked for each client – long hair, dangerous curves, narrow ankles, you name it. Now, all I had to go by was a gut call. Clearly, that dandy 'hunch' factor wasn't as fine-tuned as my sex drive.

Mental note: Work on the whole women's intuition thing.

Finally Ranger said, 'You're about the most beautiful woman I've ever seen.'

Ooh. Flattery. Right up there with chocolate. 'You're a sweetie.'

'No, I mean it. Your eyes, your smile . . . God, your tits . . .'

Hah, I'd been right. Smiling, I took another sip of champagne.

He broke away from my eyes to slowly look me over, eating me with his gaze. He ogled the swells of my breasts, the curve of my hip, the V of my crotch. As he feasted on the image of my flesh, I swallowed my drink, knowing

328

that all I was to him was eye-candy, a snapshot of sexual gratification. Nothing more.

Uber cool.

I grinned at him, my lipstick shining in the softly lit room – enticing, advertising the things I could do to him with my mouth. That's right, sweetie. You want to taste the alcohol on my lips, want to bruise my flesh with your kisses . . .

As Chris Rock once said, there's no sex in the Champagne Room. But that didn't mean I couldn't *think* about there being sex in the Champagne Room.

In the background, the music from the hidden speakers switched to Patti LaBelle's 'Lady Marmalade.' Excellent tune, sultry vocals. I let my shoulders move with the beat, felt my skin humming from the piano keys.

'Say,' Ranger said, his voice husky, 'would you mind dancing for me now?'

'Love to.' I placed my glass on the side table, then rose to my feet. With my stiletto-clad foot, I nudged his legs apart. Stepping forward so that I stood between his knees, I leaned forward, shoulders back, until my rack was inches away from his sweating face. I ran my hands over my twin mounds until they nipped out, straining against the material of my gown.

He groaned, then parted his lips as if he were dying to give suck. 'Oh, Jezebel . . . you're killing me . . .'

Heh. Not even close, sweetie. I don't do that anymore.

'I'm supposed to start in the middle of the song, charge you for a full. But I like you.' I raised my arms high and shimmied, getting all jiggly and wiggly. 'I'll just consider this a warmup. No extra charge.'

Ranger said something like 'Argghluh' and proceeded to drool.

Winking, I teased him with a teeny nip slip. Peek-a-boob.

'Jezebel,' he breathed, 'would you mind if I . . . um . . . touched myself while you dance?'

'Sweetie,' I said, lowering myself into his lap, 'I'd be honored.'

One thing about a guy coming while you're giving him a lap dance: it's damn sticky.

I dashed to the ladies' room as fast as my five-inch heels would allow me. It was one thing to give the nod to Ranger doing the hand-over-fist thing with his salami; getting his jizz on my gown was something else entirely. I'd assumed he'd have enough control to hold back until I'd stripped down to my G-string. But no – as soon as I popped my tits out of my dress, blastoff. Blech.

Not that I particularly minded being covered in bodily fluids. But I drew the line at cum dripping off my work clothes. A gal's got to have some standards. And technically, it's a no-no for customers to touch themselves, or us, even in the privacy of the Champagne Room. If any of the bouncers – or, gah, the floor manager – saw the lewinsky drying on my dress, Ranger would be banned from the club. Forcibly. Premature ejaculation aside, Ranger was a decent guy; I didn't want him to get roughed up.

Besides, the poor dear had been so embarrassed that he'd emptied his billfold to make up for it. A five-hundred-dollar tip goes a long way to forgiving such a faux pas.

I rounded the corner and saw the ladies' room at the end of the hall. One of the other dancers kept a supply of oxisomething in one of the bathroom cabinets for just such a stainage emergency. If I had another gown in my locker, I simply would have shucked the dress off, poured another one over my body, and not looked back. Problem was, all my clean gowns were currently balled up in the hamper at Paul's apartment, doing their dirty clothing impersonation. Mental note: Do laundry.

Mental note, part two: Learn how to do laundry.

Yanking open the door to the bathroom, I was greeted with a stink foul enough to curl my hair. Yow, someone recently visited the fudge factory. Waving my hand in front of my nose, I beelined it to the sink – the one farthest from the rows of toilet stalls – and was about to turn on the water when I heard a soft groan.

Breathing through my nose, I saw Circe seated in the far corner of the room, at the end of the huge vanity table. The dark-haired beauty was staring intently at her reflection in the wall mirror, clutching something to her chest. I glimpsed her pale face and baby blues in the mirror, but it was the hugely muscled man looming behind her that grabbed my attention.

Dressed in a sleeveless tank and biker shorts that left nothing to the imagination, he stood behind her, massaging her shoulders. Leonardo da Vinci would have creamed his pants to have this guy model for him; his body was perfectly proportioned, perfectly sculpted, and he radiated confidence almost to the point of arrogance. Slurp! Score one for Circe. After her shift was over, I'd have to corner her and get all the juicy details about her latest love. Last I'd heard, she'd fallen hard for some skinny blond guy. Guess that was yesterday's news.

Mister Gorgeous bent over and whispered something in Circe's ear. She sucked in a hitching breath, then let out a soft moan, closed her eyes.

Humph. Maybe there was no sex in the Champagne

Room, but it looked like the ladies' room was up for grabs. I must have missed the memo.

I opened my mouth to ask Circe how she could even think about foreplay with the smell in the bathroom as overpowering as it was, when I realized three things. One, Circe was crying. Two, Mister Gorgeous cast no reflection. And three, there was a dull-red glow around Circe. This wasn't a freshly fucked glow, either; it pulsed around her like a dying heart – slow, sickly, erratic.

Shit.

I didn't know which was worse – that the aura around my pal meant that she was perilously close to dying, or that there was a demon giving my pal a backrub. Of course, the latter explained the former.

Okay, Jesse. Play dumb. Most mortals can't see the nefarious. Ignore the obscenely huge – and hello, very turned on – demonic entity. Hmm. Actually, there was one place where he wasn't so huge. Must be the infernal equivalent of steroids.

'Circe? Sweetie, you okay?'

'Ignore her,' Mister Gorgeous said, casting me a long look. 'She couldn't possibly understand the pain he's caused you. He doesn't love you.'

Circe said, 'He doesn't love me.' Her voice cracked, shattered into a thousand pieces.

'Who doesn't?' Right keep your voice steady. Don't look at Mister Gorgeous. You don't see him, la la la . . .

'Larry.' Circe said his name with a sob.

Pasting a smile on my face, I did something very brave, and completely stupid. I walked over to her, sat in the chair next to her, within spitting distance of the hulking demon. Pay no attention to the Evil creature behind the curtain. The stench emanating from him was strong enough

332

to make my eyes water. Now I recognized it for what it was: Brimstone.

I said, 'Larry? You mean the skinny blond guy? Sweetie, you can do better than him.'

'You gave him your heart,' the demon said. 'He chewed it up and spat it at your feet. Show him how much he hurt you, how you can't live without his love.'

Circe's breath was coming in hitches. I reached over to pat her hand, and that's when I saw the bottle of prescription pills she was holding in a death grip by her chest. 'Whatcha got there, sweetie?'

'He doesn't love me,' she said again. 'I gave him my heart, and he chewed it up and spat it at my feet.'

Uh oh. Cyrano de Bergerac, infernal style. Very bad news.

'Sweetie, there are other guys out there.'

'I can't live without his love.' Her voice faded as if someone had turned the volume way down, and something went dead in her eyes. She unscrewed the bottle cap. In a tiny voice she said, 'I'll show him.'

I grabbed her arm, but she wrenched it away. Fuck, she was strong. Massaging my sore hand, I darted a glance over her shoulder. Yup, the demon still had his hands clamped onto her shoulder. Not quite possession, but definitely influencing her actions.

The cheating bastard.

'Show him you still have your pride,' Mister Gorgeous said. 'Swallow the pills. All of them.'

'I still have my pride,' she said, her voice a monotone. She took off the cap.

I touched her elbow. 'Circe, listen to me. Unrequited love is a bitch, but it's not worth dying over. Come on, girl, this is stupid.'

She spilled some blue pills into her palm.

Fuck. Okay, let's try some shock therapy. I slapped her, hard. The crack echoed in the room.

Blinking, she turned away from the mirror to look at me. My handprint stained her cheek an angry red. 'Jesse . . . ?'

'Forget about the skinny blond asshole,' I said. 'He's not worth it.'

'She doesn't understand how he hurt you,' Mister Gorgeous said.

Circe echoed, 'He hurt me . . .'

'Sweetie, he has no idea what he's missing out on. You're a sexy, funny, wonderful girl. And if he doesn't want a part of that, he's an imbecile.'

She looked down at the bottle, at the pills in her hand. 'You think so?'

'Probably impotent, too.'

That brought a faint smile to her lips. 'Yeah?'

I said, 'I read it somewhere, in one of those business magazines, that it's been proven that the higher the level of imbecileness, the higher the likelihood of impotence.'

'Imbecileness'?'

'What, it's a word.'

Her smile slipped. 'I really loved him. Why doesn't he want me?'

'Because he's an imbecile. I thought we covered this. It's not even his fault. Imbecileness runs rampant in the male sex. Comes with all the testosterone.'

'Think so?'

'Yup.' I held out my hand. 'Care if I hold your pharmaceuticals for you?'

In her ear, the demon roared: 'Swallow the pills!'

Circe frowned, turned her head. 'You hear something?'

'Just the hum of the flourescents. Know what you need?'

She shook her head.

'A glass of wine and a good vibrator.'

Circe barked out a surprised laugh. 'Jesse!'

'I'm telling you, it's a surefire cure-all to everything that ails you, from a broken heart to the common cold.'

'I thought that was chicken soup.'

'I have never heard of pleasuring yourself with chicken soup,' I said. 'But I'm willing to give it a shot.' I made a gimme gesture. 'Fork it over.'

With a sigh, she plopped the bottle into my hand, then the loose pills.

Behind her, Mister Gorgeous said nothing, radiated pure rage. Gleep.

'Come on, sweetie,' I said, doing my best not to eye the invisible demon. 'Let's cut out early. First round's on me.'

Circe stood, looking vulnerable and beautiful, like a sculpture of flowers. 'You sure?'

'I'll go tell Jerry to move us off the stage lineup, then I'll tip out.' The D.J. was a real prick about dancers missing their rotation; I'd have to slip him an extra twenty to mollify him.

'Okay.' She smiled at me. 'Thanks Jesse. I . . . Jesus, I don't know what I was thinking. Suicide's a sin.'

'Keep forgetting you're so damn religious.'

'I'll find Joey, tell him we're cutting out. Meet you back here to change?'

No freaking way was I staying in a bathroom with an angry demon. I started to get up when I felt a crushing weight press down on my shoulder, my neck. The demon squeezed, and suddenly I couldn't breathe.

I wanted to shriek at the top of my lungs. What I said in a hoarse whisper was, 'You bet.'

Circe took a deep breath, straightened her spine, and sauntered out of the ladies' room.

As soon as the door closed, something tangled in my hair and yanked my head back. I dropped the bottle, and the pills spilled from my hand, bounced on the tile floor. Over the nauseating odor of sulfur, the ripe stink of my fear clung to my nostrils. Blood roared in my ears, pounded my head, and my heart jackhammered like it wanted to break free from my chest. My arms were leaden, dead things; my feet were rooted on the floor. I couldn't run, even if the demon released me.

But as I stared up into his face, I had a sinking suspicion that the last thing Mister Gorgeous wanted to do was let me go.

'I know you,' he said, his face twisting into a leer. 'You're the slut from the Courtyard.'

Even through my overwhelming fear, I heard the capital C in Courtyard . . . and I placed him.

Tell us, is it true that all Seducers are pox-infested carriers of disease?

Oh boy. Oh boy, oh boy, oh boy. Mister Gorgeous was a demon of Pride – and he had a personal grudge against me. Granted, most creatures of Arrogance had a chip on their shoulders when it came to one of my kind . . . former kind. Pride and Lust rarely work well together, unless there's seriously strong drink involved. But he had a reason to despise me: I'd embarrassed him in front of his buddies. To one of the Arrogant, there's no worse crime.

Licking my lips, I tried for the Dumb Blonde approach, ignoring the fact that my hair was a curly brunette. 'Never saw you before.' I even spoke with the right balance of Pants-Pissing Terror and Indignant New Yorker. Maybe he'd think I was just one of those rare mortals who were able to see the supernatural. 'Let me go.'

'You're lying. You smell of sex, slut.'

'Last customer got too happy, got his splooge on me.'

'That's not a lie.' His grip on my scalp tightened, and I felt clumps of hair tearing at the roots. Between the shriek of agony atop my head and the flare of pain from me biting my lip to keep from screaming, I was one raw nerve. 'But you do know me,' he said. 'Oh yes, slut. And I know you.'

Fuck.

He grinned, and my breath strangled in my throat. Icy fingers tripped up my spine, reached out to grip my heart. The demon bent down until his mouth was inches away from mine. 'Once a fifth-level succubus, now a flesh puppet with a soul. How appropriate. The only thing lower than your type of trash is humans.'

'My soul,' I said through clenched teeth. 'It's clean.'

'You entice humans with thoughts of Lust. Your work is in the name of Sin.'

Yeah, well, old habits die hard. After four thousand years as a Seducer, what was I going to do, be a telemarketer? 'Not Sin. Entertainment.'

'A fine line.'

'Maybe. Still a line. You can't claim me.'

He growled, deep and low in his chest. 'You talk tough for a mortal slut. You don't have your Fury friend with you to keep you safe this time.'

My throat constricted as I remembered the softest brush of lips on my own. Just thinking of Meg brought angry tears to my eyes. 'Don't need her protection.'

'You think not?'

'You can't claim me for Hell. My soul's clean.' Benefit

of being only thirty days old in mortal years: that's not a lot of time to wreak havoc.

His eyes narrowed, and for a moment I glimpsed his true form swimming beneath his false human shell – charred black flesh, white holes for eyes, a maw crammed with razor-blade teeth. Then he pulled my head up until I was sitting up straight in the chair. He spun me around to face him, his hand still tangled in my hair.

'Old rules are bending, breaking.'

'I got that,' I said, far calmer than I had any right to be. 'Seems the nefarious are encouraging mortals to kill themselves. What, business is too slow?'

'Business is booming.' His dark gaze held me, explored me. 'You mortals make excuses for your sins, think you can talk your way out of damnation. As if understanding why you commit certain actions, you forgive the action itself.'

A demonic therapy session. Spare me. 'The ends don't exactly justify the means. I know that.'

'The mortal coil is steeped in Evil. Murder because of disrespect. Genocide because of disgust.' He leered. 'Lust because of entertainment.'

My heart, already careening at marathon speed, started rocketing at a pace just short of cardiac arrest. Bless me, I hated being afraid. I really preferred causing fear – which is hard to do when you're short, cute, and human. Maybe I should start carrying a big gun. 'You know what they say. The world's going to Hell in a handbasket.'

'The trip is taking too long. No more sitting back, waiting for humans to die before collecting their souls for the Pit. We're encouraging them along.'

I pushed aside my fear to sniff my disdain. Even an ex-demon has Sin standards. 'You assholes are cheating.'

'Time are changing, slut.' For a moment, his eyes closed in on themselves, faded to something old, worn. He released my hair. 'We can't let the world be more Evil than the Abyss.'

I heard the implication behind his words, and I shivered. People think that the King of Hell is the Devil. They're wrong. The Devil – the Nameless antithesis of the Almighty – has been around way, way longer than the celestials or the nefarious. The only thing keeping It from destroying all of humanity, and the world itself, is Hell. Torturing souls amuses the fuck out of the Devil.

At least, it used to.

Wrapping my arms around myself, I said, 'So your King is changing the rules. Keeping things lively.'

'You have no idea just how much has changed.' He shook himself like a dog, regained his malefic ire as he smiled a shark's grin, all teeth and appetite. 'And that means, slut, we can influence your actions more so than ever before. To put it in language even you could understand, we can seduce you.'

Arrogant prick. 'You really have to work on your pickup lines.'

'What's that pithy saying the mortals like to throw around? Oh yes. "The devil made me do it." Quaint.' His eyes gleamed. 'And now, rather accurate.'

I swallowed thickly. If the infernal really were going to be actively influencing people, encouraging them to live fast and die young, life was about to get much more interesting. Mental note: Start thinking pure thoughts.

Oh, puke, who was I kidding?

'I say with supreme confidence that I'll see you in Hell, slut. But you know,' he added, 'the Pit is a better place without you and your Fury friend.'

I frowned, wondering what he meant by that. Of course Meg was in Hell. That's where the Furies hung their hats, like most creatures who weren't inherently Good. If not in Hell, where else could she be?

Stop. Don't think about her. She betrayed you, left you to die.

Her voice, like a kiss, in my mind: *We all do what we must*.

'Until next time, slut.' Grinning like he'd eaten all the kids in a candy shop, the Arrogant disappeared in a puff of sulfur.

There's nothing worse than a demon with a grudge. And a little dick.

HOTTER THAN HELL

Daunuan was never the ambitious type. There's so much to love about his job just the way it is – mind-blowing sexual prowess, the power to seduce any human, excellent dental plan. But now Pan, the King of Lust, has offered to make Daun his right-hand incubus – a position other demons would give their left horn for. All he has to do is entice a soul destined for heaven into a damnable act of lust. Should take, oh, seven minutes, tops.

Then he meets his target, Virginia Reed. She's cute, funny, smart. And unfathomably resistant to his charms. He can't understand it. But Duan has centuries of seduction to his credit. Sooner or later, he tells himself, he'll transform this polar ice-cap of a female into a pool of molten desire. But there's one problem: the dawning realisation that he's falling in love – that unholiest of four-letter words – with the woman he's about to doom for all eternity . . .

978-0-7499-5343-0